SADDLE UP, PARD ... **AND TAKE THE RIDE OF YOUR LIFE WITH DUSTY FLANAGAN'S** *RODEO RIDERS*

Cowboy Up!
Rigged to Ride
Final Ride

AND DON'T GET THROWN OFF, 'CAUSE YOU'LL ONLY MISS

The Natural
by Dusty Richards

Praise for the *Rodeo Riders* series:

"An exceptional book . . . a great rodeo story."
—Dave Eastlake, Seven-time National Senior Pro Rodeo Association World Champion

"Anyone who ever dreamed of being a cowboy should read this book."
—Danny Newland, Seven-time announcer, International Finals Rodeo

"A must read for anyone who enjoys a good cowboy story." —Dan and Peggy Eoff, Founders, National Championship Chuckwagon Race

"A great yarn. The story of rodeo as never told before . . . by the men (and women) who live it every day." —Dr. Lynn Phillips, Rodeo announcer

Rodeo Riders #5

BUSTED RIDE

Mike Flanagan

A SIGNET BOOK

SIGNET
Published by New American Library, a division of
Penguin Putnam Inc., 375 Hudson Street,
New York, New York 10014, U.S.A.
Penguin Books Ltd, 80 Strand,
London WC2R 0RL, England
Penguin Books Australia Ltd, Ringwood,
Victoria, Australia
Penguin Books Canada Ltd, 10 Alcorn Avenue,
Toronto, Ontario, Canada M4V 3B2
Penguin Books (N.Z.) Ltd, 182–190 Wairau Road,
Auckland 10, New Zealand

Penguin Books Ltd, Registered Offices:
Harmondsworth, Middlesex, England

First published by Signet, an imprint of New American Library,
a division of Penguin Putnam Inc.

First Printing, December 2002
10 9 8 7 6 5 4 3 2 1

Copyright © Mike Flanagan, 2002

  REGISTERED TRADEMARK—MARCA REGISTRADA

Printed in the United States of America

PUBLISHER'S NOTE
This is a work of fiction. Names, characters, places, and incidents either
are the product of the author's imagination or are used fictitiously,
and any resemblance to actual persons, living or dead, business
establishments, events, or locales is entirely coincidental.

Chapter One

Will Paxton carried the pail of dirty dishwater to the ditch behind the cook shack. As he watched the water pour from the pail, run down the ditch, and disappear over the edge of the canyon, he wondered again how he'd wound up in Montana, working as a cook's helper on the Triangle T ranch.

He was reflecting on the last two years since leaving his father's farm. He hadn't become a cowboy yet, but the dream was still there. Some things just didn't die that easy. He made up his mind that somehow, someway, he was still going to make a ranch hand.

The sound of a horse's squeal and the crashing sound of four hooves coming to earth with such force it vibrated the ground under Will, brought him back to the present. Turning toward the corral, he saw Tye Garrett on the back of a line-backed dun, reins pulled tight, his spurs raking the horse's side in perfect rhythm with every jump.

Tye Garrett broke all the horses for the Triangle T. In the two years Will had been there, he had watched with fascination as Tye rode the rough string, breaking the horses to be used in the day-to-day ranch work.

Breaking horses was not a full-time job on the Triangle T ranch, so when Tye wasn't breaking horses, he was with the other hands working cattle, building fences, putting up prairie hay, or helping with the gathering and branding, until the colts were old enough to break or the ranch foreman, Charley Hicks, bought a new string of unbroken horses. The demands placed on a working ranch horse required replacements on a regular basis.

Tye's broad shoulders stretched tight the denim shirt as his arms strained against the pull of the reins. His six-foot frame was lean and fit. His face was browned by many hours in the sun, making him look older than his twenty-six years.

Will climbed the fence to watch, mesmerized by the battle before him. The dun was using every trick in the book to lose the man on his back. Leaping high, he'd turn all four feet almost to the sky, twisting his body in the air, then righting himself before coming back to earth with a stiff-legged, bone-jarring thud. Meanwhile, the rider on his back clung to the reins and raked the horse's sides with each lunge. Will could not see how it was humanly possible for anyone to remain astride a horse that could buck the way this one did. But Tye not only stayed aboard, he made it look easy. Will could swear Tye had a smile on his face during the entire ride.

The battle lasted for another five minutes, and then the dun, after one of his sunfishing slams back to earth, stopped, head down and breathing hard. Tye allowed the horse to catch his breath, then kicked him into a lope around the corral. He loped him around twice, then turned and guided him in the other direction, finally coming to a stop in front of Will.

"You wanna ride him?" Tye asked

"Sure," Will said, with such eagerness it brought a smile to Tye's face.

Will was climbing down from his perch on the fence when an angry voice reached his ears.

"Will . . . Will Paxton. Where in the blazes are you? I'm gonna tan your hide when I catch ya, boy. Lazy no-account kid, can't get an honest day's work outa ya fer nothin'."

Will looked up at Tye, regret written all over his face. "I guess I'd better get back to work. Can I ride him some other time?"

"Sure ya can," Tye said with a grin. He watched as Will climbed down the the fence and headed around to the front of the cook shack. That was a good boy, Tye thought to himself. He deserved better than to be workin' for that lazy, no-account cook. He had seen Will at night, when the boy thought no one was watching him, sneak out and ride the horses in the corral. Will had a natural ability with horses and they trusted him. That spoke a lot for the sort of person he was and it made an impression on Tye. If a horse trusted a fella, then it was a pretty sure bet he was worth his salt.

The year was 1872. Will Paxton was in his sixteenth year, nearing seventeen. He had the lean look of youth still about him, but carried it with agility, and none of the clumsiness that sometimes plagues the young. He had been working as a cook's helper at the Triangle T for the past two years since leaving his parents' farm in Kansas to follow his dream.

When he'd left the farm in Kansas, he'd left with holes in his overalls, food enough for two days, and a single-minded goal. He was going to be a cowboy, riding the range, following the cattle drives, and riding the rough string.

This had been the only thing he'd thought of ever since he'd read his first dime-store novel. His father had tanned his hide good for reading what he called trash and lies, but even the whippings hadn't quenched the fire in Will's soul, and he scrimped and saved every penny he could to buy another novel.

His dreams might have died a natural death, as dreams so often do when confronted with hard work and disappointments, if it had not been for a chance meeting with a gentleman by the name of Curly Woodson.

This particular meeting took place one day after school as Will was returning home. Will was late this day due to the garter snake found in the teacher's desk. Although it could have been placed there by any one of the twelve boys in the school, Mr. Henry affixed the blame to Will—not without good reason, since Will was usually the instigator of such pranks and even carried out most of them on his own.

On this particular day, he'd been detained after school to wash the wooden floor of the one-room schoolhouse.

Will would have preferred a whipping to the menial labor, but Mr. Henry never whipped his students; rather, he chose to keep them late after school. By arriving home late, the errant child was automatically guilty, the only question remaining was of what crime.

Will, having two brothers and one sister in school with him, knew his father would hear about the prank before he was through washing the floor. He also knew he would get the strap laid to his backside, then the lecture for his soul. He was never sure which of the two was more unbearable.

After scrubbing the floor with halfhearted wipes with the worn-out mop, and dirty water for the required half hour, Mr. Henry excused him, knowing there were chores at home for the boy.

It was on his way home that day that Will met Curly Woodson.

About a mile from the Paxton farm, and by the main road running between the scattered small farms around the area to town was a small stream. As Will approached the stream, he noticed a horse picketed under the shade of the large oak tree. The tree itself grew beside the road and was used by many a traveler as a resting place, offering a cool respite for the weary, and water for the livestock.

Will was watching the horse as he continued down the road toward home. It wasn't until he was abreast of the tree that he noticed the prone figure in the shade.

Cautiously, Will approached the stream, keeping his eyes on the figure under the tree. Upon further inspection, he noticed the man had a Stetson hat pulled over his eyes, while his head rested on his saddle.

Will had every intention of passing the stranger by and continuing on his way. He was already in trouble, and he didn't want to add to that by dallying. But as he prepared to cross the small rivulet of water, the stranger spoke, causing Will's breath to catch in his throat.

"Howdy, young fella. Where ya headed?"

Will whirled, looking at the man, who was tipping the hat back on his head and sitting up.

"Home," Will said weakly, his knees shaking slightly.

"Live around here, do ya?" the stranger asked

"Yes, sir, just down the road a spell," Will said, motioning in the direction of his home.

"You reckon a man could get somethin' to eat there? I ain't had nothin' in my stomach for two days now and my belt buckle is startin' to rub my back-bone," the stranger said, standing up and looking down at his stomach.

"I guess so," Will said hesitantly, knowing his parents were both good Christian people, who had fed weary travelers before. But he also knew they wouldn't take kindly to Will bringing home a stranger.

"Well, let me get my hoss saddled and we'll ride over and ask your folks. Worst they can do is say no," the man said as he picked up his saddle and started toward the horse.

"By the way my name's Curly Woodson. What's yours?"

"Will, Will Paxton," Will blurted out, watching the man saddle the horse.

"Pleased to meet ya, Will. Come on, Ole Smokey'll ride double."

Will walked cautiously over to the horse as the man mounted and extended his hand to Will. Will climbed up behind Curly, feeling the sharp backbone of the horse digging into his backside, evidence that Smokey had missed a few meals as well.

"Are you a cowboy?" Will asked innocently.

"Yep," Curly said. "I been in Texas workin' on a

spread down there. I had some business in Missouri to take care of and now I'm headed back."

"Wow!" Will exclaimed. "That's what I'm gonna be, a cowboy. Are there really Indians in Texas?"

Curly chuckled. "Yep, there's Injuns there all right. I've killed a passel of 'em, but there's still plenty left for you."

Will gulped. He couldn't believe his luck. Here was a real live cowboy and he was taking him home with him. He forgot all about the whipping he'd get when he got home. Here was the real thing, not something out of the novels he'd been reading.

Will's mother listened quietly as Will introduced Curly. She looked neither approving nor disapproving as she listened to her son describe Curly as a "real cowboy," who was headed to Texas. Her expression never changed as Will sheepishly admitted to inviting Curly to eat with them.

"Of course, you're welcome to eat with us, Mr. Woodson," Martha Paxton said, the sigh of resignation audible to both Will and Curly.

"Put your horse in the barn. Will, you get down to the field and help your pa."

Dinner that evening was a combination of frustration and excitement. Will's constant questioning of Curly about the places he'd been and work he'd done monopolized the conversation and exasperated Will's father, who continued to give him disparaging looks throughout the meal.

Afterward, Curly and Will's father sat on the front porch in the two worn rocking chairs, talking about the weather, crop conditions, and the state of affairs.

Will sat listening respectfully as his father and Curly talked. Once, during a lull in the conversation, he tried to steer the conversation back to Curly's exploits, but his father's stern look persuaded him to remain quiet.

Due to the large number of Paxtons, six children, Ma and Pa, and the size of the house, Curly spent the night in the barn.

"I'm sorry we ain't got no room in the house, Mr.

Woodson. I'll have the missus rustle ya up some extra blankets," Will's father had said.

"There's no need in that," Curly objected. "I'll be fine with my roll. After sleepin' under the stars, that barn will seem like the finest hotel room in St Louis. I'm much obliged to you and the missus for feedin' me and lettin' me spend the night here."

The next morning, Curly was gone before Will arose. The disappointment upon finding him gone before he had a chance to talk to him again, left Will in a solemn mood for the next week. He went to school, did his chores, and helped his father and brothers in the fields, but his heart wasn't in it.

The only thing that occupied Will's thoughts was Curly and the life he led as a cowboy.

A week later, he packed his few belongings in a worn-out suitcase, took enough food for two days, and headed west. He looked back once to see the farm before it was hidden by the rolling hills. Then turning, he headed down the road, carrying his dreams with him.

He tried to find work on every ranch between Kansas and Montana, but the story was always the same. No one wanted to hire a fourteen-year-old kid with no experience. Fortunately, all the ranchers were willing to feed him before he went on his way, which prevented him from starving as he continued his journey. He didn't plan on winding up in Montana. It seemed things just turned out that way.

Finally, he found this job as a cook's helper, the only position he'd been offered since he'd left Kansas. He had gladly accepted the job. It may not have been what he'd expected when he'd left, but it was a job and he ate regular.

Thinking back on it, Will figured things could have been a lot worse than they were. At least he was working on a ranch, and the way he looked at it, that was better than being on the farm in Kansas.

Will wasn't worried about being in trouble with the

fat cook, but he needed the job, even if it didn't pay much: ten dollars a month, plus room and board. Besides, he didn't have anywhere else to go. The next ranch was a good twenty miles away and he knew he couldn't get a job as a cowhand because he lacked the experience, and no one was gonna hire a kid still wet behind the ears. He'd learned this the hard way after nearly starving to death looking for work on ranches between Kansas and Montana. He might have been able to get a job in one of the towns along the way, but he didn't figure that would be any better than being tied to his father's farm.

Will worked from early morning until late at night. He was up before anyone else, including the lazy cook. He started each day stoking the fire in the large wood cookstove, laying out the pots and pans Cookie would need, gathering the eggs from the henhouse that would be used for the morning meal. Eggs were a real treat on a working ranch and it was said that many of the hands who worked there did so because of the eggs they got for breakfast every morning.

Once Will had gathered the eggs, he would knock on Cookie's door, which was a room off the kitchen, and roust him from bed.

Will slept in the bunkhouse with the hands, but since he was up before they were and usually went to bed after they did, he didn't get much chance to talk to them.

Will always dreaded waking the grouchy cook each morning. He'd never met a person who complained as much as the fat man did. He'd start in first thing in the morning complaining about how dirty Will had left the kitchen the night before, and continued finding fault with everything he did all through the day. He even complained about the number of eggs Will collected, as if it were his fault the chickens only laid one egg apiece.

Will continued working hard throughout the day, serving the ranch hands as they ate, keeping their coffee cups full, and bringing more food as they emptied their plates. Keeping twenty-odd plates filled kept Will running.

One thing Will learned shortly after starting to work for the Triangle T was that cowboys could put away the grub. Cookie always said, "A cowboy ain't nothin' but a appetite with a horse 'tween his legs."

Once the meal was over, Will went to work washing dishes, cleaning the long tables and benches where the ranch hands ate, sweeping the floors, chopping wood, and filling the wood box for the next meal.

While Will was busy with his chores, Cookie went back to his room and closed the door, leaving the cleanup work to Will. Though this irritated Will, he was grateful to be out from under the constant complaining and harassment of the man.

By the time Will finished his cleaning and preparation for the next meal, he had little time to himself before he had to start waiting tables again. His only break from the daily grind was when the whole outfit was gone, usually during branding time, for the spring gather. Then the cowboys just packed a couple of biscuits and some beef jerky to eat until that evening. Will had begged the ranch foreman, Charley Hicks, to let him go along, and thought the man was going to relent, until the cook intervened and said he needed Will there to help him.

"Sorry, kid," the foreman had said. "Maybe next time." But it had been the same every time. Will didn't quit trying though. He was determined to find a way to prove himself as a hand.

Will was the last one to turn in at night after making sure everything was clean and ready for the next morning. Then, if no one were around, he'd head to the horse corral to catch one of the horses. He had started out riding in the large corral, but as time progressed, he had taken to riding in the open pastures. He didn't know what would happen if someone caught him in the act, but the thrill and pleasure he got from the horses far outweighed the risk. He was going to continue riding until someone stopped him. He had learned to ride on his father's farm in Kansas, but riding the slow plow horses was a world apart from riding a working cow horse. Riding the wiry cow horses took some getting used to, especially since he rode bareback, not daring to risk borrowing a saddle from the tack room.

He loved the feel of the horses under him and they seemed to respond to him as if they knew what he was thinking. When riding, he forgot about the hard work of the day, the lazy cook, and the constant harassment. This was his time and he let his dreams carry him away as he rode. He didn't know how he was going to do it, but he knew that one day things would be different. Little did he know things would change sooner than he expected.

Will's second greatest enjoyment came from listening to the stories told by the cowhands as he waited on them during the meals. He listened as they talked about the horses they'd ridden, the tough cattle they had worked, trail drives they'd been on, and men they knew. Will liked all the cowhands and for the most part they were friendly to him. All that is, except a man by the name of Slade. His full name was Garth Slade, but since he hated his given name, he swore he'd beat anyone who used it in his presence.

Slade was a large man, standing six-foot-two and weighing over two hundred pounds. He wore a black, drooping mustache that added a sinister look to his appearance, and he was constantly stroking and twisting it to make it curl on the ends, adding to the effect.

The evil looks he cast at Will each time he filled his plate or coffee cup, sent shivers down Will's spine. And every time Will heard the call, "Hey, Dish Boy, bring me some more food," it made the hair on the back of his neck stand up on end.

Even though he was young in years, Will recognized Slade for what he was: a man who took his pleasure from bullying those who were weaker than him. He always preyed on those who were intimidated by his size and menacing looks. These were the ones who caught the brunt of Slade's sadistic humor and were constantly tormented by the man.

The cruel streak that lay beneath the surface of the man was evident to any who inspected the horses he rode. Each one carried the scars from the Mexican spurs he wore. Will had put salve on the cuts several times during his late-night visits to the horse corral.

Slate's spurs were large rowelled and sharpened to razor-sharp points in order to inflict the maximum damage and pain when used, and Slade enjoyed using them. The story had circulated around the bunkhouse, when Slade was gone, about how he had almost killed a man in a fight, using his spurs to rake the man while he was down.

Had Will known how Slade would play a major part in changing the course of his life, he might not have harbored such hatred for the man. But as it was, Will despised Slade and swore somehow he'd even the score for the pain he inflicted on defenseless horses.

The fork in the road for Will began after breakfast, as the men finished eating. Will placed their plates in the large washtub as he did every morning. He placed the last plate in the tub, lifted it off the table, and was carrying it by the handles to the kitchen, arms straining under the load. Slade was sitting at the end of the long table and Will had to pass by him on his way. With an evil grin spreading across his face, Slade stuck his foot out as Will walked by. Will, loaded down with the tub of dishes, didn't see the extended foot until it was too late. He hit Slade's boot, his feet becoming entangled as he stumbled. He tried to right himself, but to no avail. He fell headlong, sending the dishes crashing to the floor as he brought his hands down to brace himself against the fall.

The sound of breaking dishes and Slade's laughter

brought Cookie hurrying from the kitchen, cursing Will as he caught sight of the broken dishes scattered across the floor.

Will's face was burning with fury as he lunged to his feet and faced the laughing Slade. No one else in the room was laughing as Will stood there shaking with rage. He looked into cold black eyes. The grin on Slade's lips was taunting. Will knew Slade wanted him to say or do something that would give him cause to strike back.

Fighting back the urge to hurl a challenge into the grinning face, Will bent over and started picking up the broken dishes, his face burning from the anger he felt.

"What's the matter, Dish Boy? Can't you walk?" Slade asked, laughing loudly again.

Even though the urge was strong, Will knew better than to say anything. Slade wouldn't hesitate to use his enormous size and strength against him. Though anger burned through him like a hot iron, he wasn't going to lose his head and get himself into something he had no chance of winning. But he vowed someday Slade would pay.

With the cook yelling at him and Slade's laughter burning in his ears, he picked up two of the broken dishes and headed to the kitchen, the cook right behind him.

Slade was still laughing when a voice from the far end of the table brought instant silence.

"Leave the boy alone!"

Though it was spoken softly, the threat behind the words was unmistakable.

Slade's laughter died instantly and jerking his head around, he stared at the man who had spoken.

Tye Garrett sat at the end of the long bench, his elbows resting on the table. He held a cup of coffee in both hands. He didn't look at Slade as he brought the cup to his lips and slowly sipped the coffee.

"You say somethin', Garrett?" Slade asked, glaring down the table to where Tye sat.

Setting his cup down slowly and turning to meet Slade's glare, Tye spoke in an even voice. "Yeah, I said leave the boy alone!"

"And what if I don't?" Slade taunted. "You gonna do somethin' about it?"

Tye stood up, and without taking his eyes from Slade, walked the length of the table until he was opposite the bully. Leaning over and placing both hands on the table, Tye stared at him and spoke again in a quiet, even voice. "You bother that boy again and I'll show you what it's like to be treated like one of your horses. I'll take those spurs off ya and use 'em to peel your hide."

After a brief pause to let his words sink in, he continued. "If you think I'm bluffin',"—he paused again and stared into Slade's eyes—"you just try me."

Slade looked into the cold gray eyes boring into him from across the table. What he saw there unnerved him. There was no doubt in those eyes, only the assurance that this man believed he could do exactly what he had claimed. Slade had been in fights before, even enjoyed fighting. But he'd always been the aggressor intimidating smaller men until they'd done something foolish. Then, with pleasure, he'd beaten them unmercifully, almost killing one man by raking him with his spurs. But this man standing before him, even though he was smaller, wasn't weak. He meant what he said and he knew he could do it.

Slade sat there for several seconds, not saying anything. He had enjoyed his status as a dangerous man to mess with; now he was in danger of losing that status. He'd been threatened. If he backed down under the threat, no one in this room would fear him. He needed that fear to feed his ego. That was the reason he cut the horses he rode. They soon came to fear him and he fed off that fear like water to the dry prairie. The more fear he created, the more he needed. But this man standing across from him wasn't afraid. This man was threatening him over a cook's helper and Slade either had to call him

or back down. Either way, Slade felt he was going
to lose.

"Well now, Garrett," he said with a sneer on his
lips, "I didn't know the kid meant so much to you.
Why if I'd known you was so fond of cook's helpers,
I'd of gotten ya one for Christmas."

Tye didn't say a word as he continued to stare at
Slade, waiting for him to play his hand.

"All right," Slade said, the sneer leaving his face.
"If he means so much to ya, I won't pick on him no
more. But don't push me, Garrett. I might just decide
to use you for spurrin' practice."

Tye smiled for the first time, but the smile didn't
reach his eyes as he said, "Anytime you feel lucky,
Slade, just look me up. I'll be more'n happy to give
ya the chance." Tye pushed off from the table and
started to turn away. Then, as if a thought occurred
to him, he turned back to Slade.

"One more thing. If I find any more spur marks on the
horses you're riding, I'll see to it that you wear the same
scars they do." Not waiting for a reply, he turned and
walked out the door, leaving Slade glaring at his back.

Will had heard none of the exchange between the
two men. After slamming the tub of dishes on the
counter, he stormed out the back door, fuming with
anger. He was leaning on the horse corral, thinking
about Slade and the things he'd like to do to him. All
the men had seen what had taken place, and in his
mind he was sure they thought him a coward for not
doing something. He was certain Slade would have
jumped at the chance to beat him, but sometimes the
pain from a beating wasn't near as painful as the pain
of humiliation. Even Tye had seen him back down.
Will was wondering what Tye thought about him when
a hand came down on his shoulder. Thinking it was
Slade, Will swung around, fists cocked and ready.

"Whoa, partner," Tye said, holding his hands in the
air. "Looks like you're ready to pin someone's ears
to the ground."

"Sorry, I thought you was Slade," Will said, looking at the ground, feeling shame and embarrassment wash over him again.

"I know it probably don't help much, but you did the right thing in there. Slade was just lookin' for an excuse to jump on ya, and you cheated him outa that. That's the smart thing to do."

"Yeah," Will said with sarcasm. "But now everybody thinks I'm a coward."

"Are ya?" Tye asked.

"No! I'm not afraid of him," Will said, with such force that Tye couldn't help the smile that formed on his lips.

"Well, as long as you know that, it don't make no difference what anyone else thinks. But if it helps, I don't think you're a coward. I think ya got a good head on your shoulders and you kept your cool. That says a lot for someone your age. I know men older'n you who wouldn't show as much sense as you did in there."

"Thanks," Will said, feeling some of the anger leave him, but still burning over the thought of being humiliated in front of the other men.

Tye looked at Will, knowing how hard it was on the boy. Sixteen was almost a man out here, and Will needed to be accepted as a man. Acceptance was a hard thing to come by when you spent your time working in a kitchen, washing dishes and waiting tables.

"I been watchin' ya ride out at night," Tye said. "Ya catch on quick and the horses respond to ya. You got good balance and that's important if you're ever gonna make a good horse wrangler."

Will's face turned red as he heard what Tye said. He didn't think anyone had seen him on his late-night rides. The alarmed look on Will's face made Tye smile again.

"Don't worry, I'm the only one that knows about it. I've also seen ya doctorin' the horses that Slade rides. I reckon anyone who'd do that after workin' all day cain't be all bad."

"One of these days, I'm gonna give Slade a taste of his own medicine. Anyone who'd do that to a horse ought to be horsewhipped," Will said, the vehemence plain in his voice.

"You'll have to get in line to do that," Tye said. Will looked at him questioningly, but he said no more and Will knew better than to ask.

"I was wonderin' if you might want to help me with these broncs? I need someone to ride 'em for a while after I get most of the buck out of 'em."

Will looked at Tye, not sure he'd heard right.

"You want me to ride horses for ya?"

"Something wrong with your hearing?" Tye asked, fighting to keep a straight face after seeing the excitement showing on Will's.

"Uh, no, it's just that, well," Will stammered, "what about Cookie and the kitchen and all?"

"I already took care of that," Tye said. "I talked to Charley, and he said you could ride for me early in the mornin' and after meals. You'll help Cookie serve the meals and when they're over, you ride. Cookie's gettin' too lazy anyway." Tye looked thoughtful for a moment, then said, "Sure is gonna make him mad though." Then, as if dismissing the thought, he said, "Ya wanna ride or not?"

"Sure! When do I start?"

"As soon as we tell Cookie about the new arrangement. You can start on that dun over there," Tye replied, pointing to a horse standing in the corral. "Let's go tell Cookie, so we can get started."

"Yahoo," Will shouted, grinning from ear to ear.

Tye laughed and said, "I hope you're this excited a week from now when your backside's hurtin' so bad you need a feather pillow to sit on. You may wish you were back in the kitchen helpin' Cookie."

"Never," Will answered. "I don't care how sore my backside gets."

Chapter Two

Cookie didn't take the news of Will's new job well at all. He cussed and ranted for fifteen minutes about how good he'd been to Will, and he didn't see why Will would run off and leave him. When Will and Tye explained to him that he'd still be there to help during the meals, Cookie cursed even more, saying how that was the easy part. He was gonna have to do all the hard work by himself and that wasn't fair. He continued to cuss as they turned to leave, and both Tye and Will had to hold their grins until they got out the door.

Will followed Tye as he headed to the barn.

"First we got to get ya an outfit. There's some extra saddles in the barn. Let's see if we can find ya one." Then looking at Will's old farm boots, he said, "I got an old pair of boots I'll let ya wear. They may be a little big on ya, but they'll be better than those old clodhoppers you're wearin'. I'd hate to see ya hang your foot in a stirrup. You'll have to ride without chaps until we can get to town, and I don't want ya ridin' with spurs until ya get a little experience on these broncs."

They found the extra saddles in the tack room. Tye picked out a saddle with a high cantle and large swells. The stirrups were small wishbones—made for riding bucking stock he explained to Will as he carried the saddle to the corral.

"This is a good saddle for ridin' broncs. If one of 'em starts buckin', the high cantle will keep ya from

slippin' off the back, while the high swells will help
hold your legs in when ya squeeze. The small stirrups
will help keep your feet in without slippin' through."

Tye threw the saddle over the top rail of the corral
fence, and after cinching it down to the fence pole,
told Will to climb aboard. Even though Will wondered
what Tye was doing, he didn't ask. He climbed the
fence and sat in the saddle. Tye started adjusting the
stirrups' length until he had Will's knees slightly bent
when he placed his feet in the stirrups.

"That's to help cushion the shock to your back. If
your stirrups are out all the way, you can't put weight
on your feet and legs to take some of the joltin' off
your backside and spine. Now, let's saddle that dun
and see how you do."

With Will holding the halter lead and keeping the
dun calm, Tye placed the saddle pad and saddle on
his back, talking to him and soothing him all the while.
Even though the dun flinched several times while Tye
was saddling him, he never jumped or shied away.
Will credited this to Tye's soothing voice and easy
handling. Once he had the horse saddled, Tye replaced the halter with a hackamore with large,
braided-mohair reins. He explained that the reason for
using a hackamore was that the dun hadn't been broken to a bit yet. The hackamore would put pressure
on the tender bridge of his nose, and the large reins
made it easier to hold.

Once the hackamore was on, Tye led the horse off
a few steps and rechecked the saddle.

"Some horses learn real fast to suck extra air into
their bellies when ya cinch 'em up. Then when ya get
on, they let it out and you're sittin' there with a loose
saddle, which ain't a good thing to have. Always lead
your horse off a step or two and check your cinch
before gettin' on. Well, he's ready. Come on."

Even though this was what Will had dreamed of,
now that the time had come, he couldn't stop the butterflies in his stomach. He'd never ridden anything but

broke horses. This was a different story altogether. He walked up to where Tye was holding the dun.

"I'll hold him while you get on. Hold the reins and grab a handful of mane with your left hand. Grab the saddle horn with your right hand. When ya swing on, do it slowly, but all in one motion. Don't hesitate, and sit down gently."

Will, following Tye's instructions, was soon sitting astride the dun. He could feel the horse quiver beneath him as he settled himself in the saddle.

"You're the first person besides me to ride this horse. He's not used to your weight and he's nervous. Take the reins in both hands and keep them tight. He may try to buck when I turn him loose, but if you can keep his head pulled up, he won't be able to. But if you let his head get down between his legs, hang on for the ride. You ready?"

"As ready as I'll ever be," Will said, with a whole lot more confidence than he felt. Will had ridden the horses on his father's farm, and the ranch horses in the corral, but nothing had prepared him for what followed when Tye let go of the dun's head and stepped back. For a few seconds, the dun just stood there. Then realizing he wasn't being held and there was a different person on his back, he ducked his head between his legs and proceeded to leave the ground.

Will was unprepared for the power of the horse. The reins were nearly pulled from his hands as the dun ducked his head. Tye's words were ringing in his ears as he felt himself fly through the air and land facedown in the dirt of the corral. He came up spitting dust and whatever else was in there.

Tye was leaning against a corral post, chewing on a sliver of wood.

"You all right?" he asked as Will got to his feet.

"I think so," Will said.

"Well, go catch him and let's try again."

Will managed to hem the dun in a corner and finally got him caught by the reins. Mumbling some words about his ancestry, Will led him back to the middle of the corral where Tye stood waiting for him.

"Ya only made one mistake," Tye said.

"What was that?" Will asked.

"Ya got on 'im," Tye replied, a serious expression on his face.

Will looked at him with disbelief, then started grinning as he saw the lines on Tye's face relax into a smile.

"Well, I think I just learned the wrong way to do it. Any pointers on how to do it right?"

"Yep. Next time stay on," Tye said, taking the reins from Will.

"Thanks, I'll try to remember that," Will said with sarcasm.

"You just found out what kinda strength this horse has. But you have the advantage—you can outthink him. If ya can't hold his head up, use your head and body. Hold tight to those reins to pull yourself down into the saddle and squeeze with your knees and legs to hold yourself in. Use the swells of the saddle. If ya let yourself flop around like a sack of potatoes, you're gonna get throwed. Any more questions?"

"Just one," Will said as he swung into the saddle. "Is it my imagination or has Cookie's disposition just gotten better?"

Tye broke into a laugh as he stepped away and let the dun have his head.

The horse didn't hesitate, but immediately ducked his head between his legs. Will was ready this time, and instead of allowing the reins to be pulled through his hands, he pulled hard on the them, preventing the dun from getting his head to the ground. Even though the dun was able to buck, he couldn't get his head far enough down to turn it loose as he'd done before. He did manage, however, to deliver some good stiff-legged, bone-jarring bucks that knocked the wind out of Will and left him gasping for air. His tight grip on the reins and the squeezing of his legs made a great difference in the ride this time. After traveling the distance of the corral, the dun allowed Will to pull his head up. Will loped him around the corral and brought him to a stop in front of Tye.

Tye's face was unreadable as Will sat there trying to catch his breath. He had relaxed his hold on the reins and the pride in making his first ride was evident in his face. The next thing Will knew, he was flying through the air, headed for the corral fence, upside down. He struck the fence about halfway up and slammed headfirst into the ground before coming to rest in a heap. The last thing he remembered was Tye taking off his hat as if to scratch his head. The next thing, he was on a keg of dynamite.

"You keep gettin' bucked off that horse, I'm gonna have to start him all over again. You're gonna teach that bronc bad habits if ya keep that up."

Will wasn't listening to Tye as he tried to rise out of the dust. When he finally got to his feet and could focus his eyes, he looked to where Tye was picking his hat up off the ground in the middle of the corral. It looked as if it had been stepped on a time or two. It took Will a couple of seconds to make the connection between what had happened to him and Tye's hat being in the corral.

"You did that, didn't ya?" Will asked, disbelief in his voice.

"Yep!" was the only reply Will got.

"But why? I'd ridden him. Why would ya want to make him buck again?"

"I didn't want him to buck. I wanted you to learn a lesson."

"What lesson is that?" Will asked, still not believing what had happened.

"Never relax on a bronc," Tye said. "If you let your guard down, he'll know it. Always be ready for the unexpected. If you'd been ten miles out on the range and a jackrabbit had spooked him, you'd be walkin' back now. If you was able to walk, that is."

"Couldn't you have just told me that? Did you have to make your point at the expense of my body?" Will asked, rubbing his hip where he'd struck the fence.

"I reckon you wouldn't have learned the lesson as well if I'd just told ya. Remember, out here a horse can sometimes mean the difference between life and death. A man on foot could be in serious trouble. Don't take anything for granted where horses are concerned."

"Or cowboys bearing gifts," Will said, still rubbing his hip.

"You catch on fast," Tye said, grinning at Will. Will didn't feel like grinning at the moment.

"Let's go again," Tye said.

Will groaned as he walked over to the horse. By now, the dun had gotten most of his buck out. And after a few crow hops around the corral, he allowed his head to be pulled up. Will stopped him in the middle of the corral and watched Tye closely, not relaxing his grip on the reins.

"Ride him out in the horse trap until lunchtime. By then, I'll have another one ready for ya," Tye said, heading to the horse corral with his lariat.

When the sun was directly overheard, Will rode the dun up to the gate of the corral. Tye was saddling a large bay mare. She was a beautiful animal, standing just over fifteen hands and weighing about thirteen hundred pounds. Will had watched Tye ride the mare once before and the sight was something he wouldn't soon forget. He had ridden her bucking and squalling to a complete standstill. Even after he had totally exhausted her, she wouldn't give to the man on her back. Instead of stepping out when he touched her with his spurs, she sulled up and wouldn't move. Tye had dismounted and led her back to the horse pen, where the horses to be broken were kept.

Will knew he was in for another show. But not forgetting his lesson from this morning, he dismounted and put the dun in a holding pen before climbing the fence to get a better view.

Tye didn't need any help mounting the horses he rode. He would hold the hackamore and rein with his left hand, keeping the horse's head pulled around to him, while he used his right hand to grip the saddle horn and pull himself up. When he was mounted and set, he would let go of the hackamore, keeping its head pulled around with the rein. He would then play out the rein, allowing the horse to have its head.

Will held his breath as Tye mounted the mare, talking gently to her as he did. As he let go of the mare's head, she reared straight up, front feet pawing the air. Will sat rigid, fearing she was going to fall. Tye leaned forward, holding the reins and grabbing a handful of the mare's mane. After what seemed like an eternity to Will, the mare came down to earth, driving her head between her legs as she did. Her front feet had no more than touched the ground when her whole body shot skyward. She twisted her head around to her back feet in a twisting motion, a move designed to throw the rider off balance. She straightened to come back to earth with legs stiff and back arched. Will watched in fascination as Tye raked his spurs from the mare's shoulders to the cantle of the saddle with each jump she made. Never had he seen a horse that could jump as high as this mare could. Every time she came down, he could see the muscles in her legs and chest tighten as she prepared to launch herself into the air once more. Each jump she made easily cleared the top bar of the corral, and each crash back to earth was enough to lay a man up in bed for a week. But Tye rode as if he was part of the horse. Every time the mare changed tactics, he was ready for her, never anticipating, but always ready.

Will thought the ride was about over when the mare, instead of bunching herself for another jump, relaxed her muscles and lifted her head. Then, without warning, she fell over on her side. Will held his breath expecting Tye to be crushed beneath the weight of the falling horse. At the last second, Tye jerked his foot from the stirrup and held it out to meet the ground. This maneuver allowed him to step off the mare as she fell. He held tight to the reins, keeping the mare's head pulled back and around, preventing her from rising to her feet. As Will watched, Tye slackened the rein holding the mare's head, which allowed her to rise.

She gathered her hind feet beneath her, and with her forefeet out in front, the mare began to rise. At that precise moment, Tye leaped into the saddle and rode the mare up, finding his stirrups as she regained her footing. As her head went down between her forelegs, Tye was seated and ready, but the battle was over. The mare's jumps had lost most of their steam and it was taking her longer to gather herself for the next leap.

Finally, with one last lunge she stopped. Legs spread and chest heaving, she stood there. Tye waited until she got her wind, then touched her lightly with his spurs. This time, instead of sulling, she stepped out at a trot. Tye plow reined her around the corral twice before stopping her and stepping off. He patted her neck and rubbed her head, talking to her all the while.

Will climbed off the fence and waited for Tye to walk over. Blood was dripping from his nose. He looked as if he'd been in a fight and come out on the losing end.

Tye handed the reins to Will and sank down against a post.

"I'm glad they're not all like her. I'd have to find another occupation if they were."

Taking a handkerchief from his pocket, he wiped the blood from his nose and the sweat from his forehead.

"That was a great ride," Will said. The excitement of watching the ride was reflected in his voice. "I wish I could ride like that."

"When I get through with you, you'll be a better rider than I am," Tye said.

Will didn't respond to that statement. He couldn't believe he'd ever be as good as Tye, much less better.

After helping Cookie with the noon meal, Will returned to the corral to find Tye had already saddled another horse for him. This one was a large red gelding with four white stockings. He was broad across the chest and hindquarters and was built for both speed and endurance. Will had watched Tye ride this horse twice before and he liked the way the horse carried himself. He didn't buck hard like most of the other horses and he bucked in a straight line with smooth, steady jumps. Once he brought his head up, the fight was over. He would lope around the corral, responding to the commands given.

"I want ya to take good care of this horse," Tye said. "He's one of mine."

"One of yours?" Will asked.

"Yep. That's the deal I have with Cal Jenkins, the owner. I break his horses for 'im for ten dollars a head. And he lets me keep my horses here and break 'em along with his."

"How many horses do ya own?" Will asked, realizing that Tye owned more than the clothes on his back and his riggin'.

"I've got about fifteen head here," Tye answered as he rubbed the horse's neck.

"What do ya do with 'em?" Will asked.

"I break 'em and sell 'em," Tye said. "Then I buy some more. I'm always lookin' to buy some good brood mares. I got about thirty head of good blooded mares on a little place south of here."

Will stared, shocked into silence. He had had no idea Tye was anything more than a broncbuster working for wages. It just went to show you, you never really knew about men in the West. Will had heard stories of men who worked the cattle drives, or worked on ranches for forty dollars a month. Men who were doctors, lawyers, bankers, or businessmen from back East, who had, for whatever reason, given up their practices to come west. Some were looking to make their fortunes; some were just looking for the excitement; and some were running to escape whatever was behind them—business, love, or, more often than not, the law. Whatever their reason, all had one thing in common: They had all ended up pushing cattle and enduring the hardships and dangers that went along with the job.

Will mounted the red horse while Tye held his head. He wasn't able to keep its head up, but he did manage to follow the instructions Tye had given him earlier that day. He stayed aboard as the horse bucked the length of the corral. When the sorrel reached the fence on the opposite side, he lifted his head, and Will loped him around the corral twice. Stopping him in front of the gate leading out to the trap, he dismounted and led him through. Tye watched as Will remounted and started across the pasture, a thoughtful expression on his face as Will reined the horse around and rode off. After a few moments, Tye grabbed his lariat and hackamore and headed to the horse corral.

Will rode two more horses that afternoon, then went to help Cookie prepare the evening meal. The fat cook was in an unpleasant mood and continued to find fault with everything Will did, but Will was determined not to let him spoil his mood. So he smiled every time Cookie began to complain, which infuriated the chubby little man until he became so angry he stormed out of the kitchen, hurling insults at Will as he went.

When all the hands had finished eating, Tye walked back to where Will was washing dishes in the large tub.

"When ya finish with them dishes, meet me at the barn."

The fat cook was sitting on a stool by the back door,

slowly peeling potatoes and glancing at Will occasionally with glowering looks meant to spoil the good mood he was in. Even though it was only early April and the evening air was cool, Cookie's shirt and apron were soaked with sweat. Upon hearing Tye's instructions to Will, he stopped peeling a potato, and pointing his knife at Will, said, "He ain't goin' nowhere till he chops wood fer the wood box, cleans the tables, and mops the floors."

Tye walked up to the cook, stared straight into his eyes, and said, "Maybe you didn't understand me this mornin' when I explained how things was gonna be. Will here will help ya serve the meals. After that, he works for me. If you got a problem with that, talk to Charley. I'm sure he'll be more'n happy to straighten things out fer ya. Will, I'll expect you in five minutes. Don't be late!" With that, he stepped past the cook, who was sweating even more now.

"Yes, sir," Will said with a grin as Tye went out the door. He couldn't help smiling as he thought about the change his life had taken since this morning.

"You better wipe that smile from your face, you ungrateful little snot," Cookie hollered at him. "I've treated you like you was my own son, and this is the thanks I get fer it."

"Cookie," Will said, "if I was your son, I'd run away from home and change my name. You're just mad 'cause you're gonna have to work for a change." The contempt in Will's voice came through as he addressed the man.

"You better watch your mouth, boy! I'll beat the livin' daylights outa ya, if you get smart with me." Cookie's face was turning red as he glared at Will.

Will dropped the pot he'd been scrubbing back into the tub of soapy water. Then, throwing the dishrag after it, he turned and faced the man who had threatened him.

"You ever lay a hand on me, you tub of lard, they'll be needin' a new cook around here."

Cookie lumbered off the stool and walked over to where Will stood.

"You've gotten real high and mighty since you got Tye Garrett lookin' out for ya. Haven't ya, boy?"

"I don't need Tye Garrett to help me take care of you," Will said, stepping closer to the fat man. "If you think I can't handle my own affairs, start the ball rollin' and we'll see where it ends up."

Cookie stood there for a few seconds, staring into Will's eyes, expecting him to look away, but Will met the cook's stare with a steady gaze. He wasn't afraid of this man standing before him, and he wasn't about to be pushed around by him. Failing to see fear in Will's eyes, the overweight cook turned away in disgust. With hatred in his voice, he said, "Get outa my kitchen and don't come back. I won't have some damned snot-nosed kid threatenin' me. Go on, get outa here. I hope Slade rips ya to pieces if he catches ya without your bodyguard around."

Will pulled off the apron he was wearing and threw it at the cook. "With pleasure," he said, and headed out the door. He didn't know what that last comment was about and he didn't care. He was free of the kitchen and free from that fat, lazy, no-account cook. He wondered what Tye would say when he told him about the incident. Would Tye agree with what he did or would he be upset at Will for losing his job? For that matter, what was he going to do for a job? Tye had never said anything about paying him. Would Charley Hicks keep him on now that he no longer worked in the kitchen?

Chapter Three

Will found Tye in the barn, repairing tack. When he told him about his argument with Cookie, he expected anything but what happened. Tye looked at him for a moment, then asked, "What do you want outa life, Will?"

Will looked at Tye in astonishment. Here he was without a job and this man wanted to know what he wanted out of life. He stood there staring, the silence hanging heavy in the air.

"Do you want to be a cowboy for the rest of your life for forty a month, or do you want more than that?" Tye asked. The seriousness in his voice made Will wonder even more at the reason behind his question.

He didn't know what Tye was digging at so, taking a deep breath, he said, "Well this mornin' I was a cook's helper wishin' I was a cowhand. Now tonight I've been fired as a cook's helper and I don't have any idea what my future holds. And now you're askin' me what I want outa life. Right now I'd settle for a steady job and a good night's sleep. I hurt in so many places, I got pains on top of pains. Does that answer your question?"

Tye threw back his head and laughed. When his laughter finally subsided, he turned to Will and said, "Ya know, sometimes a fella can get so wrapped up in his own dreams he forgets about the things other folks is feelin'. Sorry, I forgot this was your first day ridin' broncs. I got some liniment in the bunkhouse you can use. It'll help keep some of the sore outa your walk. As far as a steady job, you got one. I'll pay ya two dollars for every horse we break. How's that?"

"That's great! Thanks, Tye," Will said, as the burden of being unemployed was lifted from his shoulders.

"Don't thank me yet. You'll earn every dollar and you may decide it ain't worth it," Tye said, watching Will's face.

"I'll be there when the last horse is broke and you're lookin' for another," Will replied.

Tye smiled at him and went back to working on the saddle leather he had in front of him.

Will lost himself in thinking about the question Tye had asked him earlier. What did he want out of life? Would he be satisfied with forty a month for the rest of his life? Is that why he'd left the farm in Kansas? It was true his mom and pop had five other children, and having one less mouth to feed was gonna make it easier on 'em. But what did *he* want? There was something driving him, and he didn't think he'd be content working for wages the rest of his life, but things were moving too fast right now for him to know just what it was he wanted.

"Why did you ask me what I wanted outa life?" Will asked.

Tye didn't look up from the lacing he was working with as he answered, "No reason. Just was wonderin', that's all."

"Well, I don't know what I want outa life right now, but I don't think I wanna work for forty a month the rest of my life. Seems to me if a fella's got a little ambition and uses his head, he can make somethin' out of himself out here. I don't know what I want yet, but when I find out, since you asked, you'll be the first to know."

Tye smiled to himself, but didn't reply. Will didn't expect one.

*   *   *

The next couple of weeks found Will working with the broncs Tye had first ridden. He managed to keep from getting himself thrown again and was even receiving nods of approval from Tye.

Several of the ranch hands had stopped by to watch Tye ride and had spoken to Will as if he was an equal instead of a cook's helper. Although they probably didn't even realize it, this had an impact on Will like nothing else could. Being accepted by the other hands was important to him and he was finally seeing that acceptance happen.

Slade made a point of avoiding him. When Will passed by him, he would just give him a baleful stare and turn away. His behavior puzzled Will. He still wasn't aware of the confrontation Slade and Tye had the morning Slade had tripped him. Will expected Slade to say something about his change in status and was surprised when he failed to do so.

Even though Slade's behavior puzzled Will, he was thankful for the reprieve he got from the constant abuse. But Slade hadn't forgotten Will, or the fact that Tye had backed him down. He swore to himself that one day both would pay. That day came a few weeks later, with unexpected results.

It was a warm day in May and Will was sitting on the corral fence, watching Tye ride a big roan gelding. Will has just finished riding one of Tye's horses and had come back for another one. Little Joe McCutchen and Lanky Thompson were sitting beside Will, watching the ride.

The roan was one of the best horses Will had seen and he knew it belonged to Tye. Standing just over sixteen hands tall and weighing fifteen hundred pounds, the roan was the biggest horse Tye owned. He'd traded for him a couple of weeks ago with a rancher who'd bought three horses from him. The rancher had traded him because none of his hands had been able to stay aboard the animal.

Tye had been riding the horse for ten minutes and

hadn't felt any give in the roan yet. He'd known he was going to be in for a tough ride when he stepped on, but he had no idea the battle was going to be this rough. The muscles in his arms and legs were starting to ache and he was tiring. At that moment, he wasn't sure he was going to be able to outlast the bronc. The big horse was trying every trick he could think of to lose the demon on his back. Every time he hit the ground, legs stiff and back arched, Tye felt as if his back would break. Then his whole body would be snapped like a whip as the horse instantly bunched itself and became airborne again, reversing ends in midair. When this failed to unseat the cowboy on his back, he'd throw his head up, rear on his hind legs, and walk backward as if he could somehow force this man to slide off. Just as it seemed he was going to fall over backward, he would throw his head forward and come down hard on his front legs. He would then bury his head between them and bring his hindquarters up into the air.

The fight had been going on longer than expected, and Tye knew he couldn't last much longer. He was considering bailing out of the saddle, when he felt the roan give a little. It wasn't much—just a slight relaxing of the muscles and a slowing between jumps—but it was enough to tell Tye that the battle was almost over for the day. The roan made a few more attempts at unseating the man on his back, but those watching could see the fight had gone out of him. With a final twist and jump, the big horse stopped, and lifted his head slightly, nostrils flaring as he fought for air. Tye let him stand for a full minute, stroking his neck and speaking softly to him. He touched him lightly with his spurs. But instead of stepping out, the roan lunged ahead, buried his head between his legs, and bucked across the length of the corral. When he reached the fence on the opposite side, Tye pulled the roan's head up. The big horse came to a stop, eyes rolling, and nostrils flaring. This time Tye didn't let him rest. He pulled him around and touched the spurs to him. The roan started at a run around the corral and Tye had to pull him down into a trot to prevent him from running into the corral fence. After trotting him twice around, Tye pulled him to a stop in front of the three spectators sitting on the fence.

"I didn't think I was gonna outlast him," Tye said. "He is without a doubt the stoutest horse I've ever ridden."

"That was some ride, Tye," Little Joe said. "I'd of paid money to see a ride like that and here I got to see it fer free. Maybe you ought to start chargin' people money to watch ya ride."

"Now there's an idea," Tye said. "Charge people money to watch some fool tangle with a bronc. I doubt you'd get enough people willin' to pay hard-earned money to see somethin' like that."

"I don't kno—" Little Joe began, but the piercing scream of a horse in pain snapped their attention to the corral where the horses Tye was breaking were kept. The first scream was followed closely by a second, and before the sound died, Tye was off the roan and over the fence, running in the direction of the corral before any of the other three could move.

When Tye turned the corner of the barn, the sight that met him made his blood run hot. Slade was mounted on Tye's big red sorrel and was using his spurs to rake the horse from shoulder to flank. Tye could see blood on the horse's side where Slade's spurs had cut into flesh. The sorrel was bucking for all he was worth, trying to unseat this man who was causing him such pain. Slade was smiling as he continued to rake the horse. The pleasure he was deriving from inflicting pain on the animal made the bile rise in Tye's throat.

Quickly gauging the line the horse would take as he worked to free himself from the lunatic on his back, Tye climbed the fence to the top rail and waited, crouched and ready. The direction the horse was bucking would bring him and his rider within three feet of where Tye perched. The horse continued his frantic bucking, screaming with each rake of the spurs. As he neared the spot where Tye was waiting, Tye tensed, the muscles in his legs tightening as he prepared for his leap. As the horse approached, Tye timed his leap to the precise moment when the horse's feet would hit the ground. Then like a wolf attacking its prey, he sprang from his perch, catching Slade around the neck in a choke hold as he went across the horse's back.

Slade, intent on riding the red horse, had not seen Tye on the top rail. He knew Tye would come running when he heard his horse cry out in pain, but he thought he would come into the corral on foot. Slade had planned to force the big horse to run Tye down and crush him beneath those sharp hooves. When he glanced up and saw Tye hurtling through the air at him, the shock of seeing his plan fail slowed his thoughts and prevented him from bracing himself for the impact as Tye hit him.

The momentum of Tye's leap carried him over the horse's back as he hit Slade with his left shoulder and grabbed him around the neck. Both men hit the ground hard, breaking Tye's hold on Slade's neck, and causing both men to roll under the horses that milled about in the corral, trying to escape the pandemonium taking place.

Tye rolled from beneath the horses, barely dodging hooves as he did. He came to his feet a second before Slade and stepped in quickly, swinging hard from his knees, catching Slade in the stomach. The air was forced from Slade's lungs as Tye stepped back and swung a roundhouse right to the face, connecting solidly and knocking Slade to the ground, splitting his lip and loosening teeth. Tye backed off, waiting for Slade to get to his feet. The blood was pounding in Tye's head. Never had he wanted to kill someone as badly as he did now. He wanted to humiliate Slade. Destroy him.

Slade got his knees under him, looking at Tye and wiping blood from his cut lip with the back of his sleeve. With a wicked smile on his lips, he said, "You've been asking for it, Garrett. Now you're gonna get a taste of what that horse got."

Tye's anger overrode any caution he might have had as he rushed in to smash Slade again. It was just what Slade wanted. Pushing himself off the ground, he drove his head into Tye's stomach, grabbing his legs as he did and pulling him off his feet. Tye hit the ground on the flat of his back, and the air was slammed out of him by the impact. Slade jumped back and brought the heel of his right boot down, trying to impale Tye with the spur. Tye twisted his body to avoid Slade's boot. He was almost fast enough, but the spur caught him on the outer thigh, tearing through his jeans and cutting a gash in the flesh of his leg. Tye rolled over and came to his feet as Slade regained his balance.

Tye knew he'd made a mistake by letting Slade taunt him into carelessness. He'd have to use his head, or Slade would cut him to ribbons with those spurs.

The two men circled each other in the dust of the corral, each looking for an opening in the other's defenses. Slade feinted with his right, then looped a left to Tye's head. Tye went under the swing, bringing a right to Slade's midsection, then driving a left to his nose. Tye wasn't set when he swung and neither blow was enough to bring Slade down, but both slowed him and Tye had the satisfaction of seeing blood come from Slade's nose.

Tye's leg was bleeding and the pain was intense. He could feel the blood running into his boot, but the heat of battle made him ignore the pain and concentrate on the enemy before him.

Slade's eyes were narrow slits as he moved in on his opponent. Tye gave ground as Slade advanced, staying away from the bigger man's reach. He knew a blow from one of those large fists could finish him.

Slade mistook Tye's retreat for weakness and rushed in with both arms swinging, triumph in his eyes as he anticipated crushing his enemy. It was the move Tye had been waiting for. Sidestepping the rush and planting his feet, he delivered a sledgehammer blow to Slade's kidneys. Slade straightened, his face a mask of pain. Tye pivoted on his feet and brought a punch over and down to Slade's jaw. Slade's eyes glazed as he went down in a heap, a groan escaping him as he hit the ground. He attempted to rise to his knees and Tye stepped in. Grabbing a handful of Slade's hair and holding him upright, he swung his fist in a full arc from behind him. He caught Slade at the point where his ear connected with his jaw. Slade hit the ground again. Then Tye grabbed him by the front of his shirt, dragged him to his knees, and hit him a smashing blow to the face. Slade went over on his back and lay there, groaning. Tye stepped back, his breath coming in gasps. He bent over, resting his hands on his knees, trying to catch his wind. Finally, he walked over to Slade, and grabbing him by the boot, he unbuckled the spur, then did the same with the other. Removing the spurs, he walked over to the horse trough, and picked up a wooden feed bucket. He filled it with water and walked back to where Slade lay.

The sounds of battle had brought all the hands to the horse corral. A fight was entertainment and none wanted to miss any of the action. No one made a move to stop the fight. It was between these two, and if one should kill the other, then it would be dealt with after the fight.

Tye took the pail of water and poured it over Slade. When he saw he was coming to, he dropped the bucket, and holding the spurs in one hand, he grabbed Slade by the back of his shirt collar. Pulling him to his feet, he dragged him to the corral gate. One of the hands standing by the gate opened it as he saw Tye's intent. Tye dragged the dazed man through the gate, then headed toward the blacksmith shop.

The blacksmith was a large German named Hanns Stuber. Everyone called him Stub. He was a large man, with arms as big as most men's legs, gained from long hours of swinging a forge hammer. He was the only other man on the ranch, besides the foreman, who had his own quarters. He lived in a small house behind the blacksmith shop with his wife and their three small children.

Stub heard the commotion coming from the horse corral and had joined the other hands to watch the fight. Now as Tye dragged Slade toward his shop, he hurried to get there first to see what Tye's intentions were and to lend a hand if needed.

Tye pulled Slade under the lean-to where Stub had his forge set up. Flinging Slade to the ground, he carried the spurs to the large anvil and picked up the tongs used for holding hot shoes. He squeezed the spur in the grips of the tongs. Placing the spur on the anvil, he took the large forge hammer in his right hand, and with a full swing, struck the rowel of the spur. The rowel shattered and flew off, sending pieces of metal flying in all directions. Then he did the same with the other spur. Slade watched as Tye not only hammered out the rowels, but beat the shanks of the spur off as well. Once he had done this, Tye walked over to Slade, who was still lying dazed in the dirt of the blacksmith shop. Dragging him up, he led him over to the anvil. Slade made one attempt to pull away from Tye's grasp, but a backhand slap to the face changed his mind. Tye placed one of Slade's arms on the anvil. Then, taking one of the spurs, he fitted it to Slade's wrist, and positioning both wrist and spur on the anvil, he grabbed the large hammer again.

"You move and I might just miss and break your arm," he said as he lifted the hammer to swing. Stub, seeing Tye's intent, stepped forward and held Slade's arm. Then looking straight into Tye's eyes, he nodded. Tye held the hammer over his head, nodded back to the big blacksmith, then swung the hammer, striking and bending the spur around Slade's wrist. Slade screamed as the metal bit into the flesh.

Once Tye finished with the first spur, he did the same with the other on the other wrist, while Stub held Slade. Then stepping back, he watched as Slade stared at his bracelets.

"You're so fond of them spurs, you can wear 'em where they can't hurt nothin' but you." With that, he handed the forge hammer to Stub, turned, and walked out of the lean-to, leaving Slade on his knees, staring wretchedly at the bracelets he now wore.

Slade then gazed at the men gathered there, his eyes pleading. But all he saw as he looked from one face to another were looks of contempt and disgust. One by one, they turned and walked away. Stub strode past him and started building up the fire in his forge. He gave Slade another look of disgust as he turned and began hammering a horseshoe into shape.

Will had watched the fight. Had seen Tye defeat Slade, a man of considerable size. It reminded him of the Bible story his mother had read to him of David and Goliath. He wondered what had possessed Slade to ride one of Tye's horses. It was evident he had done it to provoke a fight between the two of them. He'd gotten his wish, Will thought. He'd never seen a man beaten down as badly as Slade. He didn't feel sorry for what Tye had done to him, only surprised by the fact that Tye had done such a thorough job.

Will looked around for Tye and, not seeing him among the other ranch hands, he went to the horse corral to care for the sorrel. Upon entering the corral, he saw Tye pulling the saddle off the big horse, talking to him, soothing him while he examined the wounds on his sides and shoulders.

Will saw the blood on Tye's pants and boot, and noticed that Tye was favoring his leg when he walked.

"Here, let me take care of him while you see about that leg," Will said, stepping into the corral.

"I'm all right. I've got to get something on these

cuts before they get infected," Tye said, stroking the horse's neck.

"If ya don't get somethin' on your cuts, infection will set in on you," Will stated. "Go wash the blood off and get somethin' on that leg, I'll look after Red. I've had plenty of experience at this and I think I can handle it."

Tye turned away from the horse, grimacing as he placed his weight on the leg. "Yeah, I guess you have." Then looking back at the big horse, sadness washed over his face. "It's a shame some men have to hurt horses in order to feel like a man."

"Yeah, it's a shame all right," Will said bitterly. "Now go on and get that leg tended to. I'll take care of Red."

Tye hobbled off to the bunkhouse as Will began putting salve on the big horse's bloodied sides. Each time the sorrel flinched from the pain, Will remembered Slade's face as he sat in the dust of the blacksmith shop, the spurs bent around his wrists, and the look of total defeat he wore. It helped ease the pain Will felt for the horse.

Later that day, Slade saddled a horse and rode out. He wasn't missed, and the only time his name came up was when someone would start talking about the day Slade had his spurs made into bracelets. Tye was glad Slade was gone, but something told him it wasn't over between them and their paths would cross again.

It had been two weeks since the fight and things had returned to normal. Will spent his days riding the horses Tye had broken. Though most of them still bucked when first mounted, his skills had improved so much he looked forward to it.

There were three horses Tye wouldn't let Will ride, even though he'd begged for the chance: the big roan gelding, the bay mare, and a large gray stud horse. All three horses had fought and bucked hard when Tye first rode them, but were now gentled to some degree. Even though they bucked harder than the others when mounted, Will figured he'd acquired enough savvy to ride them. But Tye had said no without giving a reason, and Tye was the boss. Will knew he usually had a pretty good reason for the things he did, so he didn't push the issue.

As Will rode a black horse back up to the horse corral, Tye was putting one of the horses through his paces, working him along the fence in the corral to put a rein on him. When he looked up and saw Will, he rode over to the gate and, leaning down, unhooked the latch. Then he gently kneed the horse around, and swung the gate open for Will to ride through. He then eased the horse around again and closed the gate behind him.

"You've really got 'im workin'," Will said. "He's about ready for the ranch remuda."

"He is ready," Tye stated. "All of 'em are about ready. I figger about one more week of this and I'll be out of a job."

"Out of a job?" Will asked incredulously, not believing he'd heard right.

"Yep, out of a job. All the horses are broke," Tye replied, not looking at Will.

"Yeah, but I thought you worked cattle till they had more horses for ya to break," Will said, thinking about what this meant to him. If Tye was out of a job, that meant he was more than likely out of a job, too. He had no idea what he was going to do once the horses were broke, and he'd been too busy to talk to Tye about it. Now his future was looking even more bleak as Tye broke this last bit of news to him.

"Usually I do, but not anymore. I told Charley I was pulling out when I finished these," Tye said, now watching the expression on Will's face.

"What'cha gonna do?" Will asked, as his shoulders slumped. He was feeling about as low as a man could feel. Just when things were starting to work out for him, Tye was pulling up stakes and leaving.

"I thought I might head down to Wyoming and catch me some wild horses," Tye said, a smile coming to his face as he thought about it. "I talked to Charley about you. He said if ya wanted to stay on, he'd put ya on as a horse wrangler. He figgers ya got the makin's of a good bronc rider."

"Thanks," Will said. Even though that answered the question of his employment, it didn't ease the pain he felt at the thought of Tye's leaving.

" 'Course, I was kinda hopin' ya might want to ride along with me." Tye said it in such an offhand way that it took a moment before it sank into Will's consciousness. When he looked up, Tye had a grin on his face.

Will's spirits rose immediately, but maintaining a straight face, he said, "I don't know, a horse-wrangling job sounds pretty good. I wouldn't have to put up with a hardheaded, hot-tempered fella what tries to get me throwed every chance he gets."

Tye laughed as he watched the gleam in Will's eyes.

"Well, I was just invitin' ya along 'cause ya look so funny when ya hit the ground. I figgered you'd be good entertainment. But since ya don't want to go, well, I'll just have to find someone else to go along for entertainment. It's gonna be hard to find someone who can fall off a horse the way you do."

Will grinned at Tye and said, "Naw, I guess I better go with ya. There ain't no one else who can put up with your cantankerous ways. 'Sides that, you'll need me along to ride the rough horses fer ya. You're gettin' on in years and it won't be long till someone will have to help ya into the saddle."

"Yeah, well, Junior, I'm not ready for the grave yet, but when I get too old to fork my own broncs, it's reassuring to know that you'll be there to take care of me. Now let's go get some chow so we can finish these cayuses up before winter gets here."

Every day of the following week, the two of them worked from sunup to sundown. Both Will and Tye rode as many horses as they could, putting the finishing touches on them before turning them over to the horse wrangler to be included in the remuda of ranch horses.

Tye continued to educate Will in the proper techniques of horse training. He found Will to be a quick learner and was pleased with the results he produced on each of the horses he rode.

Chapter Four

Saturday evening, after a full day of riding, Tye took the last four horses in the string to the horse pen and turned them in with the ranch remuda. Will was in the tack room, putting away his saddle when Tye walked in.

"We'll be riding out before daylight in the mornin'," Tye said as he hefted his saddle onto the wooden rack. "Charley said to tell ya you could keep the riggin' you been usin', and he also said if ya ever needed a job, come see him. Said he'd put ya on as a cook's helper any day."

"That's mighty nice of him," Will said. "If you get to actin' mean and nasty in your old age, I'll have a place to come to."

Will put his saddle and roll on the rack. Then, with a thoughtful look at Tye, he asked, "Where we headed to in Wyoming, anyway? Here I am leaving in the mornin' and I don't even know where we're goin', or what we're gonna be doin', except catchin' wild horses."

"That's what I like about you, Will. You don't ask too many questions. We're goin' to a place in northwest Wyoming around the Yellowstone river. I was through there a few years back and I saw the wild herds runnin' in the mountains. I've had a hankerin' to go back there and catch me some of 'em ever since. I've got enough buyers now to sell all we can catch and break, if we can keep our hair long enough to get 'em out."

"Keep our hair?" Will fairly shouted. "You didn't say nothin' about keepin' our hair. I gather there's Injuns out there."

"You gather right. You're not gettin' cold feet on me now, are ya?" Tye asked, watching Will's face closely

"I ain't gettin' cold feet," Will said. "But I don't want my head to get cold without any hair on it either. How do you plan to get these horses out of there without losing both our scalps? And how do you know there's still wild horses down there?"

"Will, I just got through sayin' one of the things I liked about you was the fact that ya didn't ask a lot of foolish questions. Now here ya go askin' a whole passel of 'em. There's horses there. I've checked with folks from time to time and they tell me they're there. As for the Injuns, well, I've got me some ideas about them, too. You'll just have to trust me."

"I do trust you," Will said, with a touch of sarcasm in his voice. "It's the Injuns I don't trust. But if you say there's horses there, then they're there. And if you say we can get 'em out without our heads hangin' in some Injun's teepee, then I guess we can. I just hope you know what you're doin'." Will looked thoughtful for a second, then said, "I would like to have a gun though, if we're goin' to be ridin' into Injun country."

"You know how to use a gun?" Tye asked.

"I've used a rifle a bit on our farm back in Kansas. I got to be a pretty good shot."

"What were ya shootin' at?" Tye asked.

"Deer, rabbits, and other game," Will remarked innocently.

"You ever shoot at someone who's shootin' back at ya?" Tye asked. The question came hard and forceful.

"Never had any reason to," Will remarked hotly. "Have you?" he asked, watching Tye closely.

"Yeah, I have, a time or two and it ain't no fun," Tye replied, his voice softening as he replied. "We'll pick ya up a rifle and a Colt at Alder Gulch as we pass through. We'd better pick up enough shells for ya to do some practicin' with, too."

Gold was discovered in the 1860s in Alder Gulch (now Virginia City), as well as Grasshopper Creek, Confederate Gulch, and Last Chance Gulch (Helena). The gold rush brought a large influx of people into the area where several tribes of Indians and only a few ranchers had been.

Will and Tye left the ranch before dawn the next morning and were several miles down the trail before the sun came up. Ten head of horses were strung out between them. Tye led the first horse, with each of the others tied to the tail of the horse before it. Will brought up the rear. His job was to watch behind them and alert Tye should anyone or anything approach. Tye had warned him before they left that morning that they could encounter Indians or bandits along the way, so he'd better ride with his eyes and ears open. If he saw or heard anything, he was to sound a warning.

Will had noticed as Tye came out of the bunkhouse with his roll that he wore a Colt belted around his waist and tied down to his leg. He also carried a rifle in the boot on his saddle. Even though Will had seen the other hands wear irons when they rode the range, this was the first time he'd seen Tye wearing one. It had a quieting effect on him as he realized they could be riding into danger. There was always the threat of Indians, and they'd even had problems once or twice with them stealing horses when they were out in the large horse trap. But as far as Will was concerned, since he'd never seen any, he never felt threatened by them. Now they were riding away from the safety of the ranch and into unknown dangers. Will searched his heart and found that although he wasn't afraid, he sure would have felt better holding on to a rifle.

There were only a couple of hours of sunlight left when Will and Tye topped the hill overlooking Alder Gulch.

"Before we get to town, not that you can call that

much of a town, there's some things ya need to know," Tye told him. "Alder Gulch is what's left of a mining town. It's not much now, but there's still a lot of riffraff hanging around, preying on those that haven't given up on the gold. The big gold strikes played out several years ago, but there's still those that think there's gold to be found. There's still some traces found here and there and that keeps these fools lookin', hopin' to strike it rich. We won't have any trouble out of the miners, unless there's one lookin' to steal a horse and hightail it outa here. But as for the others, there's those that would slit your throat for the gold fillings in your teeth.

"It's best not to say too much or ask too many questions. Let me do the talking. All right?

"If prices ain't too high, we'll buy some supplies to get us down the trail. I know of a trading post in Wyoming where we'll buy most of our supplies." Tye paused, looking at Will to make sure he was understanding what was being said. Satisfied that he was, Tye went on.

"Once we're out of town, I'll fill ya in on the rest of my plans. If ya don't know anything about it, ya can't tell no one. It's not that I don't trust ya. It's just that sometimes not knowin' somethin' can keep ya outa trouble. Understand?"

"Yeah, I understand. You don't want me sayin' something that might make folks suspicious. Right?"

"You got it," Tye replied, a somber look on his face. "We'll be spending the night here and getting our supplies in the morning. I want to get as much information as I can about the country ahead of us."

Will looked around him. Then, as if he was afraid someone might hear, he grinned and whispered, "Don't forget to ask about Indians while you're at it."

Tye chuckled. "I promise ya, I won't let that slip my mind."

They rode into town and pulled up in front of the livery stable. Will swung down and opened the gate so Tye could lead the horses into the corral. After taking the halters off the horses, they unsaddled them, and rubbed them down with loose hay. Tye was glad to see that none of the locals paid them any attention. They finished rubbing their horses down, then filled the hay manger with fresh hay. When they were finished, they carried their saddles and gear into the barn. Tye dropped his gear inside the door and made his way to a door that had a faded OFFICE sign above it. Will followed close behind. Tye opened the door and Will could see a man sitting in a chair, his feet propped up on the desk, and his head tilted forward. Soft snores came from him and Tye almost hated to wake him, but he needed to be about his business, so he knocked lightly on the door. When there was no response, he knocked louder, causing the glass pane in the door to rattle. The sleeping figure came awake with a start, his feet banging loudly to the floor as they slid off the desk.

The man before them was in his mid- to late-sixties, with long gray hair, and a mustache that drooped at the corners of his mouth. His hat had seen better days. Where it had once been a well-creased Stetson, it now flopped in all directions. It looked more like a bonnet than a hat.

When he saw Will and Tye standing there, he stood up and cleared his throat. "Humph, can I help you fellas?"

"Sorry to wake ya from your nap," Tye said, extending his hand. "I'm Tye Garrett, and this is Will Paxton. We've just put some horses in your corral and we need to store our gear."

"Wiley Topps," the man said, shaking hands with Tye and Will. "How many horses ya got?"

"Twelve head," Tye said. "We've already given them hay. They don't need nothing else tonight."

"You spendin' the night in town?"

"We might," Tye replied as if the thought hadn't occurred to him until now. "Are there any good sleepin' places in town?"

"Only one. That's the Ruby Inn. It's a one-story

building and don't have no saloon with it. The other places in town have the sleepin' rooms above the saloon. Been more'n one feller gone to bed at night and woke up dead from someone shootin' through the saloon ceiling. The Ruby's got good food, too. They hired 'em a chef what came out here from back East to look fer gold and didn't have any luck. Prices ain't bad though. Not like they was awhile back when the gold strike was goin' on."

"We're gonna' be needin' some supplies," Tye said. "Is there a good mercantile in town where we can get some?"

"Yep, and prices ought to be pretty good on them, too," Wiley answered, pointing to a building across the street. "Sooner's up the street on the right has a large stock and is tryin' to get shut of it. Seems old Clyde wants to sell everything and light a shuck outa here. Too bad, too. He's a decent sort of fella. Made himself some money during the strike, but now that that's over, there ain't much here except leftovers and outlaws.

"We ain't got no sheriff and the riffraff has just about run off all the decent folks. I liked things a whole lot better before they found gold. I've made myself a pretty good livin' out of it, but I ain't got no place to spend it and pretty soon I won't have no friends left here. So what is money if ya ain't got no friends left and no place to spend it?"

"Ya got a point," Tye agreed, not really having a response to the question. "I'd be obliged to ya if you'd throw them broncs some hay in the mornin'. We may be pullin' out early, and I'd like to have 'em fed before we hit the trail."

"I'll feed 'em on my way to breakfast in the morning," the old man promised. "Since the Ruby's got that new chef, I usually eat all my meals there. Not that I can't cook. It's just that a feller don't get a chance to taste that kinda cookin' very often, and I aim to take advantage of it while it lasts."

Tye and Will laughed at the old man's statement. Tye asked, "It's about time for supper now, ain't it? I'll buy us some grub, if you don't mind sharin' some information with me."

"I don't know what kinda information you'd be wantin', but I never turned down a free meal in my life. I'll tell ya anything I know and make up a whole lot more fer a free meal. Let me lock up here and I'll be ready to go."

When Wiley had the doors shut and locked, the three walked up the rutted street to the Ruby Inn. As they walked through the front door, the aroma hit them like a rainstorm, completely drenching them in the scent of cooking food. Both Tye and Will stopped, breathing in the delicious smells lingering in the lobby of the inn.

"If you boys think it smells good, just wait till ya taste it," Wiley said, leading the way into the dining room.

There were few vacant tables in the room and they had to settle for one in the back, close to the kitchen.

"This place is always like this," Wiley declared. "Sometimes there's a waitin' line out into the street."

An exhausted waitress brought them menus and a promise to return shortly to take their orders. When she returned, all three ordered steak, potatoes, biscuits, and gravy. The smells coming from the kitchen were so overwhelming, Will thought he was going to pass out from hunger before she brought out their meal. Finally, the waitress brought out three steaming plates of food and set them down on the table, then left in a rush to take another order. All three ate in silence, attacking the plates of food like it was the first meal they'd had in a week. There was nothing left on any of their plates when they finished. Even the gravy was soaked up with the last biscuit.

"I'm so full I hurt," Will moaned. "But if they brought out another plate, I'd have to eat all of it, too."

"I know what ya mean," Tye agreed. "I don't think I've ever eaten anything that tasted so good."

"I told you boys you'd like it, didn't I? 'Course, it wasn't always like this. When this New York chef first started cookin' here, he was always tryin' to fix some of them fancy dishes like they have back East. Nobody would order the durn stuff. Liked to have closed the place down. Finally, he gave up on all that and started cookin' real food like we just ate. Business has been boomin' ever since."

Tye leaned back in his chair and crossed his legs in front of him. "How long you been around here, Wiley?"

"Since forty-eight. Been about twenty-four years. I come up from Texas with a trail herd and liked it so well I just stayed."

"What part of Texas?" Tye asked.

"North of San Antonio," Wiley replied. "My family had a small farm down there. Ma and Pa tried hard to make a go of it, but they wasn't good at raisin' nothin' but younguns. Pa finally gave up and became a clerk at a dry goods store. I hired on with one of the ranches down there. Stayed with 'em a couple a years till I got the wanderlust and hired on with a feller who wanted to come up here and start a ranch. He was bringin' a small herd with him and I figgered I'd help 'im trail them critters up here. We fought Injuns and rustlers the whole way. Lost four men along the trail. By the time we got here, I'd had enough travelin' and decided to settle down. Married me a Swedish gal. Big enough to eat hay and pull a wagon. She sure could cook though. But she got meaner'n a sore-toothed mule. I was doin' some horse tradin' and doin' all right, but it weren't good enough fer her. She'd gripe and complain every time I come home. Griped about everything. Nothin' seemed to please her. One day while I was gone, a drummer came through town, sellin' his wares and she ups and leaves with him. Folks around here figgered I'd be plum tore up over it. But to tell the truth, it was the happiest day of my life. I've been a bachelor ever since and I aim to stay that way."

It was apparent to Will and Tye that Wiley liked to talk and didn't need any coaxing.

"I come from Texas, too," Tye said. "West of Austin on the Colorado River."

Will, who had been listening to Wiley talk, now looked at Tye. This was the first time he'd heard him speak about himself or where he'd come from.

"Well, I'll be! A fella Texan, and one close to home at that. I rode through that part of the country a couple a times. Sure was nice land."

"Sure is. I got a small piece of it still down there. Someday I plan to go back and build me a spread. I haven't been there since before the war, but there's some folks down there lookin' after it for me. I'm lookin' forward to the day when I can settle down there."

"You mentioned you needed information, and since I done et the free meal ya promised, I reckon I owe ya whatever information I can give ya," Wiley said.

"I need information about the trails leadin' into Wyoming, especially the ones in the northwest part of the territory. There's a large lake that the Yellowstone River empties into. I'm interested in any information you might have on the country east of there. I'm real interested in hearin' about Indian activity."

"Wyomin', huh? You know, I wouldn't give ya a plug nickel fer the whole state of Wyomin'," Wiley said, with a sour look on his face. "You know they give women the right to vote in that state."

"I didn't know that," Tye stated. "But I don't plan to be there long. I just got a little business to do there. Then I'm headin' to Texas."

This last statement caused Will's eyebrows to rise. Tye hadn't mentioned anything to him about Texas. He didn't know if Tye really meant it, or if this was just something to throw anyone who might be interested off the track.

"If you was smart, you'd bypass Wyomin' and go

straight to Texas," Wiley said, shaking his head. In 1869, Wyoming became the first state in the Union to give women the right to vote, earning it the title "The Equality State." "Women votin'. What's this world comin' to anyway?"

Will wanted to hear about the Indians and the land and was getting impatient with Wiley's ramblings, but Tye seemed relaxed and willing to let Wiley take his time.

"I don't know that it's all that bad," Tye said. "I've known some pretty smart women who could probably make better decisions than I could when it comes to politics. 'Sides that, look at the mess we men have made of things in the last few years. If women had been allowed to vote from the beginning, we probably wouldn't have gone to war with each other."

Wiley gave Tye a look of disbelief, then said, "Son, you got a powerful lot of learnin' to do about women. We may not have done so good ourselves, but I guarantee ya if women had been runnin' this country, we'd be in a whole lot worse shape than we're in right now. But arguin' about it ain't gonna get us nowhere. You wanted to know about the trails between here and Yellowstone Lake. I can't tell ya whole lot, 'cept what I've heard. They's pretty good most of the way. Not a lot of people travel there, 'cept some trappers and some prospectors. The Injuns is the biggest problem. Captain Powell whupped the Sioux pretty good about five years ago and drove most of 'em back up here to Montana, but there's still raidin' parties and a few small villages around that part of the country. There's some Shoshone Injuns around there, but so far they ain't caused much trouble. I've talked to some fellers who have traded with 'em on a regular basis, and they say they're friendly enough. Your biggest problem will be with the young Sioux braves who are tryin' to prove themselves."

Wiley didn't ask why they were going to Wyoming or why they needed this information. That was the

way it was. A man's business was his own, and if he
wanted you to know why he was doing something or
going somewhere, he'd tell you. But you didn't ask.

Tye sat up in his chair and spoke. "You've been a
lot of help and I appreciate the information. Is there
anything else we need to know?"

"Just this," Wiley replied. "Watch yer backside here
in town. There's some mighty salty characters hangin'
out. There's some who would stick a knife in your
gizzard just for the boots yer wearin'. There's fewer
of 'em now than there were. Maybe they'll all be gone
soon, but while you're here, watch yerselves and don't
hang around dark places."

"Thanks," Tye said. "We'll remember that. I'm
gonna get us a room and turn in early, so there ain't
much chance we'll be gettin' into trouble."

Chapter Five

It was dark out when they left the dining hall. After shaking hands and saying good night, Tye and Will crossed the lobby to the hotel desk. Neither noticed the man watching from the darkness outside as Tye got the room key and they started down the hallway.

The room wasn't fancy, but it would do. It had a double bed, a washstand with a fresh pitcher of water, and a chair by the foot of the bed. There was a small window about head high that could be opened to let in fresh air. Tye crossed the room and raised it an inch. Even though it was almost June, the nights were still cool.

Will lit the coal oil lamp on the washstand, not knowing as he did that someone was watching from across the street for the glow coming from the window.

"This reminds me of back home," Will said. "It's been awhile since I shared a bed with anyone."

Tye closed the door and turned the key in the lock. Then he took the chair and wedged it under the doorknob.

"As long as you don't snore or steal the cover, I'll let ya share this one. But you do either one, and I'll kick your tail out and you'll sleep on the floor," Tye stated as he sat on the bed and started pulling off his boots.

"Like I said, you're gettin' older an' more cantankerous every day. It won't be long till I'll have to shoot ya just to put ya outa your misery," Will replied as he walked around the bed to the other side.

"Puttin' up with insolent babies makes a man old and cantankerous, and I'd almost let ya shoot me just to keep from havin' to listen to all your squawkin'," Tye complained as he pulled the covers over himself. "Now turn out the light and come to bed."

"But the light's on your side of the bed," Will cried indignantly. "Why don't you turn it out?"

" 'Cause," came the muffled reply, "I'm too old and decrepit to get back outa bed. And besides that, last one in always turns out the light."

"I'll remember that one, too," Will said as he made his way around the bed, stubbing his toe on the bed-post on his way back.

The light fading in the window was observed by the man standing below in the shadows. He watched for a few more seconds, then made his way across the street.

Will came awake to the feel of someone's hand clamped over his mouth. For a moment, he fought the smothering effect until he heard Tye whispering, "Shhh." The hand was removed. The room was dark except for the small amount of light coming through the window.

When Will's sleep-filled eyes became accustomed to the dark, he saw Tye near the door, holding a pistol. His finger rose to his lips, telling Will not to make a sound. Outside, steps were slowly approaching—not the rapid steps of someone just passing by. Will held his breath as the footsteps stopped by the door to their room. He heard the rattle of a key as it was inserted in the door lock. He held his breath as the key was turned and the knob slowly rotated.

Tye backed against the wall, gun in hand, waiting for the next move. There was a push against the door, and when it resisted, there was another push, this time with a little more force. Only the chair placed under the knob prevented the door from being opened.

Will was sitting up in the bed, looking first to Tye, then to the door and wondering what action to take. The next thing he knew, Tye was leaping across the room at him. Tye's leap caught Will in the chest and both went tumbling off the bed to the floor. To Will, it seemed as if Tye's body hit him at the same time as he heard a loud noise. It took him several seconds to realize that someone had shot at them through the door.

As the echoes of the gunfire died away, Tye leaped up and kicked the chair away and jerked open the door. He looked up and down the hallway before stepping out. Wearing nothing but his underwear, he raced to the back door of the inn, opened it, and stuck his head out, looking both left and right before stepping out into the alley. No one was around and no sound came from either direction. Upset that their would-be assassin had escaped, Tye returned to the room.

The sound of gunfire had roused the other two guests and brought the manager running. All were crowded into the small room as Will tried to explain what had happened.

When Tye pushed his way in, he noticed Will's ashen face. It wasn't hard to figure out the cause, for there in the mattress, where Will had been sleeping, were three holes left by the shots fired through the door. There was one hole in the mattress on Tye's side of the bed and one in the headboard, low enough to have taken its toll on a sleeping man.

"What's going on here?" the manager demanded. "I won't stand for gunplay in this establishment. I'm going to have to ask you to leave. Now!"

"Let me ask you something," Tye said casually, swinging the Colt up until it was aimed at the manager's midsection. "Does each room have its own key, or does one key unlock all the rooms?"

Everyone in the room turned to look at the manager..

"Each room has its own key, of course."

"Then do you mind tellin' me why it is that someone was able to unlock this door when I had the key in here with me?"

"Well, uh . . . ." the manager started, but Tye ignored him and continued.

"I'm sure you keep an extra key to each room in case one gets lost, don't you?"

"Yes, of course, we do," the manager answered, not nearly as sure of himself as he had been.

"Well, someone unlocked this door tonight from the outside. If I hadn't placed the chair under the door-knob, he would have been in here with us and the outcome would've been a lot different. Now suppose you tell me how it is that someone had a key to our room. Did you let someone have it?"

All eyes turned to look at the man again. Sweat was starting to break out on his forehead as he looked at the Colt Tye was holding. His arrogance drained from him now as he thought about the di-lemma he faced.

"I assure you, Mr. Garrett, I didn't give your room key to anyone other than yourself," he said, his voice almost rising to a whine.

"Where are the extra keys kept?"

"Behind the desk on a board."

"Well, let's just walk down there and see if there's a key missing." Tye motioned to the manager with the pistol barrel.

The manager led the way as they walked down the hall to the lobby. Will had slipped on his pants, but Tye was still dressed only in his underwear, a fact that didn't seem to bother him at all. Of course, the other two men, both who appeared to be drummers of some sort, took no notice and seemed more interested in the key situation than anything else.

When they reached the lobby, the manager went directly to the desk and, walking behind it, looked at the board until he came to Tye and Will's room num-ber. With an embarrassed look, he turned to Tye and said, "It's not here. I don't know what happened. It was here earlier this evening when I gave you your key, but now it's gone."

"Did you leave for any length of time?" Tye asked.

"I left for just a few minutes to get some coffee. I couldn't have been gone more than five minutes."

"How long do you think it would take a man to cross the lobby, get the key, and slip down the hall unnoticed?" Tye asked.

After looking from the front door to the desk, then down the hallway, the manager looked at Tye and said, "About thirty seconds, I would guess."

"And where were you when the shooting started?" Tye asked.

"I was behind the desk."

"How long after getting your coffee was it before ya heard the shots?"

"Maybe a minute."

"So what do you reckon happened?" Tye asked, staring intently at the man.

"I guess someone took the key while I was getting coffee, then slipped down the hall to your room," he answered.

"So whose fault is it that we almost got shot in our sleep?" Tye questioned.

In a weak voice, the manager replied, "Mine," then hurried on. "I'm sorry, Mr. Garrett. I never thought about anyone doing such a thing. How can I make it up to you?"

"You can start by givin' us another room. And this time I'll take both keys with me just to ensure nothin' happens to one of 'em," Tye replied.

"Of course, Mr. Garrett," the manager said, handing Tye the keys to another room. The other guests had never said a word. But when Tye asked for the extra key to his room, they both asked for theirs as well, just in case this person was someone who liked to shoot people in their beds for the fun of it.

Tye and Will returned to their room to collect their belongings and move them to the new room. This time, Tye left the window closed and didn't light the lamp. When he and Will were settled in bed, Will asked, "Who do you reckon it was that shot at us?"

"I been ponderin' that ever since it happened," Tye responded. "It wasn't someone bent on robbin' us, or he wouldn't have shot through the door. Whoever fired those shots was out to kill one or both of us, and he came real close to doing it."

"If it hadn't been for you, I'd be full of holes right now and you'd be lookin' fer someone else to entertain ya. Thanks for savin' my bacon," Will said.

"Yeah, that could have been a mistake," Tye replied, with no humor in his voice.

Will sat up in bed and, looking at Tye, asked, "Just how do you figure it was a mistake saving my life?"

"Well, think about it. If I hadn't jumped across the bed to save you, I could've shot him through the door. Then we wouldn't have to be worryin' about who it is that's tryin' to kill us. Don't you agree?"

"I don't reckon I'm too crazy about your thinking," Will answered. "But I'm sure glad ya decided to save me instead of killin' that skunk."

"Well, chalk it up to my old age," Tye said. "I just don't think as fast as I used to, or else I might have done otherwise."

"Ya might be getting old, but I gotta tell ya, you really made an impression on them ladies on the street tonight."

"What are you talkin' about?" Tye asked.

"Well, I noticed while you was talkin' with the manager in the lobby, some ladies passed by the window and looked in. I don't know what they was sayin', but they sure was gigglin' a lot and pointin' at you. It must've been them legs of yours, or your pretty drawers, I reckon."

Tye pulled the covers over his head and mumbled, "Yep. I definitely made the wrong choice. Now go to sleep before I shoot ya myself."

Will grinned as he rolled over on his side, facing away from Tye. One thing about it, life sure wasn't dull now.

*   *   *

In the alley across the street, the man watched the scene in the lobby of the Ruby Inn. He knew he'd failed when he saw Tye and Will talking to the manager. He cursed under his breath and continued watching until the group broke up and went back to their rooms. Then he headed for the Gold Nugget saloon where he proceeded to get stone drunk.

"Wake up, Slade!" the bartender said. "You wanna sleep, go on upstairs."

Slade couldn't remember what time he had passed out; only that he'd drunk a lot of whiskey trying to erase the picture of the beating he'd received from Garrett.

Slade had never hated anyone as bad as he hated Tye Garrett. Because of Tye, none of the other outfits would hire him. The news of the fight had spread through country like wildfire, branding him a troublemaker. Now he was reduced to holding up miners for what little gold dust they carried, which was usually just enough to get him drunk at night so he could drown the memories that burned in his mind.

Yesterday, when he saw Garrett and that snot-nosed kid ride in, he knew his chance had come. He'd waited outside the Ruby Inn until Garrett paid for a room. Then he waited until he saw the light come on, telling him which room they were in. All he had to do then was wait until the manager left his desk, ease across the lobby, grab the extra key, and lurk in the darkness of the hallway until the manager was back at his desk. Everything had gone like clockwork until he'd tried to open the door. He knew when it wouldn't open that a chair had been placed under the knob. So pulling out his Colt, he stepped back and emptied his pistol, aiming where he judged the bed to be. After firing, he'd run out the back door of the inn into the alley and cut around to the front, where he waited for the crowd to gather and view the bodies. Only there weren't any bodies, not dead ones anyway. And the only crowd that gathered were the ones inside. When he saw Garrett and the kid come into the lobby with the manager and two other men, who must have been guests, he'd slunk back into the shadows. When he heard footsteps approaching, he'd hidden in the darkness until two of the girls who worked for the Diamond Lil saloon passed by. He silently cursed them as they stopped in front of the window of the inn to watch the scene taking place. He heard them giggle, then walk on. Only when he was sure they were gone, did he come out of the shadows to watch from a distance until Garrett and the kid went back down the hall. He thought about trying again, but no light appeared this time and he didn't think he could get past the manager again. As he stood there in the shadows, he vowed that one day Garrett would pay for the humiliation he'd caused him.

Slade fought his way up the stairs in a drunken stupor. Finding his room was difficult, but since he had lots of experience locating it while staggering drunk, he managed once again. He didn't bother undressing, but slammed the door closed behind him and fell onto the bed. His last thoughts, before passing out, were of Tye Garrett and the revenge he would someday have.

Tye and Will were up before the sun, both feeling rested, even though their sleep had been disturbed the night before.

They ate a breakfast of eggs, biscuits, bacon, and hot coffee, shared with Wiley Topps, who offered Tye more information on the trails and the Wyoming territory. They left the Ruby Inn and headed to Sooner's, telling Wiley they would be along soon to settle up with him and collect their horses and belongings.

Clyde Sooner was just opening the doors to his mercantile as Tye and Will stepped up on the sidewalk.

"Howdy," he said as they walked in the front door. "Can I help you gentlemen?"

"We're needin' some supplies," Tye said. "I've made a list of things we need. If ya don't mind, we'll look around while you fill this list."

"Look around all ya want," Sooner said, taking the list from Tye. "If ya need any help, just holler."

Will and Tye walked along the aisles between shelves of dry goods. Most of the items they saw were for mining purposes, and since they didn't plan on doing any mining, they just passed on by. But when they came to the counter where the pistols were displayed, Will stopped to look through the glass top.

"Which of these do you think I should buy?" Will asked as Tye looked at the selection of handguns.

"Let's see what kind of rifles he's got," Tye said. "We might as well get a pistol that uses the same shells. That way, you only have to buy one kind."

They chose a rifle and pistol for Will, as well as a belt and holster for the pistol and a saddle boot for his rifle. Will also picked out a pair of boots, chaps, and a wide-brimmed Stetson. Will paid for them while Tye picked out a packsaddle and supply boxes to carry what they were purchasing.

Tye paid for the supplies and asked if they could be left there until they got their horses from the livery stable. Mr. Sooner assured him it would be all right.

"You wouldn't happen to know if old Clement Stoner still has a tradin' post up on the Yellowstone, would ya?" Tye asked.

"Clement Stoner, huh? You know him?" Sooner asked.

"I met him a few years ago," Tye answered. "I had a couple a Sioux on my tail and he persuaded 'em to leave me alone."

"Bet it wasn't through no sweet talk that he persuaded 'em either," Sooner said.

"Nope. As a matter of fact, he talked to 'em with a Sharps rifle. One of them Injuns probably won't be doin' any more talkin'. I think he hit him pretty hard and that discouraged the other one from any further thoughts he might've had about takin' my hair," Tye replied, with the hint of a smile.

"As far as I know, he's still there. I reckon he's tradin' with the Shoeshone some and what few trappers there are in the region. He likes the wilderness area up there and says he won't leave. I reckon they'll bury him in them mountains.

"It's been about six months since I last saw him. He come in here to trade me some furs he had. He should still be there, if someone or somethin' ain't killed him," Sooner said

"We may swing by that way and see him," Tye said. "I'll tell him you said 'howdy.'"

"I'd appreciate that," Sooner replied. "Tell him I'll come down that way when I get shut of this stock, and we'll play some checkers. He does love to play checkers. Cheats though. Ya gotta watch 'im like a hawk."

"Yep, you know Clement all right," Tye said. "I stayed with him for two weeks and never did win a game."

Tye and Will left the mercantile and headed down the street to the livery stable. Tye hadn't forgotten the events of the night before and was watching closely for any sign of trouble. He noticed Will was also watching and was impressed by the awareness he exhibited. Even though Will was young, he had good instincts. With a little help, he'd grow into a capable man.

Tye settled their account with Wiley Topps while Will started catching and haltering the horses. Before leaving, Tye picked the largest horse from the bunch for a packhorse. They led him to Sooner's and, after fitting the packsaddle to him, they loaded the supplies. Once they'd said good-bye to Clyde, Tye led out, leading the string of horses. Will brought up the rear, leading the packhorse. The pistol was stored in his roll, but the rifle was in the boot attached to his saddle. It gave him a secure feeling knowing he carried it. He hoped he wouldn't need it for anything other than hunting game, but after last night, he doubted that would be the case. Besides, they were heading into Indian country and who knew what was going to happen there?

Chapter Six

They were riding south at an easy gait. Tye turned often to watch back along the trail. Twice, he had called a halt and sat listening to the sounds and watching the horses. Will knew the horses would alert them if there were any other riders around.

The land in which they were traveling was rolling hills with little timber. Topping knolls, they could see a long way back down the trail from which they came. There was no sign of anyone following them.

After traveling south for about three hours, Tye turned and headed due east. Will noticed the mountain ranges ahead and wondered if they were going into the mountains.

Tye called a rest at noon and they stopped by a small stream to eat some canned peaches they'd bought at Sooner's.

"We'll make camp before reaching those mountains ahead of us," Tye said, pointing to the mountain range directly ahead of them.

"I want to be out in the open. There'll be no fire after dark. After tonight, we'll still be riding in open country, but there'll be mountains on both sides of us for a couple of days. Then we'll be in the mountains till we cross into Wyoming. We should be at Clement's tradin' post in about five days, providin' we don't have any trouble."

"Do you reckon whoever shot at us last night is followin' us?" Will asked.

"It's better to believe he is and be ready for him,

than to think he ain't and get careless. I figger anybody who'd go through the trouble he went through
last night won't quit just because we left town."

They rode the rest of the day in silence and made
camp two hours before dark. Will could see they were
entering a valley between two mountain ranges. A
man riding in between the mountains would be out of
rifle range of anyone trying to dry gulch him from
either side.

Tye made a small fire and soon had water boiling
for coffee. He and Will fixed a meal of biscuits, gravy,
bacon, and beans. After eating, they let the fire burn
down before covering it with dirt. There was a little
stream about twenty yards from the camp, and after
watering the horses, they picketed them close to the
camp where the horses could still feed on the lush
prairie grass.

"The horses will warn us if there's anyone out
there," Tye said as they came back into camp.

They rolled out their bedding and Will took his Colt
out, holding it in his hand to feel the balance.

Tye noticed Will looking at it and said, "Once we
get to Clement's, I'll give ya some pointers and let ya
practice. I don't think it would be safe to practice
here."

"How far are the wild horses from Clement's tradin'
post?" Will asked.

"About a day's ride east," Tye replied.

"How long ya reckon it'll take us to catch 'em?"

"I'm figgerin' about three weeks to trap 'em and
rough break 'em enough to get 'em out of there," Tye
said.

"How many head ya figgerin' on takin out?"

"I want at least two hundred. More, if there's some
good mares. We won't break the mares to ride though,
just halter break 'em so we can lead 'em out," Tye
said.

Will was quiet after that, lost in his thoughts about
the things that had happened to change his course in
life and where he was headed.

Tye broke the silence with a question. "You said that night in the barn that you didn't think you wanted to work the rest of your life bein' a forty-dollar-a-month cowboy. How would ya feel about bein' a rancher in Texas?"

"I ain't never been to Texas, but it sounds like the kinda place I'd like. But bein' a rancher would require some money, and that's somethin' I ain't got," Will said.

"Not yet, ya don't. But as soon as we get these horses out, we'll have a good start. And I got some other things in mind that might just pan out to put some money in our pockets. We'll have to wait and see," Tye said.

"Wait a minute. You just said 'we'. I thought I was just along workin' for you," Will replied.

Tye looked at him. Then, in a voice that left little doubt as to his seriousness, he said, "I could'a hired me a forty-dollar-a-month cowboy if I was lookin' to have someone workin' for me. I need a partner. Someone who wants to make somethin' of himself. There's a lot of fellers who can work for someone else. There's mighty few who can step out on their own and make things happen. That's why I chose you. You got good sense about ya and ya don't make quick decisions. You keep your head about ya, too. You told me ya didn't want to be workin' for someone else the rest of your life. You said you thought a man could make big tracks in this country. Well, I think so, too, if that man ain't afraid to gamble a little. If ya think you're up to it, I want ya to ride with me till we make it big or go bust. What do you say?"

Will was silent, letting Tye's words sink in. Tye wasn't just asking him to work for him. He wanted him to be a partner. Could he measure up? There was a lot he didn't know. Would Tye be willing to wet-nurse him along until he was ready?

Tye was watching Will's face, noting the changing expressions as he pondered the questions that had been raised. Finally, Will looked at him and spoke.

"You haven't really known me very long. What makes ya think I'm the person you want to partner with? And how do you know I'll stand up to what ya got in mind?"

"I don't know fer sure. Nobody ever really knows how another person will act. The only thing I can trust is my instincts and my instincts tell me you'll do to ride the river with. You got some learnin' to do, but you catch on fast and, with my help and guidance, it won't be long till you'll be a hand. 'Sides that, if ya don't work out, I can always just shoot ya and hire me someone."

"So in other words, I either work out or ya kill me?" Will asked, a smile spreading across his face.

"I reckon that's about the size of it," Tye said, grinning.

"Then let's go for it," Will said. "I don't know of anyone I'd rather partner with. I just hope I can pull my weight."

"I do, too," Tye said, still smiling as he lay down and pulled his hat over his eyes.

The next five days were uneventful as they traveled southeast into Wyoming. As they rode, Tye talked to Will about the country they were riding through and what it would be like where they were going. He showed him how to read tracks and how to identify animals by them. He talked about the horses they were going to catch, and what it would take to break them enough to move them out of the mountains. At night, they talked about Texas and Tye told Will about the ranch and his plans for expanding it. This included buying new land and stocking it with cattle and horses.

"Texas is still in bad shape from the war. If a fella's got some money and ain't scared of hard work, he can build himself an empire out there. I ain't lookin' to build an empire, but I think we can put us together a mighty fine spread."

Tye kept watching their back trail as they rode.

Once, when they topped a peak where he could see for several miles, he called a halt and watched for nearly an hour, knowing that anyone following them would have to take the same trail. There was no sign of anyone, and Tye relaxed a little, hoping maybe their close call was just a case of mistaken identity, but somehow he doubted that was the case.

It was early afternoon when they followed the Yellowstone River to Clement Stoner's trading post. Will was surprised to find it was little more than a shack with a lean-to attached to the front of it. The shack was butted up to a solid granite wall that towered a hundred feet above the basin they were in. An overhang jutting out from the wall served as protection from falling rocks. Will mentally noted the defensive position of the small cabin, which allowed a view of the clearing in front of it. A man with enough water and food could hold off his attackers for days if necessary.

There was smoke coming from the chimney, but other than that, there was no sign of life. When they were fifty yards from the shack, Tye pulled up and called out.

"Hello the camp." There was no response. Tye leaned over and spoke softly to Will.

"That old renegade should be here. There's smoke comin' from the chimney and there's fresh footprints leadin' down to the river."

Will's eyes went back to the door of the shack. Then he was startled by a flurry of action as Tye's horse, suddenly riderless, shied into his own. Tye was on the ground rolling as he landed. Will never saw him draw his gun; it just appeared in his hand. Tye came to a stop, belly down, facing back the way they'd come, pistol aimed and looking for a target between the legs of the horses. Will felt, rather than heard, the presence of another person, and after bringing his startled horse under control, he swung from the saddle, drawing the rifle from its boot as he did. He went down on one

knee, facing the woods behind him, keeping the horses
between him and whoever was there.

Laughter broke the silence of the afternoon. "I
mighta missed you Garrett, but I shore would'a got
the papoose. He's a little slow getting started. You
and me's gonna have to work with him a might if'n
he's gonna live long in this country."

Will watched as Tye came to his feet and holstered
the pistol. Will stood up and walked around the
horses, his face red, both from being called a "papoose" and knowing that what this man had said was
true. Walking out of the woods was the largest man
Will had ever seen. He stood well over six feet tall,
and could have easily weighed three hundred pounds.
He wore a beard that was as black as coal and looked
as if it hadn't been trimmed in years. He was smiling
as he walked toward them and the smile he wore
made his eyes sparkle.

Tye walked around the horses and faced the giant.

"Clement, you're too big and noisy to sneak up on
anyone. Not only that, ya smell like an old grizzly
bear. I been smellin' ya for the last mile or so. Don't
you ever take a bath?"

Clement feigned a hurt look as he held up his arms,
sniffing as he did.

"I just took one in March; here it is just now the
end of June and you're wantin' me ta take another
one. A man could wear out his skin bathin' that
often." He let out a thunderous laugh at his own
humor and grabbed Tye in a bear hug.

"You're slowin' down some, Garrett. Last time you
was up here, I couldn't get nowhere near as close to
ya as I did just now. You must'a been livin' the easy
life lately."

Stepping back from the big mountain man, Tye replied, "I heard ya a long time ago. I just wanted to
be sure it was you and not the bushwhacker that tried
to shoot us a while back."

"Bushwhacker, huh? Come on up to the house and

tell me about it over a cup of coffee," Clement said as he led the way down the trail.

They unsaddled their horses and turned them into a small pen that had been built by the river. They followed Clement up the hill into the shack.

It took Will a minute after entering to let his eyes get accustomed to the dim light. When his eyes had adjusted enough to see, he noticed the shack was bare, except for a stove, table, chairs, and a washbasin. There was a blanket across the back wall that Will figured was to cover the granite wall. He wondered where Clement slept. There wasn't a bunk. As a matter of fact, there weren't any shelves either. How could a man have a trading post and not have any goods to trade? Hadn't Tye said they would pick up more supplies here? He was still looking around when he noticed that both Tye and Clement were watching him.

"What's the matter, boy? Don't you like my home?" Clement asked, his eyes sparkling like the stars.

"It's all right, I reckon. It's just not what I expected for a tradin' post," Will responded.

"Well now, just what did you expect it to look like?" Clement asked. The grin on his face was starting to irritate Will some.

"Well, if you're a trader, where's the supplies ya trade with?" Will asked.

"Why they're right here in this house where they're suppose to be," Clement responded incredulously. "Where did you expect them to be?"

Will looked around the small room, trying to figure out if he was being made a fool of, or if this was a test. Scrutinizing the structure from top to bottom and side to side, Will's eyes finally came to rest on the blanketed wall and realization sank in. Clement had built this shack in front of a cave and the blanket covered the opening. Will walked to the blanket and gently ran his hands along the wall till he came to a place where the blanket gave under his hand. Reaching down and grabbing the blanket by the edge, he gave it a triumphant pull. As the blanket fell away from the opening, Will got a brief glimpse of the contents before he heard a "click," which was followed by a loud boom and a blinding light pierced his eyes. Will jumped three feet back into the shack, heart pounding and eyes blinded by the flash. He stumbled into the table, almost overturning it, then righted himself, only to bump into Clement. Clement reached out a big hand and steadied him as he blinked his eyes and tried to clear his vision. Tye and Clement were laughing so hard, both spilled coffee out of the cups they were holding.

When Will's eyes finally cleared enough so he could see the two men who were almost rolling on the floor, anger flooded through him.

"You two planned that, didn't ya? If I had a gun, I'd shoot both of ya and leave ya here for the buzzards."

Tye finally got his laughter under control and slapped Will on the back.

"He got me the same way. Led me like a bear to honey. I almost shot him for it, too. So don't feel too bad about bein' took in. It happens to the best of us."

"What was that?" Will asked, his temper cooling as his heart slowed its pace.

"Just a little trap I rigged up to discourage curious folks from lookin' around while I'm gone. Don't go nosin' around in there by yerself. I got some traps set in there that'll do more'n just scare ya. Couple a years ago, a feller come nosin' around here while I was gone to Jackson. I reckon he was gonna help hisself to some supplies, 'cause when I returned, there was a pile of goods here on the floor and he was still back there. I reckon he'd been there a day or two, judgin' by the smell. I buried him down by the river and put a marker on his grave, 'Caught Stealin'.' Ain't had no trouble since. My powder flash has been set off once or twice, but I figgered it was just a Shoshone lettin'

his curiosity get the better of him. Come on, I'll give
ya a guided tour of my warehouse."

Will followed Clement into the cave, wary of any
more surprises he might have in store for him.

The cave ran back a good sixty feet. It was over
eight feet high and about thirty feet wide in front,
narrowing to about twenty feet at the rear.

"This old cave weren't near this big when I first
come here," Clement said as they entered. "I worked
for over a year makin' it big enough to live in and
store my wares, too."

Will could see that Clement was well stocked with
items to trade. He had hardware for digging, climbing,
chopping, or anything else you might want to do in
the woods. He also had a large supply of pelts, which
Will figured he had traded for. Clement must have
read his mind. "I've got to take them pelts to Jackson
soon and restock. The Shoshone supply them for me
and I trade 'em tools for 'em. The Shoshone are good
farmers, which is real nice. I get all the fresh vegetables I need."

Will noticed there were bunks built along part of
one wall, and upon further inspection, noticed a small
stream in the back of the cave that came out the rocks
near the base. It ran along a shallow trough and disappeared under the rocks on the opposite wall. It served
not only as a source for drinking and cooking water,
but cooled the cave as well. The coolness helped pre-
serve the haunch of venison hanging over the stream.

Clement finished up the tour and led Will back into
the shack, where Tye was enjoying his coffee.

As Clement refilled his cup and handed one to Will,
he looked at Tye and asked, "Now what's all this
about bushwhackers after ya?"

Tye filled him in on the details about their stay in
Alder Gulch, leaving out the part where he pushed
Will off the bed.

"You have any idea who it might be?" Clement
asked.

"I've got my suspicions," Tye said

"How long ya plannin' on stayin'?" Clement asked

"Long enough to get supplies and information," Tye said, looking at Will.

"You goin' after them wild horses?" Clement asked.

"If they're still there," Tye said

"Oh, they're still there all right. I saw 'em couple weeks ago. There's even more of 'em now. I noticed some with brands on 'em. I reckon that wild bunch has taken to raidin' ranches now," Clement said.

"Either that, or they were stolen by the Sioux and he got 'em from them," Tye replied. "Speakin' of Sioux: How many of 'em are still around?"

"There's a few still raidin'. They raid the ranches and settlements in the lowlands, then hightail it back up to the mountains. Can't nobody find 'em. 'Course, ain't nobody asked me either. I don't reckon I'd tell 'em if they did. So far, the Sioux has left me alone. As long as they don't bother me, I won't bother them," Clement said.

"How close are they to where we'll be?" Tye asked.

"A little over twenty miles. But that won't matter. They'll know you're there the day after you arrive," Clement responded.

"How many of them are there?" Tye asked.

"Upwards of a hundred. 'Course, that's countin' squaws and younguns."

"Why haven't the Sioux captured these horses already?" Will asked.

"'Cause they'd rather steal 'em from folks than catch 'em and break 'em themselves. Once they know what ya'll are doin', they probably won't bother ya until ya get 'em broke and ready to move."

"That's about the way I figgered it, too," Tye said. "All we got to do is figger a way to get 'em out of there without them Injuns stealin' 'em from us.

"I think I'll ride over that way tomorrow and do a little scouting around. Find us a place to set up camp. I remember seein' a box canyon with a stream comin' out of it. I want to scout it out and see if it'll hold horses. It's east of here about fifteen miles. Sits in between two big buttes and there's a valley with good grazin' leadin' up to it. You know the place I'm talkin' about?"

"Sure. I'll ride along and show ya," Clement said.

"Thanks, but I'd rather go alone. I can travel faster, and goin' alone, maybe I won't attract as much attention."

"Well," Clement said, feigning a hurt expression, "if ya don't want us along, then me and the papoose'll just take the day off and go huntin'. We could use some fresh venison anyway."

Tye saw the pained expression in Will's eyes and knew he didn't like the idea of being left here with Clement. But he needed to scout the area and study the lay of the land and he could do that better without having to worry about Will.

"You still as sorry at checkers as you used to be?" Clement asked, breaking the tension that had suddenly filled the room.

"You still cheat?" Tye asked with a grin.

"Cheat!" Clement bellowed. "I don't need to cheat to beat the likes of you. Let me get the board set up. I'll beat the both of ya."

Will lost count of the number of games that were played that night. The only time they took a break was to stop and eat a meal of venison steaks and potatoes cooked by the odd man out, which was mostly Tye and Will, as Clement lost few games.

It was late when Tye pushed away from the table after losing another game. "It's gettin' late. I'm turnin' in for the night. I've got a lot of ridin' to do tomorrow."

"I reckon we better turn in, too," Clement said, looking at Will. "We want to get into the woods early if we wanna get there before the deer hibernate for the day."

Chapter Seven

Tye was saddled and ready to ride the next morning when Will stepped out of the cabin. He strode down to the makeshift corral as Tye led his horse through the gate.

"I sure wish I was ridin' with ya."

"I know, but like I said, I'll travel faster alone. And if I do happen to run into any hostile Injuns, all I'll have to worry about is gettin' my hide outa there. You listen to ol' Clement. He may sound kinda crazy, but he ain't. That ol' man's forgot more about these mountains and how to survive in 'em, than most folks will ever know. Listen to him and learn. What you learn could someday save your life." Tye mounted his horse as Clement came out of the cabin. Looking at Will, Tye said, "I should be back around dark if nothin' goes wrong. I expect a big venison steak when I get here, so don't disappoint me." He kneed his horse and headed off toward the east. The sun was not yet up as he rode into the woods.

Clement had been leading the way since they'd left. Not a word had been spoken since leaving the trading post. They had been climbing steadily for the last mile. Will noticed that the woods seemed to change as they continued their upward climb. The pines seemed to grow thicker and the trail narrowed, allowing only single-file passage. The trail they were on wound its way up the mountainside, and though they weren't climbing straight up, the incline of their ascent had

Will gasping for breath by the time Clement called a rest. Will noticed that Clement was breathing as if he were on a Sunday stroll.

"It's the thin air that gets ya," Clement said.

Will sat on the log next to Clement, trying to regain control of his breathing.

"A man has to take it easy till he gets used to it or it can whup 'im," Clement continued. "Ya cain't hold a rifle steady if you're breathin' hard. And if ya cain't hold it steady, ya sure cain't hit what your aimin' at. If ya got to walk very far, stop every so often and get your wind. Listen to the things around ya.

"Do ya hear that whippoorwill singin', or the sound of that stream runnin'?"

Will had to admit that he had heard neither of those things until Clement pointed them out.

"That's the things ya got to listen for," Clement said. "Those things can make the difference between survivin' or dyin'. That stream means there's water. The whippoorwill will let ya know if someone's comin'. His tone will change if somethin' threatens him."

Will straightened himself, his breathing slowly returning to normal. He looked around at the majestic mountains surrounding them. The trees rustled as a light breeze caressed their branches and danced among their leaves. In the distance, he heard the cry of a hawk and wondered if it called to its mate, or talked of lost prey. A light rain had fallen during the night, leaving the air fresh and clean smelling. The trail they traveled followed the rim of a canyon. Will had been too busy trying to catch his breath and keep up with Clement to take notice of what lay in this canyon. But now he walked to the edge to gaze onto the canyon floor. What he saw was so majestic, it nearly took his breath away again. The canyon walls had begun to separate from each other about two hundred yards back down the trail and continued to separate, forming a lush valley. The stream Will heard ran through the center of this valley, giving life to the wildflowers and grass growing along its banks. The effect was stunning in its beauty. The rainbow of colors below looked as if a master painter had chosen each hue with precise care to blend with the others in natural splendor.

Will looked in wonder at the beauty before him, knowing there was no way man could ever create anything to compare with the picture he was seeing.

As if reading his thoughts, Clement spoke. "Beautiful, ain't it? But ya can't let the beauty fool ya. These mountains is like a woman. You treat 'em right and you can live in peace. Threat 'em wrong and they'll fight ya every step of the way. You got to learn to live in harmony with nature if'n you're gonna survive. The freezing cold here can kill ya. But if you're wounded bad, it can save your life by slowing down the flow of blood and keep ya from bleedin' to death. There's plants here that can kill ya if ya eat 'em; at the same time, they can save your life if prepared properly. The Shoshone have taught me plenty about these here mountains. They say the gods dwell here. I ain't so sure they're not right. If I was a god, this is where I'd want to live."

"It's beautiful here," Will said. "I could stay right here lookin' at this forever."

"You'd get almighty tired of lookin' at it after a while. That's why there's so much land around here. It's so's a feller won't wear out one place lookin' at it too long.

"Tye says y'all are goin' to Texas," Clement said, looking quizzically at Will.

"That's what he says," Will responded. "I ain't never been to Texas. Does it have beauty like this?"

Clement scratched his beard in thought, before replying. "I was down Texas way several times. It ain't got the same kinda beauty as these mountains, but it's got beauty all right. The plains at sunset is as pretty as anything I ever seen. It's a place where a man can

swing a wide loop if he's man enough to haul in what
he catches. You and Tye can make a place fer yerselves down there. Tye's a good one to ride the river
with. You pay attention to him and he'll learn ya
things. He sets a great deal a store in ya. See to it
that ya don't disappoint 'im."

"He thinks a lot of you, too," Will said, and had
the satisfaction of seeing Clement's face flush with embarrassment. But he could see Clement was pleased
with the comment.

"We better get a move on if we're gonna have fresh
venison fer supper," Clement said, rising to his feet,
and taking up his rifle.

Tye rode warily as he scouted the mountain region
east of Clement's trading post. The only tracks he'd
seen were those of the wild horse herds. By his esti-
mate, there were over four hundred head running in
the valleys. He had found the place where he and Will
would make their first camp. It was chosen not only
for its location, but for defense as well. A small canyon branching off the larger one in which he was now
riding provided the shelter he was looking for. There
was a small cave a hundred yards from the mouth of
the canyon that would allow protection from the
weather. The area around the cave was open, offering
no cover for an approaching enemy, and could be
guarded by one person. It wasn't far from the box
canyon he planned to use as a trap for the horses.
Once they had the horses caught, they could move
their camp to the mouth of the canyon. Even though
they would be more in the open, it still offered a good
defensive position, with little chance for someone to
approach unnoticed.

Tye knew he ought to be heading back, but his urge
to see the wild horse herds was stronger than the need
to return. He knew he was getting closer to the Indian
village Clement had told him about, but he rode on,
following the tracks of the herd.

Tye remembered a small lake situated in a valley southeast of where he was. He suspected this was where the herd watered and bedded down at night. He turned his horse and headed into the woods, climbing the ridge to approach the valley from the rim rock above them.

There were only a couple hours of daylight left when Tye looked down at the small lake in the valley. He knew Will and Clement would be worried about him, but the view he looked upon now was worth the extra time he'd taken. There below him was no less than four hundred head of wild mustangs. Some were grazing, while others drank from the lake or lay upon the lush grass of the meadow. Colts ran and bucked, nipping each other in play as their mothers stood with watchful eyes, ready to sound a warning should danger approach.

Tye could not take his eyes from the scene below. This was the beginning of his dream. If he and Will could pull this off without losing their hair to the Sioux, or breaking their necks trying to break these brutes, they'd have their start. With great reluctance, Tye turned his horse and headed back down the trail in the direction from which he'd come. Glancing back over his shoulder, he saw a large stallion standing apart from the other horses. The big horse was looking in his direction and Tye could see the nostrils flaring and the ears twitching back and forth as the horse sensed his presence.

"Soon, old son, soon," Tye said as he turned in the saddle.

The horse, as if hearing Tye's words, pawed the ground, shaking his head as if accepting the challenge.

It was ten o'clock when Tye rode up to the trading post. Both Clement and Will came out when they heard him call.

"We was beginnin' to wonder if you'd gotten yourself scalped," Clement said as Tye swung down.

"I did," Tye said. "But I talked 'em into givin' it back to me."

"Well, it sure took ya long enough," Will said. The worry and disapproval in his voice wasn't lost on Tye.

"Sorry for causin' ya'll to worry, but I wanted to see the horses."

"Did ya see 'em?" Will asked, the excitement in his voice overshadowing the worry he'd shown only moments before.

"Sure did," Tye said. "Good-lookin' bunch of horses, too."

"How many are there?" Clement asked.

"I ain't tellin' ya'll another thing till I get me some venison steak," Tye said with a grin. "That is, if you two got one. Knowin' you two, you probably couldn't even find one."

"Hmmph," Clement snorted indignantly. "I'll have you know Will here downed two big ol' bucks by hisself. The boy's a pretty good shot with that rifle. We done got 'em skint and quartered. Will and I et already, but if you treat us nice, we might just cook ya up a steak with some taters and corn."

"I'm so hungry I could eat this horse while he stands here," Tye said.

"Well, I'll get the fire stirred up while you tend to 'im," Clement said and headed back to the cabin.

Over supper, Tye related the details of his trip into the mountains. Clement and Will listened with rapt attention as Tye described the area he'd ridden over, the campsite he'd picked, the box canyon where they'd trap the horses, and finally the herd itself. Will's eyes brightened when Tye talked about the stallion he'd seen.

"Are we gonna break him, too?" he asked.

"It depends," Tye said. "Some of these horses have been too long in the wild. They'll kill you and themselves before they'd allow ya to break 'em."

"When do you plan on gettin' started?" Clement asked.

"In about a week. That'll give us enough time to get our supplies together and prepare the things we'll need, like halters, lead ropes, and lairats. You got enough hemp to make about sixty or seventy halters?"

"I think so," Clement said. "How come ya need so many halters? I thought you was gonna break these horses to trail."

"I've changed my mind. I got to thinkin' on the way up there today. Rather than try to break all these horses up there in the box canyon, we're gonna halter break about sixty head and lead them out with the rest follerin'. That way we can leave quicker. We'll let the Sioux think we're gonna break all of 'em. But we'll only break a few; then we'll sneak out in the middle of the night leadin' as many as possible. We may lose a few, but that's better'n havin' to fight our way out."

"Did ya see any Injun sign?" Clement asked.

"Nope, but that don't mean they ain't there."

"That's fer sure," Clement said. "I'd rather see sign of 'em. That way, ya knows to watch fer 'em. Kinda like a rattlesnake. Ya tend to watch a little more if ya know he's around."

"Well, we're gonna act like they're around all the time. But right now I'm gonna get some shut-eye. It's been a long day and we got lots to do to get ready."

The following week went by fast as the three worked, preparing halters and lead ropes for the horses, sharpening the axes needed for chopping trees. Clement cut rawhide strips from hides. These would be used to tie the poles for the gate and fence in place. In the evening, Will practiced with the Colt.

"Don't worry about drawing fast," Tye told him. "Just concentrate on gettin' it out and hittin' what you're aimin' at."

By the end of the week, Will was not only clearing his holster with respectable speed, but hitting six out of six shots in the target Tye had nailed on a tree for him.

"Not bad for a papoose," Clement commented one evening as Will put six bullets in the circle of the target. He was thumbing the spent shells out of the cylinder as Clement spoke. Tye had been working on a packsaddle as Will practiced. All of a sudden, a thunderous roll broke the quiet. Will whirled to see Tye standing with a smoking pistol in his hand. Looking from Tye to the target, Will could see six neatly spaced holes that he could cover with the palm of his hand. The shots had come so fast, it had sounded like one shot rather than six.

"I do believe you're the fastest man I ever seen with a six-shooter," Clement said as Tye reloaded. "A man could end up gettin' hisself a bad reputation shootin' the way you do."

"Only a fool would look for a reputation as a fast man with a gun," Tye said.

"Sometimes you don't have to look for it. It just comes on ya 'cause of circumstances. I'm just tellin' ya to be careful, that's all," Clement said.

"I know," Tye said. "I shouldn't be showin' off anyway. I just thought I'd give Will somethin' to try for."

Will laughed humorously. "Maybe if I live to be as old as you two, I might get to be that good, but hangin' around with you, I doubt I'll get a chance to find out," he said, looking at the two older men.

"You might have a point there, papoose," Clement said, turning to grin at Tye.

"Don't encourage him," Tye said with a grimace. "I already have enough problems with this young upstart criticizin' my age and my habits. Now he'll start thinkin' he's right all the time."

Clement winked and grinned at Will.

Two days later, Will and Tye loaded up their supplies and prepared to leave for the "Horse Valley," as they now called it.

"We'll be back in about a month," Tye said to Clement as they mounted their horses. "I expect a good meal when we get here. I doubt this pup can cook anything but beans, and my cookin' ain't a whole lot better."

"I'll be waitin' fer ya," Clement said. "I'll try to have some good elk or moose steaks by the time ya get back. Y'all watch your backsides and keep your hair on your heads, and don't bring back no Injuns with ya neither. I ain't got enough room here fer no one else."

Tye and Will shook hands with Clement and rode away from the trading post. Will glanced back once to see Clement standing in the yard, watching them depart. He raised a hand to bid them farewell. Will returned the gesture, wondering what would happen between now and when they next saw Clement. They were setting out on an adventure that was both exhilarating and frightening at the same time. Will knew this was the beginning of fulfilling Tye's dream. Was it going to be his dream as well? Was this the beginning of Will Paxton's future, or was his road destined to take him in another direction? Many questions would be asked before the answers came. Tye knew where he was going and what he wanted to do. Will had never seen the wild horse herds. He'd never been to Texas. How could he say what his dream was? All he knew was that he trusted Tye Garrett and he'd never find a better partner, or one who would offer as much as Tye had.

They rode along in silence for the first few miles, leading the packhorses and allowing the others to move along ahead of them. The trail where they rode was in a wide canyon. This canyon eventually opened into the bigger horse canyon. The canyon they rode in was bordered by woods on both sides, sloping up to the rim rock that formed the upper edge and prevented all but the most agile animal from escaping.

"This is the route we'll be using to bring the horses out. We can keep 'em bunched here with little chance for escape. This canyon opens into the larger canyon. Our first campsite is about two miles east of there. The lake where the horses water is in another canyon, about eight miles from the box canyon where we'll trap 'em. I'll be watchin' the herds for the first few days to learn their feeding habits. Once we've established their range, then we can form a plan to drive 'em into the trap.''

It was late afternoon when they arrived at the campsite Tye had chosen. Will gathered firewood, while Tye unloaded the packhorses.

"We'll only unload what we need for the first week," Tye said as Will started the small fire they would use for cooking.

"How would you like some fresh fish for supper? I saw some nice-sized trout in the stream when I was here the other day."

"Sounds great. How we gonna catch 'em?" Will asked, looking about for some means of catching fish, and not seeing any.

"We'll do it the Indian way. Come on, I'll show ya."

They walked down to the small stream running through the canyon. Tye had cut a pine branch from a tree and was shaping it into a spear, sharpening the point with the hunting knife he now carried on his belt. Once the spear was sharpened, he pulled off his boots and rolled his pants legs above his knees, then stepped into the stream. He moved about slowly, watching the rippling water as it moved over the rocks. He worked his way toward the shallow bank, then stopped and raised the spear in his right hand. He poised there for a brief moment, then, with lightning speed, brought the spear down, plunging it beneath the surface. He held tightly to the spear with both hands, then brought it splashing out of the water, a nice brown trout impaled upon the end. With a flip of his wrists, he sent the fish flying through the air to land upon the grassy bank. Will, astonishment showing on his face, hurried to gather up the fish. Meanwhile, Tye had resumed his search in the swift water of the stream.

Will cleaned the fish as Tye threw them on the bank.

The coffee Will had started smelled good as they carried their supper to the fire. Tye broiled the fish while Will prepared potatoes in the hot coals. After cooking the fish, Tye prepared dough balls, and, using some of the corn he'd gotten from Clement, wrapped the dough balls around it and dropped it into the hot grease.

The meal that night was one of the best Will could remember, as he lay back on his bedroll. His stomach stretched his belt tight and his eyes grew heavy.

"I'll take the first watch and let you have the second one, seein' as how you're almost asleep anyway," Tye said.

"Okay by me," Will replied with a yawn.

Chapter Eight

Will woke Tye an hour before sunup. The coffee was ready and Will handed him a cup as he finished pulling on his boots, which was the only thing they took off at night. The horses were pulled in close to the cave at dusk to serve as watches, as well as a caution against being stolen by Indians.

Tye had seen several tracks around the mouth of the canyon, telling him Clement had been right in his prediction. The Sioux knew they were there and even though they hadn't bothered them during this first week, with Indians you just didn't take any risks.

During the week, they had built the fence across the opening of the box canyon. Actually, it was two large gates covered with brush to blend into the surroundings. Once the horses were herded inside, the gates could be swung closed to hold them. They had also built a fence across the large canyon, consisting of two ropes three hundred feet long, one on top of the other, with cedar stakes spaced along and tied in place with rawhide strips. This fence would be used to turn the horses into the box canyon.

Tye had scouted the horses every morning for the past week, returning by noon to help Will build the fences. He had determined where the horses grazed during the day, and the best route to stampede them in order to drive them into the trap.

Sitting by the fire the last night before the drive, Tye went over his plan one more time with Will, out-

lining in the dirt floor of the cave where the strategic
points would be.

"The horses move away from the lake during the
day, coming down the valley to graze along the river.
There are actually four different herds in this bunch,
but they stay pretty well together. There are four
canyons that offer an escape route for them between
here and the lake. Three are on this side of the valley
and one is on the other side. The three on this side
are the closest to the lake. Usually they graze past
those three. If we start them after they've grazed past
these three canyons, we only have one to worry
about. This means one of us will have to be on the
far side of the canyon when they start running in
order to head them off. That will be your job. Once
we're past that canyon, they'll run straight down this
canyon, thinking their escape is in this direction. We
won't push 'em hard until they get close. The fence
across the valley should turn 'em into the box canyon. The smart leaders in the bunch will know that's
a box canyon, but we're relying on fear and timing
to force 'em in. Once they go into the canyon, we've
got to be at the gates, swingin' 'em closed. More'n
likely some of 'em will try the gate after it's closed.
We'll have to stay by them until they settle down.
Any questions?"

Will shook his head.

"Well, let's put this fire out and get some sleep.
We've got to be on the trail early in the morning."

As the sun rose in the eastern sky the next morning,
Will and Tye sat on the rim rock above the horse
lake. Will looked in awe at the horses gathered around
the lake. He could not believe there were so many.
Colts were running in the cool morning air, kicking
and nipping each other as they ran. Mares were calling
to their young from the grassy slopes surrounding the
lake. The morning sun shining on the dew on the grass
created crystalline reflections, making the meadow
come alive in a shimmering dance.

They had left their horses tied in the woods about a mile back down the trail so the wild herd would not catch their scent, nor could their horses send a warning call upon spotting the wild ones.

Tye, keeping his voice low, spoke to Will.

"They'll start moving out in a moment. They usually move down the valley about two miles before grazing. As soon as they've moved out of sight, we'll work our way down to the bottom and follow them at a safe distance. When they've grazed past the three canyons I told you about, you'll move to the opposite side of the valley and be ready to block the fourth canyon."

Will nodded, but said nothing. This was it. There was nothing left to say.

After watching the herd move out of sight, they waited another thirty minutes before going back to their horses. Making their way to the valley below took another twenty minutes as they wound down the canyon walls, navigating boulders and trees.

Once they reached the bottom, Tye led off at a ground-eating trot. It had taken them longer to reach the valley floor than he had anticipated.

He had explained to Will the night before how all the horses didn't always follow the valley, but sometimes one or more of the herds would break off from the others and enter one of the escape canyons to graze. Each of the four herds had different leaders. Most of the leaders were wise old mares that'd been around for a spell. Tye had explained how horses established a hierarchy among themselves, much the same as humans would, with leadership going to the strongest and wisest and the others ranked according to strength and ability. He had told of one of the mares he'd watched. She was a large roan mare with scars, no doubt the result of many battles to establish and hold her position as leader. A young stallion had challenged her leadership, but she had quickly dispatched him with a series of bites and a broadside kick that had lifted him off the ground and bowled him over. This, and a quick bite to the rump as he came to his feet, had dispelled any doubts he had about her leadership role.

The stallions with each herd were there for protection. Part of their role was to be guardian and watchdog for the herd, but few actually became leaders.

Tye had watched the herd for several days and had determined which herds were led by which mare. He had graded each herd by the number of colts over two years of age, the number of mares compared to the number of stallions, and the number of horses that bore saddle marks. He had chosen the herd led by the roan mare as the best herd. There were fewer colts under two years of age and more stud horses with this herd. It was also the largest herd of the four, numbering two hundred head. This herd would be the one they would concentrate their efforts on, hoping to gather at least one of the other herds with it. If this herd took one of the escape canyons, they would postpone their drive until tomorrow.

They spotted the horses about an hour after making the descent into the valley. The horses were moving at a leisurely pace, grazing as they went. They had passed the first two canyons and were approaching the third.

Will and Tye watched from a wooded area. Concealed by the trees, they stroked their horses' necks and spoke in whispers to soothe them. If one of the horses called out, the herd would be gone before anything could be done.

Tye and Will sat their horses until the herd moved out of sight around a bend in the valley.

"They'll be up to the next canyon about ten minutes from now. We'll wait for a while, then ease up and see if they kept going or turned into it," Tye said.

As they approached the third canyon, Will could see fresh tracks leading into it. Tye studied the ground and, looking at Will, said, "We're in luck: The smallest herd cut off here, only about fifty head. Now comes the hard part. You've got to cross over to the other side of the canyon and stay under cover until ya get past the herd. I'll give ya an hour to get ahead of 'em; then I'll start 'em runnin'. You got to be at the mouth of that canyon before they get there or they'll be gone and we might not get another chance."

"I'll be there," Will said, with a look of determination.

"I'll see ya at the box canyon. Keep 'em bunched, but don't push 'em hard until we get close," Tye said.

Turning his horse, Will said, "See ya soon."

Will crossed the canyon, which was about half a mile wide at this point. Trees grew along the canyon wall. These trees offered cover for the most part, but Will knew he would have to be wary once he was even with the horse herd. One slip and they'd be off like a shot, up the canyon and gone before he could get ahead of them.

Tye sat in the shade of a tree, watching the sun move across the sky. When he judged it to be an hour since Will's leaving, he stepped into the saddle and reined his horse in the direction of the herd.

It would take him half an hour to catch up with the herd and that would give Will a little extra time to reach the mouth of the canyon.

Rounding a bend in the canyon wall a short time later, he could see the herd moving ahead of him. He estimated there were still over three hundred head. He kicked his horse into a trot and moved toward the herd. He wouldn't have to worry about spooking the horses. Once they got wind of him, they'd be off and running.

Tye was riding his favorite bay mare today. Normally, he wouldn't have ridden her on a chase such as this, knowing the chance he would be taking with her. The chase would more than likely be a race over broken and unfamiliar ground. There was the danger a horse could step into a hole, or stumble going down many of the arroyos between here and the box canyon. But he also knew he would need the speed and endurance of the mare. She was tall, with long legs, a broad chest, and powerful hindquarters. The speed she possessed could make the difference in capturing the wild herd. The risk was one Tye was willing to take.

He kicked the mare into a lope, watching the horses ahead, knowing they would soon spot him and start the wheels in motion.

He had ridden two hundred yards when the shrill call from a stallion pierced the morning stillness. It was as if each horse in the herd had one mind as they bolted away, tails and manes flying in the breeze.

The old battle-scarred mare took the lead and headed for the escape canyon. Tye spurred his mare to keep up with the herd. He flanked them on the right, hoping to push them away from the canyon, but also to be ready if they tried to force their way through.

He could see the bend in the canyon ahead and knew that the escape canyon was only yards away. He would be behind the slower of the horses and might not be able to push his way to the front if trouble started.

Even though the old mare was leading them from danger, she didn't outdistance the slower mares and colts. Tye knew if she had wanted to escape, she could have easily pulled ahead of the stragglers and been gone.

They rounded the bend and Tye could see the canyon ahead. Was Will in place? Had he made it around the herd in time? Tye couldn't see him yet. The ground swelled ahead, making it impossible to see a rider from this distance. He remained behind the herd, matching the mare's pace to theirs. He had to trust that Will was there to turn the herd down the valley.

The lead mare topped the swell and Tye could sense the hesitation in the herd. Will must be there. The horses slowed as they approached the canyon. Tye put the spurs to the mare. The herd had to be kept moving or they would double back. If that happened he wouldn't be able to stop them. Yelling and swinging his rope, he pushed the stragglers faster. The lead horses veered away from the canyon. Tye was expecting this and was already moving across the valley, urging the herd forward.

The old mare, head high, looked around at Tye. Seeing him coming from the rear, she turned and headed down the valley toward the box canyon.

As Tye topped the swell, he looked for Will. He saw him move into the right-flank position to prevent any of the horses from turning back to the canyon.

It was another three miles to the box canyon and the fence across the valley. Tye's horse was breathing hard and sweat was pouring from both horse and rider. He eased the mare down to a slow lope, knowing he'd need her speed when they reached the fence. He kept the horses in sight, not allowing his mare to fall too far behind.

It was now two miles to the box canyon. Will was riding behind the herd. Tye had fallen back to allow his horse to rest. The mare was loping smoothly with no sign of tiring. He would rest her for the next mile, and then catch up to the herd for the last mile race. They would push the herd fast for the last mile, then ease off before reaching the fence. If he drove them too fast, they might try to go through it before Tye or Will could turn them.

With a mile left, Tye spurred his mount to overtake the herd. When he got even with Will, he nodded to him and both started shouting and swinging their ropes. The herd, in response, picked up the pace. The critical moment was fast approaching as the two watched the horses race toward the fence they had built.

When they had covered three-fourths of the miles, Will moved to the right and spurred his horse. He was riding the large roan gelding and easily passed the stragglers. He pushed the roan until he had passed half the herd, keeping a distance of two hundred feet between them. His job was to turn the herd once they reached the box canyon.

Tye eased up on the mare, allowing the horses to slow a little. He could see the fence far up the valley. The lead mare, if she saw it, didn't slow her pace. Tye watched as they continued their run, following the stream as it wound its way through the valley.

Suddenly, Tye felt the herd slow as the lead horses saw the fence. They were five hundred yards from the fence now. This was the critical point. If the horses cut back, there would be no way for he and Will to stop the horse herd if they took the notion to turn back up the valley. He could only hope that the lead horses would turn into the box canyon. Fear was their strongest ally now. He hoped the horses' fear would make them seek escape from the two riders.

Will was still riding on the right side of the herd. Soon he would have to push his horse to the front and attempt to turn the leaders. The roan was tiring now as they approached the fence, but when Will touched him with his spurs, he felt the surge of power in the big horse. He waited until he was almost even with the lead horses, and then changed direction. He set his course to meet with the leaders just before they reached the fence. He and Tye had rehearsed this maneuver time after time in the evenings around the fire. As he neared the lead horse closest to him, he could see it swing away, forcing the horse next to swing left. Soon the entire lead was moving away from him.

Tye, riding in the rear, watched through the dust as Will made the move they'd discussed. He watched the lead begin to change. If they continued to change course, they would be headed directly for the box canyon before they reached the fence. Tye swung his rope and shouted at the drag horses. Now was the time to push hard.

The old mare saw the fence. She slowed. Her instincts told her she was headed for a trap. With head held high, she looked around for an avenue of escape. She saw the canyon on her left, but knew it for what it was. She looked right and saw the man on horseback coming at them. Her only hope lay in front of her. She gathered herself for the leap that would carry her to safety. She didn't think of the herd now. It was too late for that. Her only thought was to save herself. She was now fifty yards from the fence. She laid back her ears and charged ahead, intent on reaching the obstacle in front of her. She was running tired now. The long run down the valley had taken its toll. Suddenly, the horse to her right bumped her. She stumbled, but managed to stay upright. In doing so, she was pushed even farther aside. She fought to regain her position, but to no avail. The lead horses were now forcing her toward the canyon.

Will continued pushing the horses to the canyon. They were running directly for the mouth. He could see the old mare being pushed along as the rest of the herd closed around her.

Tye was riding hard now, bunching the herd as they neared the canyon. He saw Will turn them before they reached the fence. He, too, saw the lead mare being pushed toward the canyon. He rode on the heels of the drag, yelling and swinging his rope. The panic he caused forced the horses to bunch with those ahead, allowing no room for the lead horses to turn.

Suddenly the horses were through the mouth and into the canyon. Tye and Will swung from their horses and rushed to the heavy gates, swinging them closed, and placing the center pole in the hole they'd dug and covered with a large rock.

Tying the gate closed with the braided rawhide ropes he'd made, Tye stepped back and, wiping the sweat from his brow, turned to Will and grinned. "Well, we got 'em in. Now all we got to do is hold 'em till we can get 'em broke."

Will took their saddle horses and, loosening the
cinches, tied them under the shade of a large tree. He
would water them later after they'd had a chance to
cool down. Tye stayed by the gate, waiting for the
horses to come back down the canyon. He fully expected them to make a try at breaking it down.

The canyon they were in was a half mile long. At
the mouth, it was probably two hundred feet across
and narrowed to fifty feet at the other end.

They could hear the horses milling about. The
mothers were neighing for their young as they became separated.

Even though their fear was strong, the long run
down the valley had taken the fight out of the herd.
They soon stopped their milling and started the inquisitive investigation of their surroundings. Some walked
to the small stream and began drinking, while others
dropped their heads and began eating. Only the old
mare and one or two stallions continued their search
for escape. But when they ran down the canyon, none
of the herd followed.

Tye and Will watched as the mare and stud horses
came at the gate. Tye picked up his lariat and swung
it over his head, yelling at the horses as he did. Will
followed suit and the mare stopped before the gate,
rearing on her hind legs and pawing the air. The stallions stood off to one side, necks bowed and nostrils
flaring, but they ventured no closer. When the mare's
front feet came back to earth, she whirled and charged
back up the canyon. The stallions followed.

Tye and Will waited another hour before feeling it
safe to leave the gate.

"They'll all come down to check it out, but she's
the only one, I think, who'd try to come across it.
Tomorrow, we'll start building our pens and sorting
gates after we've roped some of these mares and put
halters on 'em."

After watering the saddle horses, Will stayed by the
canyon, while Tye rode to the old camp to bring back

their supplies and the other horses. They'd worked
the night before, loading everything for a quick move.
Their new camp would be just outside the gates leading into the canyon. There was an overhang on the
west side that would provide shelter. Tye had scouted
around and found a small cul-de-sac where they could
put the saddle horses. The grass wouldn't last long
and they would have to be tethered out on the lush
grass of the valley every day, but at least they could
be guarded against Indians.

Tye hadn't forgotten the threat that still lingered.
The Sioux could decide to attack and steal their horses
at their whim. He only hoped he and Clement were
right, that they would wait until he and Will had broken the wild herd before making their move. He knew
they were gambling not only the herd, but their lives
as well. He knew they were being watched. On the
pretense of hunting, he had scouted the area for signs.
He had seen the tracks of their ponies on the rim
overlooking their camp. He'd also seen a moccasin
track in the box canyon. The track had been fresh. It
had been made since the gates had been built. He
found but one, but it was enough. He hadn't mentioned it to Will. No use causing alarm at this point.

Chapter Nine

It was after dark when they finally got the horses cared for and the supplies unloaded. They had a cold camp that night, opting to turn in early after the hard day.

They were up early the next morning, cutting trees to be used for drags. These drags would be used for halter breaking the horses. Each log would weigh approximately two hundred pounds. Each horse to be halter broke would be tied to one of the logs and left to drag the weight. Tye had explained to Will, how after dragging one of these logs for three days, a horse could be led. It would also aid in gentling the horses down.

After cutting thirty logs, they set about sinking a snubbing post in the ground close to the end of the canyon. This would be used each time they roped a horse out of the herd. Several wraps around the post would help hold the fighting animal until it gave to the rope.

It was late afternoon when they tamped the last of the dirt around the post. Tye stood back and surveyed the post with satisfaction.

"We'll get a few of these critters started on the halters tomorrow, and then we'll build a fence across this end of the canyon to use as our breaking pen. We should be breakin' horses by the day after tomorrow. But first, we've got to cut out some of these mares and young colts that we ain't gonna keep. There's not enough grass in this canyon to run this many head as long as we need to hold 'em here."

"How many you gonna cut out?" Will asked, as he looked over the herd.

"I've counted about fifty head of young colts. The ones that are too small to take a hard drive outa here. We'll cut them and their mamas out. That'll leave us about three hundred head. I figure there's about fifty head of mares that I'd like to keep and maybe four stallions. We'll sell some of the mares like they are, and maybe some of the others as well. I figure there'll still be about two hundred head of horses to rough break."

"How many you aimin' on breakin' before we drive 'em outa here?" Will asked.

"About fifteen or twenty," Tye said. "That'll give us enough to hold them together."

"I'll be glad when that day comes," Will said, looking around him. "This is pretty country, but knowin' them Injuns is around don't make me any too comfortable."

"I know what ya mean," Tye said. Then picking up his rope, he motioned to Will. "You work the gate down there. I'll cut out the mares and colts and drive 'em out."

They worked the rest of the day cutting out the horses they didn't want to keep. The next morning found them building the corral they would use to break the horses. Since they were using the narrow end of the canyon for the working pen, it required less work to build a fence across than it did for the opening of the canyon.

By late afternoon, they had completed the make-shift corral and were ready to start working the wild bunch.

"Let's get a few of these mares haltered and tied to those logs we cut."

"Sounds good to me," Will said, as he picked up his rope and started for the gate.

Tye, on horseback, cut out several head of mares and drove them into the corral. Will closed the gate and waited for Tye to dismount and join him before he entered.

"I'll rope the first one. You snub the rope to the post. Once you've got her snubbed, yell and I'll move out of the way. You ready?"

"Yep," Will said as they opened the gate and entered the corral.

This was one of the dangerous tasks of working the wild horses. Once the mare was roped, she would fight for everything she was worth, attempting to crush anything or anyone in her path. It was up to the snubber to keep the rope tight at all times, preventing the mare from running him or anyone else down.

Will had helped Tye snub horses while working on the Triangle T. He had become quite adept at dallying the rope around the snubbing post and holding the fighting horses until, exhausted, they gave to the rope.

There were five mares in the corral and Tye selected a large palomino as his first choice to halter.

Tye used a technique called the "wild horse loop," or hoolihan, to catch horses in a corral. This style of roping was a method used by the vaqueros in Mexico and required a backhand swing and throw. The advantage in using it was that it cut down on the swinging of the rope, which had a tendency to excite the horses.

Tye lined the horses out down the fence, allowing each to run by him until the palomino was singled out. Then with precise accuracy, he threw his loop and braced himself as it settled over the mare's neck. Will moved in to grab the end of the rope and wrap it around the snubbing post.

Upon feeling the noose tighten around her neck, the mare went into an acrobatic dance, standing on her back hooves and throwing her head high in the air. She fought against the rope, which was beginning to close off the air to her lungs. The rope stretched taut, and continued its restricting hold until the mare finally came down. This was enough of a relief to allow her to suck air into her lungs. Immediately, she pulled against the rope again, fighting the demon that held her tight.

Tye moved beyond the reach of the mare, allowing Will to keep the rope tight. The mare would fight the rope until she wore herself down. Then he would ease up to her and put the halter on.

The fight continued for another ten minutes. The mare pulled against the rope until she could no longer breathe. Then, with reluctance, she would move forward, easing the strangling effect of the noose cutting off her wind. Finally, after one last desperate struggle to free herself, the palomino stepped forward and stood shaking as the rope slackened itself around her neck.

Tye stepped forward, placing one hand on the rope far enough from the mare to move away should she decide to attack. He worked his way down the rope, talking in soothing tones to the mare as she watched him with eyes rolling and nostrils flaring. He eased toward her, holding one hand outstretched before him, talking to her all the while. As his hand reached to touch the trembling horse, she exploded again, straining against the rope. Tye moved out of reach while Will held tight to the rope, preventing the horse from pulling away. With her wind immediately cut off, the mare soon ceased her pulling and walked forward. The lesson of the rope was quickly learned.

It took Tye two more tries before he could place his hand on the mare's neck. When he did, she stood trembling as he gently stroked her and talked in low tones. He continued to rub her neck and head as he slowly slipped the halter over her head. Tightening it down, he stepped back and held the lead rope. Will loosened the rope from around the snubbing post and opened the gate.

Tye herded the mare out the gate as Will held the rope, preventing her from bolting as he went through. Once outside, Tye rolled one of the logs to a level area. Then he tied the end of the mare's lead rope to the log after slipping the rope from around her neck.

The palomino stood trembling, ready to bolt. Only

the rope around her neck had prevented her from seeking escape. But now, as the rope was removed, she rolled her eyes and snorted as Tye moved away. Feeling the absence of the rope from her neck, she whirled and ran, only to be snapped around by the weight of the log. The log was jerked along the ground for fifteen feet before the mare was pulled to a stop, where she stared at it in bewilderment before pulling back. The log skidded along the ground as the mare continued her backward trek. Finally, tired and frightened, the mare stopped her frantic pulling and stood watching the log, confusion and fear showing in her eyes.

Tye and Will watched the mare for a moment longer. Then Tye turned to Will and said, "She'll be all right. Let's get some more staked out before it gets dark. Why don't you work the next one?"

Will looked at the mares standing in the corral, then turned to Tye.

"Maybe I should do the rest of 'em. You're lookin' a bit peaked. I wouldn't want you to wear yourself down. That could be dangerous for a person of your age."

Tye looked at Will and hid the grin that was coming to his face.

"Why don't you do that, youngster? I've had to do all the work since we got here. It'll be nice to see you carry your weight for a change."

Will grinned at Tye, enjoying the easy banter they shared as they worked.

They roped and haltered ten head before the darkness closed in on them. They ate a cold supper that night and turned in early, worn from the day's work.

The next morning they roped and haltered twenty more mares. The sight of thirty mares tied to logs was something to behold. Tye looked on with pleasure as he noted the old roan mare tethered to one of the logs. She had fought the hardest of all the mares and had come close to taking a bite out of Will's arm, ripping his shirt in the process. They had finally "eared" her down: twisting her ear and biting the tip to hold her still while they haltered her. Tye didn't intend to gentle the mare, but he wanted her as one of the lead horses when they took the other horses out.

They started breaking horses that afternoon, snubbing the broncs to the snubbing post and tying up one back foot. Tye saddled the first horse. He placed the hackamore and blindfold on the horse's head, then motioned for Will to climb aboard. Will looked shocked as he saw Tye's intent.

"You want me to ride the first one?" he asked.

"Why not?" Tye asked, grinning at the expression on Will's face.

"You wouldn't let me ride the rough horses on the ranch. I figured you'd never let me ride one of these till you'd ridden them first," Will said.

"I had other reasons for you not riding those horses. This is different. We're both gonna break these. We'll take turns riding. That way, we can break more of 'em."

Will grinned as he pulled his hat tighter on his head. He untied the horse's foot while Tye eared the horse down. Then taking hold of the reins, Will stepped into the saddle. When he was seated, he took a tight hold on the reins in each hand and said, "Let him go."

Tye removed the blindfold and let the horse have his head, moving swiftly out of the way as he did. By the time he turned to look back, the horse's head was between its legs and Will was seated firmly on his back.

Will allowed the horse to buck across the pen, getting the feel of him to find out what kinds of tricks he would use. As he got in tune with the horse, he began to use his spurs to get in rhythm with each jump. Each time the horse lunged into the air, Will would rake him with the spurs from the shoulder points to the flank. This kind of timing helped him keep his balance, and let the horse know that with each jump, it would feel the punishment of the spurs.

The horse Will was mounted on was a black stud about three years old. Tye wanted to break the younger horses first, saving the older horses until they were away from the canyon. The black was a stout horse and was giving Will a good fight. He would jump straight into the air, coming to earth stiff legged, then flex his knees and lunge forward. The combination of jarring and lunging made for a hard ride, but Will was making a good show of riding the animal. He kept his seat and followed the horse's head the way Tye had taught him, learning quickly that where the head went, the body was sure to follow.

Tye watched Will spur the horse around the corral. He was satisfied with the way Will rode the horse. Only once or twice did he feel the need to yell advice to the young man, and those were only minor corrections. He smiled inwardly as he reflected on the progress that had been accomplished in only a few short months. As he had predicted, Will had a natural ability with horses and would soon be a better bronc rider than Tye himself. As the thought came to him, he was somewhat puzzled by the fact that this didn't bother him. He had always made it a point to be the best he could possibly be at whatever he undertook. That to him meant he had to be better than everyone else. Now here was someone who was going to be better than him and he was proud of the fact, rather than envious. He thought about this for a moment, then smiled as he turned his thoughts back to the corral to shout encouragement to Will as he continued to spur the black horse.

Will had been riding the black for ten minutes when he felt it start to tire. The leaps were coming slower now and each one had less energy behind it than the one before. Finally, the horse stopped, front legs spread wide, head down and breathing hard. Will let it stand for thirty seconds, then touched him lightly with the spurs. The black lunged forward and Will pulled him around hard, forcing the horse in a circle. At last, exhausted, the horse stepped out, walking in a tight circle as Will continued to pull him around. Will turned him around in the opposite direction, kicking him around and making him respond to the reins as he guided him around the corral.

After a few minutes of working the colt around the corral, Will rode up to where Tye was standing. As he approached, he watched as Tye reached up as if to scratch his head.

"You throw that hat at me and I'm gonna run over it and stomp it flat," Will said as he watched Tye closely.

Tye chuckled as he dropped his hand to his side. "I swear you're sure gettin' suspicious these days."

"I got good reason to be suspicious," Will replied, still not taking his eyes off Tye.

Only after he was sure Tye wasn't going to try anything, did Will ease off the black colt.

"Let's unsaddle him and tie him to one of the logs for a while," Tye said. "Then we'll catch another one and I'll see if I can ride one, unless you want to ride 'em all."

"Naw, I reckon I'll let you ride a few. Don't want ya gettin' outa practice. You'd start gettin' fat and lazy. Then I'd have to do everything for ya."

"I can see where that might be a problem for you," Tye said. "Seein' as how I do most of the work around here while you lay around till noon, takin' life easy."

Will grinned and started taking the saddle off the colt, talking over his shoulder as he worked. "Sure is dark around here at noon. I guess bein' this far back in the mountains just takes the sun longer to get here, huh?"

Tye didn't respond as he walked over to one of the logs and positioned it to tie the colt. Then taking a halter, he held the black's head as Will placed the halter over his ears. Between the two of them, they herded him out the gate and tied him to the log.

Will went to his horse and, tightening the cinch,

said, "I'll pick you out one and bring him in. Reckon you can handle the gate?"

"I think I can handle it all right," Tye said. "Just don't take all day bringin' one up. I want to ride at least one more before I'm too old and decrepit."

Will cut out a nice-looking four-year-old buckskin stallion. The horse was fifteen hands tall and well developed. He herded him into the corral and watched as he cantered around the enclosure, head and tail high, sniffing the air as he went.

Tye entered the corral, rope in hand, while Will brought in his saddle and hackamore.

One throw was all it required to have the horse caught around the neck. It was soon snubbed to the post, where Tye and Will went about blindfolding and saddling it.

Once Tye had the saddle cinched down, he nodded to Will and stepped into the saddle, holding the reins tightly in his hand as Will removed the blindfold and stepped out of the way.

The buckskin stood for a moment, blinking as the sun hit his eyes. Then, realizing there was something on his back, he reared on his hind legs, pawing the air with his forelegs as he lifted.

Tye leaned forward in the saddle, holding the reins and mane in his hands until the horse started his descent back to earth, letting go of the mane and holding tight to the reins as the horse's feet hit the ground.

The buckskin was a smooth-bucking horse, bucking in a straight line around the corral. Instead of trying tricks to lose the rider on his back, he relied on brute strength to batter down the resistance. His leaps were long and the impact with the ground was bone jarring.

Tye sat the saddle, keeping rhythm with the horse's jumps, relaxing his muscles as the buckskin hit the ground to lessen the jarring on his body.

The horse bucked for another ten minutes, then leaped forward and ran around the corral. Tye pulled him around to prevent the possibility of his jumping the fence. Slowing the horse to a lope, he watched him warily, expecting him at any moment to duck his head and resume his bucking, but after loping twice around the corral, the buckskin allowed himself to be pulled to a stop.

Pulling the horse's head around and holding him by the headstall, Tye stepped off.

"That was a nice one. If the rest of 'em were like him, we'd have 'em all broke before we left here," he said as he walked over to where Will was preparing another log.

"How many do you reckon we can rough break before we pull outa here?" Will asked.

"If we can have around twenty head of these younger ones ready, I figger we'll have enough to lead the others out. With these, and the mares we'll have halter broke, we should have enough to keep the herd together."

"We should be able to have twenty head ready in a week or so. You plan on leavin' that soon?" Will asked.

"I'm figurin' on two more weeks at the most. Let's get this one started on the log, then grab a quick bite. Maybe we can get a couple more ridden this afternoon. Then we'll ride these again in the mornin' and start some more tomorrow afternoon. That way we break in a few new ones each day, and keep the ones we've already ridden from forgettin' what the saddle is all about."

"Sounds like a good plan to me. As long as I keep pickin' out the easy ones for you to ride, things ought to go along smooth and easy."

Tye looked at Will through one eye, then shook his head and grinned at him as they headed down the canyon to their camp.

Chapter Ten

The next two weeks were grueling, bone-jarring, hard days. But even though Will felt as if every muscle and bone in his body was sore and bruised, he had to admit to himself that he'd never felt more alive in his life. Breaking the wild horses was like a tonic to his soul. He had never experienced anything close to the pleasure he got while aboard a bronc, matching his newfound skills against the wild animal trying with all its will and might to rid itself of the man on its back, but fighting more to hold on to the freedom it had been born to.

Will knew they would soon be moving the herd out of the canyon and making a run for Clement's trading post. They had broken twenty-four head of the wild mustangs, and had forty mares halter broke. He hoped this would be enough to keep the herd together. It was going to be a risk moving the herd at night to keep the Sioux from stealing them.

Will had seen signs of the Indians twice while riding in the valley. Once, while riding, he had caught a glimpse of two Indians riding along the tree-lined wall of the valley. He had quickly hidden in a stand of cedar and watched until the Indians were well out of sight. After that, he kept a close watch around him, knowing they were probably being observed by the Sioux.

Will was finishing off one of the three-year-olds he had broken. The horse was responding to his commands and Will was well pleased with the young horse and thought he might keep this one for himself.

Tye was leading one of the mares they had halter broken back to the corral. It was a hot afternoon and he had removed his shirt while he worked, dragging a log up close to the corral so he could tie another horse to it.

Will rode to where Tye was struggling to pull the log into place. "We pullin' out tomorrow night?"

"What makes ya ask that?" Tye asked.

" 'Cause you been busy as a beaver gettin' all these horses up here close to the corral. I figure if you're gettin' 'em all together, then you must be plannin' something, and the only thing that could be is leavin' here."

"I'm impressed, Papoose. You're gettin' to be pretty smart for a pup still wet behind the ears."

The name Clement had called him was not lost on Will as he grinned at Tye.

"I reckon we'll pull out tomorrow night if everything looks good. You ready?"

"Yep, my hair ain't felt safe since we got here. I'm ready to put some distance between me and them Injuns. What else we got to do to get ready?"

"Nothin' today. We'll go about tomorrow just like it was any other day, just in case we're being watched."

"I guess I'll finish this one off then and get another one."

"Why don't we knock off early today and take us a swim in that deep pool down the valley? I been sweatin' so much, I'm startin' to smell like a wet saddle blanket," Tye said, as he reached for the shirt he had laid on the ground.

Will said, "So that's what that smell is. I been lookin' for somethin' dead all day long."

"Let me tell ya, Junior, you don't smell none too sweet yourself. I durn near passed out a time or two just bein' close to ya."

"I guess it is time to wash a few layers of dirt off," Will said, slapping his gloves against the legs of his jeans and watching the dust fly off.

*　　*　　*

The pool of water Tye was talking about was at the base of a small waterfall. Years of flash floods and running water had eroded the sandstone at the base of the falls, forming a natural pool with a depth of ten to twelve feet in the middle.

Will was the first one in. Taking just enough time to unbuckle his holster and lay his Colt aside. Then removing his boots, he ran to the top of the falls and giving a Comanche yell, and jumped in, clothes and all. Tye followed close behind.

The water, despite the warm days, was cold enough to take their breath away as they plunged beneath the surface, gulping for air as they came to the top.

Lying on the sandstone rocks afterward, the sun drying their clothes and warming their chilled bodies, Will watched a hawk circling overhead as it searched the valley for prey. The long gliding pattern of the bird was hypnotizing and Will was content to watch the bird as it continued its search. Suddenly, the hawk swerved upward and changed course, flying away from the valley wall.

Something had scared the hawk away and Will suspected it wasn't an animal. He glanced over at Tye, but Tye was lying on one of the flat rocks facing the opposite side of the valley. His eyes were closed and Will suspected he was dozing.

He cut his eyes back to the rim of the valley. Nothing moved, and the only sound coming to his ears was the sound of the stream as it continued its course down the valley. Will knew something was out there, but what was it? It was a pretty sure bet that whatever it was, it wasn't friendly.

Their horses were tied in a stand of trees a hundred yards from the pool. Will could see them sheltering in the shade of the aspens. They were standing with their ears up, looking at the rim rock. Will knew they could not be seen by anyone up there; but at the same time, he and Tye were out in the open. He didn't move, but continued to scan the horizon.

*   *   *

Two Eagles led the remnants of his raiding party along the rim of the valley. He was not in a pleasant mood as he rode. He was weary and wounded. The pain in his side where the bullet had struck him, reminded him of his failure.

His raiding party had started out with fifteen. They had killed three white men, stolen their horse herd and two of their women. Now they had only one of the women, none of the horses, and only eight left in the party. And of those eight, four of them, including Two Eagles himself, were wounded, all the result of encountering an army patrol returning to Fort Bridger.

Two Eagles rode staring ahead, eyes looking neither right nor left. The pain in his side reminded him of his failure. The girl on the white pony followed him, wishing she could kick the wound in his side again, as she'd done while trying to escape when the soldiers had surprised them.

She had almost escaped, except she had no way of guiding the horse she was riding when it had pulled away from the Indian leading her. The Indian brave had suffered a wound to his shoulder, causing him to drop the lead rope.

Rebecca Kincaid rode staring at the back of the Indian in front of her. He was the one who had pulled her screaming and kicking out of the house, after her father, brother, Tim and uncle John had been killed by these savages.

Hearing the gunfire shortly after the men had left the house, Rebecca had run to the window to see her uncle and Tim lying in the dust of the yard. Her father was bringing his rifle to his shoulder when his body was violently twisted around, the rifle discharging into the air.

Only her mother's holding on to her had prevented her from rushing from the house to aid her fallen family.

Mrs. Kincaid had dragged Rebecca struggling and

fighting to the closet at the back of the house. As Rebecca stood there sobbing and shaking with both fear and anger, she remembered her father building the closet for her mother and the pride he had taken in fitting the rough boards into place, the cedar shakes he had used to line the closet. The smell of the cedar reminded her of the times she had hidden from Tim in this closet while playing hide-and-seek.

Her father and Tim lay dead or dying in the front yard as she and her mother cowered in the closet, waiting.

That had been the worst part, the waiting. They heard the front door broken open. Heard the sounds as the savages overturned the kitchen table, the one her uncle John had made. They heard the crash of her mother's dishes as they were thrown to the floor. Rebecca hugged her mother tighter as a fresh sob escaped her. Those dishes had been her pride and joy. She had brought them west with her on her long trek from Virginia. They had belonged to her mother, Rebecca's grandmother. Rebecca thought of the time she had broken one of the precious plates while washing dishes. Her mother hadn't scolded her, but the sadness in her eyes at seeing her precious plate lying in pieces on the floor had been punishment enough. Now they were all destroyed, but what did it really matter? In a few moments, if they were lucky, they would be dead.

But they hadn't been lucky. The Indians had discovered them shortly thereafter. Dragged from their hiding place, Rebecca knew what would take place. She had heard of other women taken by Indians. Had heard the stories of the things that had been done to them.

She and her mother were thrown to the floor in the kitchen, all the Indians circled around them. Rebecca looked up into the faces of her captors. She had steeled herself to show them no fear, though her heart was beating so fast it felt as though it would burst from her chest at any moment. She saw the lust in each pair of eyes she looked into, both from the killing and anticipation of what was to come. She forced herself to meet the eyes staring at her, showing each the contempt she felt for them. But when her eyes passed the bloody scalp hanging from the belt of one of the savages, her resolve slipped. Her eyes blurred with tears and her heart felt as if it would stop. Then, slowly, she felt hatred such as she had never experienced enter her consciousness, and burn into her soul.

She sprang from the floor like a cougar going for a kill. She leaped on her prey, a shrill scream escaping from her as she attacked the savage brandishing the fresh scalp. Before he could react, she had raked her nails the length of his face, feeling with satisfaction the skin and flesh embedding itself under them. She was suddenly grabbed by the hair from behind and slung to the floor, scraping her knees and elbows on the hard wood. She leaped to her feet, only to be slapped hard by one of the braves standing there. She landed again on the hard floor, her eyes clouding with pain as her head hit its surface. She raised herself up on her elbows and shook the cobwebs from her brain. Her vision cleared in time to see the Indian whose face she had clawed draw his knife and start for her. She knew this was the end and she felt no regret at having hurried the process along. Her only regret was that she could do nothing for her mother.

As the brave advanced, Rebecca pushed herself up, determined to make one more attack before the animal took her life. But before she could rise, a voice from the front door of the house quieted the group and stopped the advance of her executioner.

All eyes turned to the large brave as he entered, his quick glance surveying the scene before him, his eyes going from Rebecca to the face of the brave. Rebecca could have sworn she saw a flicker of a smile cross his face as he studied the long gashes on the cheek of the Indian before him. Then instantly his face clouded and his tone was harsh and commanding.

The Indians turned from the women and started gathering things from the house. When one of the Indians reached for Rebecca, she kicked out at him, catching him on the shin and having the satisfaction of hearing his howl of pain. The next second, she saw flashes of light as she was slapped hard across the face. But the pain of being slapped was nothing compared to the humiliation she felt as she was grabbed by her long blond hair and dragged staggering out the door into the bright sunlight of the day.

She was pulled to a horse, her hands were bound, and she was lifted bodily, as if she were a child, and placed on the back of the horse. She hurled insults at the back of the Indian as he walked away from her, vowing she would even the score.

Rebecca watched as they led her mother, wrists bound together also, to another horse, and lifted to its back. Tears came to her now as she watched her mother turn to look at the bodies of her husband and son lying in the yard of their home. When she turned back, Rebecca was shocked to see the dullness in her eyes. It was if she were already dead. Rebecca called to her. "Mama, we'll be all right. We'll escape somehow. Mama. . . ." But her mother said nothing, and just sat, staring straight ahead.

They were led from the yard at a full run and all of Rebecca's concentration was centered on remaining aboard the running horse. She thought once about letting go and hoping the fall would kill her, but she couldn't bring herself to do it. As long as she lived, there was hope of escape.

When the cavalry had come upon them, Rebecca's spirits had soared. She had seen the Indian leading her mother's horse fall in the first volley of gunfire. She had seen her mother's horse run away from the gunfire and no one gave pursuit. She knew her mother had escaped. Her chance had come when the Indian leading her horse had been wounded. Although he had tried to keep his hold on the lead rope, Rebecca had dug her heels into the horse, sending it bolting ahead of her captor's horse and jerking the lead from the Indian's hand.

Rebecca held to the horse's mane as he plunged into the thick undergrowth of the wooded area. Try as she might, she couldn't turn the horse as he ran on into the woods. If she had been able to turn the frightened animal, she might have been able to reach the soldiers. But with her hands bound by the rawhide strips, she couldn't reach the lead rope as it trailed on the ground. She tried using her feet and knees to force the horse to turn. But as frightened as the animal was, it was all she could do to keep from being knocked from its back as it continued its frightened run through the trees, jumping fallen logs and crashing through thick undergrowth.

Rebecca was so intent upon remaining aboard the running animal, she didn't notice, until it was too late, the Indian in pursuit. Suddenly, he was beside her, leaning over to catch the trailing lead rope.

Recognizing the Indian who had dragged her from the house by her hair, Rebecca's fury came to her stronger than before. She saw his bloody side from the bullet wound, and grabbing a stronger hold on the horse's mane, she raised her foot and kicked out, feeling her foot connect solidly. She had the satisfaction of seeing the agony wash over him as he pulled away. For a brief moment, she thought she might have succeeded in driving him away as he pulled his horse up and bent over its neck. Then her spirits fell and her heart beat faster as he sat up and kicked his horse after hers.

This time, instead of coming alongside her, he angled his horse to meet with hers where he would be at her horse's head, allowing him to grasp the lead attached to the halter and preventing her from kicking him again.

Grabbing the lead, he headed deeper into the woods. As they pulled away, Rebecca glanced back over her shoulder, but trees were the only things she saw as she was led away from the sounds of battle.

At least Mama was safe, she thought as she glared at the back of the Indian in front of her.

Chapter Eleven

Will continued to watch the rim of the valley, some sixth sense warning him of danger. He was about to give up his vigil, figuring it was a bear or cougar, when he spotted a horse coming into view, an Indian mounted on its back. He held his position, not daring to move. Even though the distance was great, he could still make out the Indian leading a horse behind him. His breath caught in this throat as the rider of the second horse appeared. The long blond hair reflected the sunlight, and even though Will couldn't make out the features, he knew it was a woman.

Will glanced over at Tye, but Tye was nowhere in sight. He didn't move a muscle then as his eyes returned to the rim of the valley. He knew movement could be seen for miles. If he moved, the Indians might see him.

He continued to watch as seven more Indians followed the path taken by the first Indian and the woman. He observed as they rode along the rimrock, then disappeared into the woods, apparently following a trail leading to their village.

After what seemed an eternity, Will heard Tye whisper, "I think it's safe now. Move down off the rock and get up under the bank."

Slowly, Will moved off the rock, dropping to the sandy soil of the river bottom. He eased up to the bank of the river. Here, he was out of sight from those on the rimrock.

Tye crawled to where Will was lying. "How many did you count?" he asked.

"Eight, not counting the woman," Will replied, his voice weak.

"That's what I counted, too," Tye replied.

"Where do you reckon the woman came from?"

"No tellin'. That was a raiding party, judgin' by the size of it."

"What are we gonna do?" Will asked, looking back over the bank of the river in the direction the Indians had gone.

"I don't know, Will. They're takin' her to the village. They might kill her once they reach there, or they might be plannin' on makin' her a squaw. One's not much better'n the other."

"We got to do something," Will said, looking at Tye. "We can't just sit here and do nothin'. I couldn't live with myself."

"We're gonna do something," Tye said. "I just got to figure out what it is we're gonna do." Tye looked up at the sun. It was sinking into the west, leaving only a couple of hours of daylight. Turning to Will, he asked, "Are you up for a ride to that Indian village?"

After thinking for a moment, Will replied, "I'd rather fight a grizzly bear, but I don't see one around right now, so I guess I'm up to it."

"Let's ride up there and check things out. Then we'll decide what to do from there."

It took them three hours of cautious riding to reach the ridge overlooking the Indian village.

The sun had set an hour ago and darkness had closed about them as they looked down at the fires in the valley below. Both carried rifles, as well as the pistols on their belts. Their horses were tied a mile back down the trail, hidden in a cedar stand off the path.

As they watched the activity below, they could see the large fire in the center of the village where something was happening.

Several Indians were standing in front of the fire,

addressing the rest of the tribe, but speaking mostly to three older Indians seated on the ground. Tye explained that the three were probably the chiefs of the tribe, and the Indians were describing the raid.

Will was watching intently as the large Indian doing most of the talking waved his arms and made signs with his hands while he talked. Even though they were too far away to hear any of the words, and wouldn't have been able to understand if they could hear, both Will and Tye were mesmerized by the proceedings taking place before them.

Suddenly, the large Indian doing the talking turned to two braves standing outside the ring of listeners and motioned to them, while at the same time shouting orders. Both braves turned and ran to a teepee that was facing the circle.

Will watched as the Indians entered the shelter, only to return shortly dragging a kicking, screaming woman behind them.

The braves dragged the woman to where the three chiefs sat. There, they unceremoniously dumped her on the ground. She sat up and Will could hear her screaming insults at the Indians as she tried to gather her torn skirt around her. Even from the far distance, Will could make out the words the woman was hurling at the Indians and he felt his face turn red as he listened to every word. He had never heard a woman use such language before. At first, he was ashamed for the woman. Then he considered the situation she was in and wondered if he himself might not react in the same way.

The woman continued to rant and rave at the Indians until the large brave who had been doing most of the talking drew back his arm as if to strike her. She instantly hushed and held up her arms to protect herself. When the brave saw she wasn't going to say anymore, he continued his talk, pointing to the woman occasionally during his oration.

Tye tapped Will on the shoulder and motioned him

back. When they were away from the ledge, he whispered, "I've got a plan, but it's a might risky."

"I think anything to do with that bunch down there is goin' to be a might risky. What is it?" Will asked, keeping his voice low.

"If I can work my way around to where their horses are and stampede them through the village, it may cause enough of a diversion where you can sneak in and get the woman."

"I thought you said it was gonna be a *might* risky. Sounds more like it's gonna be suicide, if ya ask me," Will said, not smiling.

"If you got a better plan, let me hear it," Tye said.

"If I had one, you would have already heard it," Will said, tight lipped.

"Then I guess we go with mine, unless you can talk me out of it," He smiled at Will and Will grinned back.

"You just remember that you promised me we'd make it outa here with our hair still on our heads. I aim to hold you to that promise."

"I'm gonna do my best to keep it," Tye said.

They crawled up to the rim of the cliff and Tye pointed to a group of trees just outside the village.

"I want you to work your way down to those trees there and wait until you hear the horses coming. As soon as their attention is drawn away from the woman, you sneak in there and grab her, then head back here to the horses. Don't wait for me. Just get her on your horse and hightail it back to the canyon. I'll be right behind you as soon as I know these devils aren't following us.

"We'll pull out as soon as I get there, so start getting our things together. Any questions?"

"Nope," Will said. "You be careful. I don't want to have to find another partner."

"You do the same. Good luck."

Tye moved off into the darkness. Will waited a few seconds, then stepped away from the rim. He circled away from the valley and made his way down the mountainside, moving slowly and cautiously, stopping every few feet to listen to the sounds of the night.

As he came closer, he could hear the sounds coming from the Indian village. The talks were still going on and Will was close enough now to make out the words, though he understood none of them. He steadily worked his way through the woods until he came to the clearing before the trees. He would have to cross twenty yards of open space before he would be hidden by the trees. He would be exposed to any eyes that may be looking. He couldn't circle around and come into the trees from any direction where he wouldn't be seen. He had no choice but to cross where he was and hope none of the Indians would look his way.

Sweat broke out on his brow as he gazed across the clearing. Twenty yards had never looked so far before. He drew his pistol from its holster. If they saw him, he was going to take at least one or two before they got him.

Saying a silent prayer, he bent over and crouched as close to the ground as he possibly could, watching the encampment as he moved. It took only a few seconds to cover the twenty yards, but to Will it seemed a lifetime. He expected to hear at any moment a yell of warning come from the direction of the village. His heart stopped beating as he crossed the clearing and moved behind the trees. He released his breath as he looked from behind a large cedar. The circle of Indians was still as they were. One of the chiefs was talking now and all eyes in the village were upon him as he spoke.

Will waited, not daring to breathe for fear the sound could be heard. His heart was racing so fast, he feared it would burst from his chest at any moment. He watched the scene taking place before him and tried to imagine what the chief was saying. From where he was, he could see the face of the large brave who had been doing most of the talking earlier. It was plain he was not pleased with the words of the chief. The brave's face was downcast, and when he looked at the speaker, Will could see pain in his eyes.

The chief continued to speak for several minutes, then motioned toward the captive. Two braves stepped beside the woman and drew her to her feet. Will, seeing her up close for the first time, was shocked by the realization that this was no woman, but a girl not much older than himself. He wondered where a girl of her age had learned the kind of language he'd heard earlier.

Suddenly, the tall brave moved to the girl and, pushing the braves away, grabbed her by the arm and pulled her to him, yelling at the chief as he did so. This move seemed to excite the entire village, and they all started talking at the same time. Some seemed to side with the chief, some with the brave holding the girl.

Will was caught up in the scene before him and was unaware of anything else. He had momentarily forgotten about Tye and the horses until abruptly the Indians stopped their heated discussion. As one, they looked up the canyon and Will could hear the thunder of hooves coming toward them.

For an instant, everyone seemed riveted to the ground. Then pandemonium broke out and Indians began running in all directions.

The tall Indian holding the girl shoved her to the ground and ran in the direction of the stampeding horses.

The girl, hands still bound together, was attempting to rise to her feet. Will, realizing this was the only opportunity he was likely to get, sprinted from the trees. He closed the gap between them in a few seconds. The girl's back was to him as he approached her and he yelled at her to run. At first, she looked around, confused by the sound of his voice. Then, as if coming out of a trance, she turned and ran toward him. He grabbed her arm as she came to him. Turning, he led her toward the woods, running for all he was worth.

Will's heart was pounding as he raced toward the trees, dragging the girl behind him. He was close now. Only a few more feet and the trees would hide them. If they managed to get away undetected, it would be hard for her captors to follow.

He was almost to the woods when he heard the sound of running feet behind him. Instinctively, he knew it was one of the Indians. The moccasined feet made little noise as they moved across the ground. Will whirled to meet his pursuer, yelling at the girl as he did, "Run for the woods!"

Will saw it was the tall brave who had been holding the girl. His long knife was in his hand and his eyes blazed with anger and the lust of battle.

Will held the pistol in his hand. He started to bring it to bear on the Indian, but his mind froze his hand. A shot would alert the rest of the tribe and bring them down on him and the girl. He couldn't risk losing the slight edge he had gained. He would have to meet his attacker hand to hand.

Will's mind raced as his opponent continued toward him. He had wrestled a lot with his brothers and the other boys at school. He was a good wrestler and a fair boxer, winning most of the rough-and-tumble fights he'd been a party to. But this was different: This was for his and the girl's lives. Could he win against an opponent who outweighed him by at least forty pounds? This last question came to his mind as the Indian hurled himself through the air, knife drawn back, ready to be plunged into Will's heart.

Will watched as the Indian dove toward him. He seemed to be riveted to the spot, unable to move as the tall brave flew through the air, bent on destroying this white man who had dared come to his village and take his hostage.

Rebecca watched from the trees as Will stood his

ground. She wanted to yell at him to run, but she knew it would be too late. The brave was almost on top of him. She covered her eyes with her bound hands—partly from not wanting to see her rescuer impaled upon the sharp knife, but also from the certain dread of knowing her escape was to be thwarted.

Will stood as the hurtling figure came toward him, his heart pounding in his chest. He could see triumph in the red man's face as he started to bring his arm down for the death thrust. At the last moment, Will ducked and moved sideways, then came back to a standing position as the arm holding the knife missed his head by inches. Will was already swinging his arm, holding the pistol tight. It caught the arm with the knife just below the elbow, and Will heard the bones crack. The Indian let out a howl of pain and dropped the knife as he hit the ground.

Before the Indian could get to his feet, Will was on him, using his pistol as a club. He hit him twice. Either blow was enough to knock the man senseless, but Will wasn't taking any chances.

Rebecca, unable to stand it any longer, removed her hands from her eyes. She expected to see her would-be rescuer lying dead on the ground, her hopes of escape dead with him. Her eyes widened with delight, and her knees went weak with relief when she looked up and saw Will running toward her, the body of the Indian lying on the ground.

"Come on! We got to get outa here before some more of 'em see us," Will said, grabbing her by the arm.

"Is he dead?" Rebecca asked, looking at the prone brave.

"Nope, but he sure is gonna have one heck of a headache when he wakes up, and I want us to be a long way gone by then," Will said.

"I wished you'd killed him," Rebecca said, with such bitterness that Will stopped to look at her. He wondered for a brief second if her captivity had caused her to go insane. Looking in her eyes, he could see the hate and anger there, but otherwise she seemed to be all right.

"Come on, we got to get outa here," Will said, pulling her along after him.

He led her around through the woods and climbed to the ridge where he and Tye had watched the village.

Looking down, he could see the Indians were gathering the loose horses. He could still see the body of the big brave lying where he'd left it. If only he'd thought to drag him into the bushes, it might have given them a little more time before they realized the girl was missing. Well, it was too late now. He and the girl had to reach the horses and make it to the canyon as fast as possible.

Will wondered about Tye. Where was he? Was he all right? He had to believe he was. He couldn't stop now to worry about him.

Taking the girl by the arm again, he started off down the trail, but she pulled back.

"Just a minute. Could you possibly remove this rope from my wrists before we go any further? It's cutting into my flesh and it's hard to run with my hands tied together and you pullin' me along."

Will felt his face burn hot with shame. He should have thought about that, but in his haste to get away from the Indian village, he'd only thought about escape.

"Sure," Will said, fumbling for his pocketknife. "Sorry, I didn't do it sooner. I was in such a hurry to get us outa there, I just didn't think about it."

"That's all right," Rebecca said. "I'm beholdin' to ya for gettin' me away from those savages."

"If you wanna stay free of 'em, we better hurry. They're likely to be coming for us pretty soon," Will said, returning the knife to his pocket and coiling up the ropes he'd cut from the girl's wrists. He stuffed the ropes into his pocket, then grabbed her hand, and started down the slope to the place where the horses were tied.

Will moved cautiously through the woods, stopping

to listen from time to time. The only thing he heard was the noise coming from the Indian village. He led Rebecca to the horses, and was untying his mount when he heard a rustling in the bushes. It was coming from the same direction they'd just come. Taking Rebecca by the hand, he pulled her behind a large oak tree, drawing his pistol as he did.

Rebecca had heard the noise and tensed at the sound. She moved behind Will and held her breath as he looked around the tree. She could almost feel herself shake, and jumped when she heard a whispery voice call, "Will, over here."

Will pulled her from behind the tree and walked back to the horses.

"What took ya so long?" Tye asked, coming out of the brush.

"Had us a little trouble back there," Will said.

"You all right?" Tye asked, looking first to Will, then to Rebecca.

"I'm fine," Will said.

"I'll be fine as soon as we're away from here," Rebecca said, looking back in the direction of the village.

"Let's get goin' then," Tye said. "We still got a long ride ahead of us before the sun comes up."

Will climbed into the saddle, then extended his hand to help Rebecca up. She grabbed his hand, and pulling her dress up above her ankles, she raised her foot to the stirrup and swung up behind him.

Will felt himself blush as his eyes fell on her well-shaped calf. Then he averted his eyes to the ground as he pulled the girl up.

Rebecca caught Will's glance and smiled as she adjusted herself on the back of the horse.

"By the way, what's your name?" Will asked.

"Rebecca, Rebecca Kincaid. What's yours?"

"Will Paxton, and that's my partner, Tye Garrett."

"Pleased to make your acquaintance, gentlemen."

"Enough of these pleasantries," Tye said. "We'll all get acquainted once we're away from these red savages."

"Don't mind him," Will said, as he kicked his horse into a fast trot. "He's old and cantankerous, but he's harmless."

For the first time since she had been abducted, Rebecca giggled. Will liked the sound and grinned as he headed the horse down the trail leading to the box canyon.

Chapter Twelve

It was fifteen miles from the Indian village to the box canyon where the horses were held. Tye made sure they made it in record time, pushing them hard all the way.

The terrain over which they traveled was scattered with large rocks. Ducking and dodging the low limbs, and jumping many of the larger rocks, they raced away from the Indian village and covered the distance in little over an hour.

Tye was shouting instructions as they raced up the valley to the box canyon. "Catch you up a fresh horse and catch one for Rebecca. I'll gather the herd and tie the horses together, while you load up the gear. Hurry! I figure them redskins will be after us at first light."

It took them just over an hour to have the pack-horses loaded and Will and Rebecca mounted on fresh horses.

Rebecca had to ride bareback since there were no spare saddles. She told Will not to worry: She would ride totally nude if that was what it took to get her out of there.

Will blushed again at the thought of that, and hurried to help Tye get the horses ready to move, putting distance between himself and Rebecca before she could see his red face.

Tye was throwing his saddle on a fresh horse when Will rode up the canyon. Will could see that the horses they'd broken and the halter-broke mares were tied together, head to tail.

"You ready to go?" Tye asked, as Will rode up.

"We're ready. The packhorses are loaded. Rebecca's holdin' 'em down by the mouth of the canyon."

"We're gonna let her push the horses out. You're gonna ride back up the valley and turn any of 'em that might try to go that way. I'm gonna stay in front of 'em. I think they'll follow these that I'm leadin'. But if they don't, you'll have to ride ahead of 'em and push 'em away from the canyons till we get to the canyon leadin' to Clement's place."

"There's only two canyons between here and there, and both of 'em are on this side of the valley. I shouldn't have any trouble headin' 'em off," Will said.

"Once we get 'em headed down Clement's canyon, we're gonna pick up the pace. I'll try not to let 'em run full out. If they'll follow these horses, we'll keep to a fast lope. Don't push 'em, but don't let 'em slow down neither."

Will nodded and rode down to the mouth of the canyon to tell Rebecca their plan and instruct her on what to do. He then rode up the valley and waited.

Soon he saw Tye coming out of the canyon, leading the line of horses. Some of the mares started a nervous dance as they realized they were being led out of the canyon that had served as their prison. But with their heads being tied to the horses in front of them and their tails being held by the horses behind them, they were stopped from bolting and forced to follow.

Soon Will heard the other horses moving behind the ones Tye led. As the herd followed the lead horses out, they raised their heads and looked about, recognizing the freedom the valley offered. But as the caravan continued on down the valley, each of them turned and followed.

Will waited until Rebecca came out, then reined his horse beside hers.

"Can you push them from behind?"

"Sure. If I have any problems, I'll call ya."

"Watch your backside. If ya see any sign of Indians, forget the horses and hightail it up to where we are."

"You can count on it," Rebecca said.

Tye was leading the horses at a steady trot. Though most of the horses followed the ones Tye was leading, there were those who stopped to graze along the way. Will and Rebecca were kept busy pushing these back into the herd and keeping them moving.

They moved past the two canyons where the horses could break away. Will had ridden out around the herd to block the openings of the canyons against any horse that might decide to make a break for it. After the last canyon was behind them, he rode up to where Tye was leading the string of horses.

"They seem to be moving along fine," Will said.

"Yep, I figure we been on the trail for about two hours now, and I don't think we've lost any. As soon as we get around this bend in the river up here, I'm gonna open 'em up and see if we can't put some miles behind us. You let Rebecca know. Then ride the perimeter to keep an eye on the herd. If you have any problems, yell and I'll swing them into the wall of the canyon and slow them down."

"How long do think it will take us to reach Clement's trading post?" Will asked.

"About another four hours, if everything goes right."

"You think those Indians will follow us tonight?"

"Normally, Injuns don't like to attack at night. They think the spirits are against 'em in the dark. But after stealin' their hostage, they might just decide to chance it. On the other hand, they might figure their medicine ain't too strong, seein' as how we went into their camp and stole her away from them. Either way, it's best to keep movin' and keep your eyes and ears open. You can never predict what Injuns might do."

"I aim to," Will said. "I don't think I'll feel safe again until we're back in Montana."

"That's still a few weeks away, if everything goes

as planned," Tye said. Then, turning to look back at the herd, he asked, "What are we gonna do with her?"

"Good question," Will responded. "You reckon she's got any family around here?"

"I don't know. Why don't you ask her and see?"

"I reckon I could do that," Will said, a hint of a smile on his face. "What do we do if she ain't got any?"

"Let's cross that river when we get to it. Now get on out there and do your job before we lose what we've worked so hard to get."

"Yes, sir," Will said, grinning as he wheeled his horse and began to circle the herd.

Will circled the horses, checking for any stragglers that might be drifting away. When he rode up to Rebecca, he noticed her head was nodding as if she was dozing. The lead rope for the packhorse was tied to her wrist. He called softly to her. "Rebecca."

She came awake with a start, looking around as if expecting someone. When she saw Will, her face dropped, and Will noticed the look of disappointment and grief that touched her face.

"I'm sorry. I didn't mean to startle you," he said.

"That's all right. I shouldn't have been dozin'. It's just that I ain't had much sleep for the last three days. I guess I was plumb tuckered out."

"I've been meanin' to ask how it is that you come to be a prisoner of the Sioux," Will said, watching her face closely. He saw tears come into her eyes and hurried on. "You don't have to tell me if ya don't want to. It's just that Tye and me was wonderin' if you have any kinfolk around here that we could take ya to."

Rebecca wiped the tears from her eyes, sniffed her running nose, and said, "It's all right. I guess I need to tell someone. Maybe it'll help ease the pain."

She told Will the whole story, leaving out none of the details of her ordeal with the Indians.

"I reckon that Injun was arguin' about me belongin'

to him when ya'll come along and pulled me outa there. He don't know it but it's a good thing you and Tye come along when ya did. Otherwise, I was going to find some way to kill me one Sioux Indian."

Will smiled, believing she would have done just that. "So you figure your mother got away?"

"I'm pretty sure she did. I saw her riding away from the Indians and I don't think any of them were chasing her."

"Where do you reckon she would have gone—back to the farm?"

"I don't know. Mama's not what you'd call a real strong woman. She may have gone on to the fort with the soldiers."

"Well, we'll find her wherever she is," Will said. "You reckon you can stay awake for a spell? We've got to push these horses a might faster."

"I'll stay awake. If I don't, you just pour water on me."

"I'll keep an eye on ya. If ya start noddin' off, I'll holler at ya," Will promised, with a grin.

"Thanks," Rebecca said, smiling at him. "And Will . . ."

"Yeah?" Will replied, looking over at her.

"Thanks for saving me from those Indians. I'm beholdin' to ya. You and Tye risked your lives for me, and I won't be forgettin' that."

"You don't need to thank us," Will said. "We didn't do any more than any God-fearin' man would have done."

"Well, thanks just the same. Like I said, I won't be forgettin' it."

"You hang on to that horse," Will said. "I'll be close by." With that, he reined his horse away and moved out to the edge of the herd and whistled them to a faster pace. He stayed close enough to Rebecca where he could keep an eye on her. Her words of thanks had left him embarrassed and at a loss for words. He wondered at the feelings he was having, and wondered why all of a sudden he felt as if he had a thousand butterflies in his stomach. It must have been from the excitement of the evening, he told himself, but he knew even as he thought it, that that wasn't the reason.

Tye led the horses down the canyon at a ground-eating lope, all the time watching the herd to make sure they were all following. He kept up the pace until he estimated they'd traveled fifteen miles since leaving the box canyon, and then slowed to a walk. He wanted to have the horses calm when he brought them into Clement's.

Two hours later, they rode into the clearing of Clement's trading post.

Tye stopped the horses he was leading and the rest of the herd moved up around them.

"Hello the camp," he shouted.

Slowly the door of the shack opened slightly.

"That you, Garrett?" came Clement's sleepy voice.

"No, it's the whole Sioux nation come to have breakfast with ya. Of course, it's me. Who else ya expectin'?"

"Well, ya never know. Could be expectin' someone important," Clement grumbled as he came down the slope toward the corrals. "How many head ya got there?" Clement asked.

"Somewhere around three hundred," Tye replied.

Clement let a low whistle escape. "I'd say you had a pretty successful hunt."

"If we can just hang on to 'em now, it will have been a successful trip."

"You expectin' trouble?" Clement asked, as he swung open the gate that led into a large trap.

"Could be," Tye replied. "We had a little run-in with the Sioux."

"They huntin' you?"

"Could be. Reckon you can take a little trip and find out for us?"

"Soon's we have some breakfast, I'll head out."

Will and Rebecca herded the horses into the corral after Tye had ridden in, leading his band of halter-broke horses.

Clement studied Rebecca as she pulled up to the corral and dismounted.

"Hey, Garrett, ya picked up a stray along the way. Looks like a right purty stray though. Where'd ya get 'er?" Clement asked, as he swung the gate shut.

"Rebecca, meet Clement Stoner. He's the proprietor of this fine establishment and our host for the next few days. He may be ugly as sin, but he's really harmless, except for the smell. You'll get used to that after about a week." Tye turned to Clement, a twinkle in his eye and a smile on his lips. "Clement, meet Miss Kincaid. She was a guest of the Sioux, but got tired of the accommodations and decided to ride along with us for a spell."

Will was surprised to see Clement's face turn red as he took Rebecca's outstretched hand. What was it about women that made grown men act foolish when they were around?

"Pleased to meet ya, Miss Kincaid," Clement said, removing his hat and bowing slightly as he held Rebecca's hand.

"Please, call me Rebecca, Mr. Stoner, and it's a pleasure meeting you."

"Rebecca, that's a purty name, but please call me Clement."

"Thank you, Clement." Will could see the flush on Rebecca's cheeks as she smiled at Clement. He was surprised by the touch of jealousy that he felt as she continued to smile at Clement.

"Would you like to come up to the house and freshen up while I get us some breakfast rustled up?"

"Thank you, Clement, that would be nice. But I reckon I better help Tye and Will with the horses."

Tye nodded toward the house and said, "You go on and wash up. Will and me will take care of the horses."

Will thought he saw a look of disappointment cross Rebecca's face as she nodded and turned to follow Clement. He watched her as she walked away. Secretly, he wished she stayed to help them. Why? he wondered. Then he put her out of his mind as he turned to help Tye remove the halters from the horses.

Tye had seen Will watch the girl leave and smiled to himself as he saw the look on his face. Will was growing into a man, and it was plain Rebecca was turning his head. Tye just hoped Will would take it slow and easy. But knowing his partner the way he did, he doubted that would be the case. Will didn't seem to take anything slow and easy.

They removed the halters and unsaddled their horses, then led the packhorse up to Clement's shack and removed their supplies and packsaddle.

"I'll take the horse back down to the corral," Tye said. "You go on in and get some breakfast."

Will glanced nervously at the house, then said, "I reckon I better help ya get that horse back down to the corral."

Tye grinned and picked up the lead rope. He started back toward the corral, Will falling in behind him.

Tye led the animal into the corral and removed the halter. As he turned back to the gate, he noticed Will leaning on the fence, his face fixed with a look of worry.

"What's the problem, Will?"

"It's Rebecca," Will said. "Her mother escaped from the Sioux and Rebecca thinks she got back to the soldiers, but she doesn't know where she might be now. You reckon we can swing by their farm on the way back and see if she's there?"

"Sure! And if she ain't there, we'll swing by the fort and see if they know where she might be."

"Thanks, Tye. I know Rebecca will appreciate it."

"Well, I don't know about you, but I could eat a bear right about now. How about we head on up to the house and see if Clement's got some food ready?"

Tye asked and was glad to see a smile come across Will's face.

"Now you're talkin'," Will said. "I been eatin' your sorry cookin' for so long, I think I almost forgot what real cookin' tastes like."

"Yeah, I noticed you havin' trouble eatin' the meals I fixed," Tye replied.

"I only pretended to like your cookin' so's I wouldn't hurt your feelin's. I know how cranky ya get," Will said with a laugh.

The smell of food cooking hit both of them as they opened the door of the shack.

Clement was busy frying elk steaks, while Rebecca was flipping pancakes on the griddle.

"Y'all come on in and wash up," Clement said. "Breakfast is about ready. 'Course you two probably ain't hungry for any real food after eatin' each other's cookin' for so long."

Will and Tye grinned at each other as they headed back to the cave to wash up.

After everyone was seated around the table, plates piled high with pancakes and elk steaks, Clement asked, "What are your plans now?"

"Once we know how the Sioux situation is, then we'll know more about our plans," Tye said. "I reckon Rebecca would like to find her ma, and then we've got to get these horses up to Montana before the snow hits. I'd like to rest up here for a few days before moving out. You reckon you can put up with us for a spell?"

"I reckon I can manage to put up with ya fer a few days, as long as you don't get no ideas about makin' it permanent," Clement said as he stuck his fork into another flapjack.

"Don't worry," Tye said. "We'll be outa here just as soon as we know it's safe."

"As soon as I finish eating, I'll head back up the valley and see what I can find out," Clement said as he put half a pancake in his mouth. "If you two ain't got them Injuns too stirred up, I may be able to calm things down a might. I done some tradin' with Two Wolves. He's the head chief at the village. Me and him hit it off pretty good. I reckon I can make up some story about the girl here bein' bad medicine, and it would be better for him to leave her alone."

"That would be some trick," Tye said. "I'd dance at your wedding if you could pull that off."

"And I'd almost get married just to see ya do it, too." Clement laughed.

After all had eaten and the dishes were cleared from the table, Clement took up his Sharps rifle and his shoulder pack and walked outside. It was still dark, but the eastern sky was starting to pale a little. Tye walked alongside Clement as he started down the trail leading into the valley.

"You be careful. There's no tellin' what kind of mood those Indians will be in when ya find 'em," Tye said.

"Don't you be a-worryin' about me. I ain't lived this long without knowin' how to take care of myself." With that, he raised his hand in a farewell salute and started down the trail.

Tye watched him go until he disappeared into the woods. Then, with a sigh, he turned and went back to the cabin.

Will was washing the dishes as Tye entered and Rebecca was nowhere to be seen.

"She sleepin'?" Tye asked.

Will nodded.

"Why don't you get some shut-eye, too? I'll keep watch for a while, then wake you." Tye reached for his rifle and headed out the door.

"If you see anything, you better run up here and holler at me. I don't know if I can hear anything through these walls," Will said as Tye went out the door.

Tye woke Will later that day. The sun was already starting its western descent when Will walked outside.

Clement hadn't returned, and though they weren't

expecting him back for several more hours, both Tye and Will looked often toward the trail heading up the valley.

"I sure hope he's all right," Will said.

"He is," Tye replied. "He's a tough old coot, and he knows what he's doing. He'll be all right. I'm gonna get a couple hours sleep. Wake me when he comes back."

"Sure thing," Will said.

The sun was setting when Will heard noises coming from the trail. At first he thought it was a wild animal making the sound. But as it grew louder, he could make out the words to a song. Even though it was sung off-key, he couldn't mistake the voice behind it.

Will let out a whoop and hurried along the trail. "Clement, would you quit that caterwauling before you scare the horses plumb to death?" Will said. The grin on his face showed the relief he felt at seeing the mountain man safe.

"Caterwauling?" Clement asked indignantly. "You just don't know how to appreciate fine music, boy."

"If that's fine music, then you're right, I don't know how to appreciate it," Will said. "Did you meet with the Sioux?"

"That's what I went up there for, isn't it?"

"Well, how did it go?" Will asked impatiently.

Clement eyeballed Will for a few seconds, not saying a word. Then, with a shake of his head, he said, "You're really turning into something, aren't ya?"

"What do ya mean?" Will asked, confused by the old man's statement.

"Let's get up to the house. I don't want to have to tell this more'n once. Are the other two awake?"

"They're both asleep, but Tye said to wake him the moment you came in."

"I guarantee ya, he'll want to be awake for this," Clement said, chuckling to himself.

Clement opened the door to the cabin and walked in, yelling a loud rebel yell as he did.

Tye came bursting into the room, throwing back the blanket covering the opening to the cave. He had his pistol in his hand and he still wore his boots, ready for trouble should it come.

Rebecca was close behind and stood there blinking as the light in the room fell on her sleep-filled eyes.

"I declare, I think you'd sleep your life away if I give ya the chance," Clement said, grinning at Tye as he holstered the pistol.

"A man ought to be shot for yellin' like that. After what we been through the last couple of days, my nerves are almost shot. Then you come in here yellin' like a wild Indian. It's a wonder I didn't shoot ya first and ask questions later."

"Well, if you'd done that, you sure would've missed one of the best tales ever."

"What tale is that?" Tye asked.

"The one about the evil spirits that visited the Sioux camp last night."

"What's that?" Tye asked, a perplexed look on his face.

Clement chuckled. "Yep, it seems an evil spirit paid a visit to the Sioux camp last night and played havoc with a young brave there."

"Clement, you're not makin' a bit of sense. Would you get on with the story?" Tye said in exasperation.

"I've traveled all day long to find out what's goin' on with them Injuns. I put myself in danger goin' into their camp. Now I'm goin' to tell this story my way. So, if you want to hear it, you just hush your yap, or I'll hush my mouth and you won't hear any more."

Tye grinned at Clement's outburst, but knew better than to say any more.

"Now, if everyone will just hush up," Clement said, casting a warning glance at Tye, who then held up his hands in surrender, "I'll go on with the story."

Looking around at Will and Rebecca to make sure

they weren't going to say anything, Clement proceeded with his story.

"I had no trouble gettin' into the village, which was surpisin', considerin' the coup you two pulled off. I asked to see Two Wolves and was led to his teepee. The old chief come out and we talked for a spell about the old times and how things used to be before so many people started movin' in. Then he started talkin' about evil spirits comin' into his village and stealin' away a hostage they'd taken. I could tell by the way he talked that he didn't really believe it was evil spirits, but his son Two Eagles had been attacked by the demon and had suffered a broken arm and a couple of knots on his head. He said it must have been an evil spirit—else how could such a thing have happened to a brave warrior like Two Eagles? The old chief kinda smiled when he talked of this, but explained that they was goin' to be spendin' the next few days wardin' off evil spirits lest they be plagued by the durn things for the rest of the summer. Things like that could mess up the huntin' for the whole village and, with winter comin' on, they couldn't afford that."

Tye was looking at Will as Clement finished up his story.

"Was that the little trouble you had back there in that Indian village?"

"I didn't know who he was," Will replied with a smile. "There was this rather large Injun who didn't take kindly to me takin' his hostage. He had some idea about splittin' my gullet with a knife. I just convinced him it wasn't such a good idea."

"He laid him out cold," Rebecca interjected. "I thought that buck was going to cut him to pieces, but Will stood there cool as you please, then knocked him out with the barrel of his pistol."

Tye shook his head and smiled. "I knew you were a scrapper, boy, but I didn't know you were an Injun fighter."

"I hope that's the last one I have to fight," Will said, still blushing from all the attention he was getting.

"I don't know," Clement said, smiling, "anyone who can get the reputation of bein' an evil spirit after just one fight, might have quite a future as an Injun fighter."

Tye, Will, and Rebecca stayed with Clement for four days, resting and restocking their supplies. On the fifth day, they rode away from Clement's trading post, leading the halter-broke mares and horses. The rest, by now used to following, fell in behind, grazing along as they went.

Clement puttered around all morning, talking about how nice it was going to be to have some peace and quiet again. But when it came time to say good-bye, there were tears in his eyes as Rebecca hugged the big mountain man and thanked him for his hospitality.

"You take care of these two no-goods, ya hear? I don't want to have to come get 'em outa trouble."

"I will," Rebecca said, with a laugh. "You take care now, you hear?"

Will and Tye shook hands with the old man and thanked him for his help, promising to stop by and see him again if they were ever around that way.

As Will fell in behind the horses, he turned and looked back to see Clement standing in the doorway of his cabin. He knew he probably would never see the old mountain man again and it saddened him to know another chapter of his life was ending. But what lay over the horizon promised to be even more exciting. With that thought, he flipped the end of his rope against the rump of one of the horses and they moved up the river, heading back to Montana.

Chapter Thirteen

Three days after leaving Clement's trading post, they pulled up to the farm that had been Rebecca's home place.

As they rode into the yard, Rebecca's eyes clouded with tears as she remembered the events of that fateful day.

Will and Tye, seeing the tears, busied themselves with the horses. They knew there was nothing they could do to ease the pain she felt. It was something she would have to deal with on her own.

They turned the horses into a trap by the barn, then unsaddled and rubbed down their saddle horses. They didn't hurry to finish, neither relishing the thought of going to the house. But finally, with nothing left to do, they crossed the dusty yard and entered the front door.

Rebecca was busy preparing the evening meal. Her eyes were dry, but both Will and Tye could see the redness from tears shed for those she'd lost.

"I'll have supper ready in a little while," Rebecca said. "Why don't you two wash up? There's a well and pump out back."

"Sounds good to me," Will said, with an enthusiasm that sounded hollow.

"Yeah, I could use a good washing," Tye said as they headed out the door, both thankful for the excuse to escape.

They walked to the back of the house, locating the pump in the yard.

Will grabbed the handle and started pumping as Tye leaned down, catching the water in his hands as it poured from the pipe.

Will was in midstroke on the pump handle when he suddenly stopped.

"What the blazes . . . ?" Tye stammered, his cupped hands empty.

"Over there." Will nodded, motioning toward a large oak tree fifty yards from the back of the house.

Tye looked in the direction Will was indicating. When his eyes found the object of Will's stare, he stood upright, immediately grasping the impact of what he was seeing.

"Fresh graves," Tye stated. "I reckon that's where Rebecca's kin are buried. Soldiers from the fort probably came back and buried them."

"Tye, there's four graves there. Rebecca told us her father, brother, and uncle were killed. Who does the fourth grave belong to?"

"I don't know," Tye said soberly. "And I hate to speculate."

"We got to tell Rebecca."

"I know, but I sure hate to be the one to tell her. She's already pretty upset just bein' here. Did you see the look on her face when we rode up and her mama wasn't here?"

"Yeah, I saw it. It durn near brought me to tears."

Will looked at the fresh grave sites again. Then, turning to Tye, he said, "I'll tell Rebecca."

"All right," was all Tye could say as he stared out across the open prairie.

Will walked back to the house, dreading the task at hand.

Rebecca was mixing dough for biscuits when Will walked in the front door.

"Supper will be ready shortly," she said.

Will stood in the doorway, uncertainty flooding through him as he watched Rebecca knead the dough. He saw her back go straight and her hands stop their motion. Slowly, she turned to face him. She could see the anguish on his face.

"What is it, Will?" she asked. Her voice was calm.

"I think you better come outside with me," Will said, feeling sick to his stomach as he watched her face go white with fear.

"Why? What is it?" Rebecca asked, panic rising in her voice.

Will walked over and gently placed his hand on her arm. Then slowly he led her out of the kitchen. He could feel her trembling as they descended the steps and walked to the backyard.

Tye was standing by the pump as Will and Rebecca came around the house.

"I'll finish fixin' supper," he said.

Will nodded, but Rebecca turned to him and, with a weak smile, said, "Thank you, Tye. The biscuits are about ready to go in the oven."

Tye nodded, his face clouded with concern. Then he turned away, and walked to the house.

Will reached for Rebecca's hand and gently led her toward the big oak tree. He felt her stumble as she saw the fresh mounds of earth. He took her elbow and supported her as they walked the last few feet to the graves.

Tears were streaming down Rebecca's face. Will looked straight ahead, not daring to look at her for fear of losing control of his own emotions. Pictures of his own mother and father came to mind as he felt Rebecca's grief.

There were no markers on the graves, only hastily made crosses constructed of old lumber, at the head of each one.

Rebecca's body shook as racking sobs escaped from her. Will held tightly to her hand, trying to will his strength into her. She turned from the sight before her and buried her head into Will's shoulder. He encircled her with his arms and held her while she poured out the grief she was feeling.

Rebecca pulled away from Will. Her tear-filled eyes looked up into his. "There's four graves there, Will."

Will remained silent. There was nothing he could say.

"Will, who's in the other grave?"

The pleading in Rebecca's voice was clear to Will. Was it her mother? If so, how did she die? If it wasn't her mother, who was it?

"I don't know, Rebecca," Will replied softly.

Rebecca looked once more at the graves, then whispered softly, "Rest in peace. I love you." Then she turned and placed her hand in Will's. Together, they walked slowly to the house.

Tye had supper on the table when they entered. Rebecca looked at the food on the table, then said quietly, "I'm tired. I think I'll lie down for a while."

Will and Tye watched her go, neither saying anything. No words could ease the pain she was feeling.

Will and Tye tried to eat, but the food had little taste. Both men sat in silence, each lost in their own troubled thoughts. Finally, Tye broke the silence. "I'm gonna ride over to the fort tomorrow and see how the Indian situation is. I might even be able to sell 'em some horses while I'm there."

Will looked at Tye, but didn't say anything. He knew why Tye was really going to the fort. It was a planned stop of theirs when they left here, but now there was another purpose for his going. He wanted to find out who was in the fourth grave and what had happened.

"Would you mail a letter for me while you're there?" Will asked quietly.

"Sure!" Tye said, not needing to ask whom the letter was going to. He knew Will was thinking of his parents. He'd been thinking of his own folks, who were long dead and buried in Texas.

Tye rode out early the next morning. Will saw him off, handing him the letter to be mailed.

Rebecca was still in her room, sleeping, Will hoped. Rest and time were the only cures for the loss she had experienced.

He spent the day working some of the colts in the corral. He'd ridden two of the new ones, allowing the feel of a bucking horse under him to take his mind off the gloom he felt.

He was just finishing the second one when he looked up and saw Rebecca standing by the gate, watching him. He reined the horse over to where she stood and stepped down. "How long you been there?" he asked, smiling.

He was relieved to see her return the smile.

"I was watchin' you from the house when you got on him. I wanted to get a closer look. You make it look so easy."

Will blushed at the compliment. "Have you had any breakfast?" he asked, changing the subject.

"I fried me up a couple of eggs and some bacon," Rebecca replied.

Will stood there, not knowing what else to say. It seemed to him it was getting harder and harder to talk to this girl. He'd never had any trouble with the girls back home. In fact, it seemed they enjoyed talking to him. Now he always seemed to be stumped for what to say next.

Rebecca smiled as she noticed Will's discomfort. "Would you like me to show you around the place?" she asked.

"Sure," Will replied. "If you feel up to it."

"I think I feel up to it." Rebecca smiled again.

Will caught and saddled their horses, while Rebecca went back in the house to fix a lunch to carry with them.

They rode out of the yard, Will letting Rebecca choose the direction. She rode east, showing him the hay meadows her father had cleared. When she talked about the things her father and uncle had planned and done, Will noticed there was no sadness in her voice, only pride at what had been accomplished.

They stopped by a stream to eat the lunch Rebecca had brought. As she talked about the land and the plans her father had, Will found it easier and easier to talk. They talked about cattle and horses, and Will told her how he'd come to be in Wyoming capturing wild horses. Rebecca laughed out loud when Will told her about Tye throwing his hat under his horse. He watched her as her laughter subsided, then the words came out of his mouth before he knew it.

"I don't think I've ever seen anything as pretty as when you laugh like that."

Rebecca looked him in the eye, her face unreadable. For a second, he thought maybe he'd said something wrong and silently cursed himself for the fool he was.

"I don't think anyone has ever said anything nicer to me in my life. Thank you, Will Paxton."

Will blushed again and Rebecca laughed.

"Will Paxton, you're goin' to have to stop blushin' all the time or the blood's going to stay in your head and make you pass out."

They rode back to the farmhouse, riding slowly and talking. Will couldn't remember when he had enjoyed an afternoon as much as he had this one.

As they came into view of the house, Will saw Rebecca stiffen. Looking up, he saw Tye's horse standing in the corral. He reached over and touched Rebecca's arm. She looked at him and he saw the corners of her mouth try to smile, but the attempt failed miserably.

They rode up to the corral in silence. Will unsaddled the horses while Rebecca waited. Then they walked up to the house together.

As soon as they entered the front door, Will knew the news that Tye brought was not good. He was sitting at the kitchen table, his hat hung on the back of one of the chairs, his face solemn.

Rebecca held her head up as Tye looked into her face. Then, in a low voice, he told her the story.

"The soldiers are the ones that buried your family. They straightened up the house, too. They regretted the fact that they couldn't free you from the Sioux,

but there was only six of 'em and they couldn't risk
following them into the woods."

Rebecca stood there, holding her breath, knowing
there was more to come and dreading to hear it. Tye
took a deep breath, looked down at his hands and, in
a strained voice, said, "As God is my witness, I wish
I weren't the one to have to tell ya this, but that fourth
grave belongs to your mama. She was shot by one of
the Indians while escaping. She lived for a spell, but
without any doctor or medicine, they couldn't save
her. Her last words were, 'Tell Rebecca I love her.' "
Tye's voice broke as he said, "I'm truly sorry,
Rebecca."

There were tears in Rebecca's eyes, but she held
her head high. "Thank you, Tye. I guess I already
knew Mama was in that grave. I guess I was hopin' I
was wrong. I cried my tears for her last night. I'll be
all right. I need a few minutes by myself. Then I'll see
about fixin' us some supper."

She turned and went outside. Will and Tye knew
she was going out to the big oak tree in the back. She
was going to say farewell to her mother.

Will sat down at the table across from Tye. "Got
to be hard on her, losin' all her kinfolk like that."

Tye looked out the window toward the barn. His
eyes held a look that said he was seeing something
far away. "It's one of the hardest things there is, but
that girl's got grit. It may take some time, but she'll
be all right."

"What do you reckon she's gonna do now?" Will
asked.

"I don't know," Tye responded. "I guess we'll have
to ask her. She can't stay here. There's no cattle or
horses and I doubt she's got any money."

"You reckon she could go with us?" Will asked
hesitantly.

Tye turned to look at him questioningly, and Will
continued. "It would be nice to have someone to cook
for us, and she can ride real good. She'd be a help
with the horses and we could even pay her a little."

"I don't think the trail we'll be travelin' is a good place to be takin' a girl. Besides that, what makes you think she'd want to go with us?" Tye asked.

"Well, I don't know for sure, but I figured we could ask her. I don't see where she's had any better offers."

Tye looked thoughtful for a minute, then said, "What if she doesn't want to go with us? What do we do then?"

"I guess we mount that bronc when we get to it," Will said, with a shrug of his shoulders. "Look, Tye, she's not a fragile girl. She's been raised here where life is tough. They've scratched a living out of this place and worked hard to do it. I think she'd do all right traveling with us."

"You really like her, don't you?" Tye asked.

Will looked at him, thinking he was making fun of him, but Tye's face was serious.

"Yeah, I really like her. She's got a toughness about her that makes me believe she can do anything, but she's also soft enough to be a female. Does that make any sense?"

"More than you know," Tye said. "More than you know."

Will raised an eyebrow at Tye, but he read nothing in his expression.

"Why don't you ask her if she wants to come with us?" Tye said.

"Don't you think it would be better if we both asked her?" Will asked.

Tye grinned at him and said, "No, I don't think it would. I think she'd rather have you ask her."

Will smiled shyly. "You really think so?"

"Yeah, I think so. Go on and ask her."

Will hesitantly stood up. He pushed the chair back under the table, then stood there, leaning with both hands on the back of it. He started to turn away, then turned back to look at Tye.

Tye nodded as if to say, "Go ahead," but didn't say a word.

Finally, Will turned and walked out the front door.

He stood on the porch, surveying the grounds in front
of the house. Rebecca wasn't in sight and he knew
she was still around back, saying her good-byes to
her mother.

Rebecca wiped the tears from her eyes as she stood
over the graves. She had promised herself she
wouldn't cry anymore. She just wanted to say good-
bye to her family. She didn't know what she was going
to do now, but she knew she couldn't stay here. She
would ask Will and Tye to take her with them until
they got to a town where she could find a job. She
didn't know what kind of job, but she was sure she
could find something. She was going to miss Will and
Tye. They had come to mean so much to her in the
few short days she had been with them.

Another tear ran down her cheek as she thought
about how her life had changed so fast. Only a few
short days ago, she had been happy living here with
her family. Now her family was gone and her future
was uncertain. She dried her eyes and wiped the tears
off her cheeks with the back of her hand. Feeling sorry
for herself wouldn't get her anywhere. She would
make it. She knew she would.

Turning away from the graves, she started back
toward the house. It was time to get supper started
for Will and Tye.

Rounding the corner of the house, she saw Will
sitting on the top step of the porch. She wiped her
eyes dry one more time to make sure all the tears
were gone. With a cheery note in her voice, she asked,
"You gettin' hungry?"

"I'm always hungry," Will responded, smiling at
her resolve.

"I'll get us some supper started," she said, starting
up the steps.

"Rebecca, I need to talk to you," Will said. He had
been sitting there, wondering how to approach her
with his idea. But now that she was standing here,

he'd become tongue-tied all of a sudden. "Uh, what do you plan on doin'? I mean, uh, what are your plans now that . . . What I mean is, how are you gonna make it alone?"

Watching her as he fumbled with the words, he saw her lips turn up as she fought to keep from smiling. As he finished, she turned and looked out over the land that had been her home place for the last six years. She turned back to him and, with a sigh, said, "I don't know. I've been thinking about that very thing. I can't stay here. There's nothing left for me here. I was hoping you and Tye would give me a ride to Cody or Cheyenne, if you're headed that way. I'm sure I could find me a job somewhere."

Will came excitedly to his feet. "That's what I wanted to talk to you about," he said. "Tye and I talked it over and we want you to go with us. We'll pay ya to cook for us and help us out. It won't be easy. We'll be travelin' some rough trails, but I figure you won't have any trouble. So, what do ya say, wanna go with us?" He rushed it so fast it took Rebecca totally by surprise.

She stood still for a second, then flung her arms around Will's neck, squeezing him tightly, tears of joy running down her cheeks as she laughed. "Of course, I want to go with you," she said, hugging him even tighter.

Will stood there, his arms going around her. Then he stepped back and, looking serious, he said, "It might not look too good for a single woman to be travelin' with two men, you know."

Rebecca was tickled at the look on his face. Then, fighting to keep a straight face, she asked, "Well, what are we gonna do about it?"

"Uh . . . well, I don't know," Will stammered

"You could always marry me. That would solve the problem, wouldn't it?" Rebecca asked

Will looked at her, expecting to see her smiling at him in her mischievous way, but she wasn't smiling and that threw him. He was surprised at how the idea appealed to him. He hadn't thought about it before now. He knew he liked Rebecca, but marriage? That hadn't crossed his mind, but why not? She was pretty, smart, and he cared for her. "All right!" Will said matter-of-factly. "I'll marry ya."

Rebecca was taken aback. The shocked expression on her face surprised Will.

"I was only kidding," Rebecca said, laughing at his response. "Will, I wouldn't expect you to marry me just because of what people might think."

He stood there studying her for a moment, feeling foolish for saying it the way he did. "I wouldn't marry ya just for that reason neither," Will said, looking at his boots.

Rebecca caught the meaning of his words. Her heart beat fast as she stood there, looking at the young man in front of her. As she saw the pained look on his face, her heart went out to him. "Will, are you saying you want to marry me?" she asked.

Will looked into her eyes and she barely heard him as he said, "Yes, Rebecca, I do."

"Will, this is a serious matter, not to be taken lightly. We've only known each other a couple of days. How can you be sure you want to marry me?" Rebecca asked, feeling the heat rise to her face.

"I'm sure," Will said. "Now that I think back on it, I reckon I knew that first night we rode out of the valley. If you don't want to marry me, I'll understand. I don't want ya feelin' you're obligated or anything."

Rebecca smiled at his words, then she said, "Will, I reckon I could look for the rest of my life and not find a better person. If you want me to be your wife, it would be my honor, but only if we wait until October. That's when my parents got married and I want to get married on their wedding date."

Will looked at Rebecca, shocked by the answer she had given. When he finally found his voice, he replied weakly, "Sure, that's fine, Rebecca."

"And one more thing," Rebecca said, a smile on

her lips. "Now that we're properly engaged, would you please call me Becky?"

Will grinned and nodded. "It would be my pleasure. Becky Paxton—it has a nice sound to it."

"Yes, it does," Rebecca agreed. Then she surprised both herself and Will by standing on her toes and kissing him.

Will was so shocked, it was a second before he could react, and by that time she was pulling away. But he put his arms around her and drew her back to him, hugging her tightly. He moved away from her slightly and looked into her eyes. Still holding her in his arms, he bent and kissed her, his lips seeking hers. This time, the kiss was more passionate and both of them felt their hearts pounding as they melted into each other's embrace.

They were lost in each other, forgetting the world about them when they both heard, "Humph." They broke apart instantly, Becky almost falling as she stepped off the front step. Only Will's holding her arm prevented her from falling down the steps.

Tye was standing in the doorway, watching the two of them, a large grin spread over his face. "Have you talked her into comin' with us, or are you just now workin' up to that point?" Tye asked, as Will and Becky stood there, both red faced. " 'Cause if you're just now workin' up to it, I'm gonna go ahead and start supper. I'm gettin' hungry and it looks like you two may be out here a spell," Tye added, watching both of them turn redder and redder.

"I don't see how you two can talk though, bein' that close together. Must be some sort of Indian sign language, I reckon."

Will looked up, grinning at Tye like a little boy who got caught with his hand in the cookie jar. "She's goin' with us," he said. "We was just puttin' the finishin' touches on the deal."

Becky laughed and said, "Will and I are engaged to be married."

Tye looked from one to the other, surprise showing

on his face. Then he smiled and said to Will, "Boy, you are full of surprises. Still wet behind the ears and here you've gone and caught yourself the prettiest filly this side of the Mississippi. Allow me to be the first to kiss the bride."

Will stepped in between Becky and Tye. "Oh, no, you don't. You can kiss her at the weddin'. I ain't takin' no chances on you bein' a better kisser than I am until I got her hog-tied and married."

Becky laughed and pushed Will out of the way. Placing her arms around Tye's neck, she hugged him and kissed him lightly on the lips. Then she stepped back and looped her arm through Will's. "I may marry ya, Will Paxton, but you'll never hog-tie me."

"I reckon I won't," Will said, smiling. "I don't reckon I'd really want to."

Chapter Fourteen

Tye, Will, and Becky rode out before sunrise the following morning.

Rebecca looked back once before the house was out of sight. She felt the pain of the loss she had experienced, and the pain of leaving all that was familiar to her behind. Then Will was beside her, reaching for her hand in the darkness. She held his hand and looked ahead, head held high and a smile on her lips.

They drove the horse herd to Fort Bridger. Tye had made a deal with the commander of the fort to buy fifty head of horses for forty dollars a head. It seemed the cavalry was short on horses, losing some of their own to the Sioux raiding parties and needing replacements.

Tye had not sold any of the horses he and Will had broken. The commander believed if his men broke their own horses, they'd be a little more careful to hang on to them.

When they came into sight of the fort, Tye rode on ahead, leaving Will and Rebecca to hold the horses. He came back shortly, followed by six mounted soldiers. As they drew up, Tye introduced the man beside him as Captain Harper.

The captain touched his hat when introduced to Rebecca.

"Sorry about your folks, Miss Kincaid. I wish there was more we could have done."

"Thank you, Captain. I appreciate what you did."

The captain looked embarrassed, then turned to Tye and said, "Let's take a look at these horses."

The soldiers went to work, riding among the herd, selecting horses, and cutting them out. They cut the herd until they had sixty or seventy head separated from the rest. Then they began selecting the ones they wanted. The captain looked on, talking to Tye about each of the horses, discussing their strong points and pointing out the weak ones. It was clear to Will that the captain knew horses.

It was late in the day when the soldiers drove the fifty head back to the fort.

"You are welcome to spend the night at the fort," Captain Harper said as he paid Tye for the horses.

"Thanks," Tye said as he put the money in his saddlebag. "But we've got a long ways to go and I think it best if we get started."

They all shook hands and Captain Harper tipped his hat to Rebecca.

"You should have a safe journey to Montana. I haven't heard of any problems with Indians along the route you will be taking."

"Thank you, Captain," Tye said.

They circled the herd and Tye led out with his string, the rest falling in behind.

The next two weeks were hard work, keeping the horses bunched and moving. Will rode the sides to keep the horses from straying. He had to change horses three times a day, as the grueling work quickly tired the horses he was riding. Becky tried to help as much as possible, but leading the packhorse prevented her from being much help. Since Tye knew the trails they were to follow, he had to remain in the lead.

By the time they reached Montana, Will was worn to a frazzle. Between riding hard all day and keeping watch at night, he was done in. Rebecca worried about him, but knew there was nothing more she could do to help.

"We'll be at a resting place tomorrow," Tye said as they ate the supper Becky had cooked for them.

Will was leaning against his saddle, almost too tired to eat. "Where's that?" he asked.

"You remember me tellin' you about some mares I had?"

"Yeah, if I remember right, you said you had some folks lookin' after 'em for you."

"That's right," Tye said. "We'll be at their place tomorrow. That's where we'll keep the horses. We'll ride out to the ranches from there. That way we can find out what they want, then deliver only the horses they need. We won't have to drive the whole herd with us."

"Sounds good to me," Will said. "Wake me when we get there."

The next afternoon, they drove the horse herd into the headquarters of the Flying W ranch.

Jim Landsing was in the corral, doctoring some calves when the caravan came into sight. He shaded his eyes as he watched Tye lead his string down the road. He walked over to the gate leading to the horse trap and opened it. Then he stood back and waited as they herded the horses into the trap.

Jim Landsing was in his early thirties, but the hard lines around his eyes and the weathered skin made him look much older. He had started the Flying W ten years earlier, and had fought Indians, drought, and hard winters to make a go of it. Now he had a nice spread and was starting to see some of his hard work pay off.

"Hello, Tye," he said as Tye stepped down from his horse to shake hands. "Looks like you got yourself some fine horses. Who'd ya steal 'em from?"

"I guess you could say we stole 'em from the Sioux," Tye said as he turned to Will and Rebecca. "Jim, I'd like you to meet my partner, Will Paxton, and this young lady is Rebecca Kincaid, soon to be Mrs. Will Paxton."

Jim shook hands with Will, noting the redness of his face at the introduction.

Rebecca dismounted from her horse and walked over to him. "I'm pleased to meet you, Mr. Landsing."

"Jim will do fine. My father was Mr. Landsing."

Rebecca smiled, liking Jim immediately.

"Where's Judith?" Tye asked.

"I reckon she's up to the house, startin' supper. That woman loves to cook more than anyone I ever met. She'll be tickled to death knowin' ya'll are here. It'll give her an excuse to show off her cookin'. Hope you brought an appetite with you."

"Cullen around?" Tye asked, looking about as if hoping to see someone.

Cullen was Jim and Judith's thirteen-year-old son. Tye was his idol. The boy worshipped the ground he walked on. Tye looked on Cullen as a younger brother and enjoyed the youngster's company.

"He's over on the west range, checking on the cattle we have over there. He's sure gonna be happy to see you. Let's get your horses cared for, and then we'll go up to the house so ya'll can clean up."

Judith Landsing was a short, plump woman with exuberant energy. She hugged Tye as he came in the door, then hugged both Will and Rebecca as her husband introduced them.

"Tye Garrett, I swear you're as thin as a rail. You haven't been eating right, have you?" Then she looked at Will, shaking her head and clucking her tongue. "There's only one side to you, ain't there? You ain't got enough meat on your bones to throw a shadow." She turned to Rebecca, taking her affectionately by the arm and ushering her into the house.

"You come with me, dear. I've got water heating and we'll soon have you a nice hot bath. You look like you could use one." Then, turning to the men, she said, "Ya'll go on out to the pump and clean up. I'll have supper ready in a little while."

Rebecca turned and looked questioningly at Will. He smiled and shrugged as if to say he was no longer in control. Rebecca smiled and let herself be led into the house. Soon, she was soaking in the large bathtub, filled with hot water and perfumed soap. She regretted that she didn't have a clean dress to put on. It seemed a shame to put on her dirty dress after taking such a luxurious bath. She felt guilty soaking in the tub while Will and Tye washed up outside, but she wasn't about to argue with Judith Landsing. It wouldn't do any good anyway she thought, and smiled to herself as she slid farther down in the tub.

She soaked for the better part of an hour, then got out and toweled herself dry. She didn't see her dress anywhere in the room and was wondering what she was going to do when someone knocked on the door.

It was Rosa who was married to Ramon, who worked as a cowhand for the Landsings. She helped Judith Landsing around the house, doing the laundry and the cleaning, but Judith Landsing did all the cooking. Rosa had told Rebecca all this when she'd brought the hot water for her bath.

Rebecca opened the door and there stood Rosa, holding a beautiful dress adorned with pink roses. There was a petticoat and undergarments, as well.

Rebecca stood there, looking at the assortment of clothes, feeling embarrassed for not having any of her own.

"The *señora* wants you to have these," Rosa said. "She says these were perfect for you. I think she right. They belonged to her sister." She pronounced it "seester," in her heavy Spanish accent.

"Her sister?" Rebecca asked, looking questioningly at Rosa.

"*Sí!* Her sister. She die four years ago. She used to live with the *señor* and *señora*. She got the fever and died. Poor Mrs. Landsing, she was very sad for long time."

"But I can't wear her dress. Won't it make her sad to see someone else wearing it?"

"No, not anymore," Rosa said. "You put on the dress. It make the *señora* very happy."

Rebecca quickly dressed, then looked at herself in the mirror. She was surprised by the reflection looking back at her. The dress was made of light material, and it swirled around her as she moved. The neckline dipped down in front, revealing just enough to be decent. Rebecca was surprised at how well the dress fit her and how well she filled it out. She was curious to see what Will's reaction would be, then blushed as she realized how important it was to her to have his acceptance. Rosa helped her brush her hair, then pulled it back into a loose fall behind her, fastening it with an oyster-shell hair clamp.

Will was sitting in the large living room, listening to Jim and Tye talk about cattle and horses when Rebecca walked in. It took him a moment to realize that it was Becky standing there, and when it did dawn on him, he jumped to his feet, his eyes opening wide.

"Well, what do you think?" Rebecca asked, turning around to give a full view.

Will stood there, wide-eyed, his mouth hanging open.

Jim and Tye were on their feet staring at her, too. Neither could believe the change that had transpired.

"You're beautiful," came the throaty whisper from Will.

Rebecca's face reddened as she heard Will's comment and noticed the way he looked at her.

Tye grinned as he watched the scene before him. Then, finding his voice, he said, "I was wondering what was under all that dirt. It's nice to know there's a pretty young lady hiding under there. But how on earth are you gonna wrangle horses in that dress?"

Rebecca laughed and was about to respond in kind, when Judith Landsing came bustling into the room. She put both hands to her cheeks, pressing them together, which made her lips pucker and made her look like she had just eaten a sour lemon. "Oh, my goodness," she exclaimed. "You look like an angel." Grabbing Rebecca by the arm, she hustled her out of the room, saying, "Let's leave the men to their talk. I've got some ribbon that would make a beautiful bow for your waist, and since you're so thin, you need something. You poor dear, we have to get some meat on your bones."

Rebecca cast a glance at Will as she was being led from the room. He was still standing in the same spot, staring at her as she left.

"Boy, if you know what's good for you, you'll saddle you and that young lady a horse and hightail it outa here as fast as you can. You stay around here for very long and the missus will have that girl turned into a proper lady and you won't stand a chance. That, or she'll have her weighting two hundred pounds and nagging you about bein' skinny."

Will hardly heard Jim Landsing's caution as he continued to look down the hall where Rebecca had been led. Right now, he was wishing he could be alone with her, just to look at her and tell her how beautiful she was. The sound of laughter coming from Tye and Jim made him turn. Then he blushed again as he realized they were laughing at him.

He joined them as they went outside to look at the horses Jim had, but his thoughts remained in the house, and he kept glancing that way as Tye and Jim talked about each of the horses.

They finished examining the horses and were walking through the barn when they heard the ringing of a bell.

"That'll be the missus calling us to eat," Jim said. "Reckon we better get on up to the house before she raises a ruckus."

Will had never seen a spread of food to equal what was being served at the Landsings.' There was a roast, and a ham, and vegetables fresh from the garden.

Mrs. Landsing was rushing around, getting everyone seated and making sure things were properly placed.

Will and Rebecca were seated side by side, and Will felt the nervousness in his stomach each time he glanced at her.

Jim Landsing asked the Lord's blessing and Will

said a silent prayer himself. "Lord, let October hurry and get here." He hardly tasted the food as he kept casting shy glances toward Becky.

Cullen Landsing came in before the meal was finished, and Will noticed how he looked at Tye as the two shook hands.

Tye introduced him to Will and Becky. Cullen shyly said hello to Rebecca, ducking his head instead of looking her in the eyes. He shook hands with Will, and Will noticed he had a firm handshake and looked him in the eye while introductions were being made.

"Did you find those heifers?" Jim Landsing asked.

"Yes, sir, they were over by the sulfur springs."

"Any of 'em have calves yet?"

"No, sir, but there's a couple of 'em due any day now. I think that brindle heifer is gonna be the first one to pop."

"That'll be enough talk about cows and such at the table," Judith Landing admonished her husband and son. "You men can talk about that when you're alone."

Jim Landsing chuckled and Cullen attacked the plate of food his mother had fixed for him. When their eyes met, both father and son smiled as if sharing a secret between them.

The evening was spent with the men talking in the large living room and the women talking around the kitchen table.

As darkness settled over them, Judith lit the coal lamps in the house. The glow from the lamps cast warm shadows over the house and created a comfortable atmosphere.

The comfort of the house, along with the meal and the talk afterward, gave Will a warm, pleasant feeling. As he watched Rebecca through the open doorway, talking to Mrs. Landsing and Rosa, he hoped someday they would have a home such as this. It felt good to sit here and dream, far away from the dangers of the Sioux Indians and the rigors of the trail.

It was late when Judith Landsing showed Tye and Will to the bedroom they would share.

"At least, there are two beds in here. I don't relish sleeping in the same bed with you again," Will said, as they entered the bedroom.

"That's news that don't make me feel too bad. Seems the last time I shared a bed with you, I almost got killed."

Will sobered at the thought of their stay in Alder Gulch and how close he'd come to getting killed. If it hadn't been for Tye's quick reactions, he would be dead and buried now.

"Let's just hope nothing like that happens while we're here," Will said.

"I think we're safe. Better get some sleep. Tomorrow's going to be a rough day for you."

"How's that?" Will asked

"You're going to start riding some of those stallions we brought with us."

Will blinked at Tye's words. "I'm going to what?" he asked incredulously.

"You heard me. You're going to start riding the stallions we brought."

"I thought that's what you said. Why the stallions and why now?" Will asked, watching his partner and wondering what he was up to now.

Tye sat on the opposite bed and began pulling off his boots. "You remember when we started into Wyoming I told you I had some other plans to make us some money, besides just catching wild horses?"

"Yeah, I remember," Will said, still looking at Tye suspiciously.

"Well those plans include you being able to ride those stallions."

"Do you mind tellin' me how riding those stallions is going to make us money?"

"I'll tell ya when the time's right. Right now, I just want you to concentrate on your ridin' skills."

Will shook his head as he pulled off his own boots. "You sure do like to keep things a mystery, don't ya?"

"I just figure a young whelp like you can't handle all the grown-up things in life, so I take care of 'em for ya."

Will smiled as he pulled the covers over himself. "That makes me feel real good, knowin' an old-timer like you is takin' care of me."

"We'll see who feels like an old-timer tomorrow after you've ridden some of those stallions," Tye said, with smug satisfaction.

Will grimaced at the thought, but said nothing as he rolled on his side and thought about Becky in the other bedroom. He fell asleep thinking about their future, a large smile on his face.

Chapter Fifteen

The next morning after breakfast, the men headed to the corrals. Tye had enlisted Jim and Cullen to help cut out and drive five of the stallions into the small holding corral by the barn.

Once the horses were in the corral, Tye cut one out and moved him into the larger corral. Picking up his lariat, he shook out a loop as he approached the young horse.

The horse Tye had chosen was a large black, with a streak of white running down his face, and three white stockings. The horse had the powerful look of a stallion about him, and Will watched with a dry mouth as Tye moved to corner the animal.

The black had moved away from the man approaching him and snorted through his nostrils as he felt the danger about to entrap him. He moved into the corner and sought escape. But rather than turning and bolting as most horses would, he turned and faced his enemy, neck bowed, ears laid back, and teeth bared.

Tye approached the animal cautiously, knowing the large horse would attack if he closed in too quickly. When he felt he was at a safe distance, he brought his loop across his body, never taking his eyes from the horse. Suddenly, he spun the loop over his head, letting it go at the precise time. It opened and settled around the horse's head, and Tye pulled the slack in the rope.

The loop tightening around the big stallion's neck

had an immediate effect on him. He reared to his hind feet, shaking his head and pulling against the tightening of the rope.

Tye, expecting the black to react this way, wrapped the rope around one hip and set his feet to hold fast to the end of the rope, not allowing himself to be pulled close to the pawing hooves.

The black fought on his back hooves for a few seconds more, and then, coming to the ground, he charged his assailant. Tye moved away at the last moment, letting the large horse rush past him. He held the rope and braced himself for the impact of the jerk he knew he would take when the horse hit the end of the rope.

When it came, it pulled Tye fifteen yards along the dirt of the corral before he managed to turn the animal.

The black was now near the center of the corral where the snubbing post could be used, and Tye stepped forward and wrapped the rope's end around the post, securing the horse with two quick wraps.

Tye quickly tied off the rope end, then moved back out of the way to watch the black horse.

The stallion pulled back with the full force of his weight, fighting the rope as it continued to shut off his wind. He struggled to shake off the villain that had closed around him. It was a battle that could only have one ending. As the rope continued its constricting hold, the horse's air was cut off. Soon, the big black was wheezing as he tried to draw air into his lungs. He gave in to the rope, then fought valiantly again, only to have his air closed off. It was a hard-learned lesson, but a necessary one if the horse was to be broken to ride.

With a final struggle against the rope, the stallion walked forward and stood. Tye eased up to the snubbing post and slowly inched his way down the rope toward the big horse. He had taken only a few steps when the black charged him, ears back and teeth bared. Tye moved swiftly out of the way and the horse went by him, only to be brought up by the rope again.

Tye moved back to the snubbing post and untied the knot in the rope, but keeping it wrapped around the post. Holding the end of the rope, he eased toward the black horse once again. This time, when the horse ran at him, Tye pulled hard on the rope, pulling the horse's head to the post. The black fought for a few seconds, then stood still, trembling, sweat forming on his body.

With the stallion's head held firmly to the post, it was only a matter of minutes until Tye had his back foot tied to a loop around his neck and pulled off the ground.

Tye motioned to Will and Will picked up his saddle and carried it to the snubbing post. He eased up to the black and placed the saddle on his back. The horse trembled again, but didn't fight as Will cinched the saddle tight.

"This is going to be the toughest horse you've ever ridden. It's going to take your total concentration and strength to ride him."

Will said nothing; his mouth had gone dry. The thought of mounting this magnificent animal thrilled him as nothing ever had.

Tye blindfolded the black horse and Will untied the back foot. As Tye eared the horse down, Will stepped easily into the saddle.

"Ready!" he shouted, and Tye removed the blindfold and moved away.

The explosion beneath him was like sitting on a keg of dynamite as Will fought to gain control of the black horse. The first lunge had snapped him back, causing him to lose his right stirrup and setting him up on the cantle of the saddle. It only took two more powerful jumps and Will was flying through the air. He landed on his feet as he came off, and managed to remain upright.

"You underestimated him," Tye said as he moved to catch the black.

"I've never felt such strength," Will said as he came to help Tye corner the horse.

Tye roped the black and was in the process of moving him to the snubbing post when Jim Landsing spoke from the corral fence.

"I've got an easier way to do that if you're interested. I've got a special pen for bucking out horses. It's the one we use to break our colts in."

"Why didn't you tell us this earlier?" Tye asked, cocking one eye at the man.

"I wanted to watch you do it your way and see how good you were," Jim said, with laughter in his voice. "Besides that, I wanted Cullen to see what it was like before we got civilized."

Tye shook his head and grinned. "I hope you got your money's worth."

"I guess we did. You put on quite a show. Now open that gate over there and we'll run that horse down the alley."

Tye looked around and saw a gate leading into a small pen. Off the pen was an alley that led up to another gate. He could see that when that gate was opened, the horse would be in an enclosure just large enough for him to fit into. There was another gate coming off this enclosure that opened into another corral. A rider could mount his horse in the small pen, then be turned out into the larger corral to ride.

"Where did you get an idea like that?" Tye asked, studying the construction of the bucking chute.

"I saw one on a big ranch in Colorado. It sure saves a lot of time and hard work."

"I can see where it would," Tye said. "Let's get that horse in there and see if Will can stay on this time."

They worked the horse into the chute and closed the gate behind him. Will climbed the fence behind the horse, and eased himself down into the saddle. He felt the horse quiver as he found his stirrups and took hold of the reins.

"Just nod when you're ready and we'll open the gate for ya," Jim said.

"Pull yourself down into the saddle, keep your knees in the swells. Think about ridin' this bronc. It takes a lot of concentration to keep in the middle of him," Tye said, as he stood by the gate waiting for Will to nod.

Will grabbed the reins tighter in his hands, pressed his knees harder into the swells of the saddle, and nodded his head.

The gate swung open and the black stood there for the count of three before realizing he'd been freed from the chute. He exploded out of it like a charge of dynamite, lunging and coming down hard on his front feet.

Will felt the impact jar his back as the big horse came to the ground. He fought to maintain his seat as the horse lifted high into the air, kicking his back legs hard as he did. The impact of coming back to earth was like that of being hit by a runaway train, Will thought, as he watched the horse's head.

Will made a better showing this time, but lost his seat when the black started a fast turn to the right, then instantly switched directions to the left.

Will flew through the air and landed solidly on the ground, feeling the air leave his lungs as he hit.

"You were anticipating his moves rather than watching his head. He caught you with your guard down. Come on, let's try it again," Tye said as he reached a hand down to help him up. Will slowly accepted the outstretched hand and came to his feet.

"How many times I got to ride that devil?" he asked as he dusted his jeans with his hat.

"Till you do it right, and then till you do it better."

"Better'n what?" Will asked.

"Better'n anyone else," Tye said, opening the gate to run the horse back into the chute.

Will rode the black horse two more times before he brought him to a standstill. He had been bucked off into the fence the last time and had bruised his ribs.

They hurt now as he rode the black up to the chute and let Tye hold his head as he dismounted.

"I'll get you another one and we'll see if you learned anything with this one," Tye said, leading the black away.

Will sank to the ground, leaning against the chute fence. "I don't know what he has in mind, but if killing me is part of the plan, he's doing a pretty good job of it."

Jim and Cullen laughed at Will's misery.

"I'll tell ya one thing," Jim said to Will. "You're learning to ride broncs from the best there is. I don't know of anyone who can ride horses the way Tye Garrett does. If he thinks you're worth teachin', then you must have somethin' workin' for ya. I know a lot of fellas who'd like to have Tye teachin' them to ride broncs."

"Yeah," Will said, grinning. "Right now I'm feelin' real lucky."

Tye kept Will working steadily for the next ten days. Each day, he would bring in four or five of the stallions they had captured and coach Will on the fine points of riding each horse.

Rebecca slipped away from the house whenever she could to watch Will ride. She loved watching him ride the rough, bucking animals. Her heart seemed to stop each time he came out of the chute and didn't start again until he was safely on the ground. She was pleased by the fact that he rode so well. She noticed the improvement as Tye worked with him each day. She was disappointed in the fact that they never got to spend any time together alone, but she knew it was impossible to sneak away from Judith Landsing's watchful eye. Besides, Will was so tired by evening he usually ate supper and went directly to bed, leaving no time for them to talk then. Even though she was frustrated by the lack of time she got to spend with Will, she loved the Landsings and enjoyed being here.

She wondered if she would hate leaving. Thinking about it, she knew she would. But in her heart she knew she would rather be with Will, wherever that may be. She was surprised at her feelings. It had only been a short time that she had known him, but in that short time, her feelings for him had grown stronger and stronger until he occupied her every thought, her every purpose. This must be love, she thought, then smiled as she thought about her discovery. Yes, it was love!

Will had just finished riding a large gray stallion to a complete standstill. This was the horse that Tye had kept till last. He was the one that would test Will's skills to the utmost.

The gray stallion was six or seven, fully developed, and strong. He stood close to sixteen hands and weighed about thirteen hundred pounds.

Will had ridden the last twelve horses without once being thrown. Tye's instructions, coupled with Will's ability, had improved his riding skills to near perfection. He loved the feel of the horses beneath him, loved the rhythm as they tried to free themselves of his presence. Most of all, he loved the triumph of a successful ride, the surge of adrenaline he got as he conquered the animal beneath him.

The large gray was standing in the chute, Will's saddle cinched under his belly. Will climbed the fence and eased down on his back, the same as he'd done countless others in the last ten days. He pulled his hat down on his head, gripping the reins tightly. Then he nodded for Jim to open the gate.

The ride that followed was nothing less than spectacular as the gray came out of the chute rearing on his back legs. Will held tight to the reins to stay in the saddle. With a mighty lunge, the horse shot high into the air, clearing the top of the chute gate with all four feet. As he crashed back to earth, Will relaxed his body to absorb the impact, but he still felt as if his body were hit by a train as the horse's hooves

blasted into the hard-packed earth of the corral. He
tensed as he felt the horse bunch for another leap into
the air, watching his head all the while. The gray fell
to earth, then bunched himself for another leap. This
time, he turned his feet to the sky and attempted to
throw Will off balance, but Will leaned to his left,
digging his spur into the horse's side to hold himself
in the saddle.

As the gray came to ground again, he went into a
swirling spin to the left, then straightened out and
jumped right. Will remained in the saddle as if glued
there.

The entire household had turned out to watch this
ride. Rebecca stood on the fence, shouting encouragement to Will as he rode the gray stallion.

Judith Landsing watched between the fence railings,
a handkerchief covering her mouth and nose. She had
twice tried to pull Rebecca from the fence, fearing the
girl would come to harm should the horse come her
way. Rebecca ignored her pleas and continued to
stand on the railing, cheering Will on.

Jim and Cullen Landsing yelled encouragement to
Will as the horse bucked across the corral.

Tye stood smiling as he watched Will ride.
He shouted no words of encouragement, for none were
needed; Will was making a picture-perfect ride He
reflected briefly on the horse Will was riding. It was
without a doubt the roughest stallion of the lot. He
wondered if he himself would have been able to ride
the animal, but that didn't matter. If Will could
ride that horse, he could ride about anything with hair
on it, and that meant Tye had accomplished what he'd
set out to do.

Will watched the gray's head as it lined out to buck
in a straight line across the corral. Then instantly, its
head came around and he switched ends in mid jump,
but Will was ready and braced himself for the switch,
digging his knees into the swells and leaning with
the horse.

The battle had been going on for fifteen minutes and Will felt very little give in the big horse as he continued to watch its head. He wondered how long his strength would last. He didn't feel tired, but neither did the gray. Which one would give out first? Right now, he felt the adrenaline flowing through his body and the excitement of the ride was still with him. Then a funny thought came to him: What if the horse never did stop bucking? What if they just kept on going until the sun went down and were going at it when the sun came up? A smile came to his lips as he thought about it, and he raked the gray once more with his spurs.

Another ten minutes went by and Will felt the gray slackening a little. He spurred the horse harder, making him expend his energy.

The gray reacted to the spurs and jumped into the air, letting out a squall and rolling his eyes. As he came to earth, Will jabbed him again, causing the horse to jump forward in a lunge. This time when he landed, Will held his spurs and the big gray stopped, head up and breathing hard. Will touched him lightly with his spurs and the stallion leaped forward, bucking twice, then loped around the corral. Will pulled him to a stop, plow reined him around to the right, touching him lightly with his right spur. The animal jumped coming around, but didn't buck. Will eased up on the rein, pulled him around to the left. The big horse responded to Will's guidance and he rode him around the corral twice, reining him first to the right, then the left. Finally, he rode him up to Rebecca and sat smiling at her.

"What do you think about him?" he asked her, excitement in his voice.

"He's beautiful," she said, reaching up to stroke his nose. The horse snorted as she reached up, but didn't move as she touched his velvety nose.

"He's going to be my wedding present to you," Will said, watching Rebecca's face.

She looked up at him, astonished. She opened her mouth to speak, but nothing came out as she continued to look from the horse to Will.

Will smiled down at her, loving the surprised look on her face. He then turned the gray and rode over to where Tye was standing.

"How'd I do, partner?"

"I once told you, you'd be better'n me when I got through with ya, and by golly you are, boy," Tye said, grinning up at him.

Will beamed at Tye, feeling as though he'd just won the grand prize at the county fair.

"Now we're gonna put that skill to work," Tye said, looking into Will's face. "Day after tomorrow, you and me are gonna start sellin' horses."

"Why do I need to ride these broncs to sell horses? We gonna break everything we sell?"

"Nope, not all of 'em. Only those they pay us to break," Tye said.

"I reckon you're still not going to tell me what you have in mind," Will said.

"You'll more'n likely find out day after tomorrow. We're heading over to the Double A ranch. Lon Taylor was one of my regular customers. I told him I would see him when we got back with the horses. We'll take some of the horses with us when we go, just to show him what we got."

Chapter Sixteen

Will sat in the easy chair, listening to the idle conversations between Tye, Jim, and Cullen. His mind was wandering as he looked out the large window of the Landsings' living room at the Montana countryside. Since his ride this morning, the entire family and crew had taken the day off and made it a day of rest.

Will was thankful for the respite. The last few weeks had been grueling, but he felt good in spite of it all.

As he gazed out the window, something caught his attention. Becky was walking by the row of trees at the side of the house. He looked closely, expecting to see Mrs. Landsing or Rosa close by, but a quick glance into the kitchen showed both women busy preparing the noon meal.

Will casually stood up, and without seeming to be in a hurry, walked to the door leading outside.

"Where ya headed, Will?" Cullen asked.

"Nowhere in particular," Will said. "Just thought I might take me a little walk and stretch my legs."

"Sounds like a good idea. I think I'll take a little walk, too," Cullen said, rising to his feet.

"Uh, I'd really like to be alone, if it's all right with you," Will said, trying to sound casual about it.

"You sit down here with us, Cullen," Jim Landsing said. "Will don't need you along right now." He smiled at Cullen and Will saw Cullen return the smile. Will turned and went out the door, his face red as he realized what Cullen had been up to.

Will walked down to the row of trees where he'd last seen Becky. She wasn't by the trees and he had to look for several seconds before he located her. She had continued walking and was following a small trail that led into the woods. Probably a game trail, Will suspected.

He started to call her, but realized if he did, they would hear him at the house and Judith Landsing may come out to investigate. He followed the path, walking hurriedly to catch her.

Rebecca had just entered the tree-covered area when she heard footsteps behind her. She wheeled, fear showing on her face as the thought of her capture by the Sioux Indians flooded her. She clenched her fist and swung instinctively as she came around.

Will ducked the lethal swing and grabbed Rebecca as she fell forward from the force of it.

"Does this mean the engagement's off?" he asked as she looked up, a startled expression on her face.

"Will," she said, relief rushing through her as she slumped against him. "Why did you sneak up on me like that? I thought you were an Indian or something."

"Sorry, I didn't want to call out to you. I was afraid Mrs. Landsing would hear and come tearing out of the house to save you."

Rebecca laughed. "She's not an ogre, Will. As a matter of fact, she sent me out here."

"She did?" Will asked, not believing he'd heard right.

Rebecca laughed again. "Yes, she did. She knew you'd come out after me."

"She was right. I was beginning to wonder if I'd ever get to spend any time alone with you."

"Well, we're alone now. Would you like to walk with me?" Rebecca asked, smiling at him.

"Yes, I'd like that very much, but first there's something else I want to do," Will said, looking into her eyes.

"What's that?" she asked, smiling coyly.

"This," he said, taking her in his arms and kissing her deeply.

Rebecca melted against him. She had longed for this every day since he'd first kissed her on the porch of her parents' house. She felt her heart race as he pulled her closer to him and his mouth hungrily covered hers. He kissed her longingly and she felt the passion of his kiss. It carried her along on a tide of emotions such as she'd never felt before.

Will forced himself to push away from her. His emotions raged as he looked at her, yearning for her, yet not totally comfortable with the feeling he now felt.

Rebecca's breathing was starting to slow as she stood there watching him. "Let's take that walk now," she said, taking his hand and leading him along the path.

"I think that's a good idea," Will said, trying to bring himself under control.

They walked along the wooded trail, talking of the many events that had taken place and the things that were yet to come. They returned to the trail leading to the house. Walking hand in hand, they strolled along, lost in each other's company for the moment.

"I know you want to wait until October to get married, but it's only July and I'm not sure I can wait that long," Will said as they approached the house.

"I'm not sure I can either," Rebecca said. "When I said I wanted to wait until October, it was really an excuse to give us more time, to make sure we were doing the right thing. I don't need that excuse anymore. If you want to get married sooner, I'm ready."

Will looked at Rebecca, a slow smile spreading over his face. "I'm ready right now. I was ready the night we helped you escape from the Sioux, but I want you to be sure. Are you?"

Rebecca looked into his eyes, her arms going around his waist. "I've never been as sure of anything as I am of this. I can't wait to be Mrs. Will Paxton."

"As soon as I find out where a preacher is, we'll be married," Will said, holding her tight.

"Make it soon. I don't want to have to wait too long," Rebecca said, smiling up into his face.

"I will, I promise."

Two days later, Will and Tye rode out of the Landsing place before daylight. They led six of the young horses they had broken to saddle. Their destination was the Double A ranch, ten miles to the north. As they rode, Tye talked of his plans for their ranch in Texas.

"I want to head down that way before winter sets in. I figure that gives us about two months to sell these horses and prepare for the trip."

"Is that going to be a problem?" Will asked.

"No, it shouldn't be," Tye responded. "But we're still going to need more money than these horses will bring if we're going to get started right."

"How much do you reckon we're gonna need?" Will asked.

"I'd like to have about twenty thousand. But if we can put together fifteen, I figure we can pull it off."

"I hear there are wild cattle in Texas," Will said. "Are you plannin' on catchin' some of 'em?"

"Those are my plans. The demand for beef since the war has provided an opportunity for men who are willing to take a risk. Some of them built empires by rounding up wild cattle from the breaks and trailing them to the Kansas railheads. There aren't as many cattle still roaming free, but there are enough, if a man works hard to round up a herd. If we can find enough cows and heifers, we can use those to start a herd. Any bulls we find, we can sell and use the money to buy more cows."

"What about the mares we're keeping?" Will asked.

"I figure where there's cattle, there's always going to be a need for horses. I want us to be the ones to supply those horses."

"How much land do you plan on acquiring?" Will asked.

"I already have fifteen sections of land that belonged to my family. It was part of a land grant given to my grandfather by the government of Mexico. I want at least that many more. The land in Texas isn't like this land. It takes more acres to run cows down there than it does up here."

"That's a lot of land," Will said. "How do you plan on the two of us taking care of that much land?"

"I reckon we'll just have to hire us some help," Tye said, with a grin. "That's one of the reasons we need money."

They rode into the Double A headquarters, leading the six horses. Will was still thinking about the things Tye had said and the plans that were being laid.

Tye pulled up in front of the large barn where a blacksmith was in the process of shoeing one of the ranch horses. "Is Lon Taylor around?" Tye asked, stepping down from his horse.

"He's around here someplace. Try the corral around back. They're workin' some horses out there."

They tied their horses to the hitching post in front of the barn and walked around back. They found three men working a horse on the ground. The horse had been roped and thrown and his legs tied to keep him from kicking the men as they worked to doctor a large gash on his neck.

Tye and Will stood back and waited until the men were through with the horse and turned him loose. One of the men looked up and saw the two of them standing there. He turned and said something to one of the other men. He looked up and grinning, started toward them. Will took this to be Lon Taylor.

Lon Taylor walked up to Tye, the grin still on his face. "Well, I'll be, I figured the Indians would have your scalp hanging in some teepee."

"I can't believe your lack of faith, Lon. I told ya I'd be back with some horses to sell. Lon, I'd like ya to meet Will Paxton. He's helping with the horses."

Will shook hands with the man, noting that Tye didn't introduce him as his partner.

"You still in the market for those horses I promised ya?" Tye asked.

Lon looked back at the men and the horses. Then motioning with his thumb, he said, "If we don't get these mountain lions under control, I'm not going to have any horses or cattle left. I've lost six horses and twenty head of calves in the last two months."

"That's tough," Tye said. "Have ya thought about hiring professional hunters to get rid of 'em?"

"Yeah, as a matter of fact, me and some of the other ranchers hired three just the other day. They've killed two already, but that's only the tip of the iceberg. By my calculations, there's probably between twenty to thirty of the large cats roaming the mountain areas around here. I hope those three hurry and kill 'em. I'm not sure which I distrust most, mountain lions or those hunters. They're a bad lot, I'm here to tell ya."

"Most of 'em I've seen are," Tye said. "You wanna look at some of the horses we brought back with us?" Tye asked, changing the subject.

"You bring some with ya?" Lon asked, surprised by the fact.

"Brought six with us, so's you could get a flavor of the type horses they are," Tye said.

"Let's look at 'em. I want to see what kind of horses they got down there in Wyomin'."

They walked back to the front of the barn where the horses were tied. Lon walked around them, looking them over with a keen eye.

"These the best of the lot?" he asked.

"Nope, the others are just as good. Some are even better. These are just a few that's been broke," Tye said.

"What ya askin' for 'em?"

"Forty if they ain't broke. Fifty-five if they are," Tye said.

"That your bottom dollar, or is there room to do some horse tradin'?" Lon asked, smiling at Tye.

"You know me, Lon. I always quote you my best offer. Saves both of us time and nobody feels like they got out-traded."

"How many you got broke?"

"About twenty head."

"I'll take all twenty and I'll take twenty of 'em that ain't broke, if they're as good as these."

"They are," Tye said. "When do ya want 'em?"

"Can you have 'em to me day after tomorrow? I want to have 'em ready by fall gatherin'."

"We'll deliver 'em," Tye said. Then, with a thoughtful look, he asked, "You got any bad ones that cain't be ridden?"

"Boy, howdy, do I," Lon said, chuckling. "I got one that's a real humdinger. He's managed to buck off every one of my hands so far. I got him in with a bunch of horses I bought a couple of months ago. You wouldn't want to do a little horse trading, would you?"

"I'm afraid I'm not in the market for that kind of horse right now, but I might try to ride him for ya when I bring your other horses over."

"I'm not even sure you could ride this one, Tye," Lon said, his face serious.

"You want to put a little wager on that?" Tye asked.

"I might," Lon said, smiling at Tye.

"Well, if you do, I'll have a go at him," Tye said, matching his smile.

"We'll see day after tomorrow when you bring the other horses."

"Why don't you have your hands hang around that day? Maybe they'd like to see the fun. We might even have ourselves a little bucking contest," Tye said.

"You gone to showboatin'?" Lon asked.

"Naw, nothin' like that. It's just that I enjoy a good contest, that's all," Tye said, his face blank and innocent.

Lon Taylor looked suspiciously at Tye, then shrugged. "We'll see," was all he would commit to.

Once they were away from the ranch and they couldn't be heard, Will pulled his horse up beside Tye's. "You gonna ride that horse?" he asked.

"Nope. You are," Tye said, with a grin.

"That's what I suspected," Will said. "You sure set the bait back there. You reckon they'll bite?"

"You can count on it. If there's one thing I know about cowhands, they love a chance to compete, and they love a chance to bet."

They spent the rest of the afternoon and the next day riding to some of the small ranches around the area. They sold another sixty head of unbroken horses at forty dollars a head, with a promise they would deliver them in the next few days.

The day they were to take the horses to the Double A, they were on the trail before daylight. It turned out to be a family event, with Jim and Cullen helping with the horses, and Ramon driving the team and wagon over. Rebecca, Rosa, and Judith Landsing all rode in the wagon, even though Rebecca had argued that she wanted to ride horseback. Judith Landsing had finally convinced her it was more proper for her to ride with her in the wagon.

They had packed a large lunch in a basket and Judith had worked all the day before baking pies and such to take to Lon's wife, Meredith.

The caravan reached the Double A shortly after sunrise. Tye had purposely planned it that way so the hands would still be around the headquarters when they arrived.

Tye had let Jim and Cullen in on his plan, but had purposely excluded Judith and Rebecca. He stated that once women started talking, there was no telling what they might say to one another. Will had managed to sneak away with Rebecca on one of their walks and had told her of their plans, vowing her to silence. Her excitement at what was taking place came close to equaling Will's, and she smiled a knowing smile at him each time their eyes met.

Once the horses were corralled and the Taylors and Landsings had greeted each other, Lon had Ramon drive the women to the house.

The men watched as the wagon rolled away, Lon Taylor smiling as it went. "I reckon there'll be more gigglin' and cacklin' goin' on up there than there's been in a coon's age. I'm glad you brought them gals along. Ma's been hankerin' for some women to talk to."

They walked back to the corral where the horses had been put and Lon walked in, surveying each animal, never commenting, but studying each one carefully. He finished his inspection, then came to where Tye was standing. "I reckon you was right. These are as good as the others you brought. We'll go up to the house in a spell and I'll get you your money."

They moved away from the corral and were walking around the barn, when one of the hands came from the bunkhouse toward them. Tye stopped and waited for the man to come up to him.

"Howdy, Tye," the man said as he extended his hand.

"Johnny," Tye said in the way of a greeting, shaking his hand. "I thought you was workin' for the Bar OM ranch."

"I was, until a couple of months ago. I got the itch to travel a little, so I packed up and headed west till I run outa money. Then I come back here and hired on with Mr. Taylor. I think this time I'll stay put."

Lon Taylor smiled and said, "Yeah, until he gets a little money set aside. Then he'll be gone again."

Johnny Day smiled and looked down, kicking the ground with the toe of his boot. Then looking up at Tye, he asked, "You gonna try to ride Ol' Widow Maker?"

Tye looked sharply at Lon Taylor. "Widow Maker?" he asked, suddenly suspicious.

Lon chuckled and said, "That's the name they gave that horse when they found out you was gonna attempt to ride it. As far as I know, he ain't killed no one that was married.''

Tye looked at Lon and saw the grin on his face. Then he looked at Will and saw that the color was slowly coming back to his face. He started talking to keep eyes away from Will.

"Where is this horse that's got ya'll so buffaloed?"

Johnny pointed in the direction of the barn. "We got him in the corral by himself. He's so mean, we can't put no other horses in there with him. He durn near killed four or five of 'em so far. We been kept busy tryin' to keep the poor devils alive.''

Will smiled at that, remembering the horse that was being doctored the day he and Tye were here. Clearly, Johnny was trying to build the horse's reputation to hedge any bet he might be making.

As they walked to the corral, cowboys started ambling over. It looked to Will as if all the hands had stayed at the headquarters that day. He mentally counted fifteen cowboys, not including the blacksmith and Lon Taylor.

Tye climbed the corral fence and looked at the lone horse standing there.

Will looked through the railing at a dark brown horse, with a black mane and tail. The horse stood watching the people on the fence, his eyes rolling. He was broad across the chest with powerful withers. He had a thickly muscled neck and strong hindquarters. Will thought he was the kind of horse any cowhand would like to have in his string.

"He don't look like much of a horse to me," Tye said.

Lon Taylor cast a sideways glance at him and said, "I thought you were a good judge of horseflesh, Garrett.''

"I don't mean he ain't a good-lookin' animal. I just don't think he looks like much of a bucker.''

Several cowhands started laughing at that statement.

"He can buck all right," one of the cowboys said.

"Ain't nobody been able to ride him yet, and there's been some pretty good bronc riders try."

"I still say he don't look that bad," Tye said, looking back at the horse.

"Well, why don't you try him and see?" another hand shouted.

"I don't know," Tye said thoughtfully. "I thought you had a real bad one here. I bet this youngun here could ride that horse," he said, pointing to Will.

This brought a round of laughter from all the hands. Even Lon Taylor was chuckling. "I'll bet you twenty dollars you can't ride that bronc," said a cowboy standing by the fence.

"I'll bet ya thirty," another cowboy shouted.

"Wait a minute," Tye said, holding up his hands. "Ya'll want to wager, then I'll make it interesting. I've got five hundred dollars here that says this youngster here can ride that horse."

The silence that followed was intense as all the hands looked at Tye as if he'd lost his mind. Then at once they began talking, each one pulling money out of his pockets, pooling their dollars.

"We've only got two hundred ninety-five. Will you cover that?"

"I'll cover the other two hundred and five," Lon Taylor said.

Tye looked at the rancher in surprise, but said nothing.

Will's mouth had gone dry. He looked again at the horse, then at the hands. "If I ride him," he said to Lon Taylor, "I get to keep him." It was a statement, rather than a question.

"That's fair," Lon said. "I don't reckon you're gonna ride him, though. So I ain't riskin' anything."

Will smiled to himself and went to get his saddle, while one of the Double A hands walked into the corral with a rope.

Chapter Seventeen

The Double A cowboy had the bay horse snubbed and a hackamore on his head when Will returned with his saddle. Tye walked into the corral with him.

"Remember what you learned. This is a stout horse, but he ain't nothin' compared to the gray you rode the other day. Don't let him pull you down over the front of the saddle. I figure that's what makes him hard to ride. He has so much strength, he pulls a fella out of the saddle. Give him his head enough to keep him from jerkin' ya, but not enough so's you don't have a good hold. You'll have to learn him quick." Tye was talking in a low voice as they walked through the corral. He stopped as soon as they were within hearing range of the cowhands.

Will eased up to the horse and set the saddle on his back. The big horse remained calm as Will reached beneath him, and found his girth, evidence of the number of times the horse had been tried. The cowhand holding him grinned and said, "He's gentle as a baby while you're saddlin' him, but once you get aboard, he's like a keg o' dynamite. Who's your next of kin so's we can notify 'em!"

He chuckled at his own humor, but Will just glanced at him and said, "I'll sell him to ya when I get through with him." Grabbing the hackamore rein and saddle horn, he mounted the horse.

The cowboy stepped back and ran to the corral fence, climbing to the top to get a good view.

For a brief moment the big bay stood there, not moving a muscle. Then Will felt him bunch and tightened his legs against the swells of the saddle. The next instant, it was as if the world had exploded beneath him. The bay lunged forward, springing into the air and driving his head between his legs. The force of the big horse almost pulled the reins from Will's hands. Only his quick reflexes prevented him from being pulled over the front of the saddle. He grasped the reins tightly and held to the horse's head, remembering the advice Tye had given him.

As the bay's big hooves met with the hard-packed dirt of the corral, Will relaxed his body. But he instantly tensed as he watched the horse's head come around to the right. Knowing the horse was going to reverse himself in a twisting motion, he dug his right heel into the horse's side and tightened his knee against the swell of the saddle.

When the reverse came, the speed with which the large horse moved surprised Will. He knew he was going to have to use all his skills to stay astride the horse until he could wear him down.

Rebecca had heard the shouts and yells coming from the corral and rushed outside, paying no attention to Judith Landsing's call as she went. She hurried to the corral and climbed to the top rail, heedless of the dress she was wearing. The cowboys sitting on the fence watched with shocked expressions, but she paid no attention as she shouted words of encouragement to Will.

Will rode hard for the next fifteen minutes, learning the horse's maneuvers and adjusting to each. The big horse was using all his tricks to lose the rider on his back, but Will stuck to him, raking him each time he jumped.

Will knew the horse was tiring. He'd known for the last few minutes that he was going to ride the big horse to the finish, and was certain he wouldn't buck much longer. He had been hard to ride at first. But once Will had learned how to use the horse's own power against him, the rest had been an easy ride.

With nothing left, the bay stopped, sweat dripping

from his flanks, his breath coming in large wheezes. Will touched his spurs to him and he balked. Will dug in a little harder and the bay stepped forward two steps and halted again. This time, Will dug his spurs in really hard and the horse lunged into a running lope.

Will pulled up at the corral gate and stepped off the tired horse. He pulled his saddle from its back and laid it on the ground. Turning to Lon Taylor, he asked, "Have you got a halter I can use? I'll return it in a few days."

Lon stared at Will. "Son, you just cost me two hundred and five dollars and a horse. And you want to borrow a halter?"

Will looked at the rancher and saw a smile slowly spread across his face. "After the ride you just made, I'll *give* you a halter. I've never seen anything like it. Where did you learn to ride like that?" Then, looking at Tye, his grin widened. "No need to answer that. I reckon we been set up."

Tye protested, "I never claimed the boy couldn't ride. You boys just took it for granted that he couldn't."

Johnny Day came up to Tye, holding out the money from the other hands. Then, turning to Will, he said, "That was some kind of ride you put on there. You earned your money." Turning to Tye, he said, "You're a cool operator. There wasn't a one of us thought you could ride that horse, much less the youngster. You reeled us in like suckers."

"I just gave you enough rope to hang yourselves," Tye said, smiling at Johnny.

"One thing's for sure," Johnny said, "we'll be talkin' about this for months to come. It don't make it so hard to lose when you see someone as good as Will here make a ride like that."

"I'm glad there's no hard feelings," Tye said. He shook hands with Johnny, and the rest of the hands came by, shaking Will's hand, slapping him on the back, and telling him what a great ride he'd made. All the attention had Will blushing, but at the same time it was a great feeling to be accepted by men such as these. It hadn't been that long ago that he was just a cook's helper longing to be like them. He looked at Tye and shook his head as he thought again about how this man had changed his life.

The ride back to the Landsings' ranch was a joyous one as Cullen recounted Will's ride time and again. The bay was tied to the back of the wagon, while Will rode alongside. He and Rebecca smiled at each other each time one would catch the other glancing his or her way.

Tye smiled all the way home, basking in the glory of his successful planning.

The next two weeks kept Will and Tye busy, delivering horses and riding to other ranches to sell more.

When they had sold and delivered to all the ranches in the area, Tye announced it was time to move out. They still had a hundred and fifty horses left. Tye reserved seventy-five of these to build their herd when they reached Texas, leaving seventy-five horses to sell along the way.

Judith Landsing cried the night before they left, promising she'd have Jim ride to the small town of Three Forks and bring back a preacher so they could have the wedding at her home. Will and Rebecca expressed their gratitude, saying how they'd like nothing better than to have their wedding there, but if they waited any longer, they might not make it over the mountains before snowfall. They were cutting it close as it was.

It was still dark the next morning as they saddled their horses and prepared to leave. Judith Landsing cried as she hugged each of them. Tye and Will shook hands with Jim and Cullen, thanking them for their help and hospitality, promising them the same if they ever got down Texas way.

Rebecca hugged Jim and Cullen. Cullen blushed

red, then blushed even more as Will, Tye, and Jim laughed at his discomfort. Rebecca scolded each of them, but the laughter in her eyes softened the chastening.

With shouts of good-bye and tears flowing from the women, they started the herd of horses moving. Rebecca smiled through her tears, thankful to be on the trail again, unaware of what lay ahead.

They had been on the trail for a day and a half, following the Yellowstone River. They would follow the Yellowstone until they came to Powder River, then turn south to Wyoming.

Tye was riding point, leading the packhorse and two other horses, one being the old scarred mare, since most of the herd still looked to her as their leader. Free from the packhorse, Rebecca was able to help hold the horses in a herd. Tye was keeping them mainly to open country, avoiding wooded areas when possible, and making it easier to keep the herd bunched. Will had put Rebecca on the river side, because it was less work to keep the horses from wandering away on that side. If one did wander, it couldn't go far. Locating it and bringing it back to the herd was the hardest part. Will, on the other hand, was working the side away from the river, keeping the horses out of the woods.

By now, the horses were fairly well trail broken and, except for the occasional one that wandered away to find grazing, the herd stayed together, following closely behind the old mare.

By noon of the second day, they were riding through thickly wooded land. Will and Rebecca were working hard to keep the herd bunched, preventing any from straying. Will was tracking a dapple-gray mare that had left the herd to find better grazing. Riding through the trees and undergrowth, he was out of sight of the herd before he managed to get around the mare. He turned the mare back and headed her toward the herd, knowing her instincts would take her to them.

Will was watching the rump of the mare moving before him, but his mind was on other things. The leisurely pace they were taking and the movement of the herd, gave him time for thinking and planning. He was thinking of Rebecca, as he looked up and noticed the herd had stopped. He pulled his horse up and listened. He thought he heard voices. He sat still, the gray mare moving back to the herd. He was in the dense woods, covered by thick trees. Before him was a small clearing through which the mare had just passed. He could see the horse herd about a hundred yards past the clearing. All the horses were standing still, heads up and ears forward.

Will looked around for Rebecca, but saw no sign of her. His view was limited by the dense growth around him. He couldn't see Tye or the horses he was leading.

Suddenly Will's body went stiff as he heard Tye's voice raised to a near shout.

"I suggest you let her go and move away."

Will heard a reply, but couldn't make out the words. Slipping quietly from his horse, Will knelt and began pulling off his boots and spurs. He knew he would have to move quietly.

Moving slowly, careful not to step on any branch or twig, Will scrambled through the woods, using the trees for cover. He moved parallel to the herd, circling around to come behind whoever was there.

Will kept his pistol holstered, wanting his hands free for the moment. He'd left his rifle in his saddle boot, knowing there would be no chance to use it in the dense woods. His only chance was to come from behind and surprise whoever was there. But what about Rebecca? He knew they had her. Tye's warning had been clear. He couldn't shoot if they were holding her.

He walked cautiously now, the voices growing louder. He could make out some of the words.

"Nice herd you got there, but not near as nice as

this here filly." Will heard Rebecca's muffled cry and
felt his blood chill.

"Where's your dish boy? Don't tell me you got tired
of baby-sittin' and got rid of him." Will tensed as he
heard the voice and the words spoken. It was Slade.
How had he found them? He couldn't have been trailing them, or he'd know Will was here. He must have
come upon them by accident, but how did he get the
drop on Tye? The answer came to him as soon as
the question formed in his mind: Rebecca. They had
somehow gotten Rebecca, then used her to get Tye.

"You're making a big mistake, Slade. You know
what will happen to you if you harm that girl."

Slade laughed, and Will felt himself shiver as he
heard the sound. Old memories flooded back to him.

"Ain't nobody gonna do nothin', cause nobody's
gonna know. By the time they discover your bodies,
there won't be nothin' left but a few bones. But first,
we're gonna have us some fun. I've waited a long time
to get even with you and now I'm gonna make up for
the waitin'. You're gonna die real slow, Garrett. But
first, you're gonna get to watch what happens to your
woman here." Slade laughed again and Will heard Rebecca scream.

It was all Will could do to keep himself from drawing his pistol and charging into the clearing. He forced
himself to think. He had to get behind them. He
started working his way through the trees, stepping
carefully, making himself concentrate on the ground
before him. He heard the voices, but ignored the
words. He was now even with them and, peering out
from the brush, he took in the scene before him.

Slade was holding Rebecca by the hair, twisting her
golden tresses in his large dirty hand. Will had never
before felt such an urge to kill—not only kill, but inflict pain, such pain that the man before him would
beg him to kill him.

Will noticed Slade had grown a beard. It was matted
and dirty, as were his clothes, giving him an even more
sinister look than Will remembered.

Tye was on his knees, blood dripping from his nose and a cut on his lip. Two other men stood beside him and, as Will watched, they dragged Tye to his feet. While they held him between them, Slade hit him; first in the stomach, then swinging an uppercut, catching him on the chin and snapping his head back. Slade had held to Rebecca's hair, using his free hand to beat Tye, making Rebecca scream each time he jerked her hair.

Will turned his face from the scene, feeling sick to his stomach. He had to move. He had to do something before they killed Tye. He turned and started working his way through the woods again. He had picked a spot where he would be behind the intruders. His brain worked frantically for a plan, something that would move Rebecca away from Slade. He needed a diversion, but what? He could think of nothing that would reduce the risk to all their lives.

Will crept stealthily through the trees to the point he had chosen. He had chosen this particular place for several reasons: It was directly behind the group, as well as being above them. It had taken half an hour since he'd seen Slade beating Tye. He was well hidden by the dense trees, but could still look down on them without being seen himself.

As he peered through the trees, he saw Tye sitting on the ground, his back against a tree, his face bloody and swollen. He at first appeared to be unconscious; but as Will watched, he saw him open one eye and look about. The three men were standing several feet away from him, and seemed to be arguing about something. Rebecca was still being held by Slade. Only now he had her in front of him, holding her with his arm across her throat. Will trembled with rage as he saw the fear in her eyes, but quickly brought it under control. Now was not the time to lose his head. He had to think, had to wait for his chance. If only Rebecca was out of the way. He could move in on the three and have them covered. But as long as Slade held her, Will could do nothing.

Will's hiding spot was thirty feet from the group of people. He knew he would have to move closer. If a chance came to catch Slade off balance, he had to be close enough to take advantage of it.

He moved forward, his pistol still in its holster. He needed his hands free to move closer. Sometimes he crawled on the ground to maneuver around a low-hanging branch or through the undergrowth. Keeping himself close to the ground, he came to within fifteen feet of the three men. He could hear their voices clearly now, but couldn't see them for the knoll in front of him. From his position, he could still see Tye leaning against the tree.

"I say we kill him now, take the horses and the girl, and get out of here," one of the men was saying.

"Yeah, I agree with Hank," the other man said. "If we hang around here, someone's liable to come along."

"There ain't nobody comin' this way," Slade shouted. "And we ain't killin' Garrett till I'm good and ready. He ain't come close to bein' paid for what he done to me. As for the little lady here—well, we may just have ourselves a little party and let the mighty Tye Garrett watch." Slade's laughter sent chills through Will and he glanced over to where Tye was.

Will went rigid as he looked at Tye's face. Tye was looking directly at him. As Will watched him, Tye shifted his eyes to the ground ten feet away. Will followed Tye's line of vision and saw what he was looking at. There in the dirt lay Tye's pistol. They must have had him toss it away and forgotten about it. As Will looked back to Tye, he saw a barely perceptible nod. What did it mean? Could Tye get to the pistol if a fight started? Will nodded at him, then moved back where he could watch the three men.

Slade held Rebecca by the arm now. He was giving orders to the other two. Will positioned himself where he could be in the clearing in two steps. Still hidden by the trees, he watched as the two men moved to Tye's horse. He saw them remove the saddlebags tied to Tye's saddle and bring them back to the spot where Slade and Rebecca stood. As the man holding the saddlebags untied the leather straps binding the flap, Will saw Slade relax his grip on Rebecca's wrist, saw her look at the hand holding her. Then she looked around. Was she looking for him, or was she looking for a place to run? Then her eyes stopped. She was facing in his direction. Did she see him? Then the thought came to him: Somehow, Tye had let her know.

Will watched as her eyes searched the trees where he was waiting. The men were concentrating on the saddlebags, their attention momentarily drawn from Rebecca. Will held his breath, then shook his head. Rebecca's eyes widened slightly and he looked into them, knowing she had seen him. If only she could do something to distract them.

The thought had hardly entered his head when Rebecca turned back to look at the men holding her hostage. It was at this moment that Slade reached into the bag and found the money Will and Tye had gotten from selling the horses.

With a shout, he pulled the cash from the bag, staring at it with a triumphant look in his eyes.

Rebecca, seeing his attention diverted from her, wrenched her arm free with such force it pulled Slade off balance, almost causing him to lose his footing, and making him drop the money. Free from Slade's grip, she ran toward the horse herd, drawing the men's attention away from Will's position.

Slade regained his footing, yelling a curse as he did. His eyes burned with anger as he came around and was reaching for the pistol at his side when Will's voice stopped him.

"Don't do it, Slade."

Will had stepped from the woods and now stood directly behind Slade. He still had his pistol holstered. He knew he could have opened fire and killed all three as they stood with their backs to him, but he couldn't do that. He knew he would be no better than the men before him if he allowed himself to.

Slade stopped in midstride, his hand poised over the butt of his pistol. Then slowly he turned, his lips curling into the sneering grin Will had seen so many times before.

"Well, well, what have we here? A dish boy that thinks he's a man now. Looks like I'm goin' to get to kill two birds with one stone."

Will stood facing Slade, his feet spread slightly apart. He felt his heart beating, the steady rhythm pulsing in his ears. He watched Slade's eyes, knowing any move he made would show there first. He felt calm, his arms tingling slightly as he relaxed his muscles. He was going to kill Slade. It didn't matter if Slade got a slug into him first—he was going to kill him. It was the only way he could save Rebecca and Tye. With Slade dead, the other two would cut and run. If he got Slade without going down, he would go for the man on his right next. He didn't have time to think about Tye. He knew he was hurt, probably hurt bad. Rebecca was out of harm's way. All he had to do was kill Slade.

Slade's smile disappeared from his face, replaced by a sneer that made him look even more evil. His feet were spread slightly. His right hand relaxed at his side. "I'm gonna enjoy killin' you, boy. Then I'm gonna kill your guardian angel over there. I missed ya both in that hotel, but I won't miss this time."

Will saw the slightest twitch in Slade's eye, and then he heard the crashing sound of gunfire. He saw the surprised look on Slade's face and the red stain that started to spread over the front of his shirt. Then gunfire sounded again and Slade jerked, straightened on his toes, and fell backward, his gun barrel still in its holster. Two more shots rang out, and Will whirled about. The two men with Slade were on the ground, one clutching his shoulder, the other shot through the head. He looked at the gun in his hand, the barrel still smoking. He didn't remember drawing, didn't remember pulling the trigger.

He looked around. Tye lay on the ground, a pistol clutched in his hand. He heard the sound of running feet and swung around in time to catch Rebecca as she dropped a rifle and threw herself into his arms, crying and laughing at the same time. Will held her close for a few moments, then gently pushed her away. He walked over to where Slade lay. The man was still alive, but barely. He looked up at Will, his face a mask of confusion.

"You beat me. A stinkin' cook's helper beat me. How'd you do it?"

Will looked down at the dying man. He felt no sorrow for what he had done. "You made a mistake by thinking I was just a cook's helper. I've been over the mountain and done some growin' since we last saw each other."

Slade peered into Will's face. He fought to say something, but his eyes closed as the last breath from his body mixed with the mountain air.

Will took a last look at Slade, then reached down and picked up the dead man's gun. He looked around, found the pistols belonging to the other two, and tucked them into his waistband. He walked over to the wounded man sitting on the ground.

The man groaned and looked up as Will approached. "My arm's busted. You got to help me."

Will stared down at the man in disgust. "Mister, you were going to kill us. You beat my partner and you were plannin' to harm the woman I'm gonna marry. So what makes you think you got any help comin' from me? Tell me why I shouldn't shoot you and leave you for the buzzards."

The man looked into Will's eyes, then turned away as he saw the anger burning in them.

"Where are your horses?" Will asked.

"Down by the river about a hundred yards. They're

tied in a clearing over there," he said, motioning with his good hand.

"You sit real still while I check on my partner. You make one move and you'll be joining the other two."

Will walked to where Rebecca had Tye leaning against a tree. His face was swollen and battered, his breathing labored.

"You look terrible," Will said, trying to smile.

"You ought to see me from this side. It looks a whole lot worse," Tye said. "But I feel a lot better'n those two gents over there."

"How bad ya hurt?" Will asked.

"Not as bad as it looks. I've got a couple of busted ribs, but I don't think they did any damage. My face feels like a bronc stepped on it with all four feet but, other than that, I feel fine."

"Let me take care of these fellas and I'll come back and start a fire to heat some water."

He located the horses without trouble. There were three saddle horses, a packhorse for their supplies, and a horse carrying pelts—cougar pelts. These must be the hunters Lon Taylor had hired, Will thought as he led the horses back to the clearing.

He loaded the two dead men on their horses, tying their hands and feet together underneath. Then he hefted the wounded man to his feet and helped him mount his horse, feeling no sympathy for the man as he groaned with pain. When Will had all the horses tied together, he said to the injured man, "You head on outa here. I ever see you again, I'll kill you on sight."

"What about them?" the man asked, looking at the bodies.

"They're beyond caring," Will said. "You can either bury them or take them with you. I don't care one way or the other." He slapped the horse on the rump and stood back as the caravan moved down the trail. Will watched it until it was out of sight, then turned back to Tye. Suddenly he felt very tired.

Chapter Eighteen

Will built a fire and started heating water. He had found the packhorse and Tye's horse still ground hitched where they'd been left. The other horses had run off at the sound of the gunfire, and he knew he would have to find them before dark if he were to have any chance of finding them at all.

He rummaged through the pack and found some liniment and salve Clement had given them. The Shoshone Indians made the medicine and Clement swore it could cure whatever ailed a man.

Will gave them to Rebecca and told her how to apply each one.

"I've got to go get my horse and boots," he said, looking at his stocking feet.

Rebecca smiled and Tye squinted at him through swollen eyes. "I don't know what to think about a cowboy who loses his boots and goes traipsin' about in the woods barefooted."

"Yeah, well, it seems that's the only way I can keep this here hardheaded, bad-tempered fella outa trouble." Will grinned.

Tye turned his head to get a better look at Will. Looking him in the eye, he tried to smile, his face twisting with the effort. "You sure pulled our bacon outa the fire." He paused, watching Will. "You ain't a boy no more. You've more than proved yourself a man, and I want you to know I couldn't be prouder than to have you as a partner."

Will's eyes misted as he heard the words Tye spoke.

A large lump came into his throat and he couldn't speak, couldn't find any words to respond to the statement just made. He looked at the ground, trying to swallow. Finally, he looked up, the hint of a smile touching his lips. He reached out a hand and laid it on Tye's shoulder.

"Thanks, partner. You get some rest. I'll look after the horses and be back as soon as I can."

After retrieving his horse and boots, Will set about finding the horse herd. He followed the tracks through the woods. The horses were staying together, following the same trail. Will rode another half mile down the trail before finding them.

Topping a rise, he saw horses grazing. The scarred mare was standing next to the trail, the end of her lead rope lodged between two rocks. Other horses stood near her. The herd must have been following her lead and now waited for her.

Will untangled the mare's lead from the rocks and, with her behind him, he circled the others. He started them toward camp, then moved to the front. The horses followed the scarred mare as Will led off. He had seen a small canyon close to the camp; hopefully, he could enclose it to keep the horses in, at least for the night. He was tired and felt the need to rest. Tomorrow, he would find a better place, if one was needed.

It was growing dark when Will returned to Rebecca and Tye.

Rebecca had bathed Tye's wounds and treated them with the ointment and salve. Tye seemed to be resting. His breathing came easier, though still somewhat labored. She had managed to get Tye's roll off his saddle and he lay on it now, sleeping.

Rebecca had a stew simmering over the fire and she handed Will a bowl as he sat down.

"Did you find the horses?" she asked.

"Yeah, I've got 'em in a canyon a little ways up the trail. How's Tye doin'?"

"He's resting quietly. I gave him some of Clement's elixir. I think it's some sort of whiskey. It seemed to help his breathing."

Rebecca watched Will closely. His mind seemed to be elsewhere and he only half listened to her as she talked, nodding from time to time.

"Will, are you okay?" Rebecca asked tentatively.

"I've never killed anyone before," Will said, his voice filled with remorse.

Rebecca moved around the fire until she was sitting at Will's side.

"I'd never even shot at anyone until today, either," she said. "I was aiming to kill that man, and I'm thankful I only wounded him. I know how you feel. I don't think I would care as much for you if you felt any other way. Taking another man's life is nothing to feel good about. But if you hadn't killed him, he would have killed all of us. I shudder to think what he and the other two would have done to me."

She paused to look at him. He was looking into the fire. Gently, she placed her hands on both sides of his face and turned his head until he was looking into her eyes. "You did the only thing you could do, Will Paxton. You saved our lives. It's all right to feel bad about killin' a man, but don't you for one second blame yourself for what happened. Those men brought about their own destiny and nobody could have prevented what took place here today."

Will looked into Rebecca's eyes. Her words soothed the anguish of the torment he felt. He wrapped his arms around her and pulled her close to him, burying his head into the soft hair that lay on her shoulder.

"Thank you, Rebecca. I guess I knew that all along. I just needed to hear it. I needed you to tell me you understood." Then softly he whispered, "I love you, Rebecca Kincaid."

Rebecca smiled as tears ran down her cheeks. The tension of the day eased out of her, as she held tight to Will.

                              *   *   *

It was five days before Rebecca pronounced Tye fit
enough to ride. During those five days, Will moved
their camp down by the river, where it would be more
convenient to water. He spent his days looking after
the horses and providing wood and water for the
camp. He was restless and wanted to be on the trail,
away from this place that had brought nothing but
misery to them. He held himself in check, knowing
Tye needed the rest and couldn't ride until he was
well.

Tye was a terrible patient and would have mounted
a horse and ridden out the next day. Rebecca put her
foot down and threatened to take his boots and saddle
away if he even attempted to mount a horse until he'd
had time to heal.

Tye pleaded with Will to intercede for him, but Will
held up his hands and told Tye he was on his own.
He wasn't about to take sides in a fight that he knew
he couldn't win.

Tye finally relented, but only because he feared Rebecca would carry out her threat. He remained sullen
and complained daily about losing time and having to
get out of the mountains before snow fell if they were
to reach Texas before the spring.

Rebecca ignored his complaints and continued to
nurse his wounds. She bandaged his broken ribs with
strips torn from her dress, binding them tight to hold
them in place until they could heal.

On the morning of the fifth day, they broke camp
before daylight. Tye led the way with the packhorse
and the old mare. His face was almost back to normal;
most of the swelling had gone down. His ribs were
bandaged and didn't hurt with every breath drawn,
but he winced every time his horse stumbled or
jumped over obstacles along the trail.

Three days later they rode into Bozeman. The town
was a hub of activity.

They found a small ranch on the outskirts of town

where they could leave the horses, and the three rode into town.

They pulled up in front of a brick building bearing the sign of the BOZEMAN EMPORIUM.

"Let's get some rooms. Then we'll find a livery stable for the horses. I want to find out if the army at Fort Ellis needs any horses," Tye said.

Tye asked for and got the keys for three rooms, asking for a bath to be delivered to Rebecca's room as soon as possible. He and Will would find a bath-house after taking care of the horses.

The three rooms were on the second floor, side by side. Tye took the first one, Rebecca the second, leaving the last for Will. After dropping his roll in his room, Will locked the door behind him, then knocked on Rebecca's door.

"Who's there?" Rebecca asked.

"It's me, Rebecca, open the door," Will responded.

Rebecca opened the door an inch, looking into Will's face. "It's not proper for a young lady to allow a man into her room."

"Rebecca, would you quit foolin' around?" Will said impatiently. "I've got something to give ya. Will ya open the dadburn door?"

Laughing, Rebecca stepped back, opening the door for Will to enter. As Will stepped in, she closed the door behind him, wrapping her arms around his neck as he turned to face her. "I've got something to give you, too," she said as she pulled his head down and kissed him.

Will pulled her close to him and kissed her hungrily. Then, remembering his reason for being there, he pushed her away and stood holding her at arm's length.

"I swear I could forget my name when I'm in your arms, but I've got to meet Tye in the lobby. I wanted to give ya this," he said, pulling a pistol from his belt. "I don't think there'll be any need for it, but just in case I wanted you to have it."

Rebecca smiled and took the pistol from him. "Will Paxton, you really know how to sweep a girl off her feet. Why, I'll bet you give one of these to every girl you meet."

Will smiled back. "Naw, just the ones I want to keep around for a while. I've got to go. We should be back in a couple of hours. You keep your door locked." He kissed her quickly and went out the door. Rebecca smiled as she put the pistol in the dresser drawer.

Tye was waiting in the lobby as Will came down the stairs. He gave Will an impatient look as he approached. "I thought maybe you was takin' a nap or something," Tye said.

"I had something to give Rebecca," Will said in way of explanation.

"There's a stable down the other end of town," Tye said, as they walked through the front door and into the street.

They led their horses down the street, watching the activity taking place. The livery was marked with a hanging sign and they walked up to the front of the large barn. The big man standing there watched them as they came up.

"Howdy," Tye said. "You got room for our horses?"

"Sure do," the man said. "Fifty cents a day per horse and I give 'em grain and hay twice a day."

"That sounds reasonable," Tye said. "We'll probably be in town a couple of days. My name's Tye Garrett, and this here is Will Paxton."

Tye held out his hand and the big man took it, saying, "I'm Hal Bonner, owner and operator of this here fine establishment."

"Pleasure to meet ya," Will said, shaking his hand.

"How's the horse market around here?" Tye asked.

"Depends on whether you're buyin' or sellin'," Hal said.

"Sellin'," Tye responded.

"Well, you're on the right side then, especially if ya got any plow horses."

"Nope, we ain't got any of those," Tye remarked. "But we got the makin's of some good saddle horses."

"Young stuff?" Hal asked.

"Some of it is," Tye said. "Some of 'em are upwards of seven years."

"How many head ya got?"

"About a hundred and fifty head."

Hal let out a whistle. "Where'd you get that many horses?"

"We captured 'em," Tye said.

"Wild horses, huh?"

"Yep, but they're the best of the herd. We cut out the culls. Everything left is top grade."

"I might be interested in a few of 'em. Are any of 'em broke?"

"We've already sold all the ones we had broke," Will said.

"How much you wantin' for 'em?" Hal asked.

"Forty a head, and that's the bottom dollar," Tye said. He liked the look of this man and felt an instant trust. He knew it was just instinct, but his instincts were seldom wrong.

"If they're good solid horses, I might take ten or fifteen head. I'm always gettin' folks in here lookin' for a horse. I know a man I can get to break 'em for me. Unless you fellas want to break 'em. I'll pay ya ten dollars a head extra."

"Thanks," Tye said. "But we won't be here long enough. How about the army at Fort Ellis? Reckon they might be in need of some horses?"

"If I was guessin', I'd say they needed some. The way they have to ride over the territory, lookin' after these nesters comin' in here, I'd say they probably need a whole bunch of horses. Ever since John Bozeman blazed that trail from Wyomin' up here, we've had more nesters comin' in here than you can shake a stick at. I think most of 'em hope to find gold, but some of 'em are settlin' in and farmin' this country. Doin' real good at it, too. That's why I was wonderin' if ya had any plow horses."

"I heard about Bozeman. He brought some settlers up through the Sioux territory, didn't he?"

"Yep, and others followed. That trail is marked with graves all the way. They've closed the trail now, but there's still those who try to make it across. Nelson Story brought a herd of longhorns up that way a few years ago. I wouldn't try it. Those Sioux are mighty protective of their hunting grounds and don't like folks traipsin' through there."

"Thanks for the information. I think we'll ride out to the fort in the morning and see if they're in need of some horses. We'll pick you out fifteen or twenty of the best ones and bring 'em in to ya."

"I appreciate that," Hal said. "I'll take care of your horses for ya and stow your gear in the tack room."

"Thanks," Tye said. "By the way, is there a bank in town with a safe? I've got some papers I'd like to store until we leave town."

"Yeah, sure. The Bozeman Bank down the street has a safe."

Will and Tye headed down the street. Tye had his saddlebags over his shoulders.

The Bozeman Bank was in one of the older buildings in town. Tye asked to see their safe and was pleasantly surprised to find a large one just recently installed.

"We had it brought in from St. Louis," the bank teller remarked as Will and Tye looked at the large vault with a door two feet thick.

Tye took six envelopes out of his saddlebags. All six were tied together with a piece of string.

"I've got some important papers I'd like to put in your safe until we leave," he said, handing the bundle of envelopes over to the clerk.

"Yes, sir. The charge is twenty-five cents a week or seventy-five for a month."

"I'll only be leaving 'em here for a couple of days, but here's twenty-five cents. I'd like a receipt for the envelopes, please, and a wax seal put on the string."

Tye got what he asked for and they left the bank to find a bathhouse.

An hour later, they emerged from the bathhouse and started toward the Bozeman Emporium, when Will stopped, looking up and down the street.

"What ya lookin' for?" Tye asked.

"Nothin' in particular. You go on back to the hotel. I'll be along in a minute. There's something I need to do."

"All right, but don't be too long. I'm startin' to get hungry."

"I won't be long. If you see Rebecca, tell her I'll be along directly."

Tye turned and made his way to the hotel, while Will started down Main Street, looking at the businesses on the way. He went into the Main Street Dry Goods Store and came out a few minutes later. Crossing the street, he entered a small shop with a sign out front saying: MISS LETTIE'S ALTERATIONS AND SEWING. He emerged from there twenty minutes later, a big smile on his face. He whistled as he made his way back to the Bozeman Emporium.

Chapter Nineteen

As they ate supper in the hotel dining room that evening, Tye talked of their plans for the next day.

"We'll ride out to Fort Ellis and see if they need some horses. We may also see if they got any rank ones." He smiled as he said this, looking at Will to see what his reaction would be.

Will grinned and asked, "You reckon those soldiers are as eager to wager on the outcome of a bronc ride as those cowboys were?"

"I figure they like a little excitement every now and again," Tye said.

Rebecca had been sitting quietly, listening to the exchange between the two men. She smiled as she saw the light in Will's eyes at the thought of riding rough horses. "I don't know what it is that makes a man want to climb on one of those brutes and risk breaking his fool neck," she said, rolling her eyes in mock disbelief.

"I wish I could tell you what it was," Tye responded. "But to tell the truth, I don't know myself."

"Well, while you two are out at the fort tomorrow, I think I'll do a little shopping. If you'll give me a list of the supplies we need, I'll go ahead and have the mercantile get them ready."

"That sounds like a good plan to me," Will said. "And while you're at it, stop by Miss Lettie's. It's a dress shop across from the dry goods store. I stopped in today to see if they could make you a couple of dresses. They need your measurements." Will reddened slightly. "And I didn't know what they were. I told the lady I'd have you stop by."

Rebecca's face lit up and the smile she gave Will was one of pure joy. "Why, Will Paxton, you are full of surprises. Can I pick out the material?"

"Sure you can. I asked the lady if she could have 'em ready in two days and she assured me she could, if you came by early in the morning."

Rebecca leaned over and kissed Will on the cheek. "I think being captured by the Sioux was the best thing that ever happened to me."

Will blushed again and looked around to see if anyone in the room had witnessed the scene. An older couple, sitting at the table next to them, smiled as Will glanced their way and his face burned even hotter as he quickly turned away.

Tye had been quietly observing Will and Rebecca. A smile played on his lips as he watched Will's embarrassment.

Will and Tye left for the fort early the next morning. Before leaving, Will had given Rebecca some money and told her to buy anything she might be needing for the trip to Texas.

Fort Ellis was about a mile north of Bozeman. Will and Tye arrived late in the morning. The sentry at the gate let them pass after directing them to the post commander.

Entering the commander's office, they were introduced to Captain Terry, a tall, thin man, with locks of blond hair, and a blond mustache that curled at the ends. His blue eyes sparkled as Tye introduced Will and himself, and explained the reason for their visit.

"You've come at a most opportune time, Mr. Garrett. We are indeed in need of horses. The only problem is that at the moment I don't have the funds to pay for them. Indians attacked the supply train from Fort Laramie four days ago. Our payroll and operating funds were on that train. The Indians didn't get the money, but the supply train had to turn back, and I'm afraid it will be another three to four days before a dispatch will reach us. The local banks have been good enough to lend us money to meet payroll, and the local stores have supplied us with enough staples to keep the men and horses fed. But there is no extra money for purchasing such things as additional horses, as much as we need them. It's very hard to find horses right now with the gold strikes and the rush of people coming in. If you're willing to wait a few days, I'll have the money."

Tye looked thoughtful for a moment, then spoke. "Well, Captain, I wish I could wait, but we've got a long way to go and not much time to get there. I think there may be a way around your problem, though. We're going to be traveling south through Wyoming on our way to Texas. We'll be passing close to Fort Laramie. If you'd give us a voucher for the sale of the horses, we could pick up our money there."

"That would work fine," Captain Terry said. "Where are the horses now?"

"We've got them held on a small spread west of town," Will replied. "How many would you be in need of, Captain?"

"How many have you got?"

"I think we got about fifty-five or sixty head, depending on how many Mr. Bonner wants."

"I'll take all of them," Terry replied. "If the price is right."

"Fifty dollars a head," Will replied.

Tye looked up, surprise showing briefly on his face, then he turned to look at the captain.

"How many of them are broke to ride?" Terry asked.

"None of them," Will replied. "They're all green, but they're tough stock and they'll make good mounts for your men."

"If they're all sound horses, you have a deal. How soon can you deliver them?"

"We can have them here tomorrow, if that'll suit you," Will said.

"Tomorrow will be fine."

They started for the door, but before they reached it, Tye turned back. "Captain, you wouldn't happen to have any horses too rough to ride, would you?"

Captain Terry looked thoughtful. "Rough stock, huh? We don't have any what you call 'rough stock,' but we do have one that's bucked off every new recruit we bring in. The men love it when a new recruit arrives at the fort. It makes for a little sport when they put them on Ol' Brownie."

"Ol' Brownie, huh? Sounds like a ringer name for sure."

Captain Terry chuckled. "Yep, it's a ringer all right. He's bucked off lots of good riders."

"Do you think the men would be up for a little sport with a wager tied to it?" Tye asked.

"You mean, in other words, you would like to attempt to ride Ol' Brownie and would like to put some money on it?"

"That's about the gist of it," Tye said. "Only it'll be the kid here riding, not me."

Captain Terry lifted an eyebrow as he looked at Will. "He doesn't look old enough to be riding rough stock. But, then again, half the kids that join up aren't old enough to be fighting Indians either. If you want a shot at riding our ringer, I'll set it up for you. How about tomorrow when you bring the horses?"

"That'll be fine," Tye said. "We'll see you tomorrow."

When they had ridden away from the fort, Tye turned to Will. "Fifty dollars a head? What made you think he would pay that much for horses?"

"He did," Will replied, smiling.

Tye looked at him questioningly.

"He said he wasn't able to buy horses because of the gold strike and immigrants. That meant that horses must be going for a premium. I figured if I said fifty, and he thought it was too high, he would have haggled over the price. If we'd had to come down to forty, we still would not have lost anything."

"How about the horses we sold to Hal Bonner? We sold those for forty dollars a head. What if the captain finds out we sold them to Hal cheaper than we sold them to him?"

"I don't reckon Hal's going to be to eager to tell anyone what he gave for those horses. After all, he's in the business of selling them, too."

"You're right about that. Well, partner, you just made us ten dollars more a head than we hoped for. I'd say that calls for a special celebration. I think a steak supper would be in order for tonight."

"Don't forget Rebecca's been shopping all day. It may take the extra money we made today to pay for everything she bought."

They both laughed as they kicked their horses into a lope and headed back to town.

The evening was a festive event. They enjoyed a steak dinner at the finest restaurant in town. Tye bought a bottle of wine and the three toasted to the success of the sale. They had sold all the horses they had, with the exception of the ones they were keeping to start their herd in Texas. Rebecca had made arrangements for all their supplies to be ready in two days and had been fitted for two dresses.

"I bought each of you a present, as well," she said, smiling in anticipation.

"What did you get us?" Will asked.

Rebecca reached into her new handbag and pulled out two small packages wrapped in paper, and handed one to each of them.

Tye looked embarrassed as he took his package. He looked it over as if expecting something to jump out at him.

"Go ahead, open them," Rebecca said.

Will tore the paper away to reveal a small box. Cautiously, he opened the box to see its hidden secret. As he peered at the contents, a smile slowly spread across his face. Reaching in, he pulled out a silver belt buckle with a bronc rider etched in the center. Turning it over, he saw something inscribed on the back. Looking closely, he saw the words: TO WILL PAXTON, WITH ALL MY LOVE, REBECCA. 1872.

Tye's present was a gold watch attached to a chain. It played the "Lover's Waltz" when the cover was opened. Inside the cover was the inscription: TO TYE GARRETT. MAY ALL YOUR DAYS BE BLESSED WITH HAPPINESS. REBECCA. 1872.

Tye stared at his watch, listening to the melody that it played. "Thank you, Rebecca. It's beautiful. I'll cherish it always."

Will thanked Rebecca for his buckle and promised to wear it always.

They finished the evening by attending a Shakespeare play that had arrived in town. Both Will and Tye fell asleep before the last act began, but Rebecca sat enthralled by the costumes the actors wore.

The following morning, all three rode out early to the ranch where the horses were being kept. Tye had sold Hal fifteen head of horses, leaving them with sixty head to sell to the army. They cut out the ones they were going to keep, plus the fifteen to be delivered to Hal, and then started the others on the road to the fort.

Will waited until the horses were strung out, and leaving Rebecca to bring up the rear, rode up to the front where Tye was leading the scarred mare.

As he rode alongside Tye, he said, "I know you wanted to leave tomorrow, but I really need for us to stay one more day."

Tye looked at him questioningly. "You got a good reason?" he asked.

"Yep, I've set up Rebecca's and my wedding for tomorrow. The wedding dress I'm having made for her won't be ready until this afternoon."

Tye smiled. "I reckon a man's wedding is a good enough reason to wait around an extra day."

Will returned the smile. "Thanks, Tye. By the way, I'd like for you to be my best man. Will you?"

"Sure," Tye said, as if there shouldn't have been any doubt. "Are you ready for the ride today?" Tye asked, changing the subject.

"The way I feel, I'm ready for anything," Will responded.

"Well, don't get too cocky. I got a feeling there's something about this horse that's different from the ones you've ridden before."

"What would that be?" Will asked, sobering at Tye's warning.

"I don't know," Tye responded. "But the army doesn't keep bad horses around very long. They don't have time to mess with 'em. If they get a bad one, they usually get rid of him real quick. This horse has been around for a while, if what the captain told us is true."

Will thought about this as he made his way to the back of the herd where Rebecca was working to keep the horses moving. Riding up beside her, he smiled and asked, "How would you feel about getting married tomorrow?"

Rebecca looked at him in astonishment. "Do you mean it? Do you really mean it?"

"Nope, I just wanted to see your reaction when I asked you," Will said.

"Well, in that case, the answer is no," Rebecca said, matching his smile.

"I talked Tye into sticking around for another day. I've already made arrangements with a pastor to marry us. I thought you might like to have a church wedding, since I don't think there'll be many churches around where we're headed to."

Rebecca reached over and laid her hand on top of Will's. Their horses moved closer together as she squeezed his hand gently. "Thank you, Will. I've always wanted a church wedding. But I wouldn't care if it was out on the open plains, as long as you're the man I'm marrying."

"Well, if I'd known that, I could have saved myself two dollars and had that minister meet us out on the plains." His mischievous smile caused Rebecca to laugh.

Chapter Twenty

They entered the fort and turned the horses into the large round pen used for that purpose. As they pushed the last horse in and closed the gate, Captain Terry came walking across the parade ground toward them.

Tye and Will turned to greet the captain as he came up to the corral. "We got 'em here. There's sixty head of tough mustangs. They'll make your men some good mounts once they're broke," Tye said, motioning to the horses in the corral.

"They look to be top grade," Captain Terry said, looking over the rail at the horses milling around in the corral. "You wouldn't be interested in working a deal to break them for me, would you?"

"I surely wish we could," Tye said. "But we've got to get on down to Texas before it gets too cold."

Terry nodded. "I remember you telling me that. I just thought I'd give it a shot. Let's get a closer look at these wild horses you brought me."

The captain walked around the corral, looking at each horse and commenting on each one's conformation. "They're everything you said they were, gentlemen. Come on up to my office and I'll give you a voucher for them."

Rebecca, who had remained mounted during the inspection of the horses, now dismounted and joined Will as they started to go to the main building. Captain Terry removed his hat as Rebecca came up. "Ma'am," he said, nodding at her.

Will, suddenly remembering his manners, stammered, "Uh, Captain Terry, I'd like to introduce you to my fiancée, Rebecca Kincaid."

"Pleased to meet you, Miss Kincaid." The captain took her hand and brought it to his lips. Will, standing beside Rebecca, felt a stab of jealousy as Rebecca flushed and giggled nervously.

"It's not often that we have someone as beautiful as yourself grace our post. If there is anything you need while you're here, please do not hesitate to ask."

Rebecca removed her hand from the captain's grasp. "Thank you, Captain. That's very kind of you."

Captain Terry led them to his office, stepping aside to allow Rebecca to enter first. Will followed, scowling at Terry's back as the officer went to his desk and pulled open one of the drawers. He retrieved a sheet of paper, and after filling in the proper spaces, signed his name and handed the paper to Tye.

"I believe you will find everything in order, Mr. Garrett. Just present this draft to the commanding officer at Fort Laramie and you'll be given your money."

Tye took the draft, and after looking it over carefully, folded it and put it in his shirt pocket. Then, extending his hand to the captain, he said, "Thank you, Captain Terry. We appreciate doing business with the army. Did you set up our little wager with the men?"

"They are anxiously awaiting you now at the north corral. I believe they have Ol' Brownie ready."

"Well, we shouldn't keep the men waiting, should we?" Tye asked, smiling.

As they left the office, Will took Rebecca's hand in his and guided her through the front door. Rebecca smiled to herself and squeezed Will's hand.

Captain Terry led them to the corral at the north end of the post. As they approached, they could see about thirty men gathered around. Some were already seated on the top rail of the fence in order to have a good view when the show began.

In the center of the corral stood a soldier holding a large brown horse. Will noted that the horse was really unimpressive, standing about fifteen hands tall, with too broad a chest and hindquarters and large hooves. His body was short and powerfully built, but he looked as if he would fit more into a harness than a saddle.

Will and Tye walked to the horse, looking him over from all angles.

The soldier holding the animal didn't say a word until they had finished their inspection, then remarked, "Ol' Brownie's really a sweetheart."

The brown horse stood stone still as Will and Tye walked around him. The soldier scratched and petted him and the horse's eyes began to close with pleasure.

"Let's go get your saddle, Will," Tye said as he looked suspiciously at the animal before him.

They walked down to the corral where Will had left his horse tied. Once out of hearing range of the crowd, Tye spoke in a low voice. "Something's not right about this. That horse is like a big ol' puppy. Did you see the saddle marks on him?"

"Yeah, I noticed 'em. Somebody's been riding that horse on a regular basis. He's been well cared for, too. Did you notice how good his coat looked, like it's been brushed regularly?"

"Uh-huh," Tye responded. "But I'll bet you my bottom dollar that horse can buck a blue streak."

"I reckon we're about to find out," Will commented, with a smile.

They walked toward the corral where the soldiers were waiting. The captain came forward as they approached and said, "The men have put together a sizable pot to wager against young Will here. They're willing to give you two-to-one odds that he can't ride Ol' Brownie to a standstill."

"How much have they got?" Will asked.

"Two thousand dollars," Captain Terry said, showing a roll of bills.

"Two thousand?" Tye asked, astonished at the amount. "Where in the world did soldiers get that amount of money?"

Captain Terry chuckled. "It seems they got some of their friends in town to invest a little of their money as well. And I don't mind telling you, I put a few dollars into the pot myself."

"I sure hope we don't get run out of town on a rail after I ride that horse of yours," Will commented, looking around at the soldiers lining the fence.

Captain Terry chuckled again. "I doubt you'll ride Ol' Brownie, but if you do succeed, I give you my word there will be no reprisals against you."

"What are the rules here?" Tye asked, as they made their way to the corral.

"Very simple," Captain Terry responded. "You are allowed one buck off. After that, if you fail to ride Ol' Brownie to a standstill, you lose."

"That's fair enough," Will responded. "Let's do it."

Will removed the saddle from his horse and carried it into the corral where the brown horse stood, looking as docile as a pet dog. Will placed his blanket and saddle on the horse's back and noticed that he stood as if it were an everyday experience to him. Once Will had the saddle on, the soldier handed him the reins and started walking away, but Will stopped him. "Just a minute."

The soldier stopped and turned back to Will.

"Will you hold him for me for a minute?"

The soldier, looking uncertain, walked back to the horse and took the reins from Will.

Will walked out of the corral to where his horse stood tied to the hitching post. Taking his lariat from the saddle, he slipped the hackamore from the horse's head and fashioned a halter from his lariat and tied the horse back to the hitching rail. Taking the hacka-more back to the corral, he slipped the bridle from Ol' Brownie's head and handed it to the soldier. Then he slipped his hackamore over Brownie's ears.

"I like to ride with my own rig," Will commented as the soldier looked at him. "Leather reins ain't much account on a bucking horse. You going to hold him for me while I get on?" Will asked.

"He don't need to be held," the soldier said, with a grin that hinted he knew something Will didn't.

Will was about to step into the saddle when he heard a commotion coming from the front gate of the fort. Stepping away from the horse, he watched as a procession of wagons and riders entered.

"What's this?" Tye asked as he looked up and saw the assemblage entering the gate.

There were three wagons loaded with men, women, and boys. Riding alongside were no less than twenty men mounted on horses.

"These are the people from town, coming to watch. I guess they want to check on their investment," Captain Terry said, with a smile.

Will waited in the center of the corral until all the people found themselves a viewing area and the grounds grew quiet.

"I feel like a rooster on parade," he mumbled to himself as he took the reins in his hand and mounted.

He fully expected the brown horse to explode beneath him when he settled in the saddle, but, to his surprise, nothing happened. The horse stood there, quiet as could be.

The crowd began to laugh at the sight of Will sitting there, his muscles tight, looking expectantly at Brownie's ears, his feet extended, ready for the first lunge. But Brownie just stood there, looking around as if this were an everyday occurrence and nothing more was expected of him.

Will, feeling like a fool, relaxed his seat, allowing his feet to hang at Brownie's sides.

Brownie still stood, totally unconcerned at the events taking place.

Tye and Rebecca exchanged glances, and Tye shrugged his shoulders.

Will sat in the center of the corral, and heard the laughter coming from the spectators. He clicked his tongue, hoping to draw a response from the horse beneath him, but Brownie just stood, totally unconcerned.

Will, feeling the humiliation of the laughter, dug his spurs into Brownie's sides. The next thing he knew, he was somersaulting off Brownie's rump, landing hard on his back in the packed dirt of the corral, the air knocked out of him.

The crowd was roaring with laughter as Will lay in the corral, trying to breathe. Catcalls and whistles reached his ears as he forced his lungs to suck in precious air.

A soldier led the brown horse up to him as he slowly came to his feet. His back felt as if it had been broken and his head hurt where it had come in contact with the ground.

Will looked up to see the soldier smiling at him and holding out the reins.

"You got one more chance, cowboy. Better make it a good one. These people came to see a show and they're going to be mighty disappointed if that's the best they get to see."

Will wanted to say he didn't give a hoot about what they wanted to see. All he wanted was to sit down until the pain in his head subsided. Instead, he just nodded and took the reins from the soldier and looked at the brown horse in front of him.

Brownie stood there as calmly as ever. No malice showed in his eyes as Will gazed at him. Will had expected to see the horse wild eyed and nervous, but there was none of that in the animal.

Will gathered up the reins and mounted the brown horse once again.

Tye stood watching through the corral fence. He was nervous as he thought about the wager they'd made. Will had already been thrown once. If it happened again, they would lose a thousand hard-earned dollars. He didn't blame Will. He doubted anyone could have stayed aboard Ol' Brownie in that situation. The horse had literally blown Will out of the saddle. Of course, Will had been relaxed, a mistake he wouldn't make again. But the power and quickness of the horse were amazing.

Will sat in the saddle, adjusting his mind and body to ride the horse. He knew when he touched the horse's sides, he was going to have to be ready, both mentally and physically.

Taking the reins in both hands and pulling Brownie's head up as far as he could, Will touched his spurs to the horse's sides. Instantly, Brownie snorted and leaped forward, his front feet coming off the ground, his back feet propelling him. The saddle horn was the only thing that kept Will from having a repeat of the previous ride. It was what cowboys call grabbing leather and Will grabbed for everything he was worth.

Brownie's front hooves came to the ground and Will felt himself being pushed forward by the power of the horse's hindquarters coming up into the air. Will fought to regain control and get in rhythm with the horse, but he was finding it a difficult thing to do. The left rein had slack, and his right hand, while holding the rein, was also holding the saddle horn in a desperate attempt to stay aboard.

He forced his mind to concentrate on the task before him. He willed himself to look at Brownie's ears and follow his direction. Glancing down, he worked the left rein through his fingers, taking the slack out of it. It took him three more jumps and a lot of punishment before he managed to get the rein tight in his hand. Using his left hand to pull himself into the saddle, he began working the right rein through his fingers, letting go of the saddle horn. This maneuver forced Brownie's head to the left and pulled him into a bucking circle, which was Will's intent. By keeping the horse turning left, it took the pressure off his right side, allowing him to work the rein up faster.

Brownie bellowed each time his front feet hit the ground. Will had his left spur dug into his side and was holding on for everything he was worth. Finally, he worked the slack out of the right rein and pulled himself down into the saddle. He released the pressure on the left rein, allowing Brownie to pull his head around and straighten out.

Will felt for the first time since mounting the horse that he had control of the situation. He had both reins now held tightly in his hands and was seated firmly in the saddle. Even though he'd taken some punishment during the first of the ride, he now felt he might finish.

Brownie leaped high in the air, twisting his body as he did. Since the horse was so short, the quick turns were more like a series of jerks, rather than smooth turns. These caused Will to move in the saddle more than he would have liked.

Each time the brown horse hit the ground, Will would dig in with his spurs. Brownie would then bellow and skyrocket forward, snapping Will's neck.

The crowd was shouting and yelling, cheering for the horse. Will heard their shouts through the din of sound about him, but he paid no attention to them. It was taking all his concentration to stay aboard the horse under him.

Rebecca watched from the top rail as Will fought to stay on Ol' Brownie. She could see that it was a punishing ride and it was beginning to take its toll on him. There was blood coming from his nose—no doubt a result of the stiff-legged jolts to the ground. She had never seen a horse leap so high in the air, nor come down so stiff legged when it hit. There was no give in the horse's legs when he hit the ground in the corral. His legs were so large and muscular, he could take the punishment without injuring himself. But how long could Will take that kind of punishment? She held her fist to her mouth as Will rode, biting into her hand each time the horse came down. She would gladly have paid the thousand dollars, if she had it, to end this ride now before Will got hurt any worse.

Twenty minutes into the ride, Will still felt no give in the brown horse. He was not riding well, for the horse had no rhythm. One time he would jump straight up, coming down hard. The next, he would spin, then lunge forward without warning, only to come to earth and jump either left or right. Each time the horse's feet hit the ground, Will would dig in his spurs, preparing for the next leap. Will knew he couldn't last much longer. His body was aching all over and the blood from his nose was getting into his eyes, making it difficult to watch the horse's head. He was going to lose, he knew that. No one could ride a horse such as this. . . . But someone did ride him. Why then did he buck the way he did?

Will's mind was churning. What made Ol' Brownie buck? Why could he be mounted and ridden? What made him change? Will was thinking fast, remembering the horse when he first sat him, and watching its head at the same time to be ready for the next jump.

Spurs! That's what it was! Brownie bucked when touched with spurs. The question now was, would he quit if Will quit using his spurs?

As the horse lunged again, Will held his feet away from his sides, not touching him as he hit the ground. This time, Brownie didn't bellow and Will thought he felt a slight difference in the horse's power.

It was all he could do to keep his spurs away from the horse's sides. It meant he had to change his entire riding style in midride. This threw him out of rhythm with the horse and made it even more difficult to remain seated, but Will knew it was the only way to win.

He was riding with pure strength now, using the power in his arms to hold himself in the saddle since he couldn't squeeze with his legs for fear of digging his spurs into the horse's flanks.

Brownie had taken four more leaps without the touch of the spurs and Will could definitely feel a difference. The anger was gone. There were no more angry bellows as the horse's hooves hit the ground. His bucks weren't as strong as they had been.

Will started talking to the horse as he fought his own awkwardness to remain in the saddle. "Easy, Brownie, easy boy. Hold up now, steady, whoa. That's it, easy now."

The brown horse slowed his leaps, blowing through his nostrils, releasing his rage. After three more half-hearted bucks, he brought up his head and stopped. Will groaned, but just sat there, feet well away from the horse's sides. After he was sure the horse wasn't going to buck anymore, he looked at Captain Terry and saw the captain nod. The ride was over.

Will tried to swing his leg over the horse's hips and found he didn't have the strength to lift it. Rebecca opened the gate and was running to his side, Tye right behind her.

"I can't lift my leg over," Will said, trying to smile.

"We'll give you a hand. Just slide off. I'll catch ya," Tye said.

"Not until you take my spurs off," Will said. "I don't want any more of what I just had."

"Spurs, huh?" Tye smiled. "So that's what made a gentle saddle horse turn into a mad bronc. I was wondering what you were doing there at the end."

Rebecca unbuckled Will's spurs, and then helped Tye hold him upright as he slid off Brownie's back. Will's knees wouldn't support him as he tried to stand. Rebecca held him on one side and Tye on the other until he could manage to stand.

"I'm walking out of here on my own," Will said. "Just give me a moment to catch my wind and still the shaking in my legs."

Rebecca and Tye continued to hold Will until the shaking left his body. Rebecca took her kerchief and wiped his face, spitting on the cloth to wash off the dried blood.

Finally, Will stood and walked to where the brown

horse was. He was obediently ground hitched and stood waiting patiently. Other than the sweat dripping from his coat, there was no sign from him that there had ever been a battle. He allowed Will to remove his saddle and hackamore, never giving the slightest sign that he distrusted the man who had ridden him.

Will removed his gear and, setting it aside, rubbed the horse's neck, talking in low tones to him as he did. Turning away, he picked up his gear and made his way to the gate, swaying slightly as he went.

Chapter Twenty-one

The crowd was silent as Will walked through the gate being held open by one of the soldiers. Rebecca and Tye followed him out.

"Captain," Will spoke, as he walked toward him, "I believe you're holding our money."

Captain Terry unbuttoned the breast pocket on his tunic, and taking the roll of bills, handed it to Will.

"You earned every penny of that money, young man. You're the only man to ride Ol' Brownie while wearing spurs. I didn't think you were going to catch on, but you fooled me. Me and a lot of other folks as well. You rode one heck of a ride though, before you figured it out. There's some folks here that were making side bets you wouldn't last the first five minutes."

"I almost didn't. I can easily say that is the toughest horse I've ever been on."

Captain Terry glanced at the people standing around the corral. No one had made a move to leave and concern clouded his eyes as he watched the crowd.

"You've created a small part of history for yourself here today," the captain continued. "Ol' Brownie has bucked off more than three hundred riders. Of course, not all of them were seasoned riders, but plenty of them were. I don't know how people are going to react to you now that you've ridden him. People around here put a lot of stock in having a legend in their midst. They might resent you for spoiling it."

Tye stepped in between Will and the captain. Staring into the commander's eyes, he spoke quietly.

"Captain, you gave us your word there'd be no trouble over this. Are you backing out of that promise now?"

"No, no, of course not. You have my word as an officer and a gentleman. No one will make a move against you. I was merely informing you that you might not be the most popular people around Bozeman."

Will looked at the people still gathered around the corral. Most of them were talking in low tones and watching him. He picked up his rig and walked over to where his horse was tied. Removing the lariat, he put the hackamore over the horse's head and began saddling him. His back was to the crowd and he didn't notice the three men coming up behind him until he heard one of them clear his throat.

"Humph."

Will turned around cautiously, wondering what to expect, but the three men standing there didn't look menacing. Actually, they looked friendly.

"What can I do for you, gentlemen?" Will asked, hesitantly.

"I think the question is more what can we do for you?" the tall man in the middle asked.

"What do you mean?" Will asked, confusion clouding his face.

"Son, you put on quite a show out there today, and even though most of us lost money on you, it was worth it to see you ride Ol' Brownie. Now we want to show you our hospitality. We hear you're plannin' on gettin' married tomorrow and we'd sure be happy if you'd allow us to give you and your bride a wedding reception after the ceremony."

Will stood staring at the three men, hardly believing his ears. "Uh, that would be great," he responded. "But let's not tell my fiancée about it. We'll let it be a surprise."

The three men smiled at Will's request. Then, one by one, they held out their hands and introduced themselves.

"I'm John Oates," the spokesman of the group said. "This here is Oatum Grant. Claims to be related to Ulysses S. Grant, but he cain't prove it. This other gent is Hiram Walker. He owns the Bozeman Emporium where you're staying."

Mr. Walker extended his hand and gripped Will's in a firm handshake. "Anything you need while staying with us, just be sure to ask."

Will nodded.

"By the way," Walker continued. "I'm taking the liberty of having your things moved to our finest suite while you're at the church tomorrow. Consider it a wedding present. And don't worry. I won't say anything to your fiancée. We'll let that be a surprise as well."

"Thank you, Mr. Walker. That's mighty nice of you."

"Why don't you come on over and let us introduce you to the rest of the townsfolk?"

Will followed the three men to the wagons where the other people from town were gathered. He met each of them, and each in turn expressed his appreciation of the ride he'd made.

Rebecca and Tye stood with Captain Terry and watched as Will went among the townsfolk, shaking hands with each. The fort commander shook his head and laughed. "It looks as if we were worried for nothing. Seems young Will has impressed everyone. I must say I am relieved to see they bear him no ill will. Why don't you come up to my office and we'll have some refreshments?" Even though the invitation was extended to both Rebecca and Tye, it was Rebecca the captain was looking at.

Rebecca smiled. Looking back into the captain's eyes, she replied, "Thank you very much, Captain, but I'm afraid we must be getting back to town. Tomorrow is my wedding day and I have preparations to make. You are, of course, invited to the wedding. I do hope you will come."

Captain Terry had the decency to redden at Rebecca's mention of her wedding. "I would be most delighted to attend. I was wondering, is there anyone to give the bride away?"

Rebecca stopped short, her heart catching as she thought about her parents. She recovered quickly, determined not to let anything spoil this joyous occasion. She responded, "No, there isn't, Captain. My parents are both deceased."

"I am sorry, Miss Kincaid. I did not mean to bring up unpleasant memories. I was wondering if you would allow me the honor of giving you away?"

Rebecca smiled. "I would be grateful, Captain Terry. Thank you for your kindness and your hospitality. I think we should be going. If we can pull Will away from his new friends."

The ride back to town was an agonizing one for Will. It seemed as if every bone in his body was bruised. What hurt the most was his tailbone where he'd slammed against the saddle trying to stay seated on Ol' Brownie. It was only later, after soaking in the hotel's bathtub, compliments of Hiram Walker, that the soreness began to leave his body. He fell asleep while soaking and woke only after Rebecca banged on his door so loudly the other guests came into the hall to see what the racket was about.

They ate an early supper in the hotel dining room, but the conversation was mainly between Rebecca and Tye, as Will's eyelids grew heavy. Rebecca laughed as Will fought to stay awake during dessert. Finally, she took Will by the hand and said, "Come on, cowboy. We'd better get you to bed. I don't want you falling asleep during the ceremony tomorrow."

"I've got to stop by the desk first," Will said, letting go of Rebecca's hand.

He caught up with Rebecca and Tye at the head of the stairs. Walking beside them, he smiled to himself.

"What are you so happy about?" Rebecca asked.

"It's just great to be alive. I rode the toughest horse of my life today, we made two thousand dollars, and tomorrow I'm marryin' the most beautiful girl in the world. What more could a man ask for?"

Rebecca kissed his cheek as they walked down the hallway to their rooms.

"How about a good night's sleep?" Tye asked.

"That would be good," Will responded, stopping in front of Rebecca's door.

"You did real good today, Will," Tye said. "I thought there for a while we'd lost a thousand dollars, but you came through and won. You know how much money we got now?"

"I figure somewhere around twelve thousand, but I haven't really been keeping up with it. You're the banker. I thought I'd let you handle that end of it. At least until you start getting too old and feeble to count. I reckon that'll be at least another year or two." Will grinned and Rebecca hid her mouth to suppress a giggle.

"We now have just over fifteen thousand dollars. The minimum we need to start our operation. If we can set up another two or three rides between here and Texas, we'll be in great shape. That is, if I can keep you two kids outa trouble long enough to make it outa here." He smiled as he unlocked the door to his room. "Ya'll get a good night's sleep. Tomorrow's your big day and I want it to be the best possible."

"Thanks, Tye," Will and Rebecca said simultaneously.

"Good night, you two," Tye said as he entered his room, chuckling to himself.

Will took the key from Rebecca and opened her door. Then, leaning down, he kissed her longingly before pulling away and whispering good night. He left her and opened the door to his room. He lay on his bed, thinking about the things that had happened that day and the things that lay ahead of him. He fell asleep with his clothes on, and was still dressed the next morning at six o'clock when the desk clerk knocked on his door.

Will opened his eyes and tried to block out the

pounding noise vibrating in his head. It took him several seconds to realize that the pounding was coming from the door. He rolled off the bed, groaning as the soreness in his body reminded him of his ride the day before. He opened the door to see the clerk standing in the hallway.

"It's six o'clock, sir."

"Thank you," Will said, fishing in his pocket for a tip. "Will you have the cook fix me steak and eggs for breakfast? I'll be down in about fifteen minutes."

"Yes, sir, Mr. Paxton. I'll see that it's taken care of."

Will closed the door, and then turned to the task of shaving and packing his clothes in his travel bag. After he had finished, he took a piece of hotel stationary and wrote Rebecca a brief note. He slipped it under her door as he walked by on his way to the dining room.

He was just finishing his breakfast when Tye entered the dining room.

"You're up awful early. What's the matter? You got the jitters or something?"

"Nope, just got some things I got to take care of before the weddin'."

"Need me to do anything for ya?" Tye asked.

"Just be there when the music starts playin'," Will said.

"I'll be there. Are you sure you're goin' to be there?" Tye asked with a mischievous grin.

"Wild horses couldn't keep me away. I've got to run. Got a lot to do. I'll see you in about three hours. If you see Rebecca, tell her I've gone to take care of some business, will ya?"

"I'll tell her you chickened out and ran away with one of the local dance hall girls. That'll fix ya up real good," Tye said, grinning wider at the thought.

"Thanks, partner," Will said. "I hope I can return the favor someday."

Will left the hotel, whistling a tune as he stepped through the front door. His first stop was the livery stable. He had a lot to do before one o'clock and it was going to be rushing things to get them all done.

At eleven thirty, Rebecca was pacing the floor in her room. She hadn't seen Will all morning and was beginning to wonder if perhaps he had decided to run away. The note he'd left said he would see her around eleven. She was considering asking Tye to go look for him when someone knocked on her door. She opened the door, expecting to find Will standing there. Instead, it was a delivery boy carrying a package.

"Miss Kincaid?"

"Yes," Rebecca replied.

"I was told to deliver this to you," he said, handing Rebecca the package.

"What is it?" Rebecca asked, her brow wrinkling in a questioning look.

"I have no idea, ma'am. I was just told to bring it to you."

Rebecca took the package, thanking the boy as she closed the door. She set the delivery on the bed and looked for a card. There was nothing to indicate where it had come from. She pulled the wrapping paper from the package to discover a long slender box beneath. Untying the string from around the box, she slowly lifted the lid to peer at its contents. As realization of what was inside struck her, tears streamed down her cheeks. She was trying to stop the flow of tears when another knock on the door drew her attention away from the package. Walking to the door, still dabbing at her tears, she opened it to find Will standing there, a grin on his face from ear to ear. Without saying a word, she threw herself into his arms, burying her face into his shirt.

Will stood there holding her, not knowing what had brought this about. He was wondering if she thought he might have changed his mind, when he spotted the box on the bed.

"Do you like it?" he asked.

"I love it," she said softly.

"Does it fit?"

Rebecca laughed. "I haven't tried it on yet. I haven't even taken it out of the box." She took him by the hand and led him into the room. She walked over to the package and pulled out the contents. Holding it up, tears started forming in her eyes again.

"How did you do it?" she asked.

"A man's got to have some secrets or else it takes away the appeal."

"You just better not have too many secrets," Rebecca said, laughing as she took the white wedding dress and held it in front of her. "How does it look?"

"You look beautiful," Will replied, staring at her as she held the dress to her body. "I've never seen anything more beautiful in my life." He pulled her to him, kissing her passionately. Rebecca responded, wrapping her arms around his neck and clinging to him as their lips met. The dress was crushed between them as they clung to each other.

A sharp intake of breath from the door took them by surprise and they broke apart as they realized the door had been left open. Standing in the hallway was an elderly couple. The woman wore a look of shock on her face, and was holding a handkerchief to her mouth. The man was openly gaping, apparently enjoying the scene before him.

Rebecca turned, holding the dress before her. "It's our wedding day!" she said, laughing.

Relief flooded through the lady's face. "Oh," she exclaimed. Then, almost timidly, she spoke to Will. "Young man, don't you know it's bad luck to see the bride before the wedding?"

Grinning, Will walked out the door, addressing the woman as he went. "No, ma'am, I sure didn't, but as you can see, a man would be hard pressed to stay away from something that beautiful. I'm sorry if we embarrassed you." The grin remained on his face as the couple smiled and nodded. Will watched them walk away. The man turned and smiled, giving Will a wink as he did.

Chapter Twenty-two

If Will was surprised at the number of people who attended the wedding in the small Methodist church, shock could be the only word to describe what Rebecca felt as she entered the front door and saw the packed pews and people standing in the aisles.

"Where did all these people come from?" she asked Tye as he led her into the church.

"I told them Will was a famous evangelist. They've come to hear him preach," Tye said, keeping a straight face.

Rebecca covered her mouth to smother the laughter that threatened to bubble out. "I'd like to see that myself," she said as Tye left to join Will at the front of the church. Will was wearing a new black suit, with a new white shirt and string tie. His boots were polished and his hair was slicked down. She noticed he had even gotten a haircut this morning.

Captain Terry led her down the aisle and placed her hand in Will's, then stepped back as the minister began to speak.

Rebecca tried to follow the ceremony, but the butterflies in her stomach prevented her from concentrating as she leaned on Will for support. She remembered Captain Terry giving her away and remembered answering the preacher as he asked her questions. Then Will slipped a beautiful gold band on her finger. She stared at the ring as it reflected the light from the candles on the altar. Then Will was taking her in his arms and kissing her and walking her down the aisle to the bright sunshine outside.

The reception, planned and held by the townspeople, was held in the theater where, only a few nights ago, Rebecca, Will, and Tye had watched a play.

The women had gone all out in their planning and preparation. There was food of every kind and lots of presents for the bride, most of them handmade by the women themselves, and even a wedding cake that was large enough for everyone to get a piece.

Someone had brought a guitar, while another had brought a banjo. A fiddle was pulled from its case and soon there was music being played while the floor was cleared for dancing.

Will stood beside Rebecca as she opened each of her gifts, tears of joy filling her eyes as she smiled and laughed. Will felt as if he were going to choke to death in the stiff collar and was relieved when his new bride, noticing his discomfort by the redness of his face, stood up and loosened the button on the starched collar.

Will took a deep breath, rubbing his neck where the collar had dug into it. "Now I know how it feels to be hung."

The party was still going strong when Will, after dancing another waltz with Mrs. Walker, spotted Rebecca alone at the punch bowl and made his way to her. He had sought out a young boy earlier and whispered something in his ear, then handed him a quarter. The boy shoved the coin in his pocket and made his way through the crowd to the front door. Will waited until he saw the boy return and give him a nod before saying to Rebecca: "I still haven't given you your wedding present."

Rebecca looked at him, searching his face to see if he was joking. "You have given me the greatest gift I could ever hope to have," she said, with such emotion Will had to swallow before he could speak.

"Well, I have another one for you."

"What is it, Will?" Rebecca asked excitedly.

"Are you ready to leave?"

"Heavens, yes! I've been ready to leave for the last

hour. My feet are killing me, tops and bottoms. I've had my toes stepped on so many times tonight, it may be a week before I can put on a pair of boots."

"Let's find Mr. Oates and thank him before we leave," Will said, looking around the room and spotting him.

Will almost regretted his decision to thank John Oates. As soon as he said good night, Mr. Oates quieted the crowd to announce their intentions. This caused a pandemonium of shouts, cheers, and a few comments that made both Will and Rebecca blush.

"Now, now," Mr. Oates said, smiling. "Let's wish this young couple a prosperous and healthy life." With that, he lifted his glass in a toast, smiling at Will and Rebecca.

They had to shake hands with everyone as they left and Will didn't think they were ever going to make it out the front door. But finally they were through the crowd and outside.

The sun was starting to sink low in the west when they stepped through the doors, waving to the last of the well-wishers. Will took hold of Rebecca's hand and led her down the steps of the theater.

Standing at the hitching rail was the gray stallion Will had ridden at the Landsings'. "I promised you I would give him to you as a wedding present. Remember?"

"I thought you'd forgotten," Rebecca said, smiling in delight as she walked up to the horse.

"Nope, I've just been breaking him in for you. He's still got a ways to go, but I figure you can handle him."

Rebecca looked at the beautiful animal standing there. As her eyes took in the saddle on its back, she turned to Will, a questioning look on her face.

"I didn't reckon you'd want to ride a western saddle with a wedding gown on, so I had the livery stable put a sidesaddle on for you."

"You mean I can ride him now?" Rebecca asked excitedly.

"That's what I planned on," Will said, untying the reins and handing them to her. Rebecca didn't hesitate, but took the reins from his hand and with Will lending a hand, she was soon seated on the stallion's back. Will stepped to the next hitching rail and untied the large bay he always rode. It was the first time Rebecca had noticed the horse standing there, and it brought a smile to her lips as she realized the plans Will had made.

People on the dusty street turned to stare as Rebecca, in her long wedding dress, and Will, in his black suit, rode side by side, oblivious to those around them. Many smiles followed them as they rode out of town, heading toward the open range, following the setting sun.

Will and Rebecca spent most of the next day riding the countryside around Bozeman. The hotel had packed them a lunch that included a bottle of wine. They found a cottonwood grove at noon and stopped to eat the lunch and drink the wine. It was a relaxed time as they planned their future, talking of things they both wanted and reveling in each other's company.

Meanwhile, Tye was busy preparing for their departure the next day. He loaded up the supplies Rebecca had arranged for at the local mercantile. He went to the bank and withdrew the funds they had deposited in the safe and placed them in the hotel safe for the night, making arrangements to remove them early the next morning. Then he rode out to the ranch where the remaining horses were being held and, after paying the rancher for caring for them, he drove them back to the livery stable where he'd made arrangements to keep them for the night.

Completing all the preparation for the trip, he decided to do a little shopping for himself, buying new shirts, new jeans, a new pair of boots, and a new hat.

It was late afternoon when he paid for his purchases

at the mercantile and stepped through the door and onto the wooden walkway. Shading his eyes against the setting sun, he glanced up and down the street, then started walking toward the hotel. He didn't notice the two men in blue uniforms following him. As he stepped down from the walk to cross an alley, the two men closed the distance. One of the men walked up on Tye's left side and, as they came abreast of the alley, he quickly turned and pushed Tye into the area between the buildings. The other soldier glanced quickly around, making sure no one saw, and stood guard at the head of the alley.

Tye cursed himself as he staggered and almost fell. He should have seen the men. He had dropped the packages as he stumbled. Regaining his balance, he wheeled to meet his attackers, but one soldier stepped close and swung as Tye came around. The blow crashed into the side of his head. The soldier's swing was short and without full power, but lights exploded in Tye's head, and he staggered backward, flailing his arms to balance himself. The man didn't give him a chance. He came in swinging a roundhouse blow aimed at Tye's head. Tye saw the swing coming and, though he was off balance, he managed to bring his arm up and partially deflect it. Even still, the large fist glanced off the top of his head, sending pain shooting through him. Tye planted his feet and shook his head. It was going to take all his skill and wits to come out of this alive.

"Come on, Clyde," the soldier who had hit Tye, yelled.

"I'm coming. I just wanted to make sure no one saw us come in here." The other soldier came into the alley.

Tye looked around the alley they were in. It was a dead end with buildings on three sides. There were no windows in any of the buildings that he could use for escape. The only way out was through the two soldiers standing before him. He glanced around for some sort of weapon he might use. His pistol was back in the hotel room and he cursed himself again for leaving it there. The two soldiers before him both carried side arms.

They had drawn back from him a little in order to set themselves before beginning their attack.

"Why are you doing this?" Tye asked, knowing the reason, but trying to buy some time.

"You took our money the other day. We don't like losing. Now we want it back," the soldier who had hit Tye said.

"I don't have it with me. It's at the hotel. Let me go get it and I'll give it back to you," Tye said, knowing they wouldn't agree to it, but he was buying time, his mind working all the while.

The soldier doing the talking threw back his head and laughed, but there was no humor in it. "Sure, we're just going to let you walk outa here and go get our money for us. You must think we're stupid, mister."

A smile came across Tye's lips and his eyes closed slightly.

"Well, now that you mention it, I guess I do think you're stupid."

Both men stiffened at Tye's words. The one named Clyde spoke first. "Lyle, I think this gent needs to be taught a lesson." He started forward, but the one named Lyle put out an arm and restrained him.

"He's mine!"

Lyle stood two inches taller than Tye and outweighed him by at least thirty pounds. Tye could see the paunch around his middle and knew that he was soft from lack of work.

Tye stood relaxed, his arms hanging loose at his sides, the smile still on his face.

Lyle moved toward Tye, drawing his arms up as he moved. Tye could see he was confident in his size and power as he came closer.

Lyle stepped to within four feet of Tye and then,

lunging, he swung a large fist at Tye's head. Tye saw
the blow coming and ducked under the blow. He had
set his feet as he ducked and as the punch sailed harm-
lessly over his head, he brought his own fist from the
ground into Lyle's stomach. He had the satisfaction of
hearing the air whoosh from the soldier's lungs as he
set himself and threw a short punch to the jaw. Lyle
went down, but rolled and came to his feet. Tye had
turned to watch Clyde, ensuring that the other soldier
was not coming in. Clyde had started forward upon
seeing his companion hit the ground, but had backed
off as Tye turned toward him.

Lyle came off the ground in a lunge, driving his
head into Tye's stomach, knocking the air from his
lungs and forcing him into the building behind him.
Tye felt a stab of pain as the impact with the building
jarred his backbone.

Lyle stepped back to set himself. Tye had just an
instant to raise his arm and block the roundhouse
blow as it came at his head. The raised arm partially
deflected the blow, but the main force caught Tye
above the ear, making his head ring and knocking him
to his knees.

Lyle smiled wickedly. Seeing his opponent on the
ground, he raised his foot to aim a kick at Tye's
midsection.

The haze cleared from Tye's vision as Lyle brought
his foot back. Tye saw his opportunity and swung another right to Lyle's midsection. The blow was timed
perfectly. As Lyle's foot came off the ground, Tye's
fist connected to the spot above his buckle. Lyle's face
lost its color as he bent over, gagging for air.

Tye wasted no time. Coming to his feet, he swung
an uppercut to Lyle's nose, feeling the bones crush
under the force.

Lyle's head snapped back, his eyes starting to glaze,
but Tye didn't wait. He stepped in and threw two
wicked blows to the smashed nose, feeling bones
crunch with each blow as it connected. He swung an-

other fist to Lyle's stomach, then pivoted on his heel and drove a wicked punch to his kidneys. The large man groaned and tried to straighten, but Tye had already moved to his left and timed a swinging blow to Lyle's jaw. Then he swung around to face Clyde as he saw the light go out in Lyle's eyes.

Clyde was standing there, his mouth hanging open, his face registering disbelief at what he had just witnessed. When Tye turned toward him, realization struck him and he started clawing for the revolver at his side. As the pistol came out of its holster, Tye's hand clamped on Clyde's wrist, preventing him from bringing it up. Tye grabbed the pistol with his free hand and twisted it from Clyde's grip. Then throwing it aside, he swung a short jab to Clyde's mouth, feeling a small amount of satisfaction as he saw blood gush from the cut lips. The man hit the ground, holding his arms in front of his face and cowering.

"Don't hit me. It was his idea," he said, pointing to Lyle's prone figure.

Tye retrieved the pistol from where he'd thrown it and turned back to Clyde, leveling the barrel at him. Clyde threw up his arms, closing his eyes and turning his head away from Tye. Whimpers came from him as he began to beg. "Please, don't shoot me. I didn't want to do it. He made me come along. I promise."

Tye looked at the quaking figure with disgust. "Get up. I'm not going to shoot you."

Clyde opened one eye and looked cautiously at Tye, seeing the pistol was not aimed at him, but held loosely at his side. He lowered his arms and tried to regain a little of his dignity. "What are you gonna do?" he asked, his voice sounding more fretful.

"I'm turning you over to the local authorities. They can hold you until Captain Terry comes for you. I reckon he'll deal with you properly, since he gave his word there would be no action taken against us. Now get to your feet."

Clyde pushed himself to his feet, staggering slightly as he stood.

"Pick up your friend over there and let's go," Tye said, motioning with the barrel of the pistol.

Clyde walked over to where Lyle lay on the ground, looking warily at the pistol in Tye's hand.

"Pick him up and let's go," Tye repeated.

Clyde pulled Lyle's inert form to a standing position. Then he bent slightly, allowing Lyle to fall over his shoulder. It was all he could do to straighten under the load. He staggered under the weight, looking pitifully at Tye, but the motion of the pistol told him there was nothing to do but start walking.

Tye fell in behind Clyde as he started out of the alley, bending to retrieve his fallen packages. He kept the pistol leveled at Clyde's back.

It was this strange procession as Tye marched his prisoners down the street to the sheriff's office. People stopped to stare at the spectacle as Clyde staggered under his load, while Tye walked behind, carrying his packages.

The door to the sheriff's office was standing open. As Clyde maneuvered his load through the opening, a man wearing a tin star on his vest and a surprised look on his face came swiftly to his feet.

"What the . . .?" he exclaimed, coming around his desk and facing the three.

"It seems these two decided they didn't like the way things came out at the fort the other day, so they decided they'd rearrange my face and body a little to make up for it," Tye said, still holding the gun on Clyde. "I thought I'd bring 'em to you and let you hold 'em till Captain Terry could collect 'em."

"You pressing charges, Mister?" the sheriff asked.

"I am," Tye responded. "If you'll send someone to the fort with a message to Captain Terry, we can probably get this taken care of right now."

The sheriff looked thoughtfully at Tye. Then, walking to the open door, he looked around until he spotted the person he was looking for.

"Sam, Sam, come here. I got an errand for you."

A boy of about thirteen came running at the sheriff's call, and a few minutes later was mounted on a horse, galloping out of town toward the fort.

Clyde was standing in the center of the office, Lyle's limp form still on his shoulder. "What do I do with him?" he asked plaintively.

"I ought to make you hold him till the captain arrives," the sheriff said. "Because of you, I'm gonna be late for supper. My wife's gonna be madder'n a wet hen. Put him in the cell over there."

When the sheriff had both prisoners locked up, he turned to Tye. "Looks like they got a few blows in on ya. You might ought to have the doc look at that cut on your head."

Tye reached up and felt his scalp where Lyle's big fist had connected. He felt the blood that had started to dry, matting his hair. His fingers came away red and he rubbed them on his pants leg. "I'll be all right. I'm going to my room at the hotel and clean up a little. I'll be back before the captain arrives."

The sheriff just nodded as he threw the keys to the cell on the desk.

Captain Terry arrived an hour later with a two-man escort. He listened as Tye told his side of the story, then asked the two men in the cell for their version. Lyle attempted to lie his way out of it and might have been convincing had it not been for Clyde breaking down and telling the truth.

The prisoners were led handcuffed from the jail. As they were placed on their mounts, Captain Terry turned to Tye.

"Please accept my apology for this incident, and rest assured these two will be dealt with in the strictest manner possible."

Tye smiled at the captain. "I just hope there aren't any more of your men who are upset over losing. I don't think I could take another battle like this one."

"After what happens to these two, I don't think you'll have to worry," the captain said, looking after the departing soldiers. He held out his hand and Tye shook it. He stood watching as the captain rode out of town, then walked back to the hotel. He felt in need of a hot bath and a soft bed.

Chapter Twenty-three

Rebecca stretched and yawned as Will tickled her nose with the feather he'd pulled from the pillow. The sun was still two hours from rising and the moonlight reflected through the window, casting a warm glow across the bed.

Will smiled as Rebecca wriggled her nose, fighting to stay asleep. He couldn't blame her. It had been late in the night before they had finally drifted off to sleep. His smile deepened as he thought about their second night together. The nervousness they had felt on the first night was gone, replaced by a new closeness.

"Wake up, sleepyhead," Will said, shaking Rebecca slightly. "We've got to meet Tye in half an hour and you haven't even packed yet."

Rebecca opened her eyes, smiling up into Will's face. "I don't ever want to leave this wonderful bed."

"I'm afraid it would be hard to carry you and the bed all the way to Texas."

Rebecca laughed, wrapping her arms around him. She pulled him down and kissed him longingly.

Tye was waiting in the dining room when Will and Rebecca descended the stairs. "I thought I was going to have to come up and get you two. I waited to order breakfast. Are you two hungry, or are you still living on love?"

"You sure know how to ask a loaded question, don't you?" Will asked, smiling.

"Well, I'm still in love, but I'm starving to death," Rebecca said. Looking closely at Tye, she asked, "What happened to your head?"

Tye reached a hand up to touch his scalp. "Oh, nothing much. Just a couple of soldiers who were a little upset over Will riding their horse. Seems they didn't care too much for us walking away with their money and decided to take it back. I convinced them that wasn't a smart thing to do."

Will looked questioningly at him, but Tye had already turned to his menu and was studying it. The subject was closed.

Will picked up his menu and asked, "How long do you reckon it'll take us to reach your place in Texas?"

Tye looked up from his menu. "I figure it'll take us about five weeks. That'll put us there about the middle of September. We won't have much time to prepare for winter, but the winters aren't that bad there. And it's not my place. It's *our* place! We're partners now!"

Will and Rebecca looked at each other, surprise showing on both their faces. Will was the first to speak. "I knew we were partners in the horses, but that land belongs to you."

"It belongs to us. We're partners. You two own forty-nine percent of everything. I've written it all down and I plan to file it as soon as I get to Texas," Tye said.

"I don't know what to say," Will responded.

"There's nothing to say," Tye said. "We're partners. We work together and split everything. Now let's order breakfast and get on down the trail."

They left Bozeman as the sun was coming up. Tye was leading the packhorse and the scarred mare. Will and Rebecca brought up the rear.

They traveled south into Wyoming, keeping to the flat lands as much as possible. The only Indians they saw were a small band moving east. They held up until they were out of sight. Then Tye altered their course to skirt wide around them.

They rode into Fort Laramie twelve days after leaving Bozeman. Tye presented his voucher for the horses sold at Fort Ellis, and the quartermaster paid without question.

They stopped in Cheyenne for two days, spending two nights in a hotel. All three enjoyed the layover, but were ready to take to the trail on the third day.

They crossed into Colorado, north of Fort Collins and stopped to gather information about the southern trails and any Indians in the area. Fifty miles north of Denver, they stopped at a ranch owned by Sam Starr. He had settled in the area ten years before and was building himself a nice spread.

Sam's wife, Katie, took Rebecca under her wing and the two of them spent the evening looking over the gifts Rebecca had received in Bozeman and talking about the wedding.

The next day, Will rode a bronc that had bucked off several good riders. The ride added another two hundred dollars to their roll, and all the hands talked Will into riding another horse, exhibition only.

They left at noon the following day. Rebecca promised to write the Starrs once they reached Texas.

They spent one night in Denver, enjoying the excitement of the booming city, but eager to be on their way.

Tye led them southeast out of Denver. There were fewer towns this way, but the plains were rolling and this route missed the mountains, which meant there was less chance of running into Cheyenne Indians that way. William Bent's half-breed sons were still leading their band of renegades against the white settlers, making travel hazardous in the mountainous regions of Colorado.

They passed through Las Animas, spending two nights in town while Tye had the blacksmith shoe

several of their saddle horses. This task would fall
to Will and Tye once they reached Texas, but for
now, they didn't have the time or the tools.

They crossed the Oklahoma panhandle, breathing
the dust as the dry, arid earth blew across the plains,
coating everything in its path and blinding those who
rode against it.

They arrived in Texas three weeks after leaving
Bozeman. The wind and dust still blew as they continued their southward journey toward Austin.

They made camp on the south bank of the Canadian River. There were makeshift holding pens here
that were used by ranchers in the area to hold their
cattle before swimming the river. After grazing the
horses for a while, they herded them into the pens
for the night.

Rebecca cooked up a stew with some potatoes,
jerked beef, and wild onions. It tasted as good as the
steak they had eaten in Bozeman.

The night breeze was blowing through the long
prairie grass, making the plains come alive as if in a
slow, willowy dance.

Will walked to the river and washed the evening
dishes as Tye took one last look at the horses.

As they all settled down to enjoy the warmth of
the fire, Rebecca looked to Tye and asked, "How
much longer till we reach Austin?"

Tye studied the grass stem he was chewing on before answering. "It'll probably take us another two
and a half to three weeks, if everything goes right."

Rebecca's face registered disbelief and Will looked
up in surprise.

"But I thought you said we were in Texas,"
Rebecca said.

Tye chuckled. "We are! But Texas is a big state
and we're at the very top of it. We have a long ways
to go to reach Austin."

Rebecca looked crestfallen as she heard the news.

Tye, noting her look of disappointment, asked,
"You're not gettin' tired of travelin', are you?"

"Yes, I am!" Rebecca stated boldly. "I'm ready to get someplace and start buildin' a home. I want to sit on something that's not moving for a change."

Will and Tye both laughed at her outburst, and Rebecca couldn't help but grin, though her words were spoken in earnest.

Tye looked thoughtful for a moment, then said, "It's going to take a while to build a home. The houses out here are built out of adobe bricks. That's mud and straw mixed together and formed into a brick, then dried in the sun. We'll have to find us some Mexicans who can make 'em. That may be the hardest part."

Rebecca looked surprised once again. "You mean there's no house on the land now? I thought this was your family's place?"

She had spoken the last softly, almost reverently, understanding the need to tread softly on the subject.

Tye had never spoken of his family or his past, and Rebecca had seen pain in his eyes each time she had broached the subject.

Tye stared into the fire, not answering Rebecca's question. She felt pangs of guilt for bringing up the matter and was trying to think of a way to change the subject when Tye spoke. "My father was one of the first settlers to come into Texas with Stephen Austin. He came first, leaving my mother, sister, brother, and one slave in Louisiana until he had established a homestead. I wasn't born at the time.

"He received fourteen hundred and eighty acres under the grant laws of the colony. That was six hundred and forty for him, three hundred and twenty for my mother, one hundred and forty for my sister, and the same for my brother, plus eighty acres for each slave. He had three slaves at the time.

"My father was a visionary. He established his claim in 1823. With the help of the two slaves with him, he built a cabin for the family, a barn for the livestock, and slave quarters. Leaving the slaves to tend to the land in Texas, he returned to Louisiana and brought his family back. But before he left for Texas, he traded the one slave in Louisiana for sixty-five head of cattle. He somehow managed to trade for another fifty head before they left Louisiana. My mother drove the wagon, while my brother, sister, and father drove the cattle to Texas.

"Cattle were scarce in Texas in those days. There were plenty of wild horses roaming the ranges. These horses were descendants of horses brought to Mexico by Cortez in the early 1500s. During the first years, as many as one hundred horses were eaten by the early settlers and, of course, everyone owned several head.

"The land cost each settler twelve and a half cents per acre, but most of the settlers couldn't even afford that much.

"My father was selling beef to the Mexicans in San Antonio at twenty-five to thirty dollars a head, delivered. It was a dangerous journey between Austin and San Antonio in those days. There were several tribes of hostile Indians roaming the plains, and there was no protection in the beginning. My brother was killed by Caranchahua Indians during one of the drives. I never met him, but my mother had a lithograph of him that she kept on the mantel.

"My father claimed more land under the Mexican Colonization law of 1823. This allowed him forty-four hundred more acres, since he was running cattle. He was one of the few who could afford to pay the twelve and a half cents per acre. The rest bartered with corn, cattle, and swine, or just failed to pay. It made things very difficult for Stephen Austin, who was responsible for payments to Mexico.

"There was continuing strife between Texas and Mexico, as Mexico changed leaders, and leaders changed the laws governing Texas. My father was caught in the middle many times because he traded with the Mexicans, but his loyalties were always with the Texans. He fought for Texas independence and was with Houston at the San Jacinto River where Santa Anna was defeated.

"After Texas won her independence from Mexico in 1836, my father came home to tend to his land. He had spent much of his money helping finance the Texas army, but he had managed to hold on to some of it. My mother and sister had managed to keep things going with the help of the two slaves. They had planted corn, potatoes, and cotton in my father's absence and had managed to take care of things properly. My father freed the two slaves, keeping them with him and paying them wages. He continued to raise beef and eventually was able to ship it to New York from Galveston.

"Ten years after Texas won her independence, I came along. I was a total surprise to both my father and mother. My father was in his fifties by this time and my mother was in her late thirties, but my younger brother coming three years later was even more of a surprise. My older sister had married by the time I came along. She and her family had built a house on my father's land. Her husband was helping him with his business. By now, my father had acquired over nine thousand acres, some of it farmland, but most of it was used for grazing cattle."

Tye quit talking and was staring into the flames. Will and Rebecca remained quiet, each wondering if Tye would continue, or if there were memories too painful to talk about.

Without looking up, Tye continued. "I met Robin on a trip to San Antonio. She was the daughter of a shopkeeper where we bought supplies. We fell in love and married three months later. I had just turned seventeen and she was sixteen. The War Between the States had been going for two years, but we had taken no part in it. It seemed so remote to us. My father didn't agree with Secession, but he wouldn't fight against Texas.

"I was restless at that age. I loved my wife and wanted to be with her, but I had to have excitement as well. By now, my father's operation had grown quite large and, even with the war going on, he was managing to ship beef to New York. He was using contacts on both sides to get the beef through and sometimes he would receive payments in Confederate currency and sometimes in Union dollars. It was a dangerous game he was playing, but I think that's the reason he did it.

"I started making the trail drives to Galveston. I was ramrod, and the excitement of being on the trail was just what I needed. We fought Comanches, rustlers, and Confederate deserters, but we always got the herd through." Tye's voice broke as he continued. "I was away on one of the drives when our place was hit by Comanches. They came early one morning as the sun was coming up. We hadn't had any trouble with them for quite some time, which should have been warning enough. So the defenses were slack and they hit unexpectedly. My father was killed in the first rush, along with my older sister and her husband. They killed four of the six hired hands in that rush. They burned the house where my wife, mother, and younger brother were holed up. They stood back and shot arrows into them as they ran out of the burning house. My wife and mother weren't dead when the Comanche found them. Robin was three months pregnant with our first baby. It was a boy. I know because they had cut her open and taken the baby out."

Rebecca gasped as Tye related the events of his wife and unborn son's death.

"There were four survivors of that raid: the two Negroes that had been slaves and two hired hands. The Indians had burned all the buildings, and run off most of the stock. When I returned and saw what had happened, I tried to go on, but I had no heart to rebuild. I blamed myself for Robin's death. If I hadn't been gone, maybe I could have made a difference. At least, if I'd been there, I could've died with her. It would have been better than living without her. I left the place in care of some longtime family friends, who promised to look after it until I returned, if I ever did. I joined the Texas Rangers to help fight the Indians until I could quench my guilt and hatred. I traveled north, riding for various ranches, breaking horses and working cattle. The horses are really what saved me. They brought back to life something that had died. Anyway, I wound up in Montana and when Will here showed up, he reminded me of myself. I started getting homesick for Texas. The rest you know."

Will and Rebecca glanced at one another. There were tears in Rebecca's eyes and a lump in each of their throats.

"It must have been awful for you," Rebecca said.

"It was, but you two have made it easier. I've never told anyone about my past before this. It feels good to get it out. I think it means I'm about over it."

Tye still stared into the fire, memories of the past flooding his thoughts, but at least they didn't torment him as they once had. They didn't enter his dreams and cause him to wake in a cold sweat, yelling Robin's name.

Will watched Tye, noting the look on his face. He had seen the anguish there as Tye talked about his family But now that anguish was gone, replaced by a look that was sad, but at the same time peaceful.

"What kind of shape do you think the place is in?" Will asked.

"I don't know for sure, but I'd say it was going to need a lot of work. The Burkes have been keeping an eye on it for me, but no one has worked the place since I left. I don't know what became of the two Negroes. I reckon they drifted once I left."

"Well," Will said, with a grin, "I reckon we'll find

out in a couple more weeks if we can keep Rebecca in the saddle."

Rebecca gave Will a look of indignation. "I've managed to stay in the saddle this far. I figure I can make it the rest of the way without any problems."

"Well, we better turn in for the night," Tye said, "or none of us will be able to stay in the saddle tomorrow."

Chapter Twenty-four

As they continued their southward journey, Rebecca and Will noted how the country around them changed daily. Leaving the flat prairie of the Texas panhandle behind them, they moved into rolling plains, sparsely covered with mesquite bushes.

The night had been cool when they had crossed the Canadian River, but as they traveled southward, the nights and days became warmer.

They had been following the Chisholm Trail since crossing into the panhandle, so it was no surprise when they encountered a large herd of cattle being brought up from San Antonio. It gave them a chance to catch up on the news from Austin and surrounding areas. Tye was pleased to find the Texas Pacific railroad had laid track to Austin the year before. It meant Austin would grow. Already, there was a large migration of people from the southern states causing Austin to boom.

Reconstruction since the war was officially over, though Texas wasn't as devastated by the fighting as most of the other Southern states, since no major battles had been fought within her boundaries.

No one with the herd had any news about the area where Tye's ranch was located. There was talk of outlaws roaming the area: Confederate outcasts with no homes to return to, had turned to rustling and looting to survive.

Rebecca sat by the fire, listening to the men talk of the changes taking place. An excitement filled her as she thought of the challenges facing them in this vast land with opportunity for those bold enough to tackle it.

Will listened with half an ear as he watched the glances from the cowhands being directed toward his new wife. His attention was grabbed when he heard the ramrod mention a bad horse they had acquired.

"I got him with a bunch I bought back down the trail. I've been tempted to shoot him on several occasions. He stampeded the herd once when he bucked into the middle of 'em. He broke the leg of one of the best hands I had. I had to leave him back down the trail. It's left me shorthanded."

"Sounds like a bad one," Tye said.

"He's as bad as I've seen."

"I'll bet ya five hundred dollars Will over there can ride him," Tye said.

Will looked up in total surprise. He hadn't expected to find a ride out here in the middle of the plains.

"If I had five hundred dollars, I'd take that bet," the ramrod said.

Tye shrugged. "Too bad. I think it would have been an interesting match. I don't suppose your hands would want to wager anything?"

The ramrod threw back his head and laughed. "I doubt you could find two dollars between the lot of 'em. I gave 'em a two-day layover in Austin and they spent all their money doin' the town."

Tye glanced in the direction of the herd as a thought came to him. "You own any of these cattle you're pushing?"

Tye saw a veiled look come over the man's eyes. Then, with a grin, he said, "Yeah, I own about four hundred head."

"What are they worth?" Tye asked.

"About thirty dollars a head delivered to the rail-head in Kansas."

"You got any cows in the herd, or are they all steers and bulls?"

"There's probably a hundred cows," he said.

"How about you put up forty head of cows against our five hundred dollars?" Tye asked, watching the man closely. He could see his mind working as he thought about the wager.

"Those cows would be worth twelve hundred dollars in Abilene," the ramrod said.

"But you're not in Kansas yet, and you've got a long ways to go. Besides, if that horse is as bad as you say, then you'll be five hundred dollars ahead."

The cowman was mulling it over when one of the hands sitting by the fire said, "Come on, Lou, I want to see Ol' Strawberry throw this feller here."

"All right, you got yourself a bet, mister. We'll hold up long enough in the morning for this young feller to give it a try."

Tye, Will, and Rebecca left shortly after dawn the next morning, driving forty head of cattle behind the horse herd.

Tye wasn't sure they were going to leave without a fight. Lou had ranted and raved about being taken advantage of. It was beginning to look as if he wasn't going to cut out the forty cows, until three of the hands rode in and started cutting the herd, in spite of Lou's scowling face.

When they had driven the cattle and horses four miles, Tye pulled up and rode back to where Will and Rebecca were pushing the stragglers.

"That was a good ride you put on back there. How do you feel?"

"Fine," Will said. "That horse couldn't hold a candle to Ol' Brownie."

"Nope, but he was still a rank horse and you rode him to a standstill," Tye said. The pride he felt was reflected in his voice.

"You reckon we'll be able to find horses like that to ride when we reach Austin?" Will asked. " 'Cause I sure wouldn't want to sit around getting fat and lazy."

"I reckon we can find us some broncs to play with. But you sure won't have time to get fat and lazy. We're going to be busy for a long time just getting things in order and turning the place back into a working ranch."

Two weeks later, they came within sight of Austin. Rebecca couldn't contain her excitement as she looked at the town before her. "It's just as I imagined it would be," she said.

Tye let his gaze roam over the city. "It's grown quite a bit since I was last here. It's bound to grow even bigger over the next few years, with the railroad being here and the number of Southerners looking for a better place to live."

"How far is our place from here?" Will asked.

"About twelve miles west," Tye answered, noting Will's use of the word "our." It gave him a good feeling to know Will now accepted the fact that they were partners. "I want to see a few people in town. We'll spend the night and head out to the ranch tomorrow."

Tye rode on ahead to find a suitable place to hold the stock. Rebecca and Will stayed with the herd. While they were waiting for Tye to return, they let the horses and cattle graze on the lush prairie grass and rode out a short distance to inspect the surrounding land.

"It is beautiful," Rebecca commented.

"I remember Clement tellin' me how Texas didn't have the mountains, but it still had beauty of its own. I see what he meant now. Looking at all this makes me feel kind of small; but, at the same time, it makes me feel like I could do anything."

"I think you could do anything," Rebecca said. "Providing you have the right woman with you to make sure you do it right." She laughed at her words.

Will grinned and said, "Well, it looks as if nothing can stop me then, 'cause I sure picked the right woman."

Tye returned in less than an hour, having found a place to hold the cattle and horses for the night. He led them into Austin. Riding up to a livery stable, he stepped down and hailed the proprietor. A man walked slowly out of the barn, looking them over as he came.

"What can I do for you?"

Tye looked at the man for a moment, and then said, "I heard some horse thief named Orrin Taggert owned this livery stable. We were thinking about boarding our horses here for the night, but I'm not sure they'd be here in the morning when we came to get them."

The man looked Tye up and down, "I know you, don't I?" he asked.

Tye grinned at him. "Yeah, you know me. It's been awhile, but I didn't think you'd forget the man that rode your red stallion for you."

Recognition lit up the man's face. "Tye Garrett. Well, I'll be." He grabbed Tye in a bear hug and the two men laughed as they slapped each other on the back and shook hands.

"I never would have known you," Orrin said as he stepped back and looked at him. "You've aged some, but it looks good on ya."

"Well, you're still as ugly as ever," Tye said. "Orrin, I'd like to introduce you to my partners. These are the Paxtons, Will and Rebecca."

Orrin shook hands with Will and took Rebecca's hand in his, holding it gently. "I'm pleased to meet you, but if you two are partnered up with this sidewinder, you better hang on to your purse."

Tye was standing to one side, a grin on his face. "Orrin, are you still upset over losing that money to me?"

"Nope, I'm not upset, but I'll tell you one thing. I'll never make another bet with you as long as I live. I still don't see how you rode that bronc, but by golly, you did. And it cost me a thousand dollars to see it."

Will looked at Tye. "A thousand dollars?"

"Yeah, that's what he bet. I'll tell ya about it some-time. Right now, you two need to find us a room while I talk to Orrin here a little while."

Sitting in Orrin's office after Will and Rebecca had left, Tye looked at Orrin and asked, "So how are things around here these days?"

"Business is great. I can't keep enough horses on hand to meet the demand."

"How is all this new growth affecting the old-timers around here?" Tye asked.

"Some like it, some don't," Orrin said. "But the growth is good for Austin. There are some problems, though. I guess you got to take the good with the bad."

"What kind of problems?" Tye asked, raising an eyebrow.

"Well . . ." Orrin hesitated. "It seems there's a band of outlaws operating somewhere around here. They're led by a Confederate deserter named Lomas Cantrell. They hit ranches in a hundred-mile radius, stealing cattle and horses. They take them into Mexico and sell 'em. There's even rumors that they steal from the Mexican side and sell over here as well. They've hit a few stagecoaches, and there's even been a couple of train robberies credited to them."

"Doesn't the law do anything about them?"

"They try. But by the time the law gets a posse together and heads off after 'em, they've done crossed the border."

"Do they hit ranches around here?" Tye asked.

"Here most often. That's why some folks think their headquarters must be around here somewhere."

"What about the Cattlemen's Association? Have they been able to do any good?"

"Oh, they put up a big reward, but that ain't done nothing to stop the stealin'. When Lomas heard about the reward, he sent a message to every town. He'd kill anyone trying to collect the reward and burn the ranch of anyone trying to stop him. That pretty well quenched any desires at attempting to collect the reward. A couple of bounty hunters tried. Their horses came back to town with them strapped belly down on 'em."

"Sounds like a tough customer," Tye said. "Have you been out to my place lately?"

"It's been over a year since I been out that way. John Burke's still looking after it for ya. Not that there's that much to look after anymore. You plannin' on stayin', or you just passin' through?"

"We're gonna stay. We've got us some horses and cattle bein' held on the Thomas ranch north of town. We're gonna move 'em out to the home place tomorrow and start rebuildin'."

"I'm glad to hear it," Orrin said. "I know how hard it was on ya, losin' all your family that way. And I know you had to get it outa your system. But that's a mighty fine spread out there and it needs someone to care for it."

"You're right," Tye agreed. "And that's just what I intend to do. I'm gonna need some more cattle. Do you know where I can get some?"

"If you're smart, you'll register yourself a brand and head into the breaks and find yourself some of them strays. There's men who are gettin' rich drivin' cattle out of the wilds, brandin' 'em, and drivin' 'em to market. I know someone who'd be willin' to hire on with an outfit. He knows more about chasin' them ol' mossy-horned cattle than anyone around."

"Good! I'm lookin' to hire some hands. Can he meet me here in the mornin'?"

Orrin grinned. "I'll have him here first thing."

"Thanks, Orrin. It's good to be back. One more thing: Is Henry Lawrence still practicin' law?"

"Yep, he's got his shingle hangin' in an office just west of the courthouse."

"Thanks again, Orrin. I'll see ya in the mornin'."

Tye walked up the street until he saw a sign hanging

outside an office: HENRY LAWRENCE, ATTORNEY-AT-
LAW. He opened the door and went in.

Over dinner that evening, Tye talked to Will and
Rebecca about hiring help and going after the
longhorns.

"If we're going to build a ranch, we might as well
get started right away. I plan to take three men and
head southwest about fifty miles. I hear there's still
a fair amount of cattle in the breaks down there.
Orrin knows a fella that's willin' to show me where
they are. You two can start the buildings while
I'm gone."

"How long will you be away?" Will asked.

"I'm not sure, but probably about two months."

"We should be able to get quite a bit done in two
months," Rebecca said.

"If you can find some help, you should," Tye
responded.

They talked late into the evening, making plans for
the gather, and deciding what building supplies they
would need for the ranch.

"I'll talk to Orrin tomorrow about buying a wagon.
We'll need one if we're going to be hauling supplies
out to the ranch. We'll have to break about six horses
to harness, but that shouldn't be too difficult." Tye
smiled at Will's dubious look.

The next morning, Tye and Will went to the livery
stable to meet with Orrin and the man he'd recom-
mended to Tye. Rebecca took the list of supplies they
would need to the local mercantile.

Orrin was waiting for them in his office. With him
was a man wearing a large black hat. The brim was
flat and the crown tall, but what caught their eye was
how tall and thin the stranger was. He topped six feet
by at least four inches and looked like a fence post
with a hat on.

Orrin stood when they came in and introduced the

man. "Tye, Will, I'd like you to meet Rowdy. He's lookin' for a job wranglin' cattle. He's been roamin' around the country for the last few months, tryin' other things. Now he's come back lookin' for a job."

Tye shook hands with Rowdy and, looking up into the grinning face, he asked, "You know how to gather longhorns out of the brush?"

Rowdy smiled, showing a row of white teeth. "I choused a few of those critters out before I started roamin' around."

"Good," Tye said. "I'm lookin' for some hands to gather about a thousand head. You know where we can round up that many?"

"Yeah, I know a spot where there's that many and more. It's rough country, but if a man has enough horses to ride, he can get 'em."

"We've got the horses. Do you know anyone else worth their salt who might be lookin' for a job?"

"I know three or four fellas who're lookin'. I might be able to find a couple more. How many you want?"

"We'll hire five, including you."

"When do you want 'em?" Rowdy asked.

"Day after tomorrow," Tye said. "Do you know where the Garrett ranch is?"

"Are you kin to the Garretts that had a place northwest of here?"

"I'm Abel Garrett's son."

"I remember you now. You joined up with the rangers after that Comanche raid. Then you just kinda disappeared. Folks around here wondered what happened to you. It was too bad about your family. They was good folks."

"Thanks," Tye said. "Why don't you meet me back here in about two hours? I'll lay out our plans then."

"All right. You want me to bring the other hands around, so you can meet 'em?"

"If you can round 'em up," Tye said.

"I'll round 'em up," Rowdy said with a grin as he left the office.

Will and Tye talked with Orrin for another hour.
They traded for a wagon and a team of horses, after
Will persuaded Tye that they would need a team im-
mediately and he wouldn't have time to break one in.

They walked to the mercantile, where Rebecca was
still ordering supplies.

"They've got almost everything we need," she said
as Will and Tye came in. "They've got to order some
of the things, but they promised they would be here
within a week."

"Fine," Tye said. "We'll have Rowdy bring the
things out day after tomorrow when he comes."

"He's the guy we just hired," Will said, in response
to Rebecca's questioning look.

"Oh, is he good looking?" Rebecca asked, her eyes
twinkling with merriment.

"He's real handsome," Tye said. "If you like 'em
short and broad."

"He's almost as wide as he is tall," Will said, picking
up on the mood.

"I want to leave town by noon. Can you two be
ready?" Tye asked.

"We'll be ready," Rebecca said.

Tye and Will met Rowdy at Orrin's livery stable
two hours later. He had four other men with him.

"Will, Tye, I'd like you to meet Shorty, Wayne,
Curly, and Bo. They're all top hands and they're lookin' for work."

Will and Tye shook hands with each of the hands.
Shorty fit his name. He was short of stature, but broad
across the shoulders and lean in the waist. There was a
strength about him that could be felt in his handshake.
Wayne was of average height and build, while Curly,
not as tall as Rowdy, stood at just six feet, without a
hair on his head. Bo was the youngest of the four,
maybe seventeen or eighteen. He still had the look of
youth about his face, but his eyes told a different
story—he'd seen plenty and ridden the trails.

Tye hired all four men, then laid out his plans, telling them to drive the wagon and supplies out to the home place the day after tomorrow. They would leave from there in a week.

Chapter Twenty-five

Tye, Will, and Rebecca gathered the horses and cattle from the ranch where they'd been left and, with Tye leading the packhorse and the scarred mare, they began the last leg of the trip that would end one journey and start another.

Pushing the horses and cattle, it took them two hours to reach the canyon overlooking the Garrett homestead.

Rebecca caught her breath as she looked into the valley at the charred remains of what had once been a house and barn. Even the ruins, and the story behind them, could not diminish the beauty of the valley and its surroundings.

Tye pulled up and sat his horse, looking at what had once been his home. He had wondered how he would feel upon seeing this place again. Would those who had died here while he was away still haunt him? He sat waiting for the emotions to envelop him, but they didn't come. Gone was the guilt; most of it anyway. Gone was the feeling of hopelessness. He found he could look at the burned house and see the future, not the past.

Will and Rebecca remained behind the herd, understanding Tye's need to face this alone.

Tye touched his spurs to the horse's side and started down the road. He was home and he was starting over. It was a good feeling.

Tye led them to what had been the house. All that was left to identify it as such, were the two rock-formed chimneys that stood among the charred ruins.

"Orrin is sending out two Mexicans tomorrow. They know how to make and lay adobe bricks. I figure if we clean up this mess, we can build upon the foundation of the original house. We'll build two living quarters with the kitchen being the center for both. That way, we can each have our private quarters. How does that sound to you two?"

Will looked at Rebecca and she nodded agreement. "That's fine with us," he said. "As soon as Rowdy gets here with the wagon, I think I'll get a load of lumber and start building us some corrals. We're going to need some to break the rest of these horses we got."

"That sounds like a good idea," Tye said. "Why don't we set us up a camp over by the river, and tomorrow I'll show you two around the place. We can let the horses and cattle graze here in the valley for a while. I don't think they'll wander off too far."

After building a lean-to and setting up camp, Will and Tye helped Rebecca prepare supper.

They were sitting around the fire, having finished eating and washing the dishes when Tye cleared his throat. "I registered us two brands while I was in Austin. One I figure we'll need for a trail brand; the other will be for the ranch stock. I registered a turkey track for the trail brand and for a ranch brand I registered a rafter *TP*, the *T* for my first name and a *P* for Paxton. The *P* will connect to the leg of the *T,* like this." He drew the brand in the dirt of the ground to show them what he meant.

"I went ahead and had Orrin start making our irons. We'll need them for the herd we're going after. What do you think?"

Will looked at the drawing on the ground, and then looking at Tye he said, "Well, I think it should have been the Rafter *PT,* since I have to do most of the work around here. But since you already ordered the irons, I guess we'll stay with the brand the way it is."

"I appreciate that, Will," Tye said with mock sincerity. "And since you do most of the work around here, why don't you go get us some more firewood for the night. It feels like it may be getting colder and my old bones can't take the cold the way they used to."

Rebecca smiled as Will went in search of more firewood.

"You two are just alike. You know it? You'd rather dig a spur into each other than eat."

"I know," Tye said, returning her smile. "It's what makes it possible for us to be close. You married yourself a good man there. He's gonna make a name for himself out here."

"I know he is," Rebecca said, looking in the direction Will had gone. "So are you, Tye Garrett. That's what I meant when I said you two were just alike."

The next day was spent riding as much of the property as possible. Tye outlined the boundaries and pointed out where the best grazing and watering places were. The traps that had been fenced would need some work to hold stock and Will made a list of the things he would need to make the repairs.

Returning late in the afternoon, they were surprised to find two Mexicans cleaning up the charred timbers and removing the debris from the old homestead.

"*Señor* Taggert tell us you want to build a new house here," the older of the two men said, as they rode up. "We start cleaning this up. You tell us what you want us to build and we build it for you."

Tye outlined the house plans for the Mexicans, whose names were Pedro and Felipe, with some minor modifications made by Rebecca.

Pedro and Felipe made their camp by the river, sleeping under the wagon they had brought. The wagon contained the tools they would use to build the adobe bricks needed for the house.

Shortly after sunrise the next morning they heard the rattle of a wagon, making its way down the canyon road. Shading their eyes against the sun, they saw

Rowdy sitting in the wagon seat, foot pushed hard against the brake. Shorty, Wayne, Curly, and Bo rode beside the wagon, which made them wonder who sat on the seat beside Rowdy. As they forded the river and came up the bank, Will got his first look at the man sitting there. At first glance, he thought the man old enough to be his grandfather. His hair and mustache were shocking white. But as they drew up to the camp and stepped down, Will could see he wasn't as old as he'd first suspected.

"Howdy," Tye said as the group pulled up.

"Hey, boss," Rowdy said, jumping down off the wagon. "I brought along another hand. I figured if we was goin' to be out in the breaks for a spell, it might be nice to have a cook along with us. This here is Ringo. The Comanche captured him when he was a youngster. When the cavalry raided the village he was in, they found him there, his hair as white as snow. No one knows what made it turn white, as he won't talk about what took place. He can outride, outshoot, and outfight any two hands, but his specialty is cookin'. He can cook some of the tastiest meals you ever put in your mouth."

Tye and Will each shook hands with the newcomer, noting that he had yet to speak a word.

"I'm pleased to have ya," Tye said. "I hadn't thought about a cook, but I know I don't want to chase longhorns all day, then come in at night and eat my own cookin'."

Rebecca had been standing by the lean-to, looking at the new arrivals, but now she stepped forward. "You must be Rowdy. You don't look anything like what I was expecting." She looked at Will and Tye and they both cast their eyes to the ground to cover their smiles.

"Yes, ma'am, that's me," Rowdy said, taking off his hat.

"I'm Rebecca Paxton. We're glad to have you here," she said, offering her hand.

"Pleased to meet ya, Mrs. Paxton." He introduced her to the other five men. She shook hands with each of them, welcoming each to the Rafter TP. Ringo took her hand, but looked shyly at the ground as she smiled and shook his hand.

"Let's get this wagon unloaded and start getting ready," Tye said. "Ringo, you tell Rebecca what you'll need in the way of groceries and she and Will will pick them up when they go to town. Let's go pick out the horses we'll be taking with us."

Will and Rebecca took the wagon to town the next day to pick up a load of lumber for the corrals, as well as the list of supplies Ringo needed.

Tye stayed at the ranch with the new hands and started preparation for the trip to the breaks. The horses they had chosen needed to be shod. This job fell to Wayne, who had worked as a blacksmith for a spell.

Each of the horses chosen was ridden to determine how well they would handle in the rough brushy area. It was going to be grueling work and it would take a horse with a lot of stamina to maintain the pace required to chase the longhorn cattle out of the dense brush. The horses had to be strong enough to hold the cattle once they were roped. Cowboys used one of two methods for roping and holding the rangy cattle. A single rider would rope a steer or cow around the horns, then spurring his horse, he would ride by, flipping the rope around the animal's rear as he went by. When the horse hit the end of the rope, it would jerk the back legs from under the cow, thus sending it crashing to the ground in a pile of thrashing horns and feet. The rider would then jump from his horse's back, run to the downed bovine, and tie its front and back legs with strips of leather or rope. The beast would then be left to thrash and bellow on the ground until it wore itself out, enabling the cowboys to drive it to a holding pen.

The other method was to double up. One cowboy roped the horns, turning the cow back, while the other rode in and threw a heel loop, snagging the two back feet and stretching the animal out. The header would then dismount and tie the legs in like fashion, achieving the same results. Although this method required teams and sometimes slowed the gathering process, it took a lot of the danger out of subduing the cattle. Tye decided this would be the option they would use. He wanted to reduce the risk of injury as much as possible. The trip would have enough dangers, with the threat of Indians and rustlers. He didn't want to add to it by having them all riding single. This way there would always be two riders together, leaving one man to watch the herd and Ringo to look after the camp.

Tye doubted that would bother the man. He seemed to enjoy his solitude, talking very little to those around him and staying mostly to himself. The only person he had talked to at any length was Will. Will had mentioned he was building corrals in order to break the remaining horses. Ringo asked about the corrals and the horses, making suggestions that would make the corrals more versatile. Will had told him about the chute he was going to build, modeled after the one Jim Landsing had in Montana. Ringo's interest was piqued by the "bucking chute," as Will called it, asking questions and making more suggestions. Tye made a mental note of Ringo's interest in the horses. It might come in handy at some time.

A week later, the six men rode out. Rowdy led the way, with Curly and Wayne bringing the remuda of horses. They had chosen twenty head of young strong stock to take with them. Some of the horses had only been ridden once or twice, but would be seasoned ranch horses by the time they returned. Ringo led two packhorses loaded with supplies to carry them through for the two months they would be gone.

Bo stayed behind to help Will with the cattle they had traded for and gather strays on the range. Tye had spotted cattle on his rides out to inspect the ranch. He hadn't seen any brands on the cattle and suspected they might have been some strays lost by the cattle drives or left from earlier gathers. Bo and Will would spend part of their time catching any unbranded cattle.

After two weeks, Will and Bo had about completed the corrals and were working on the bucking chute. Once they had the chute finished, they would begin breaking the remaining horses. First they had to repair the fences in each of the traps in order to hold any cattle they rounded up.

Pedro and Felipe were making good progress with the adobe bricks, having several hundred already drying in the sun.

"We will start the building of the house in a few days," Pedro said to Rebecca one day. "As soon as we have enough bricks dried, I will bring out my two sons and two nephews from town. They will continue making the bricks and mixing the mud for the bonding, while Felipe and I lay the bricks. We will have you a fine home in about one month."

Meanwhile, Rebecca had set up housekeeping in the canvas-covered lean-to Will and Tye had built for her. The thought of having a house to live in made Rebecca smile with pleasure.

A week later Pedro came to tell her he was going to town to pick up his sons and nephews. "If it's all right with the *señora,* I would like to bring my family back with me. My Juanita does not like being alone without me. She could help the *señora* with the cooking and the washing of clothes."

Rebecca was taken back by Pedro's request. The surprise showed on her face. Pedro, seeing the look, was immediately embarrassed.

"I am sorry, *señora,* I should not have made such a request. She will have to wait until I am finished with the work here."

"No, no," Rebecca exclaimed, hurrying to explain her thoughts. "I would love to have your wife come out here with you. I am just surprised is all. I wouldn't have thought she would want to come out here. She is welcome to come with you. I would love to have her."

Pedro's pleasure showed in the broad smile on his face. "*Gracias, señora.* Juanita will be so happy. I will bring her back with me two days from now. *Gracias, señora.*"

Rebecca laughed at Pedro's pleasure. She was thankful she would have another woman to talk to.

Will and Bo completed the corrals and chute and were repairing the traps. They spent each day riding to the various locations, stringing new wire or repairing broken ones. Rebecca packed food for them to take with them, knowing they would not be back until the sun was setting.

She enjoyed the evenings with Will and Bo as they talked of the work they had done that day and their plans for the next day's work, but she felt the loneliness of the days. She had ridden out with them on two occasions, but found she was of little help. She opted to stay at the lean-to in order to have their supper ready when they returned.

Will had told her the night before that most of the repairs had been made, and soon he and Bo would start gathering strays. She asked to go along with them when they started the gather and Will had relented. Good sense told her the best thing she could do was to have a hot supper ready for them when they came home. But she did want to ride out at least once or twice. Maybe she could make arrangements to have Pedro's wife cook for them. She smiled at the thought of spending her days with Will, even if they would be hard, grueling days with little time for conversation.

Pedro arrived at the ranch with his two sons, two nephews, and wife, Juanita. Rebecca went out to greet the newcomers, smiling as Pedro introduced each one of them. There was nothing shy about his wife. She immediately wrapped her arms around Rebecca, giving her a hug and thanking her for letting her come to be with Pedro.

"You know how these men are: They don't like to be away from us for very long." She smiled as she stepped back, looking Rebecca over from top to bottom. She said, "If I had known you were so beautiful, I would have been jealous of my Pedro being out here." Pedro smiled and shook his head at Rebecca. She returned his smile behind Juanita's back. She took an immediate liking to Juanita.

"Would you like to sit down for a spell?" Rebecca asked, pointing to the lean-to.

"Eeee, I don't know if I will be able to sit again for a whole week," Juanita said, rubbing her backside. "That wagon seat ees as hard as a beeg rock and I think Pedro heet every hole een the road." Rebecca laughed in understanding, taking Juanita by the arm and leading her to the lean-to.

"At least you can enjoy a cup of coffee. I just put on a fresh pot."

"*Sí*, that would be very nice." She turned and called to one of the boys standing by the wagon. "Manuel, bring me the basket I feexed for *señora* Paxton."

"Yes, Mama," the young boy said, hurrying to follow his mother's orders.

When Will and Bo returned that evening, they were pleasantly surprised to find a meal of homemade tamales, venison burritos wrapped in flour tortillas, and stuffed chili rellenos. Both Will and Bo were sweating from the hot peppers, but continued to eat them, fanning their mouths and drinking water by the glassful.

"I've asked Juanita to help me with the cooking so I can ride out with you," Rebecca said.

Will looked up from his plate, not sure of how to respond. He spoke hesitantly. "That's great."

Rebecca picked up on the hesitancy in his voice. "Don't you want me to ride with you?" she asked.

"Of course, I love for you to ride along. It's just that I figured you'd be tired of riding after the trip here from Montana and with Juanita here now, I guess I figured you'd want to stay around."

Rebecca looked at her husband, wondering if that was all that was behind his hesitation. "I don't want to ride every day, but I would like to ride out some times. With Juanita here, I won't have to worry about the meals. But if you don't want me along, I'll stay here."

"No, no, I want you along," Will hurried to say. "I think it's great that you want to go along. Tomorrow we're going to start gathering cattle. You can be a big help to us."

Rebecca smiled and put her arm through Will's. "I'll be the best help you ever had." She laughed as Will blushed and Bo turned to look out the opening of the lean-to.

Chapter Twenty-six

Tye spurred his horse after the rangy longhorn Rowdy had flushed from the dense thicket. His loop built and swinging over his head, he pursued the thousand-pound animal at breakneck speed. He had to rope it before it reached the thicket on the far side of the opening. His horse, a stout quarter horse with abundant speed, closed the gap between them in a short distance. Tye threw his loop with well-practiced accuracy, watching with satisfaction as it settled over the expansive horn spread. Jerking his slack, he reined the horse around and waited for the inevitable jerk that came an instant later.

Days of roping wild cattle had trained the horse to brace for the impact. He lowered his body and leaned away as the big steer hit the end of the rope. The steer was pulled around as the horse dug his feet into the ground and kept the rope taut.

Rowdy was close behind Tye as the steer was pulled around. He swung in behind it, swinging his rope as the animal was forced forward. He threw his loop at the back feet, watching as it encircled both hooves.

Tye spurred his horse forward until the longhorn was stretched between the two horses. Stepping to the ground, his horse keeping the rope tight, he raced to the animal's tail and, pulling hard, forced the animal to its side. Taking two lengths of rawhide from his belt, he tied first the back legs, then the front, securing the steer until they came to retrieve him later.

They had been working the dense thickets for the

past four weeks, gathering over five hundred head of longhorns. It was hard, grueling work, fighting the thickets to force the rangy cattle out into the openings where they could be roped and tied until later in the day. After a day of fighting the rawhide bindings, the cattle were more subdued and could be driven to the waiting herd.

Ringo was cooking meals, and true to Rowdy's compliments, the food they ate was excellent. They alternated days watching the herd, which was held in a box canyon close to the camp.

Curly and Wayne both proved to be top hands, roping and tying as many longhorns as Rowdy and Tye. It was a contest to see which team could bring in the most cattle during the day. Each time it was close, with one team having more one day, and the other team having more the next.

Driving the longhorns from the thickets of mesquite and yucca cactus was hard on both horse and rider. It was becoming routine to pick thorns out of both after each chase.

One of the biggest dangers came from the longhorns. Releasing one required skill, agility, and a good horse. A loop was placed around the back legs of the animal and held tight by one man on horseback, while the other removed the rawhide bindings. The man on the ground then had to make it back on his horse while the other held the longhorn at bay.

Wayne was knocked from his horse and received a blow to the head when one of the steers managed to get free before Wayne was fully mounted. The horse, reacting in terror, reared as the steer came at him. Wayne, with one foot in the stirrup and hanging on to a handful of mane and the saddle horn was helpless and could only hold on and pray for the best. Luckily, the horn spread on the thousand-pound animal was so wide, the horse missed being gored as a horn passed on either side of him. But the impact of the collision toppled him over backward. Wayne was thrown into the air and brought up short by a mesquite tree, hitting his head and bruising his body. Curly managed to get a rope around the steer before he could do any more damage, but Wayne nursed a headache for the rest of the day.

There were no signs of Indians, but each man rode with his Colt at his side and was constantly watching for signs. The only tracks seen so far were those of shod horses. This in itself worried Tye, for he remembered Orrin's warning about Lomas Cantrell. He could be in the area. No one knew where he was holed up. Tye warned the other riders to keep their eyes opened for tracks.

Though it was November, the days were warm. The grass was still green and plentiful along the Llano River where they were holding the herd.

Tye was pleased with the gather so far. They were ahead of schedule and if things continued to go as well as they had, they should finish the gather with more cattle than they had anticipated.

Meanwhile, Will and Bo were working from sunup to sundown, gathering strays on the Rafter TP and driving them into the trap close to headquarters.

The work went about the same as with the men gathering in the breaks. He and Bo would double team a rangy longhorn, heading and heeling it, then tying its legs until later in the afternoon, when they would release it and drive it with the others to the trap.

The most difficult part of the job was locating the strays. This job fell to Rebecca. Finding a high point where she had a good view of the countryside and could still see Will and Bo, she would spot one of the longhorns standing in the thick brush, attempting to blend in with the foliage. She would direct the two men to it with a series of hand and arm signals. She waited with her breath held as the two men roped it and had it securely tied. Then she would resume her search for another. The system had worked well, saving Will and Bo countless hours of riding the thickets in search of the elusive longhorned cattle.

It was an overcast day as Rebecca watched from her vantage point as Will and Bo closed in on a large bull. They had tried once before to capture this particular animal, but he had managed to escape by doubling back on them and lying down in the brush. Rebecca had not been able to see where he had gone. It was only by luck that they had come across him again and Will was determined not to let him escape. He and Bo were closing the space, working their way through the thick mesquite, pushing the bull toward a clearing twenty feet away.

Rebecca's full attention was on the scene before her and she didn't notice the man who had ridden up, until he spoke.

"If they get a rope on that one, they better have a good horse under 'em."

Rebecca let out a startled gasp as she whirled in the saddle to stare at the man. He wasn't a large man, but for some reason he seemed big. He was dressed in a black shirt and wore a black vest and hat. His black mustache was neatly trimmed, but the eyes were what caught Rebecca's attention. They were light gray and held her mesmerized as she continued to stare. He allowed her to sit there like that for several moments, returning her stare. Then he spoke again.

"I didn't mean to startle you. I was just riding through when I saw you sitting here. I thought you might be in trouble or something so I rode over to check on you. My name is Lomas Cantrell."

There was no way he could miss the sharp intake of breath at the mention of his name. Tye had told her about this man and now he sat calmly talking to her. Her first instinct was to scream, but she thought about the results and willed herself to become calm.

Lomas chuckled. "I see you've heard of me. Well, have no fear. I don't have the reputation of harming

beautiful women. You are quite safe, I assure you."
He smiled as he sat there looking at her and her fears
calmed as she watched him. He had done nothing to
threaten her so far, and with Will and Bo close by,
she doubted he would try anything.

"They've got him in the opening." He motioned
toward the thicket where Will and Bo were in pursuit
of the longhorn. She had momentarily forgotten the
bull and was surprised when he turned to watch the
episode below.

Will was closing the space between him and the
bull, swinging his loop as his horse pounded across
the open ground, ears laid back, intent on overtaking
the running animal before him. As the gap narrowed
to fifteen feet, Will threw his loop and pulled the slack
as it settled neatly over the wide horns.

Will was riding the large bay he'd won at the Double A ranch in Montana. The horse had a lot of "cow
smarts" and could handle the toughest longhorns. He
turned and braced himself as the big bull hit the end
of the forty-foot lariat. The large bull was jerked
around as Bo moved in to throw the heel loop. But
instead of resisting the pull of the rope as most did,
the large bull charged straight ahead, running at Will,
intent upon using his horns to impale both horse and
rider. Will felt the slack in the rope and turned in
time to see the bull close the distance behind them.
The bay sensed rather than saw the bull advancing
and immediately swung to the right. Only this move
saved both him and Will as the big bull brushed past
them and was brought up short again as he hit the
end of the rope. This time, Bo was in position and
throwing a perfect heel loop, catching the bull's back
legs and holding the slack until the animal was
stretched between the two horses. Will wasted no time
in tying the front and back legs, taking caution to tie
them extra tight.

Lomas smiled as Will finished the job of securing
the big bull.

"That's some horse he's riding. If he hadn't moved when he did, that cowboy would be hurting mighty bad right about now."

Rebecca looked over at the outlaw and was surprised to see admiration on his face.

"That's my husband, Will Paxton. He and his partner, Tye Garrett, own this ranch."

Lomas Cantrell looked surprised. "Own this place? I thought this was open range."

"No, it belonged to Tye's folks. They're dead and he's been away for a while, but he's back now." She noticed his eyes take on a troubled look, but he instantly smiled.

"Sure is a nice place. I'm glad to see someone's going to be making good use of it."

Rebecca didn't respond, but continued to watch him, wondering what his purpose in being here was.

"Well, I better be going. It was a pleasure meeting you, Mrs. Paxton. Perhaps we'll see each other again sometime," Cantrell said, touching his hat and smiling at her.

"Perhaps we will," she responded coolly.

She watched him as he turned his horse and rode away, noticing how he rode in a direction that would keep him out of Will and Bo's line of sight. She didn't suspect it was from fear, for she doubted the man she just met feared any man.

Later that afternoon, she told Will about her meeting with Cantrell. He was shocked that the man would so boldly ride in the open.

"I don't like the thought of him comin' upon you like that," Will said to Rebecca as they were pushing the cattle toward home.

"I don't either," Rebecca said. "But something tells me he wouldn't have harmed me. He might be an outlaw, but I think he has morals about him. I don't think he would harm any woman."

"Just the same, I'd feel a whole lot better if you'd stay at the lean-to," Will said.

"And what if he comes there?" Rebecca asked. "Pedro and Felipe aren't any hands with a gun. I doubt they would be able to do anything should this man decide to harm me."

"I guess you're right," Will conceded. "I just wish I knew why he was riding out here."

"I don't know, but he seemed surprised that someone had moved in and was running the place now," Rebecca said.

"We'll just have to keep our eyes open and be on the watch. I don't like the feel of this. Tye should be back with the rest of the group in about a week. Maybe we can do a little scouting around and find out if there's anything going on around here. I doubt there is, but it won't hurt to check. He was probably passing through and heard us thrashing in the brush. I doubt we'll ever see or hear from him again."

Rebecca nodded at Will's reassurance, but she had the feeling they had not heard the last of Lomas Cantrell.

Five days later, Will and Bo were riding out to look for strays. Pedro and Felipe were finishing the roof on the house today and Rebecca was going to start moving things into it.

They had rounded up three hundred head of cattle in the last few weeks, but had found only five head in the last three days.

"I think we've gathered about all we're going to get," Bo said as they watched for fresh tracks along the stream they were traveling.

"I think you're right," Will said. "Unless there's some further west of here. We haven't tried that part of the range yet."

"I thought Tye said to stay within the bounds of this here creek," Bo said.

"He did," Will said. "And I reckon we better listen to him. Let's ride over to that draw south of here and see if we can pick up any sign."

"I don't think we'll find any. But at least we can get a good view of things from the top of that peak."

They rode, watching for sign as they went, but saw no fresh tracks. As they approached the peak, Will looked off to the west. Pointing in that direction, he asked, "I wonder what's raising so much dust over that way?"

"Could be a duster blowing in," Bo commented, speaking about the hard blows that sometimes came upon the prairie, covering everything with dust and drying up water holes.

"I don't think so," Will said. "It's too even, and seems to be following a path."

"How far off do you reckon it is?" Bo asked.

"Ten, maybe twelve miles."

"Why don't we ride over and find out?"

Will looked at the sun. It was still early in the day. It wouldn't take long to find out the cause of the dust. They could be back home before dark.

"All right. Let's ride over and check it out. If it's what I think it is, we may be needed anyway."

They set out at a ground-eating trot, saving their horses, but covering the miles.

Will watched the dust as he rode. It was moving south at a crawling pace. His first thought had been of the herd that was being driven in by Tye and Rowdy, but the more he thought about it, the more he was sure it wasn't them. They wouldn't have been this far south.

As the distance between them and the dust cloud narrowed, both Will and Bo could hear the bawling cattle and shouting men. They seemed to be moving at a brisk pace. But why south? Will wondered.

"Something doesn't feel right about this," Will said as they drew near. "See that rise over there? Let's see if we can work our way around where we can't be seen."

Will turned his horse and headed for the rise. It was nothing more than a sand drift that had built over the years until it rose out of the prairie to stand twenty feet above the land. A washout draw followed along the base of the rise, offering Will and Bo natural cover.

The herd had not yet reached the point where they waited. Hidden by the mesquite shrubs growing sparsely along the rim of the rise, they tied their horses in the draw several yards back.

Lying on their stomachs, they could see the cattle being driven hard by twelve men. Their faces were covered with bandanas to keep the dust out.

Will watched as the lead cattle approached the spot directly beneath him, the dust boiling up as the cattle's hooves tore into the ground beneath them. Will peered through the dust as the first animal came even with him. He guessed there to be somewhere between a thousand and twelve hundred head. As his eyes searched the herd moving before him, his breath caught: There on the left hip was a turkey track brand. It was the brand Tye had registered for their trail brand. He looked to the horse remuda that was moving on the other side of the herd. It was hard to see through the dust, but watching closely, he saw several head of horses that he could identify as those from their stock. The large gray mare that Tye favored was there, along with a stocky black that Rowdy had chosen to be part of his string.

Pulling back from the edge of the rise, Will motioned for Bo to follow him. Easing along the draw, cautious not to be seen, Will waited until they were well away from the herd before he spoke. "Where does this trail lead to?"

"I don't know for sure, but I imagine it leads to Mexico," Bo said.

"How long would it take this herd to reach Mexico?" Will asked, looking around nervously.

"Three days, if they were pushed hard," Bo replied. "Why're you asking?"

"Because that's our herd," Will responded with anger. "Someone's stole the herd from Tye and the boys. I don't know how, but they've got it and that means something has happened to Tye."

Bo looked toward the herd as the impact of Will's words sunk in. "What are we going to do?"

"I'm thinking," Will answered. "Can you draw me a map to get to the place where Tye and the rest of them went?"

"Yeah, it's pretty easy. But why do you need a map?"

" 'Cause one of us has to go find out what happened to the others and one of us has to stay with the herd."

"I guess I'm elected to stay with the herd," Bo said, trying to grin, but not carrying it off very well.

"I have to find Tye," Will said. "Where's a place we can meet three days from now?"

"There's an inn at Uvalde that would be about three days ride from here. I imagine the herd will pass close to there."

"Good, I'll meet you there in there days, if I can find the others. If I'm not there, you hightail it back to the ranch. Don't take any chances. Stay away from the herd. Just stay close enough to make sure it's still heading south."

"Don't worry, I ain't about to tackle twelve men by myself," Bo said, handing Will the map he had drawn on a tally sheet.

"All right, here's my canteen and the lunch Rebecca packed for me. I wish I had more. Maybe you can find a village along the way to buy some supplies. Here's twenty dollars, in case you need it." Will looked over at Bo, then held out his hand. "Good luck."

Bo took Will's hand in a firm grip. "I'll see you in Uvalde. We'll show these thieves it ain't healthy to mess with the Rafter TP."

"You bet we will," Will said, with more confidence than he felt.

Chapter Twenty-seven

Will slowed his horse to a trot, giving it a chance to blow. He estimated he had covered half the distance to the ranch since leaving Bo at the draw. He was going to the ranch first. There, he would get extra horses and weapons; then he would set out to find the others. He had been running his horse as much as he possibly dared. He couldn't afford to break him down at this point: too many lives depended on him. That is, if they were still alive.

Riding, he pondered the situation. How did the thieves manage to steal the herd? Had they killed Tye and the others? Were they now lying in the hot sun, dead or dying? How much time since the herd had been stolen? Estimating the distance the herd was from where Tye and the others had started, Will figured they had been on the trail at least two days, possibly three. If he rode hard, he could be at the breaks in a day and a half. Would he be in time? He would have to try!

It was another two hours of hard riding before he came in sight of the house. Pedro and Felipe were on the roof, putting the last of the tin in place as he ran his horse into the yard, yelling for Rebecca.

Rebecca had just finished placing her mother's tablecloth on the kitchen table when she heard the pounding hooves and Will calling her name. She hurried outside, knowing that for Will to be riding that way, something had to be wrong.

Will dismounted from the weary horse before it came to a complete stop. Rebecca was standing in the doorway of the house, clutching her apron.

"We've got to gather the horses. The cattle have been stolen and we have to find Tye."

All this came out in a rush as Will hurried to Rebecca. She didn't waste any time with foolish questions, but rushed into the house to change into a pair of riding pants, giving instructions to Juanita to pack some food, water, and bandages.

Pedro and Felipe came down from the roof, hurrying to assist Will in gathering the horses from the trap.

By the time Rebecca emerged from the house, Will had the horses in the corral. With Pedro and Felipe's help, he was frantically saddling seven good mounts.

Rebecca hurriedly saddled her gray, then helped Will tie each of the horses, head to tail. Juanita came out with the food and several canteens of water, as well as medicine and bandages. She and Rebecca distributed the supplies in the saddlebags of each horse.

Will was working in a frenzy, knowing each moment lost could mean the difference between life and death.

"Pedro, I want you and Felipe to go to town and buy as many rifles and pistols as you can. Also buy ammunition for each. If you have any problems, tell Orrin Taggert our herd has been stolen, and Tye and the boys are missing. He'll help. Take the wagon and team. When you leave town, head toward Llano." Will showed him the map Bo had drawn. "Meet us here. If Tye and the boys are all right and headed this way, we should run into them before they reach this point. If not, I'll send Rebecca back to get you, but you wait here. *¿Comprende?*"

"*Sí señor,* we will be there. It will take us one day to reach this spot. We will wait for you there. I have a cousin who lives in Llano."

"I will be there also," Juanita said.

"*Gracias,* Juanita, we may need your help," Will

said. Then, handing Pedro a handful of coins, he said, "If this isn't enough, tell them to put it on our bill."

"Sí señor. Vaya con Dios."

Turning to Rebecca, Will asked, "Are you ready?"

"Let's go," she said. "Tye's waiting for us."

Will smiled as he gathered the reins of his horse. Climbing into the saddle, he turned to Pedro. "We'll see you tomorrow." Then, spurring his horse, he led the other horses out of the corral, Rebecca following, yelling at the horses as they broke into a lope.

As the sun sank slowly behind the Texas hills, Will and Rebecca were twenty miles away from the ranch. They alternated between a slow lope and a trot to conserve the horses. Will knew he couldn't wear the horses down. If they found Tye, they would have to go after the herd. He forced himself to believe Tye was all right.

Will pulled up as the darkness settled around them. "There'll be a full moon tonight. It'll help, but we won't be able to travel as fast. How are you holding up?"

Rebecca was tired and sore, but she smiled and said, "I'm fine. You just set the pace and I'll keep up with you."

Will took her hand in his. "I don't know what we'll find up ahead, but I'm glad you're here with me. If you get tired, let me know and we'll rest."

Rebecca squeezed his hand. "We'll have plenty of time to rest after we find Tye and the others. Let's keep moving. I'll keep up."

Will followed the Colorado River, keeping it to his right as they rode. The moon was casting its glow on the trail, providing enough light to follow the trail Bo had laid out for them.

They had been traveling northwest. Now upon reaching the Pedernales River, Will turned due west. The Johnson ranch lay on this path, and he planned to stop in. There might be a chance Tye had made it this far.

The Johnson ranch was the gathering point for seven counties, and a stopover for those driving cattle to the railheads in Kansas. If Tye had been able to make it this far, Will was sure he would have received help and may now be on his way after the herd.

It was after midnight when Will and Rebecca pulled up to the gates leading up to the Johnson headquarters.

"Hello the house," Will shouted, knowing it could be unhealthy to ride in unannounced.

Several moments later a light appeared in the bunkhouse. Then a voice called out, "Who's there?"

"Will and Rebecca Paxton. We have a spread over on the Colorado north of Austin. We're hunting our partner. We believe he was ambushed by cattle thieves and could be in danger."

"Hold on a minute," the man in the bunkhouse called down.

Soon afterward, a man came to the gate, carrying a lantern. He held it up to get a better view of Will and Rebecca.

"You say your partner was ambushed by rustlers?"

"We believe so. I saw a herd wearing our brand being driven toward the border. Our partner, Tye Garrett, was gathering cattle in the breaks west of here. Some of our horses were with the herd. I believe rustlers stole them. I don't know what has happened, but I'm trying to find out. Have you seen anyone come by this way?"

"Nope, but one of the hands saw a group of about twelve or thirteen men riding west four days ago."

"That sounds like the men we saw with the herd," Will said.

"Sounds like Lomas Cantrell's bunch. If it was, you'll be lucky if your partner is still alive."

"How far is it over to the breaks?" Will asked.

"Half a day's ride from here."

"If I miss them on the trail, they'll probably try to get to this ranch. If they do, tell them to head to Llano. I'll meet them there tomorrow," Will said.

"If they make it here, we'll take care of them. If you need any help going after your herd, send word to us. We'll ride with you."

"Much obliged," Will said, as he reined his horse around. "Sorry to wake you."

They rode through the night, watching the trail as best they could for signs of cattle or men. An hour before dawn, Will veered off to the north, heading for a hill half a mile away.

"I want to be on high ground come daylight," Will told Rebecca. "Maybe we can spot 'em."

They were resting on the hilltop as the sun rose. Will had unsaddled both his and Rebecca's horses and built a small fire to warm them. Rebecca dug in her saddlebags and brought out some biscuits and cold steak.

"It ain't much, but right now it tastes like a New York restaurant dinner," Rebecca said as she bit into one of the biscuits.

"It does taste good," Will agreed.

They sat by the fire, watching the lower regions for a sign of life. Will saw deer moving about in the early morning, feeding on the lush prairie grass, but never far from the thickets. There were three does and a buck grazing in a clearing not far from a washout that led into a draw. One of the does lifted her head, looking in the direction of the draw. Will followed her line of vision. He could see nothing to cause alarm. Suddenly, all four deer bolted across the clearing, disappearing into the thicket on this side. Will continued to watch the draw, but nothing moved. There was something there, though. Something was in that draw.

Walking to his horse, Will lifted his saddle to its back, and then saddled Rebecca's horse, too.

"There's something down there. I'm going to go down to check it out. I want you to stay here with the horses. I'll wave to you if it's clear."

"Will, you be careful. If there is something down there, it might not be friendly. There's still Indians around here and I don't want you losing your scalp to one of 'em. I never did cotton to a bald-headed husband." She smiled as she said it, but the concern in her eyes was easy to read as Will took her in his arms and kissed her.

"I'm glad you're here with me," he said. "I better go before I forget what I came here for."

He mounted his horse and started off down the hill. He planned to circle around and come up from the northwest side. This would put him below whatever it was the deer had seen.

He rode cautiously, watching the surrounding area for signs of anything out of the ordinary. When he was within two hundred yards of the draw, he stopped and tied his horse to a mesquite tree, keeping him out of sight. Proceeding on foot, he worked his way to within a few yards of the edge of the draw. Getting down on his hands and knees, he crawled to the edge and peered over.

The draw was about ten feet deep and three feet wide. Will could see only partway up toward the mouth. A curve in the bank blocked his view.

Crouching down, he went along the edge, watching the bottom as he moved. Working his way around the bend, he stopped short. There, under a washout in the bank, he saw a boot sticking out, but shadows from the bank prevented him from seeing any farther inside the washout. He eased farther along the bank, drawing his pistol as he moved. He had to make his way around the bend in order to get a view of the area where the boot was.

The bend in the draw was caused by a large boulder that blocked the rushing waters during the spring and fall rains. As Will moved along the bend, he kept his eyes on the floor of the draw. He eased up to the lip once again, peering over the edge of the washout where the boot had been. Only it wasn't there any-more. He moved closer to the edge and looked at the sandy bottom where waters had eroded the soil over the years. He saw footprints made by boots, apparently more than one pair, for there were several prints. Peering into where the water had eroded the sides and left a natural cave, he could see where the dirt had been packed as if one or more persons had bedded down there.

Will was looking up the draw, trying to follow the footprints in the sand. Suddenly, he spun around, his gun coming level with the surprised face of Curly, who was holding a large mesquite branch over his head, apparently intent on denting Will's hat and head.

Both men stood there, each shocked by the other's presence. Curly was hatless, his shirt torn, and dried blood showed on several scratches, but otherwise he looked unharmed. As they stood there looking at each other, Will with his gun drawn and Curly holding his club high, each of them began to smile—Curly with relief that it was Will, and Will with relief at finding at least one of them alive.

Lowering his pistol, Will asked, "Where are the others?"

Curly lowered his club, leaning on it as if in need of the support.

"They're down in the draw. Wayne took a slug in the shoulder and Ringo's got a sprained ankle. Tye's behind ya."

Will whirled around to see Tye standing three feet from him, his hunting knife held lightly in his hand. Will grinned at the sight of him. His shirt was in shreds, his hat was missing and his jeans looked as if he had been dragged in them.

"You all right?" Will asked.

"I've been better, but I sure am glad to see you. How did you know we were in trouble?"

"Bo and I saw the herd with our trail brand. It was heading south toward Mexico. I also saw several of our horses in the remuda, so I figured something must have happened. What did happen?"

Tye shook his head. "It all happened so fast I'm

still not sure. We had finished gathering and branding the cattle. We were holding about thirteen hundred head. We were just starting them on the trail. It was hard work getting them broken to the trail. We were in the saddle sixteen to eighteen hours a day. On the third day, we were breaking camp when ten men on horses rode up and got the drop on us. Wayne and Ringo were on night watch. They shot Wayne in the arm. Ringo got off a couple of shots, but a bullet nicked his horse and he was thrown into some rocks. He's bruised up some and has a sprained ankle, but other than that, he's all right. We've all got bruised feet and scratches from working our way through the thickets, but Wayne's the only one in bad shape."

"I've got horses for you," Will said. "Pedro will meet us this afternoon at Llano with the wagon. Bo's following the herd."

"I always knew picking you for a partner was a smart thing to do," Tye said. "Where are the horses?"

"Rebecca's got 'em up on the hill over there. I guess I better let her know everything's all right."

"I think you're a little late," Curly said, pointing in the direction of the hill.

Will looked up to see Rebecca leading the horses down the hill toward them.

"That girl can't follow directions any better than you can," Will said, looking at Tye. Tye grinned at him.

It was two hours before they got Wayne bandaged up and able to ride. The food that Rebecca had brought disappeared soon after it was brought out.

Will looked at the sun. "We're going to have to push it if we're going to get to Llano before dark."

"We'll make it," Tye said. "Then we'll get our herd back."

Chapter Twenty-eight

The eight riders made it to Llano by late afternoon. The ride had been hard on Wayne and his face was drawn and haggard from the long hours in the saddle. But each time Tye had suggested a rest, he had protested, "Keep going. We got to get the herd back. I worked too hard to see those thieving skunks get away with our cattle."

Pedro was waiting on the outskirts of town. Juanita sat beside him on the wagon seat, the worry and anxiety draining from her face as she spotted the riders. Seeing Wayne, she immediately began giving instructions to Pedro and Felipe. A bed was made in the wagon from blankets she had brought and Wayne was laid upon them. From a large bag, she brought forth medicine and began cleansing his wound as the others were handed food.

Tye looked at the group of riders. The events of the last few days had taken their toll. Each face was gray and weary from lack of rest.

"We've got to rest before going after the herd. Pedro, is there an inn in Llano?"

"*Sí, señor,* there is such a place, but it is a bad place. There is a lot of fighting and shooting there. My cousin and his family live close by, *señor.* It would be better if we went there."

"Are you sure they would welcome this many?" Tye asked, looking at the number of people who would be staying there.

"*Sí, señor.* My cousin is a good man and he has a good wife. They will put us all up for the night."

"We won't be there all night; just long enough to get a little rest, then we'll be on our way. I see you brought the rifles and pistols. That is good. We need to go into town and buy supplies and some hats. The sun has already burned our heads enough. Is there a doctor in town?"

Juanita, who had been listening to the exchange between Tye and her husband, spoke up at the mention of a doctor. "What for you want a doctor? I can take care of thees one. No doctor can fix him better than Juanita."

Tye looked questioningly at Pedro, who nodded vigorously. "*Sí, patron.* She is medicine woman. She knows the herbs with healing power. She will have Meester Wayne fixed up in no time."

Tye smiled. "Sorry, Juanita. I did not mean to offend you. Of course, you are the one to care for him."

Juanita returned Tye's smile, then went back to caring for her patient.

Night had fallen by the time the group had bought supplies and ridden to Pedro's cousin's house. Pedro's cousin, Miguel, welcomed them to his humble house, assuring them that they would be no inconvenience.

Rebecca brought in some of the food she had bought in town and soon Juanita and Miguel's wife, Maria, had the delicious smells of cooking filling the house. It was a small house, with one large room that served as the living room and kitchen, and one room serving as the bedroom. Miguel's three small children slept on pallets in the large room close to the fireplace. Wayne was now laid on a pallet here, enjoying the warmth as Juanita's herbs worked their power on his wounds.

After a quick meal of flour tortillas filled with steak cuts and spices, washed down with cold milk, all of them lay down in the large room on pallets made from the blankets Juanita had brought and straw ticking Maria provided.

Will and Rebecca lay next to each other, exhausted but happy. They had found Tye and the others, and all were alive. Ringo and Curly had spoken little since the morning and Will knew they were thinking about the men who had stolen the cattle and the revenge they wished for.

Tye had left instructions to be woke up in four hours, at which time they would leave, heading south to find Bo and retake the herd. It would take them at least a day and a half to reach Uvalde, and only then if they rested little and rode hard.

Pedro woke them four hours later. Will felt as if he had just closed his eyes. Rebecca stirred and sat up.

"Are we leaving?"

Will looked at her, knowing he was going to be in for a battle.

"Rebecca, I want you to stay with Pedro and Juanita."

"Well, you can want all you care to, but I'm going with you. I'm not about to sit at the ranch and wonder what is happening to you while you chase those outlaws. I promise you I will stay behind when the fighting begins, but I'm going with you. Besides, I can help bring the herd back."

Will looked at her in exasperation. He knew there was no use arguing with her, but he had hoped she would be reasonable about it.

"All right," he relented. "You can come. But you'll stay behind when we get to the herd. You have to promise me that, or I'll hog-tie you and send you back right now with Juanita."

Rebecca looked at him and smiled. "I promise, as long as you promise not to get yourself killed."

Will couldn't help the smile that came to his face. "I promise you I will do my best to honor your wish."

An hour later, they left from Miguel's house, riding south at a brisk lope. They rode for six hours before stopping to rest the horses and eat. The country they traveled was rolling hills covered with mesquite brush and yucca cactus.

They passed by Kerrville, the frontier post started

by the Frenchman Charles A. Schreiner, now a cattle-
man who was reported to own over six hundred thousand acres. Tye had served with Schreiner in the Texas
Rangers and had considered enlisting his help, but decided against it. This was his and Will's fight, theirs
and the men who rode with them. There was no use
involving outsiders.

They rode late into the night, pacing the horses. At
midnight, Tye called a halt. They built a small fire and
heated tortillas and beans for supper. They rolled out
their blankets and were instantly asleep. No watch was
posted, trusting to the horses to wake them should
anyone approach their camp.

Three hours later, Tye woke them. Everyone rolled
out. Nobody complained and nobody spoke as they
saddled their horses. Each one drank hot, black coffee
and ate the remaining flour tortillas. Then they
mounted and rode out.

It was a weary group that rode down the streets of
Uvalde that afternoon. They pulled up in front of the
only inn in town and dismounted, knocking the dust
from their clothes. Heads turned to look at the group
of trail-weary strangers who had ridden in.

Will entered the inn, looking around the lobby. As
his eyes adjusted to the darkness of the room, he
found what he was looking for. Bo was sitting in one
of the two chairs against the wall, a paper in front of
him. Will walked over and stood over him, waiting for
him to look up.

It took Bo a moment to realize someone was standing before him. He lowered the paper to look at the
man standing before him. He was covered with dust
and looked bone weary. It took Bo a second or two
to recognize Will. When he did, he came instantly to
his feet.

"Did you find the others?" he asked excitedly.

"They're waiting outside," Will said. "Where's the
herd?"

"South of town about five miles. They've got 'em

held on the Nueces River. They got there yesterday afternoon. Three gents left the herd and rode south. I figure they've gone to contact the buyer. I think they're going to move the herd in the morning. I heard two of 'em talkin' about it.''

They walked outside where Tye and the others were waiting. Will told him what Bo had said.

"Let's get us some rooms and get some rest. We'll meet in the lobby at eight o'clock tonight and plan what we're going to do. Bo, you take our horses down to the livery stable and grain 'em down good. Did you get a good night's sleep?''

"Yeah, I spent the night here, waiting for ya'll to show up."

"Good. I want you to stay awake in case any of those men show up. Wake us up at seven thirty.''

Will awoke feeling better, but still tired. He left Rebecca sleeping and slipped quietly out of the room.

Tye was sitting in the lobby, looking rested and fit. Will almost resented him.

"You feelin' better?" Tye asked as Will poured himself a cup of coffee from the pot on the stove.

"Define better," Will said. Tye grinned at him, but said nothing.

Curly, Shorty, and Ringo walked into the lobby a few minutes later, all looking better for the rest.

"Where's Bo?" Will asked.

"He's getting our horses ready. We're riding out in an hour."

Will sipped his coffee and waited for Curly, Shorty and Ringo to join them. Bo came in shortly afterward.

After everyone was seated around the table in the lobby of the inn, Tye looked at each one of them in turn. "If we do this right, we can take the herd back the same way they took it from us. Bo, how many men do they have with the herd?''

"Nine, with the other three gone."

"How many guard the herd at night?''

"They usually have four nighthawking."

"That leaves five sleeping. We're going to take those five first, then we'll get the four nighthawks. How long are their shifts?" Tye asked.

"Four hours."

"That'll give us enough time to put our plan into place. Drink your coffee. We ride in fifteen minutes."

Will went back to the room he shared with Rebecca. She was sleeping, but woke as he came into the room.

"Are you leaving now?" she asked.

"Yeah, we got to move while it's dark. We've got a good plan and if all goes well, we should have the herd back by morning."

Rebecca looked into his eyes. "Come daylight, I'm riding south to the herd. Don't make me ride too far, okay?" Tears were threatening as she hugged him to her.

"I'll have them right outside of town for you." He hugged her once more. Then, pushing her away, he turned and went out the door.

The moon was low in the eastern sky as they rode out of town. It provided enough light to show them the way. Bo led, taking them around the herd. Tye wanted to come upon them from the south. If there were guards posted, they would be expecting trouble from the north, not the south.

They could hear the cattle lowing long before they sighted them. Bo took them across the river and followed the low-lying hills until they were close to the herd.

"Their camp is east of the herd," Bo said. "It's about three hundred yards away from the cattle. They don't have a wagon, just packhorses. You can see their camp fire from the hill over there."

Tye looked around, locating a place where he could watch the camp.

"All right, Ringo, I want you to take the first watch. The rest of us will catch some sleep while we can.

Wake me in two hours if they haven't changed nightriders. We'll make our move after the next change. Wake me when the change is made."

They picketed their horses well away from the herd, not taking a chance on them picking up the scent of the remuda. Ringo made his way to the top of the hill, which was well covered with mesquite trees. He could watch the camp below without being seen. The others rolled into their blankets, gaining whatever rest they could before the action started.

A hand shook Tye's shoulder. He was awake instantly, pulling on his hat.

"They changed riders fifteen minutes ago," Ringo said. "Four rode out and four rode in. They have no guard posted. They must not be expecting any trouble."

"Let's go look at the camp," Tye said, pulling his blanket about his shoulders.

Will was sleeping fitfully when Tye shook him awake.

"It's time to ride, partner."

No one spoke as they started toward the camp on foot, moving slowly, careful not to make even the slightest noise.

Tye had worked out their approach from the hill overlooking the camp. Now he led the way, using the soft sand of the riverbed as much as possible. Leaving the riverbed, he led them around mesquite trees and yuccas until they were within thirty feet of the camp. With hand signals, he directed them to the sleeping forms on the ground.

The fire had died down to coals, which was a good thing because that would prevent any of them from being seen by those riding herd.

Each man moved cautiously, expecting at any moment a challenge or warning to be sounded, but none came as they came into the camp.

Will crept toward one of the men sleeping on the

ground. The man's pistol was in its holster, looped around his saddle horn. Will moved quietly, lifting the gun and holster and looping them over his shoulder. He didn't see any rifles, but knew they were around somewhere. After he had taken the pistol, he moved back into the shadows. The others soon joined him, each one, except Tye, who had stood guard, had a pistol and belt around their arms.

They unloaded their burdens, and then turned to the sleeping men, drawing their pistols as they walked back into the camp. Each one chose a man and moved in, kicking them with the toes of their boots. One man started to protest, but a pistol barrel upside his head quieted him instantly. The others moved as directed. Tye faded into the darkness and returned shortly with five ropes. Each man was tied to a tree and gagged, some with their own socks. That had been Ringo's idea.

Tye, Will, Ringo, Shorty, and Curly went to the picketed horses, each carrying one of the outlaw's saddles. They led the horses back into the circle where Bo was watching their captives. Shorty took watch outside the camp should Cantrell return.

"We should be back shortly. If anyone rides in alone, it's probably one of them so be careful," Tye said to Bo. They mounted their horses and rode out, each knowing what to do.

When the four riders reached the cattle, they split up, Tye and Curly going in one direction, Will and Ringo in the other. If all went well, they would meet back in less than thirty minutes.

Will and Ringo rode side by side, their hats pulled down low over their eyes. They had ridden a short distance when they heard singing. Many cowhands sang while on night watch. It helped to calm both cattle and rider, as well as letting other riders know your whereabouts. Will looked at Ringo, who was grinning. This particular rider was more likely to spook the cattle with his singing than calm them.

Will and Ringo saw the rider as he came toward them. He stopped his singing, pulling his horse up and taking out the makings for a cigarette.

"I'm sure glad you came along. I've run out of matches and haven't had a smoke in two hours."

The man was busy pouring tobacco into the paper when Will rode up beside him. Will was carrying his pistol across his lap and, as the man looked up, Will brought it down across his head. The man let out a moan and slid from the saddle. Ringo tied him with his rope and gagged him with his neckerchief, then dragged him into the brush as Will led his horse into a clump of trees and tied it up.

Will rode on alone, Ringo following at a distance. The next rider was whistling a tune as Will came upon him.

"What took you so long?" the man asked as he saw Will.

Will grunted as he came up beside him.

The man pulled up alongside, peering through the darkness, trying to see Will's face. He couldn't see the pistol in Will's right hand.

"Hey, you're not Lon," the man exclaimed, reaching for the pistol at his side. Will brought the gun in his hand up to within inches of the man's nose. The ominous click of the cocking hammer stilled the man's motion. He went stiff as Will softly said, "Mister, if you want to live to see daylight, let that pistol drop to the dirt."

Will heard the pistol as it hit the ground.

"Now ride toward the camp, and don't make a sound. If you do, it'll be the last sound you ever make."

Ringo came out of the darkness. "I'll go get the one we left under the tree."

"We'll meet you there," Will said, riding behind his captive.

Ringo and Will arrived at the spot where the four of them had split up. Tye and Curly weren't there, but showed up a few minutes later, two riders in front of them. One was bleeding from a gash on his jaw and Curly was rubbing a bruised knuckle and smiling.

They took their prisoners back to the camp. Tye threw wood on the fire, building it up until they had good enough light to see all their captives.

"Well, boys, it looks like we're going to have a good night for a necktie party," Tye said, taking a rope from his saddle. Curly grinned and Ringo grabbed one man by the arm, leading him over to the center of the camp.

"This one goes first. He's the one that shot Wayne."

The outlaw's eyes grew to twice their normal size as Ringo threw the rope over a branch and brought the loop down to the man's neck. He looked around at the five men standing there. There was no mercy in any face, only hard lines.

Bo led a saddled horse up to where Ringo held the prisoner. Together, they lifted the outlaw to the horse's back. His hands were now tied behind him.

Tye threw another loop over the branch of the mesquite tree and another man was brought forward, his hands bound behind him. He was lifted onto the back of his horse. When they had four of them lined up, each with a rope around his neck, Tye spoke. "Do any of you have anything to say before you go to meet your maker?"

One of the men, the one Will had hit with his pistol, spoke up. "You're going to regret this when Lomas Cantrell catches up with you."

Tye looked up at the man. "We might, but, mister, you won't be around to see it," he said as he slapped the horse with his hat. The rider swung from the saddle, his neck broken. As if on cue, each of the other three horses bolted, leaving their burdens swinging from the mesquite branch.

The other five were dealt with in the same manner, quickly and with no regrets.

"Let's get this herd moving north," Tye said as the last outlaw swung from the tree.

Bo brought up the horses they had left tied by the

river. He turned them loose with the rest of the remuda and each man chose a fresh mount.

The sun was still two hours from rising when they
started the herd moving north. Most of the cattle were
trail broke now, and with a full day's grazing and
plenty of water, they were easily managed by the
five riders.

With the herd moving easily along, it still took them
three hours to reach the outskirts of Uvalde. Rebecca
had caught up with them as the sun cleared the horizon, but had said nothing after seeing the grim expression on each of their faces.

Chapter Twenty-nine

Will found a place to hold the cattle outside Uvalde. They bedded them down and Tye left them to go into Uvalde to find extra men. Everyone needed rest and he needed at least six men to hold the herd at night.

He found eight men to do the job and help take them to the Rafter TP. He told them to be there at six that evening and rode back to help set up camp.

The lack of sleep and the ordeal of the last three days left them all with little reserve. Will was dozing in the saddle when Tye rode up.

"Hang in there, partner. I've got help coming. We'll rest here for two days, then move the herd. I want to ride out tomorrow and look for water and a place to bed the herd down. We'll have to scout for places each day. I figure it'll take us four days to drive them to the ranch. I don't want to push them any harder than we have to. Why don't you go on in and get some rest? I'll ride herd for a while. Curly and Ringo are already sacked out. Rowdy, Bo, and I will ride for a couple of hours."

Will grinned. "I'd argue with you, but I'm too tired." He started to ride away, but pulled up. "Do you think Cantrell will try something?"

Tye shook his head. "I don't think he will. He doesn't have a gang anymore and I don't think he'll be able to get another one together. Thieves are superstitious. They don't like to follow someone that got all his men hung. He might try to get revenge, but I don't look for it."

"Well, I don't know about you, but I'm going to watch my backside for a while. Something tells me Cantrell won't like the fact that we took back the herd and hung his men."

The men Tye hired showed up at six that evening. They rode night herd, while Tye, Will, Rowdy, Ringo, and Bo slept the first full night in three days.

The next morning, Tye and Will rode out to scout the trail leading back to Austin. Fifteen miles from Uvalde, they found both water and grazing for the longhorns. Returning to the herd they made plans for the drive.

Rebecca, checking the supplies, said, "We'll need more since you've hired extra men."

"We'll ride into town this afternoon and get what we need. How many of the new hands have rifles?" Tye asked.

"Six of them," Rowdy said.

"We'll pick up two more. I want everyone to have a rifle. I hope we don't need 'em, but you never know."

The sun was high as Will, Rebecca, and Tye rode into town, their horses kicking up dust as they trotted down the only street in Uvalde. Pulling up in front of the general store, they dismounted and walked up the wooden steps that elevated the sidewalk above the street.

"While you two are getting supplies, I'm going over to that little shop over there and see if I can get some material for curtains," Rebecca said, pointing across the street.

"All right," Will said. "Just make sure you get some material with horses on it."

Rebecca looked at him in astonishment. "Horses? Are you crazy? If you want horses, you can sleep in the corral. I'm not about to have anything with horses hanging in my house."

Will feigned a hurt expression as Tye walked into the store, hiding his smile as he went.

"I think horses would be nice hanging over the

kitchen window. That way, when you're washing dishes, you would be able to see them," Will said.

Rebecca shook her head. "Will Paxton, you've lost your mind if you think I'm hanging curtains with horses on them over my kitchen window."

Will grinned at her as she stood there, hands on her hips and a look of determination in her eyes.

"Well, if you don't want horses, how about somethin' with a cow on it?"

"A cow? Why I never . . ." She stopped in midsentence, seeing the grin on Will's face. "Will Paxton, I ought to shoot you right here and now. You've been pullin' my leg all along, haven't you?"

Will's face showed mock surprise. "Why, Becky, how can you say such a thing?" He smiled, pulling her to him, but she pulled back from him.

With a serious look in her eye, she looked up at him. "Just for that I'm buying pink material to put on every window in the house." She turned and started across the street. Will stood there, a truly shocked expression on his face. He turned and walked into the store, wondering if she'd really do it. Rebecca hid the smile on her face as she walked across the street. That would teach him to fool around with her.

Tye was looking over the shelves of stocked goods when Will came through the door. Neither saw the three men turn the corner at the edge of town.

Lomas Cantrell was filled with cold fury. The picture of the nine men hanging from the mesquite tree was still fresh in his mind. He had ruled these parts for three years now, no one daring to challenge him. He had made his threats and backed them up. He had reaped the rewards of being an outlaw, but he knew it wasn't luck. It was careful planning and forethought to which he attributed his success. He knew whom to steal from and whom to leave alone. He never stole from the large spreads, but hit the small ones instead, holding the stolen cattle and horses until he had enough to drive to Mexico. He had a buyer that enjoyed receiving cattle from those "stupid Nortamericanos," no questions asked. Of course, stealing cattle from the small Mexican spreads and selling them on this side of the border was just as lucrative.

The two men riding beside him were Jake Black and Bart Tombs, both hardened gunmen, who had been useful in keeping order among the men, as well as ensuring Cantrell's safe passage in and out of Mexico. They had been very helpful in obtaining information from the cowboy at the herd. Hiding in the brush, they had grabbed the cowhand as he passed by. It took them only a matter of moments to find out who was responsible for the hangings, and where they were. They had left the cowboy unconscious, hidden in the brush, his horse tied to a mesquite out of sight of anyone passing by.

Now they were looking for two men: Tye Garrett and Will Paxton. Cantrell wondered why the name Paxton sounded familiar to him, but dismissed it. It didn't matter. Paxton would be a dead man soon.

Rebecca was looking at a bolt of cloth on a stand by the window. She looked up as the three men rode to the general store, looking at the horses tied there. Her heart froze as she recognized the man in the middle. Though she had seen him only once, his face was imprinted on her mind and now he was here.

Dismounting in front of the general store, Lomas Cantrell looked around, making sure there was no one on the street. He motioned to the other two and they started up the steps ahead of him.

Will heard the footsteps as the two men walked through the door. Turning from a counter where he had been looking at the rifles, a sixth sense sent a warning to his brain. The men had moved apart as they entered, intentionally putting space between them.

Tye was behind a shelf, looking at the rolls of hemp. The owner was in the back getting the hundred pounds of flour Rebecca needed.

Will watched as one man stopped three feet inside the door, while the other moved to his right and walked up the aisle until he was even with Will. Will noticed that the move put him in a position where he couldn't watch both men at once.

His mind racing, he turned back to the counter as if the men held no interest for him. He picked up a box of shells and, lifting the top, he took a handful out, pretending to inspect them as he mentally took stock of the situation. The counter where he stood was located at the back of the store. It was at the end of the wide aisle leading from the door. Slightly to his left, and about four feet behind him, the shelves of goods began. The next aisle between the shelves was a good ten feet away. There was no way he could make it to the cover of the shelves before one or both of the gunmen nailed him. If he could distract the one closest to him, he might have a chance to make it around the shelves before the one standing in the aisle could get him.

Will heard the wooden floor squeak as the man standing close to him shifted his weight. Glancing in that direction, Will saw the man standing there had his feet slightly spread. His hand was inches away from the pistol at his side. Will turned to look at the open doorway, his eyes widening as he looked. It had the desired effect, as both men turned slightly to follow his gaze.

Will reacted instantly, throwing the box of shells at the gunman closest to him. The gunman, turning back at that instant, instinctively ducked as the shells, coming out of the box, flew in his direction. It provided Will the time he needed as he drew and fired, moving toward the row of shelves as he did. He felt the force of a bullet as it hit him in the upper part of his leg. He threw himself sideways, landing on the floor behind the shelf.

Tye rounded the corner of the aisle in time to see Will fall between the shelves. He saw a man down on one knee, blood covering the front of his shirt. At that

instant, another man came around the end shelf. The
man was apparently so intent upon getting Will that
he didn't see Tye standing there, gun drawn, feet
spread. When realization struck, surprise showed on
the man's face. He shifted his feet and brought his
gun hand around, but he never made it. Tye's gun
belched flame, once, twice, three times, and the man
was hurled backward into the aisle. His only move-
ments were the jerking spasms of death.

Tye looked at the remaining gunman. Still on one
knee, he was struggling to rise, a look of disbelief on
his face as he stared at Tye. Then slowly, he fell to
his side, his pistol still in its holster.

Tye walked to where Will was trying to rise, blood
running down his pants leg.

"Here, let me help you," Tye said, taking him by
the arm and pulling him to a standing position.
"Looks like Juanita will have another patient for a
while."

Will grimaced at the thought. "I don't mind being
laid up, but who's going to look after you and keep
you outa trouble? I hate to think of all the things
you'll be getting into without me there to watch out
for ya."

Tye bent and put Will's arm over his shoulder and,
with his other arm around his waist, he let Will lean
against him as they headed for the door.

Lomas Cantrell watched as Jake took Will's bullet.
He saw Bart get off a shot as Will jumped behind the
shelves and figured Will for dead as Bart ran around
the shelves to finish him. The sight of Bart dead in
the middle of the floor stunned him. He was standing
there in shock when Will and Tye came around the
corner of the shelves, but instantly he came to life,
drawing his pistol and stepping into the doorway. He
brought the pistol to bear as the large man looked up
and saw him. He stopped in his tracks and the other
man, who looked familiar to Lomas, looked up at the
gun pointing in his direction.

"Gentlemen, you have cost me dearly, but you shall pay for it with your lives, so I guess that will be compensation enough," Lomas Cantrell said as he pulled back the hammer on the pistol.

Never in his life had he heard anything that sounded as loud as the cocking of that pistol, Tye thought. But the absolute feeling of helplessness, knowing there was nothing he could do was the worst part, as he looked into the cold gray eyes of his executioner.

Cantrell smiled as if reading Tye's mind. He was enjoying the moment. First, he would shoot the wounded man and, as he was falling, he would kill the other one. He tried to shift the gun to the right, but his vision blurred and his arm suddenly felt heavy. There was a pain in his back that seemed to spread to his chest. The gun in his hand slipped from his fingers and fell heavily to the floor. He stood there looking down at it. All he had to do was reach down and get it. He had to kill the two men standing there. He heard footsteps on the walk behind him. Slowly, he turned, staggering as he did. He saw the woman standing there, a rifle in her hand. He knew this woman, but who was she? Where had he seen her before? Then it came to him: Mrs. Paxton. He'd met her out on the range just before they had stolen the herd. Why was she holding that rifle and why did she have it pointed at him? Then the realization struck him as he sank slowly to his knees.

"You shot me, Mrs. Paxton. Why?" he asked, his face a cloud of confusion.

"Because you were going to shoot my husband, Mr. Cantrell, and I couldn't let you do that."

He eased himself down to the floor, as if lying down would ease the pain spreading through his body.

"I knew I'd seen him somewhere before. It was out on the range that day. He rode the big bay horse. I sure wish I owned that horse." He smiled then. "Your husband is a lucky man. He owns a fine horse and has a beautiful wife. A man can't ask for more than that, can he?" His face contorted in pain and his body arched, then relaxed and he lay motionless, his eyes staring at the ceiling.

Rebecca stood there for a moment, too stunned to move. Then leaning the rifle against the door, she stepped around the prone body of Lomas Cantrell and walked to Will's side.

"Can we go home now?" she asked.

"Yeah, I think it's time," Will said.

"Me, too," said Tye.

Chapter Thirty

July 4, 1874

Five of the larger ranches in the area had gathered at the Rafter TP for the Fourth of July celebration.

All hands of the Rafter TP, as well as several from neighboring ranches were gathered around the corral, waiting for the Fourth of July festivities to begin. A large steer had been cooking in a pit for a full day now and was filling the air with mouth-watering aromas. The women had prepared their favorite recipes and were now in the house, putting the finishing touches on their dishes.

The men stood around in groups, talking about horses, cattle, and the lack of rain. Some talked about the depression that had gripped the country and what it was doing to the cattle market.

As usual when cowmen gathered in Texas, the talk turned to those blankety-blank sheep that had invaded the ranges. Cattlemen as a rule hated the "woolies," and were convinced in their minds that sheep would overgraze the grasslands, thus starving out the cattle.

Rebecca knew she herself was the topic of many conversations when these cattlemen gathered, but this neither bothered her nor deterred her from her plans.

When Tye had driven the herd of longhorns to the Kansas railhead at Abilene, leaving Will at home nursing the wound in his leg, he never imagined what Rebecca would do with part of the proceeds from the herd. Had he known, he doubted he would have done anything different.

Rebecca had taken a part of the money after convincing Will that sheep would be more profitable than cattle one day, and bought one thousand head of sheep. She had hired two Mexican herders to look after the sheep for her, and chose the roughest part of the Rafter TP range to run her flock.

Will and Tye, meanwhile, had bought more land and cattle, and were now running just over five thousand head on forty thousand acres.

Tye had ridden a train to the East after selling the herd. There he had bought five hundred head of Hereford cattle to crossbreed to the Texas longhorns. They were waiting for the first calves now, with much anticipation.

They had made two more gathers in the breaks, gathering over twenty-five hundred head of longhorns. Combining these with the ones they already had, they bought some from small ranches around the area.

Both Will and Tye managed the horse operation, breeding the best mares to the best studs and keeping detailed records. They had contracts with several ranches to supply both green and broken horses. Tye was working with some contacts he'd made in the East to supply trained horses to eastern buyers.

More and more people were moving into Texas, looking for work. Since Texas was growing and felt the depression very little, word got out through eastern papers that it was the land of opportunity and wealth. But those who came, found out that the wealth was only there for those who were willing to work for it.

The Texas legislature was opening up more government land to homesteaders, but most of the land was in the dry arid climate of West Texas, where cattle had been king for some time. The land didn't take well to the plow, but eventually the people learned which crops would do well in the dry soil. Cotton proved to be the best crop to grow in the Texas soil, and since there was a high demand for the crop, it didn't take long for cotton to replace cattle as king.

Will had been one of the first to recognize the value of cotton and had set aside three hundred acres of river land to be cultivated for cotton. He had hired two black families from Mississippi to oversee the production and harvest.

Overall, the operation of the Rafter TP flowed smoothly. Rebecca's sheep proved to be more profitable than the cattle. The first cotton would be ready for picking this fall, and Will felt it would be a good cash crop if prices held.

Cattle prices were still low, but Will and Tye knew they could hold their cattle until prices came back up. They even planned to buy more while prices were low. It would prove to be a good investment.

They now had six full-time hands and a full-time cook working for them.

Not only had the house been completed, but a bunkhouse, two barns, and a house for Pedro and Juanita had been built.

Rebecca had talked Tye and Will into hiring Pedro to help with the horses. He had proved to be a good blacksmith, as well as an able hand with the mares and colts.

While Rebecca was the center of conversation in many circles because of her sheep, men spoke of her with respect. And it never failed, when her name was brought up, that someone didn't bring up the fact that she had been the one to put an end to the notorious outlaw Lomas Cantrell.

After the gunfight in Uvalde, Rebecca's fame had spread over Texas like wildfire. Several of the small ranchers who had been hit by Cantrell's band of thieves, stopped by the Rafter TP to see her and thank her and tell her they were beholdin' to her for ridding the range of such a scourge. Of course, Will and Tye received praises, too, but it was Rebecca of whom most spoke when Cantrell's name was mentioned.

Rebecca wished the whole event would just be forgotten. She never regretted her actions or the results, but neither did she want the notoriety that followed her. She hated the stares that followed her each time she went to Austin and the many questions by inquisitive people who wanted to meet the beautiful Mrs. Paxton.

As Rebecca worked in the kitchen this day, assisting the ladies in preparing the food and directing the setup of the tables, she thought about the day and what it would bring. Will and Tye had brought in several head of young horses that were due to be broken in the next few weeks. There would be contests between the hands to see who could ride the best. There would be roping contests held in the large corral, as well as several races. A large feast and a dance would follow all of these later in the day.

Since such big events were held only once or twice a year, the festivities would go well into the night, with some of the folks spending the night in wagons or in the barn, and returning home tomorrow.

Rebecca smiled as she thought about the day and the impact it would have on her and Will. This was indeed a happy day and she was eager to sneak away and join Will at the corral. Spying Juanita bustling about the kitchen, she made her way through the crowded area until she was beside her. Rebecca whispered something in her ear and Juanita smiled and nodded vigorously.

Slipping out the back door, Rebecca walked down to the corral, looking for Will. She spotted him sitting on the top rail of the corral, watching a young cowhand attempt to ride a rather mean-tempered grulla horse. Rebecca made her way through the crowd, smiling and returning greetings as she went. Watching through the poles on the corral, she stood on the ground, waiting for the ride to end before getting Will's attention.

The ride ended shortly, with the young man flying off over the horse's head when he did a sudden cutback, planting his front feet, ducking his head, and sliding backward. The young man got to his feet and

was rewarded with applause, whistles and good-
natured gibes from the crowd.

Will looked down and saw Rebecca standing beneath him.

"Did you come to wish me luck on my ride?" he
asked, jumping down beside her.

"Not exactly, but since I'm here, I guess I might as
well," she said, smiling at him.

"You better not be wishin' anybody else good
luck," he said, returning the smile.

She said coyly, "Oh, I don't know. There's a lot of
handsome cowboys here today. I might just find me
one to root for."

Will, with mock seriousness in his voice, said,
"Yeah, but none of 'em will give ya half the excitement I do, so you might as well forget about 'em and
stick with me."

Laughing, Rebecca said, "You're right! Life would
be plumb boring without you around. You better go
on and ride your horse, I see Tye waving to you."

He bent down and kissed her lightly on the lips,
then hurried off to the bucking chute to mount his
horse.

Will had drawn a large strawberry roan with four
white stockings. It was one of his favorites among the
young horses on the ranch. Rebecca watched as Will
rode the horse to a standstill, dismounting to the
cheers of the crowd.

Tye rode next, drawing a smaller, stout, black filly.
She reared as she came out of the chute, then lunged
forward giving Tye a good ride as she tried her best
to throw him, but he rode her to a standstill as well.
The crowd cheered as loudly for Tye as he dismounted
as they had for Will.

The final contest came down to four riders: Will,
Tye, a cowboy from the Circle C, and another cowboy
from the Two Deuces. The judging committee chose
the horses and each rider drew a horse's number from
a hat, making the competition fair. The final rides

would be judged on style and toughness by two judges picked from the local ranch owners. Each judge would score the horse and rider. Scoring between one and fifty, the two scores would be added. The rider with the highest score would be declared the winner. Each rider had to ride his horse to a complete standstill before the judge would award a score.

It was a great contest, with the first cowboy getting bucked off after four minutes of riding. Will, Tye, and the cowboy from the Circle C, rode their horses to a standstill, but Will won the contest. He had ridden with reckless abandonment, spurring his horse at every jump, and even riding with one hand in the air for a good portion of the ride.

Rebecca watched with her heart in her throat as Will rode. Now was not the time for him to be getting himself hurt.

When the bronc riding was over, Rebecca found Will among several cowhands, talking about the rides they'd made, the horses that had been ridden, and those that hadn't. Standing off to one side, she tried unsuccessfully to get his attention. Finally, in frustration, she walked into the circle of men, elbowing her way until she was face-to-face with Will.

"Excuse me, gentlemen, but I need to talk to my husband," she said, taking him by the arm and ushering him away to the laughs and jeers of the others.

Will allowed himself to be led reluctantly from the group. He was puzzled by Rebecca's behavior. She had never acted like this before and he wondered what could possibly be wrong.

"Where are we going?" he asked, noticing she was leading him away to a secluded spot behind the barn.

"We're getting away from the crowd," she said. "We've been so busy the last week getting ready for this that we haven't had a moment to ourselves, and there's something I got to tell you."

Hearing the seriousness in her tone, Will became alarmed. "Is there anything wrong?" he asked, concern in his voice.

Seeing the worry on his face, Rebecca laughed. "No, sweetheart, nothing is wrong. In fact, everything is wonderful."

"Then what is it?" he asked, still perplexed.

"Calm down," Rebecca said. "I've got something to tell you and I want it to be just right."

Will cocked an eyebrow, looking intently at her. He waited for her to go on.

Smiling, she walked up to him and wrapped her arms around his waist, leaning her head against his chest.

"Are you happy, Will?"

The question took him by surprise and it took him a moment to answer.

"Of course, I'm happy. I've got you, this ranch, a great partner. What else could a man ask for?"

"A baby?" Rebecca said, looking into his face.

It took a moment for Will to realize the implication of what she had said. "A baby! Is that what you're tellin' me? We're havin' a baby?"

Rebecca searched his face. "Do you want a baby?" she asked.

The shock was still evident as he answered, "Of course, I want a baby. I want a whole houseful of babies. I want six boys and six girls, and I want all the girls to look just like you."

Rebecca laughed. "How about we start with one and see where it goes from there?"

"That's fine with me," Will said. "When did you find out?"

"I've been pretty sure for about a month, but I knew for sure last week. I've just been waiting for the right time to tell you."

He pulled her tight against him. "I love you, Becky. I'll always love you."

She smiled as she clung to him, tears of joy running down her cheeks.

His face pressed against her cheek, she almost didn't hear him whisper his request. "If it's a boy, can we name him Tye?"

Laughing, she pulled away from him. "I couldn't think of a better name."

They stood there holding each other, oblivious of the other people, each lost in the other's presence.

Will felt as if his heart would burst. He now had everything a man could ask for. With Tye and Rebecca's help, he would build something that would last, something that would be there for future generations of Paxtons. He would lay the foundation for them to build on. He looked around him and pictured Paxtons in the future: raising cattle, working the land. But what made him smile was his mind's picture of future Paxtons riding the horses. He could see his son as he gave him pointers, watched him ride the rough broncs to a standstill. He felt the pride he knew he would feel when that day came. He kissed Rebecca one more time, and then, taking her by the arm, he started back to the house. He couldn't wait to tell Tye.

Epilogue

By the turn of the century, Texas had continued its growth as an agricultural state, but it was also striving to remove the stigma of being a backwoods state with nothing but ruffians and wild Indians.

Austin was now the state capital and was the center for business. Houston was establishing itself as a port of trade.

Cotton was a major export for Texas, supplying many of the world markets and helping establish the U.S. once again as a leader in the cotton industry.

Cattle were still a major part of Texas growth, only now it wasn't the large cattle drives that were making history, but the building of cattle empires. The King ranch was now established in the southern part of the state. The XIT ranch had been established with the building of the state capitol. Mudro Mckenzie was operating the Matador, and the Scottish syndicate that owned the ranch was well pleased. Many other ranches had been started on the vast plains of this magnificent state, some to succeed, some doomed to failure. But when one failed, there was always someone willing to step in and try again. It was this determination that built Texas and kept it proud.

Texas was number one in oil production. Railroads were spreading all over the state, bringing economic prosperity to all corners.

The turn of the century was the beginning of the progressive era for the cattle state known as Texas, and those willing to take the risks and put forth the effort, reaped the benefits of the times. Will Paxton and Tye Garrett never held back, but continued to build and strengthen their holdings.

The Rafter TP was thriving. Cotton and sheep had proven to be more lucrative than cattle. Not to say that cattle had not played a large part in the building of the ranch, nor would they ever be replaced. Both Will and Tye devoted most of their time and energies into building strong herds. They began by crossing the rangy longhorns with the Herefords. The results of their labors had produced more pounds of beef on the same amount of range. They had continued their crossbreeding, researching different breeds of cattle to cross with their herds and importing the best. But both Will and Tye's first love was the horses.

They had built a reputation for producing some of the best horses to come out of Texas. With the Eastern markets Tye had opened up, as well as the Texas ranches that sought their stock, they had more orders than they could fill.

Pedro was still responsible for the daily care of the horse herds. Pedro, now in his seventies, worked alongside his sons and grandsons to ensure that the stock was well cared for, and all provisions stocked appropriately. Juanita still worked in the kitchen, helping with the daily cooking to feed the twenty ranch hands now employed by the Rafter TP.

Rowdy was the ranch foreman, looking after the day-to-day operation of the ranch and managing the hundred thousand-plus acres that made up the Rafter TP. Now in his late sixties, he would not consider retirement.

Will was in his early sixties, Tye in his seventies, yet both worked from sunup to sundown. Even though neither rode the rough stock anymore, their most enjoyable moments were sitting by the large fireplace in the main house and reminiscing about the horses they'd ridden, or a bad one that had been ridden by one of the hands.

Rebecca, as beautiful in her later years as she had been in her youth, loved to listen to the two of them talk, and even joined in the conversation, mainly to keep the statistics accurate and not allow their imaginations to embellish the stories beyond a point of credibility.

She spent most of her time working with the accounts of the ranch, turning over the sheep operation to Ringo, who turned out to be the best hand with sheep, preferring the quiet solitude to the everyday workings of the ranch. She had more than four thousand of the woolies running in the broken hills on the westernmost region of the ranch.

Will's dream of a son came true, but only after two daughters were born first. Even though he had tried his best to turn both Katie Lynn, named after Rebecca's mother, and Cory Jo into the boys he wanted, both had married and moved from the ranch. Katie lived in Dallas with her husband, who was an attorney in his father's law firm. Cory lived in Austin and came often to the ranch. Her husband was part owner in the local newspaper and was well on his way to a successful career.

Tye Paxton came along late in both Will and Rebecca's life. Will and Rebecca were in their forties when Tye was born, surprising both of them.

While Will and Rebecca doted on their only male child, it was Tye Garrett who seemed the proudest of his namesake. Having never married again, but devoting his life to the ranch, he took young Tye, who had been nicknamed "Boots," under his wing, teaching him the things he would have taught his own son. Will and Rebecca often wondered if Boots didn't sometimes regard Tye as a parent rather than the godfather he was, but they did not interfere in the relationship. As far as they could see, Boots was getting the best of all.

On his sixteenth birthday, Tye led him down to the corral and presented him with a two-year-old, dapple-

gray colt, the best of the young stock on the ranch.
While Will and Rebecca looked on, Tye moved the
young horse into the bucking chute and set Boots's
saddle on its back, then motioned for Boots to climb
on. It was his first try at riding an untried horse. He
had ridden many horses on the ranch, and been
thrown on several occasions, but both Will and Tye
had forbidden him to break the young colts, leaving
that to the hired hands. Now, with Will and Rebecca's
consent, Boots was about to try his first true bronc.

As the young horse bolted from the chute, Boots
gripped the saddle tight with his knees, trying to remember the instructions both his dad and Tye had
given him.

The gray planted his front feet in the ground and
bunched his knees, then shot skyward, clearing the
ground by a good six feet. Boots hung on to the reins
and gripped with his knees, bracing himself for the
impact to come.

Boots managed to ride the young horse through six
more leaps, before a twisting lunge unseated him and
sent him crashing to the earth. He came up slowly
from the ground, smiling as he straightened up.

"Can I try him again?" he asked, looking first at
his father, then to Tye.

Rebecca had been standing with her fist in her
mouth, watching her son ride. She felt relief flood
through her as he stood up and dusted himself off.
She opened her mouth to protest when he made his
request, but instantly closed it, shutting off the words
she wanted to speak, knowing she would accomplish
nothing by denying him his wish.

Two hands herded the colt back into the chute and
Boots hurriedly climbed the rails to take his place in
the saddle.

Will put his arm around Rebecca, his mind wandering back to a day many years ago, the day Rebecca
had told him she was pregnant. He remembered his
thoughts of that day, the day he would see his son

ride the rough string. Things had changed, the days of breaking horses the rough way were about gone. Now they broke most horses slowly, training them with more patience. There were still exhibitions being held and Will was reading more and more about the rodeos that were being held around the country. He didn't know if it was something that would take hold, but it sounded exciting.

Boots made his second ride and managed to ride longer, but still plowed up the dirt of the large corral.

"I think it's time we taught this boy to ride broncs," Tye said, as Will came into the corral to talk to Boots.

Will looked at his son, and the look of excitement and anticipation in his eyes reminded him of someone he had known long ago. Smiling, he said, "I think you're right. There's nothing wrong with knowing how to stay aboard a rank one. When do you think we should start? How about after the spring gather? We'll have more time then." He smiled at Tye without Boots seeing him.

"But Dad, that's a month away. Can't we start now?" Boots asked, his voice pleading.

Will and Tye laughed, each recalling another youth who was eager to ride the wild broncs.

"All right, Tye," Will said, reverting back to his son's given name. "We'll start in the morning. I know what it's like to want to ride. I hope this country doesn't become so tame that there's no more rough stock to ride. It would be a shame to see the desire to climb on the back of one more bronc die because there are no more broncs to be ridden."

The young man looked at his father, seeing the sadness that came into his eyes, and said, "Don't worry, Dad. As long as there are Paxtons on this earth, there will always be broncs to ride."

Father and son looked at each other, and both smiled, one thinking about the past, the other thinking about the future.

SIGNET

Charles G. West

Medicine Creek   0-451-19955-3

The white-born, Cheyenne-raised warrior Little Wolf
has left the warpath behind to create a prosperous
life with his wife Rain Song. But when a renegade
army slaughters his tribe and takes Rain Song
captive, Little Wolf's dreams for peace are overrun
by the need for bloody vengeance.

Mountain Hawk   0-451-20215-5

Mountain man Trace McCall must rescue his
beloved from a kidnapper without getting caught
in a growing conflict between white homesteaders
and Indians.

Son of the Hawk   0-451-20457-3

When a war party of renegade Sioux slaughters his
Shoshoni tribe, the young brave White Eagle has no
choice but to venture into the world of the white
man to find mountain man Trace McCall—the father
he never knew.

To order call: 1-800-788-6262

Ralph Cotton

"Gun-smoked, blood-stained, gritty believabilty...
Ralph Cotton writes the sort of story we all hope
to find within us." —Terry Johnston

"Authentic Old West detail." —*Wild West Magazine*

HANGMAN'S CHOICE   20143-4
They gunned down his father in cold blood. They are his
most elusive enemies, the outlaws known as *Los Pistoleros*,
and they're still at large. But Federal Deputy Hart will not
give up...

MISERY EXPRESS   19999-5
Ranger Sam Burrack is once again driving the jailwagon
filled with a motley cargo of deadly outlaws, whose
buddies are plotting to set them free. But with the Ranger
driving, they're in for quite a ride.

Also available:

BADLANDS	19495-0
BORDER DOGS	19815-8
JUSTICE	19496-9
BLOOD ROCK	20256-2